THE CHASM

THE CHASM

A NOVEL BY

GEORGE CRAM COOK

※

*"I love those who sacrifice themselves to
the earth, that the earth may be one day
the Superman's."*
SO SPAKE ZARATHUSTRA

*"Come shoulder to shoulder ere earth
grows older! The Cause spreads over
land and sea."*
THE VOICE OF TOIL

※

NEW YORK
FREDERICK A. STOKES COMPANY
PUBLISHERS

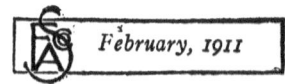

February, 1911

THE CHASM

PART I

MOLINE

I

THE nine-fifteen train was speeding toward Moline on the Mississippi. At the window of one
of the Pullman staterooms, a girl, lifting her
eyes from her book, looked out across black, fall-
plowed furrows, russet plains cut with barbed-wire
fences, wet fields full of broken and withered corn-
stalks tramped by cattle. The sky was covered with
gray, amorphous cloud.

"How dismal this country is," said the girl.

"We should have stayed in Italy till May at least,"
answered her middle-aged mother in the chair opposite.

The girl's tightened lips marked her inward denial.

"You must learn, Marion, to find your sunshine in
your own soul," preached the lady. "Roman palazzo or desert island are all one to me."

"If you mean that first palazzo we tried to exist
in—give me the island."

"Some day you will learn to make yourself independent of the external world and be complete in yourself," the other continued, not to be diverted by frivolous exaggerations.

"You have to depend on external dressmakers, though. And what about food, Mama?"

"The day may come when we learn to nourish our bodies spiritually," the mother maintained.

Marion reopened her book—Fogazzaro's "Il Santo" printed in Italian and privately bound in hand-tooled crimson levant. On the title-page, in Russian-looking script was written the name of Marion Moulton and that of Feodor de Hohenfels.

As soon as her mother became immersed in her new thought pamphlet, the girl let her head sink back and closed her eyelids.

The Italian maid on the other side of the room laid down her needlework and brought a small cushion.

"You're very thoughtful," said Marion, speaking Italian.

"If the signorina would let me take off that great hat?" suggested Mathilde. "The cinders do not come in any more." Brown veil and green velvet hat removed, the girl's red-gold hair showed circlewise around her head in a massive coil like a garland or a crown. Without taking off her long brown gloves, she had slipped her right hand free to turn the leaves of her book. For ring, so soft it could be molded to her finger, she wore a thick band of gold, from which, in gypsy setting, the highest point of light in her color scheme, gleamed a vivid yellow diamond.

"What does the word *abaco* mean, Mathilde?" asked Marion. She suspected it of being an abacus.

Of course she must know what an abacus was, only
—she found she didn't. Mathilde also had to convince herself of her ignorance and was looking the
word up in an Italian dictionary when she was interrupted by a knock at the stateroom door. The por-
ter gave her a card, which she handed to Marion.

"George Pearson," she read.

Asked to come in, a correctly attired young man
with thin brown hair, aquiline nose and narrow chin
greeted the ladies effusively. "We'd begun to think
you were never coming back," he said, seating himself. "To think of my being on the same train! I
didn't see you get on. The conductor asked me if I
knew you were on board. Not that I'm in the habit
of talking to conductors, but this one used to know
me when I was a small boy, so of course——" He
stopped, judging he had said enough to justify the
intimacy of the trainman.

Marion did not look very sympathetic, and Mr.
Pearson concluded he must be careful not to offend
her presumable new standards of exclusiveness acquired in her recent contact with the European aristocracy.

"How is Lady Diotima, George?"

"Lady Diotima? Oh, yes, that's what you used
to call my mother. Why, she's well, thank you.
She will want to see you right away."

"I have strange tales for her sympathetic ears."

"I'd like to hear a little of that, myself," the young
man suggested, glancing at Mrs. Moulton, and then
at his watch. "I want you folks to take lunch with
me. They have a new diner—a beauty, finished in
mission style."

"They're waiting lunch for us at home," Marion explained. "Won't papa be cross by two?" she added to her mother.

"Thank you, though, George," said Mrs. Moulton.

"Don't let us keep you from *your* lunch," put in Marion.

"Why-uh, there's no hurry. I'm awfully anxious to find out if some things I've heard are true."

"I am going to take just a peep at that mission car," announced Mrs. Moulton.

"Mother!" Marion remonstrated, but Mrs. Moulton was undeterred and left.

"Your mother is a brick," said George enthusiastically. "Quickest person. She knew I wanted to ask you some things."

"Naturally—since you said so. But did she know I wanted you to ask them?"

"Why, don't you? Seems to me I have pretty near a right to, Marion."

"Do you believe much in 'rights' of that sort? If you want me to do anything, make me want to."

"What kind of a moral standard is that—doing only what you want to?" demanded George, looking severe.

"That is all we do anyway. One way is to do things honestly because we want to. The other is to find some lofty moral ground for doing the very same things."

"What becomes of the will-power of a person who does only what he wants to?"

"Is there such a person? Well, I should say

strength is developed by doing things rather than by not doing them."

"Are those European ideas?" demanded George.

"Not particularly. They are Marionian ideas. Your mother shares them."

"Oh, mother! It's all talk with her. She acts just like everybody else. I'm afraid you wouldn't."

"I haven't the faintest desire to! Do you suppose I would be guilty of acting just like anybody else— by cut and dried formulas—rules of propriety— with never a guiding emotion of my own—never one spontaneous 'yes' or 'no' out of my own heart— a clockwork dummy wound up to do the proper thing?"

"Why, who in the world are you talking about, Marion? You don't mean my mother, do you?"

"Your mother, you idiot! Bless your heart, no! I mean about everybody *but* her. She is a live person in the midst of a lot of social automata."

Mr. Pearson rose abruptly. "I don't think I care to ask you, Miss Moulton, about your reported engagement to that foreigner, since you consider me an idiot!"

"I didn't suppose you were *really* one!"

"I never had a girl call me that in my life. I don't propose to give any girl the chance to do it twice."

"Don't be a baby, George! Sit down here. Must I really explain that we feminine mortals call no one but our intimates idiots?"

"I would prefer to be excluded from that select circle."

"That's *clever!*" She smiled at him winningly, but her unflattering surprise at his cleverness irritated him still more and he refused to relax. "Oh, well," she said, settling herself in her chair and preparing to dismiss him from her thoughts.

"If those are European ideas and manners of yours, young lady, I think you'd better stay in Moline and lose a little polish." He threw loose the curtain. Looking out of the corner of his eye to see how Marion was taking his departure, he had the misfortune to collide with Mrs. Moulton returning from her peep at the mission car.

"It didn't take you long, Marion," commented Mrs. Moulton, resuming her chair.

"No, I was abominably rude to him and he didn't know it. Then I made amends by being nice and he thought I was insulting him. All he can hear is words. Mr. G. Pearson shows me what a dungeon Moline would be to me. Oh, I hate papa every time I think of it!"

"Marion!"

"And I think about it all the time. Even when I'm asleep some of my mind still burns with the humiliation of that cablegram."

"It would have worked out all right if you hadn't insisted on leaving. You gave Feodor no chance to forgive you."

"I can't bear to be forgiven. I won't be. If papa won't write and apologize I shall contrive somehow to make my own living. I will have nothing more to do with papa—never in my life!"

"If you would leave it to me everything would work out all right. I have been sending the right influence into your father's mind every night and morning since we left Rome."

The girl picked up an alligator hand-purse, glanced at a miniature watch set in the leather and realized that in another half hour she would be facing her father. The tension of her nerves grew painful. A stop in East Moline seemed prolonged wantonly. When the air-brake fell in Moline she reached the station platform and located the driver of the motor-car before her mother and Mathilde appeared.

The driver, Eldridge, affected by her tense atmosphere, sent his machine recklessly through the dingy brick business section crowded with workingmen, past the great factories, up the hill on the high power, between the terra cotta pillars at the gate of Hillcrest, along the curving driveway, past the conservatory and under the archway of the *porte cochère* where the heavy car skidded a little on the concrete flags and stopped.

A footman in livery and white gloves opened the door—the end of their five thousand mile journey—the door of "Dave" Moulton, plow manufacturer, the great man of Moline.

Mr. Moulton was just coming downstairs as they entered—a big, slow-moving man of fifty with well-trimmed, reddish brown beard and florid cheeks. He was unconsciously chewing the end of a thick, unlighted cigar. His high forehead was a little flushed and moist, his blue eyes keen behind rimless gold spectacles. "I'm glad to see you, Anne," he said. His voice was deep and convincing. He evidently wished to have no more made of this than if his wife had been away only a day. He returned her kiss perfunctorily and turned to Marion. "How are you, daughter?" he said, extending his hand.

"I don't feel like shaking hands with you," she said.

His hand drew back abruptly, his lips and eyes ominously hardening. "Oh, is that the way you feel?" He turned toward the library as though there were nothing more to be said.

The girl matched his effect of indifference by giving Mathilde some directions in Italian; and then, without looking at her father, she crossed to the foot of the stairs. Having expected some involuntary word or sign indicating her desire not to let her first greeting go unmodified, he gave her a curious look as he saw her sticking to it. "Oh, Marion!" he called.

She stopped and looked back.

"We'll have to fight it out—you and I," he said incisively. "It will be better if we do it at once."

She decided it was too much like an order and went on, followed by Mathilde. "I shall be in the library a few minutes before lunch," she said.

"I suppose I am to await your pleasure there," he remarked.

"If you choose," she answered, as she disappeared.

He felt that he had lost the key to her mind. "That seems to be a high and mighty daughter of yours, Mrs. Moulton," he observed. "I find the Illinois legislature somewhat easier to control."

He was not in the library when Marion came

down. Rather than sit face to face with him at table she decided to have luncheon in her own rooms, and telephoned her Lady Diotima to come quick and keep her company. "There is war," she announced. "I'm blue and lonesome and dying to see you. I need your moral support. I'll tell you my troubles and I'll even let you give me advice."

"Will you promise to follow it if it's exactly what you think yourself?" Mrs. Pearson demanded. "Oh, I can't wait to see you, Marion. I'll be over instantly."

Half an hour later the Lady Diotima, coming into the large, book-lined room which Marion called her "lair," set her eyes of unfaded blue upon a physically radiant creature, fresh from her bath, in a silvery-looking negligee revealing white rondures of throat and shoulder. For a moment the girl's face glowed with welcome in the sumptuous light of a drift-wood fire, and then she flew into the woman's arms and hugged her. "Oh, Diotima, you are worth all the rest of America!" she crooned. "I would perish here if it weren't for you! Do you still love me?"

"Against my conscience—yes, you vagabond! You deserve nothing of the sort. I've been shamefully neglected—left here to age and ossify with never a letter from Rome—and all sorts of fascinating rumors unverified."

"What has age to do with your young soul? I won't waste breath apologizing. You know the Marionian psychology too well to expect a letter when you ought to have it." She put her arm around

Lady Diotima's shoulder, intending to take off her mink stole, but forgot and let her hand linger stroking the smooth fur.

"Eat, child," commanded Mrs. Pearson, tossing her muff on the window-seat and taking off her toque. "You must be famished."

"I am," admitted Marion, and seated herself at a little table set with chafing dish and charcoal-heated samovar. The dark green curtain behind her was in shadow, the girl in firelight. One white, high-heeled slipper was outlined in startling beauty on the dark, highly polished floor that almost mirrored it. Lady Diotima watched the girl's graceful, leisurely hands as she drew a cup of tea and balanced across it a spoon containing a lump of sugar which she saturated with brandy from a flask cased in silver filigree, and ignited with a gold-handled alcohol lighter. Mathilde carefully set for the visitor this cup over which the blue and fragrant flame danced as with feet that rose and fell. "That's your flame-fairy," explained Marion. "Isn't he nice—this chilly day?"

"Charming as he is, I'm no salamander," protested the lady. "He'll have to die before I drink him."

"Oh, he doesn't die. He reincarnates himself in the tea."

The Lady Diotima looked dreamily at the flame, then thoughtfully at Marion, who glanced at Mathilde and told her she would not be needed.

"You speak Italian unconsciously!" Mrs. Pearson commented with a little note of envy.

"Yes, isn't that nice? I have even accomplished the feat of dreaming in Italian."

"I suppose you've forgotten you learned your first Italian phrases from my phonograph?"

"Could I ever forget that mournful invalid who always wanted a bed or a cab or a room or a doctor and for twenty-six lessons refused to eat one single bite? Which reminds me——" Uncovering the chafing dish, she served herself with creamed sweetbreads.

The flame-fairy having danced himself and his sugar pedestal away, Lady Diotima turned so she could see the fireplace and the play of light on the bronze replica of Rodin's "The Thinker" who sat in silent power above the tiers of books, and musing sipped her tea.

Twice in the six years of their intimacy she had turned the current of the girl's life.

When Marion was seventeen her awakened nature, under her mother's influence, had thrown itself ardently into one of the modern cults of spiritual mysticism. Being a rebel by nature the girl had delighted in that revolt against "orthodoxy." She had attempted to convert Mrs. Pearson and had given her some of the wonderful literature of her cult. Mrs. Pearson began skillfully to preach the beauty of accurate thinking, with the result that the girl, fired with the passion for study, had tutors to prepare her for college and became a Vassar grind.

Contact with scholarly women developed a habit of mind that freed her from the spell of the esoteric, but two years of safe, sane Vassar began to make her dull. Then the Lady Diotima, named by Marion after that wise woman who was the teacher of Socrates, cried down mere intellect and preached life; disparaged knowledge and taught power. To be a social, an intellectual, even a political force—a power behind the throne—to have influence through charm—to modernize the rôle of Madame Ré-camier—the ideal of the old French salon—all this the Lady Diotima preached.

The two of them tried it in Washington one win-ter—but not two.   Not men, but soulless "interests" being there the real power, there was in Washington no significant rôle for a woman, however gifted with beauty or brains or charm.   Wealth did count, but not for its esthetic use, the only use that Marion knew or cared for.

"My face is set toward Europe," then said Mar-ion.

Mr. Pearson's health failing, Lady Diotima did not make the European campaign, and now, as she drank her tea she was keen for history.

"Marion Moulton," she broke out, "do you in-tend to tell me of your own free will and accord whether you are engaged?   It's your last chance."

"How unflattering!" said Marion, buttering a French roll.

"Stupid!   Your last chance to *tell*—except under torture."

"Unfortunately I'm not—thanks to my tactful papa."

"Do tell what happened."

"From the beginning?"

"No, the end first.   I couldn't stand the suspense. And before you tell the end tell me if it is the end."

"Papa again.   If I can make him do what he should——"

"Ah-hem! Financially?"

"No, confound him! That's what *he* thought! That's what he took for granted. That's what he cabled to Feodor—right out of a blue sky—that insulting assumption. And now you too! I thought you would take it for granted that I had brains enough to tell the difference between a man and a fortune hunter!"

"Well, well, Marion, we all know European marriage customs."

"The mistake you both make is in assuming that Feodor de Hohenfels is a creature of custom. I know him and I know myself and I flatter myself I can afford not to be jealous of my own dot."

"What made your father send this cablegram?"

"I didn't consider it necessary to beat about the bush with him. I wrote him that De Hohenfels had made me a proposal of marriage and I intended to accept it. I told him what kind of a man De Hohenfels was—brilliant, talented, a daring steeple-chaser, good-looking, influential, estates in Russia, winter residence in Rome—a quaint old Palazzo and garden, and above all—I didn't tell papa this—a man who had just about outlived his enthusiasms when he met me."

"And naturally they revived," said Lady Diotima dryly. "Very good incense. What form is his revived ambition going to take?"

"That doesn't particularly matter. I'm told he is a wonderful stylist in Russian. He could be eminent in musical criticism. He has the position and the brains to make himself a leader of the younger nobility. He is a candidate for the new Duma and

may become a power for progress in Russia."
"He certainly sounds wonderful," said Mrs. Pear-
son, trying to decide how much allowance should be
made for Marion's friendly and imaginative vision.
If the half were true she saw the futility of her son
George's hopes of Marion.

"I didn't like him a bit the night I first met him,"
Marion confided. "You see, mama and I started
wrong in Rome. Mama met one of her old friends
whom she considered 'most patrician.' She had married an Italian. I was foolish enough to believe in
the lady and let her plan a reception for us. We had
everything wrong—wrong place, wrong people,
people invited whom the 'most patrician' person
imagined she knew, or her husband knew—and he
was a joke, and—oh, it was awful! so awful the
swagger people came for a lark—and De Hohenfels
put them up to that. Of course I became aware of
his attitude as soon as he was introduced. Maybe I
didn't know the ropes of Roman society, but I
knew how to deal with a man who accepted my hospitality for the purpose of making fun of it. He
thought he was doing it so subtly! He was nice and
frank when I cornered him, and you should have
seen him make amends. He told everybody the
Titian American was a social treasure. They who
came to scoff remained et cetera, and I was not
butchered to make a Roman holiday. Little Marion
became the thing, was invited everywhere, and a
month later, with the guidance of Feodor's mother,
the Countess Xenia, and her brother Prince Razinsky, we gave a ball—oh, beautifully right. You

couldn't have thrown a cat without hitting an ambassador or a prince or a duchess—those funny Roman nobles, ruined in land speculation, who come with splendid carriages and empty stomachs."

"Well, talk about luck!" exclaimed Lady Diotima. "But you started to tell me about your father's cablegram."

"In my letter to papa I came square out about my dot. I wanted a big one and asked how big he would make it. I simply said it was the custom in Europe, and a girl marrying in Europe ought to do it right."

"In Rome as the Russians do," Mrs. Pearson suggested sympathetically.

"Exactly. What does papa do but send a cablegram to mama, and get Feodor's address; and the next thing—I suppose the first time Fedya realized there was such a person as papa—came this message saying: 'Do not care to purchase European title for my daughter. Much obliged for offer.' "

"How did the count take that?"

"How could he? It made him furious!"

"Did it make him break things off with you?"

"Nonsense, Diotima. I simply couldn't stand it. It was such a hopeless, crude, horrible, uncalled-for piece of impertinence! If you only knew how incongruous—that message and that man!"

"But what happened? What did you say? What did you do?"

"I couldn't say anything. I was dazed—and more humiliated—more than I shall ever allow myself to be again!"

"Was the man angry with you?"

"With me—no. He wanted me to marry him that day—to show papa."

"Well, that was correct. Really I'm glad you didn't, but—why didn't you? Your father would have respected both of you for that. Now you have apparently confirmed his suspicions."

"It won't take me long to disabuse his mind of that particular delusion."

"But how did you leave things, Marion? What understanding have you with De Hohenfels?"

"None. I simply fled. Mother and I left Rome that night."

"Well Marion Moulton! You certainly did lose your head. Do you know what you are here for?"

"To make papa take it back!" said the girl grimly.

II

MRS. MOULTON interrupted Lady Diotima's visit with the information that Marion's father was alone in the library.

"Did he send for me?" the girl demanded.

"No. He didn't even mention your name all through luncheon, but I know from the quality of the thought-force he radiated that—— Would you like it, Mrs. Pearson, if you hadn't seen your son for over a year and he refused even to shake hands with you?"

"I am told that even pugilists shake hands before they fight," agreed Lady Diotima.

"Oh, dear!" exclaimed Marion impatiently. "I do often bow to custom and treat people hypocritically—but not papa. And not you, Lady Diotima. Whenever I feel like quarrelling with you I intend to do it." She rose abruptly. "I might as well see him and have it over," she said, and called Mathilde. After promising Mrs. Pearson to come to see her next day, Marion dressed for the afternoon and went down to her father's study.

As she entered, Mr. Moulton appeared to be absorbed in the pages of "The Iron Age."

"Am I interrupting you?" she inquired.

17

"Oh, come in."

She seated herself without hurry in the big leather chair on the opposite side of her father's wide, orderly table. "I suppose we might as well have it out," she said.

"Good! Well, what is it we are to quarrel about?"

Marion found it difficult to avoid liking him. "As if you didn't know perfectly!"

"You forget. I am not the mind-reading member of the family."

"You know you sent an insulting cablegram to Feodor de Hohenfels and that he and I were on the point of engaging ourselves to marry."

"You didn't—did you?"

"He would have married me that day, but I wished first to have him receive from you a letter of apology. I came home to ask you to write it. Will you do it?"

"Suppose I will not?"

"There's no use going into that until it is certain you will not."

"I hope I shall not find it necessary."

"What, in your opinion, will make it unnecessary?"

"Your own decision that I acted wisely."

"Wisely! You acted without the slightest knowledge of facts, persons, or circumstances. You blazed away with your eyes shut. You were governed by a provincial prejudice against the European nobility —some platitude you read in a funny paper when you were a boy. If you did things like that in your business you'd be bankrupt in a week. You took it for granted I was a fool. I know what kind of a man a man is. And yet you—five thousand miles away— you over-rule my judgment in a case where I have all the facts and you haven't one!"

"That's a good many charges to answer all at once, Marion. At least it brought you home—without the gentleman—and that was what I wanted."

"Why did you *want* to play the devil with my life?"

"In the first place an American girl is a fool to marry into nations that have a lower ideal of women than her own."

"Sheer provincial ignorance, I tell you. I have studied exactly what rôle a woman can play here and abroad. In America an ornament, in Europe a power. I prefer to be a power."

"You do? I'm glad to hear it. That is exactly what I hoped. I respect your preference. You want power. You are running to the ends of the earth for it. You don't know exactly what it is yet, but you want it. You think of it as social, intellectual, political. As a matter of fact, in the modern world these are merely the shadows of power. The real power is industrial."

"Industrial power doesn't happen to appeal to me personally. I suppose it's a good foundation, but need I concern myself about it?"

Letting his finger slip from the page it had been marking, he thoughtfully broke into a tray the long ash from his cigar, and swung his chair to face her squarely. "Do you know," he asked, "what is happening here in the shops and offices of Moline and Rock Island—in all these miles of factories that you have looked at all your life and never seen? It's a fascinating, big, slow battle between various sets of powerful, determined men. Do you know what it means? It means that in a few years one man will control the plow manufacturing business of the United States. Every furrow that is turned across eight million farms will send its share of tribute in to him. Men in mines, steel-mills, shops, men on railroads and on farms, will depend on him for work and life. Millions of men will collaborate in pouring in to him a stream of wealth so great the imagination cannot conceive it. If I can, I am going to be that man. If I am—well, in the natural course of events that stream of wealth will flow to you. You—Marion Moulton! A young lady who has decided that in America there is no power to be had. She is looking for it in Europe, in Rome, a city whose chief industries are a wax bead factory for peasant's rosaries and the business of manufacturing saints' relics out of mutton bones."

"*What* a view of eternal Rome!" Marion exclaimed. "Oh, in spite of your narrowness, your blindness to everything in life but 'business,' you do make me feel how big and real your power is and may become. I suppose it's too bad I'm not a man. But I'm not. You don't want me to remain unmarried and go to work in your office, do you?"

"I want you to realize your position. Did they say nobility imposes obligation? That motto has died. The motto that is alive to-day is this: Ownership imposes obligation. Your marriage is not, as you seem to suppose, a thing that concerns you alone. It is of direct concern to thousands."

"Just for curiosity, Papa,—whom do you want me to marry?"

"You ought to know I have no intention of trying to dictate to you. If you did decide to carry out your original intention of marrying George Pearson, I should make no objection."

"When I did think of doing that, you said George didn't have brains enough to be a corporal of industry."

"I *was* doubtful about George's having the head to carry on a great industry, but it has recently developed that Dick Pearson, supposed to be in poor health and thinking only of retiring from business, has really been putting through some tremendous deals in lumber. The rise in timber lands is going to make his holdings simply colossal. The Pearson interests are now so secure that——" He hesitated.

"That your respect for George's brain power has increased?" Marion suggested innocently.

He scrutinized her, making sure she was conscious of her irony. "He will have advisers and managers. The Pearsons are going to have vast capital to invest in other lines than lumber. The plow industry is attractive. If that capital should back up United States Plow we could ultimately absorb our competitors. We may do it single-handed. But any young person looking for power should consider attentively a proposition that would result in one of the great fortunes of the modern world."

"Don't you see your inconsistency?" said Marion. "You attribute a mercenary motive to De Hohenfels, reproach him for it, and in the next breath you advise me to marry George Pearson for his money!"

"One of these propositions is to your disadvantage, the other to your advantage. I advise you accordingly."

"Assuming that there's no sort of advantage but the economic. No, Papa. You can make business your own God if you like, but you can't make it mine."

"You are not in a position to assume ethical superiority in this matter. As a matter of fact you have no moral right to throw away the immense resources that may be yours on any little foreign landowner."

"Feodor de Hohenfels is not little in any sense of the word."

"Economically he is exactly that. He owns some farms in Russia. Perhaps he employs a villageful of muzhiks who scratch the ground with wooden plows. What does it amount to? He naturally will have the prejudices and mental limitations of his medieval, land-holding class."

Marion smiled. " 'Mental limitations' sounds funny, Papa, in connection with the gentleman you are talking about—without knowing anything about him. A man has certain aspects besides the economic. This man is not exactly a pauper at that. There are several million roubles' worth of timber lands, for instance, that make him decidedly richer than I am, for at present I have nothing. Of course if you're going to throw in all the plows and farms and mines and things in America that you may own some day——"

The thrust angered Dave Moulton. "The twenty-five odd million dollars' worth of them I do at present own I may feel compelled to place beyond the reach of Mr. de Hohenfels. Possibly if he is given to understand this, the problem will solve itself."

"There you go again!" exclaimed Marion, spring-ing to her-feet. "I'd rather earn my living by my own hands than be in a position where anyone in this world can take the right to talk to me like that!"

"Don't be a fool, Marion."

"If it's fool or slave, I prefer to be fool!"

"You needn't be either."

"I needn't? Oh, no! All I have to do is let you decide such little matters as whom I shall marry and whom not!"

"You are mistaken. Marry whom you please. If the man happens to be one I don't want in control of the United States Plow Company he shan't con-trol it—that's all."

"The Count de Hohenfels does not happen to be consumed with a burning passion for the United States Plow Company. It's very doubtful if he knows there is such a thing. It's that assumption of yours which has caused all the trouble, and I'm simply asking you to straighten things out again by a letter to him."

"Doesn't know there is such a thing, eh? Do you know we send over a million dollars' worth of agri-cultural machinery a year through the port of Riga? You'll find he has read a little something about us in Bradstreet's."

"What's the use of making that statement? All there is to the whole question is that you insulted us. I want to know whether or not you are going to be decent and write that letter?"

"A letter of apology?"

"Exactly."

"Which would result in the gentleman's taking the next steamer for America?"

"I don't know how it would result. I do know you owe him that reparation. You owe it to *me*. Can't you see it doesn't put me in a very good light —your taking it for granted that the only reason a man would want to marry me is for your money?"

"Being married for money is a distinct danger of any girl in your position—especially when she develops an affair with a man of a notoriously money marrying class. The newspapers are full of how such marriages turn out."

"The newspapers! Papa, are you going to write that letter?"

"Not to-day."

"When are you going to write it?"

"When you tell me you'd rather have that letter written than inherit control of the United States Plow Company."

"Well, I'll tell you that right now!" blazed Marion. "Please write the letter." She went rapidly to the door.

"Just a moment," said Mr. Moulton. "I do not intend to accept a decision of such magnitude made by you on the spur of the moment and in the heat of argument. I will accept no decision one way or the other for——" He glanced at the calendar on his desk. "This is Tuesday the twentieth. A fortnight is none too much. You may give me your answer on April third, two weeks from to-day."

"I should very much like to see the letter before you send it," said Marion, and out she walked.

III

NEVER in her life having felt the lack of it, wealth meant little to Miss Moulton. To have every luxury, to do whatever one pleased without reckoning the cost, seemed simply the normal state of things. She had no conception of the thing she was ready to throw away; and yet before she reached the end of the hall as she left her father's study, she stopped with a pang. "Fedya!" She voiced the name involuntarily. "I can't let you marry me without a penny!" she thought. Walking slowly on, she turned absent-mindedly into the conservatory.

From the west, blown clear of cloud by a northwest wind, the low sun was sending red lances and arrows of light through fronds of palm. In front of a dark green wall of ferns a bed of orchids blazed fantastic, over rich—a sense impression of so violent beauty as to draw the attention of the girl even with her life-problem burning in her thoughts! She remembered a certain rustic seat and passed down a tessellated aisle between fragrant walls of verdure and bloom that rose from shining jardinieres and trailed from hanging baskets. From that artificial splendor of sumptuous nooks and graceful bowers she entered a place of massive rocks and moss run wild and great ferns growing. There was the tinkle and gurgle of a rivulet, a rustic bridge, a pool of Japanese pond-lilies.

With a welcome sense of seclusion she dropped upon the rustic seat to think things out. She was wondering whether among her dabblings of art and knowledge there was anything substantial enough to make a living for her. Hearing a curious swish near a high rock of an island in the pond, she looked and to her amazement beheld there, knee-deep among the lilies, a man in shirt-sleeves and hip-boots. He was stooping over and carefully touching with a brush the center of certain blossoms.

"Where in the world did you come from?" the girl exclaimed.

The man straightened up hastily and stared at her. "Excuse me for having a better right to the question," he said. "I've been here two hours on this job."

"Oh," said the girl, her curiosity satisfied. "You're one of the gardeners."

"That's all," said the man. Smiling privately at his elimination in her mind from the category of human beings, he resumed his occupation.

Something in his tone modified her preconception of him as simply a specimen of the genus gardener, but she did not wish to think about him. She tried to get back her interrupted train of thought, but found herself mechanically watching the movements of the gardener and his brush. The result was a slight irritation that he should be doing it.

"Why are you doing that?" she demanded, not really thinking of what she was saying.

"To cross-fertilize the flowers," he answered without looking up.

She felt that she had displayed her ignorance, and social inferior though he was, she did not care to leave that impression on the man. She gave the subject her full consideration for a moment, groping among shadowy recollections of freshman botany. "Have you ever looked at the pollen through a microscope?" Her malicious hope was that he had not.

"Oh, yes," he answered in a matter of course tone.

Her failure to make him feel ignorant roused her interest. The glance he gave her seemed to be one of lessening hostility. He drew a pocket lens from his corduroys, and bent down with it looking at various flowers. She noticed his fine wavy brown hair and fair complexion slightly tanned by his artificial summer under glass.

"Here's a grain of pollen on the tip of this pistil," he said. "It's likely to open and send a little liquid filament down to the eggs of the flower. Would you care to watch it?"

"Not having any hip-boots at hand, I think I won't," she answered, wondering how a man in his station had managed to acquire such diction.

He took a knife, cut the stem of the gorgeous lily, brought it ashore to her, and offered her the lens.

She hesitated an instant, then took the flower and looked. The young man went back to his work without waiting for her comment, so she was free to forget him and lose herself in contemplation of the wonderful structure and still more wonderful func-, tion of that minute, amorous grain of living dust.

She watched it with real interest. When she lowered
the lens she looked at the whole flower with a new
wonder—a sudden realization of the depth and
beauty of sex in the life of the world. "What a
pity the stem is cut!" she thought. "That wonderful event will do no good."

With a start she remembered the presence of the
gardener, felt that he was looking, glanced quickly
to read his expression, and to her surprise encountered an inadvertent look of sympathetic understanding. For a purely human instant it disarmed her
and drew a like look to her eyes. But what right
had he to understand? "Very interesting, I'm sure,"
she said coldly.

He turned without answering and bent over the
next lily, but she saw a curious little smile. What
sort of man was he anyhow with his rough hands
and scholar's speech? Her eye went back to the
lily.

"Tell me," she said, "do women ever do this sort
of work?"

"Gardening? My mother has slaved at it all her
life."

She dismissed her half-formed idea that he might
be a man of good family reduced to working his way
through college. "It seems to me I have heard of
girls fitting themselves as horticulturalists in a college founded by Lady Warwick," she mused. "How
decent a living could one make at it anyway?"

"At gardening?" He looked at her and smiled.
"If you think of going into the business, you'd better
put in plenty of capital and hire me."

She did not respond to his humor, but as he started to laugh she noticed with approval his excellent, clean teeth. "I wished to know what one could do without capital—by one's own work."

"Starve," said the gardener.

"Indeed? *You* do not look emaciated. How much do you earn a month?"

"I get fifty and board."

The girl's eyebrows lifted at the meagerness of the wage. Her own personal yearly expenses were supposed to be limited to twenty thousand a year. "Are you the head gardener?" she pursued.

"No. He draws a hundred."

"And you think that I, for instance, couldn't aspire to fifty?"

"It takes physical strength," said the man eyeing her sceptically.

That made little impression on her, for she felt that she had it.

"It also takes patience," he added—"an ox-like physical endurance such as nothing in your life can possibly have given you."

"Oh, as to that—!" she said, waving it aside. "If others acquire it, I could."

He thought a moment. "My father and mother have slaved at truck-farming all their lives, Miss Moulton—they and their children—often sixteen hours a day and sometimes in emergencies twenty hours. They have produced pretty near enough to feed Moline, and they haven't cleared fifty a month year in, year out, for the whole family. Of course a job like this—after a technical course and some years' experience—you might get a hundred raising useless things for rich people to look at once or twice a year."

Her expression hardened with dislike of his tone.

"You gardening!" he repeated, not at all worrying about the effect of his words on her. "It's as though a nightingale who could fill the heart of the night with fire should—want to live in a hen-house and lay eggs for somebody's breakfast."

Her mind drew from the speaker to the poetic phrase. His voice's indisputable knowledge of how to give it the value of truthful music affected her only unconsciously.

"What gives you that romantic idea—as to the heart of the night?" she said, her disparaging tone not successfully concealing the pleasure the romantic idea gave her.

"The things open to you! Your boundless freedom for development. Some who have that have nothing to develop; but it's evident that——"

"I have no freedom whatever!" she exclaimed bitterly. "I was thinking of that very thing when I came in here!"

Seeing his interest in her exclamation, she pulled up, wondering how she had come to drift so far into things personal. Her unconscious feeling that her social superiority was too obviously secure to bother thinking about or demonstrating was there to reassure her. The man went carelessly on in his tone of dispassionate analysis. "Of course you haven't much sense yet," he said, "—but doubtless that's inexperience."

For a moment Miss Moulton was too astonished to answer. "I admit that what I am doing just now shows lack of good sense," said she, scathingly.

"In talking to me?" smiled the gardener, straightening up. "Oh, no,—*that's* sensible."

"I think," said she with an air of finality, "that there is a little too much ego in your cosmos."

"On the contrary—to reverse your quotation of Kipling—most everyone you meet has so much cosmos in his ego that the ego is all squeezed out."

What arrested her was the fact that that very thought, turned that very way, might have come from—Feodor de Hohenfels! "One thing would be interesting to know," she said. "Did you borrow that egoistic pose from someone you've heard or from something you've read?"

"Neither. Oh, I have read Max Stirner and found him in possession of a few distorted fragments of my philosophy. But it isn't an egoistic pose, Miss Moulton. It's *real* egoism."

The surprise of this turn and his smile as he said it were too much for her. She had to smile back.

"I have simply accepted myself," he explained. "Most people accept instead some fool ideal and then belittle themselves for differing therefrom. I reflect that nature has been twenty or a hundred million years or so at the job of making me as I am. I'm not egotist enough to frame up some ideal conception of what I should be and imagine that shadow of my brain superior to nature's actual achievement in me."

She was silent following and weighing the idea.

"Yes," she decided. "It's strange, but this man does think like Feodor." And then she asked, "Have you read Bernard Shaw?"

"Some," he answered.

"Did you learn that trick of turning things inside out from him?"

"It seems hard for you to conceive that a man can be his own thinker."

She looked at him with the sudden respect of a stung child for a bee.

"Your question," he said, "entitles me to ask if you think when Shaw turns an old idea inside out that he's wantonly twisting that he knows to be true into something clever and different?"

"My dear Mr. ——" began Marion.

"Bradfield."

"Thank you. Anyone who knows that a man may say a thing wittily and nevertheless believe what he says will not debate the banal question of Mr. Shaw's sincerity. Which do you prefer, Mr. Bradfield: Shall I imitate you and tell you plainly that I am an intelligent person, or shall I pay you the compliment of supposing you able to perceive it?"

"Hoist with my own petard!" chuckled Mr. Bradfield. "I believe there's no one else in Moline who could have come back at me outegotizing the egoist."

She found herself not resenting his putting himself with her in a class from which the rest of Moline was somewhat naturally excluded. Feeling that she might find clarification in the atmosphere of this remarkable individual, she had a sudden instinctive impulse to test and seize and use his thinking power as a tool for her own purposes—very much as her family was using his power of muscular labor. "I'm into this too deep to báck out now," was the way she put it to herself. "If you are as clear-headed a person as you think you are——" she began. "Please come up out of that pond and sit down here and tell me why you said I have no sense. If you can prove it——"

He came ashore. "Any one with the enormous economic power that will be yours—to talk of gardening for a living!" he scoffed.

"Suppose I find the price I must pay for that power too high?"

"Well—it must be a staggering price!"

"Do you think slavery too high a price?"

"Slavery!" he echoed. "You don't know what it means! Go ask my mother what it is!" After a moment he added: "Your father's conditions are nothing to the thing you want to put your neck into."

"My father's conditions!" Marion gasped. "How did you—what makes you say that?"

"An obvious inference from slavery as the price of economic power."

"Do you call that obvious? It strikes me as uncanny. Sit down. How much more do you infer?"

"More would be guessing." He glanced at the low sun, sat down, and turned down the tops of his boots. "Still—was it some little point of honor—a difficulty you could have smoothed out in a minute if it was not for what your friends call your 'high spirit'?"

Marion sat back abruptly. That letter she had come to America to have written—was that so all-important? Incidentally Bradfield no longer reminded her of Feodor. The Russian prized that same high spirit more than anything else. It was that in her which had attracted him and fired him with the passion of conquest. "I *was* high-handed with papa," she thought. "And what did I gain by it? Why don't I steer straight for the big thing?" Completely absorbed in viewing the whole affair of De Hohenfels and her father from this sudden new angle, she rose and started toward the bridge.

Looking after her, Bradfield the gardener thought she was going to leave without another word; but remembering him, she turned and, not really letting go the new threads of her thought, she murmured, "That suggests things. Thank you. I wish to think them out." So she walked on slowly out of the gardener's sight.

IV

MARION showed a desire after dinner that evening to talk again with her father on the subject of the letter to De Hohenfels. Mr. Moulton saw with satisfaction that it must mean modification—sooner than he had hoped—of her demand, but he felt it necessary to maintain his resolution to accept no answer before the specified time; and Marion had to resign herself to a fortnight of unsettledness. She chafed at what she felt to be the sheer tyranny of the unnecessary delay, characterizing it as springing from a senseless, old-fashioned habit of parental rigidity toward children.

The letters to Feodor which she began were necessarily so unsatisfactory that they all went into the fire.

Everything at Hillcrest irritated her. When it occurred to her the second morning after her arrival to go to the conservatory and talk again with Bradfield, her knowledge that her father would neither understand nor sympathize was anything but a deterrent. And when she began to think of Bradfield, whom she had left so brusquely, she became really curious. He was an unusual phenomenon she wished to understand. She decided to get him talking, hear his history, explore his range, and find his

limits, which were still quite vague to her. She felt
that very likely her first surprise at finding an intellectual man in his station had caused her to overesti-
mate him. On her way to the conservatory, for the
satisfaction of her own, not her father's, sense of
decorum, she considered pretty carefully the tone she
ought to adopt. To treat him simply as a gardener,
she felt, would be absurd, since merely as a gardener
he had practically no interest for her. About right,
she decided, would be that nuance of conduct she
had been taught to observe with governesses and
tutors and middle-class people of culture, not servants, who for any reason mingle with the family
yet are paid for being there.

When Bradfield, however, looked up at her, returning her greeting, from his kneeling posture before a velvet slope of moss he was creating on a bare
spot among the rocks, a sudden spirit of mischief
somewhat disarranged Miss Moulton's predeter-
mined program.

"Sir Oracle," she said in a tone of amiable mockery, "I think perhaps you did me a service the other
day, and for all I know I may now be seeking more
wisdom."

"What shall I enlighten you about?" he inquired,
straightening up on his knees.

"I haven't just decided. You disapprove of gardening, so of course I have dropped that. As I remember it your alternative was to fill the heart of
the night with fire. The idea appeals to me re-
markably. I'm sure I should like nothing better.
But on reflection I find myself just a little uncertain
how it is done."

"Of course I couldn't be explicit for you," he said, taking another square of moss from his basket.

"Be so for *you* then. How would you go about filling it?"

He took the question seriously—thinking for a moment.

"I suppose I would have to go about it mainly with pen and ink—I mean a typewriter. But meanwhile I would study, think, travel, observe. I would get my philosophy down to unshakeable bedrock. I would stiffen it with multitudes of exactly gauged facts. Above all—I would become personally acquainted with the men in every land who are fighting for freedom—find out what they want done—and help them do it." For a moment he was absorbed in the vision of what his life would be if he had her opportunity. The ring in his voice as he spoke of the fight for freedom must have stirred something deep in her, for he heard her saying self-unconsciously:

"My version of that feeling seems narrower but more definite—to rouse and guide the ambition of a gifted man adrift on life: to waken him into a power for the liberalization, not of every land, but of one belated country—Russia."

"The liberalization of Russia?" said Bradfield dubiously.

"Yes. To transform it into a free government."

"Like ours?"

Her mind busy with his trend, she seated herself sidewise on the rustic bench and turned looking over the back of it to talk to him—the whole graceful process the flower of long training become unconscious. "I suppose you think liberalizing Russia as much too big as gardening is too small," she said.

"No. I am thinking it wouldn't be worth while."

She repeated that phrase in amazement.

"You see only the outward form, not the substance of modern tyranny," he explained, going on with his work. "The men in your father's mills—and the men who are not allowed to work in them—are oppressed with the real oppression, which is economic. The people of Russia would be practically no better off under a republic if all the sources of wealth remained as now both in Russia and America, in the hands of a few."

"You don't know Russia, my friend, or you would not talk like that."

"I know America, though, and you do not."

"Don't you think that rather arrogant? I have lived most of my life in America. I've kept my eyes open and have thought some. How comes it that you know America and I do not?"

"Because you've not had to know it. I have. You and your friends have tabooed the subject of the people's misery. You live like the uncaring gods of Epicurus—in places like this." The fernery was full of gorgeous glooms and gleams, ripplings and tinklings of sound and light. "You never see the unbeautiful homes of the workmen who make this beauty possible," he said. "If you did, you'd think their squalor good enough. Where they are concerned you are afflicted with the myopia of your class, whose dominance is based on systematic injustice to mine."

"I simply don't believe it," said Marion.

"Shall I tell you why you don't?" said he, forgetting moss. "Because the class philosophy you have breathed since babyhood is full of lies born of your class-interests—the self-interest of profit-taking men and dividend-spending women. Dividends are holy things—not to be cut—no matter how much or how wide-spread suffering it costs to maintain them. You bourgeois have believed your own lies about this condition until you have lost the power of seeing straight in anything. The foggy new religions you go wild over prove the decadence of your intellect. You affect looking down on intellect—it is so dead against you. Whatever you deal with you show yourselves muddleheads. We workers see things straight. We have to. Economic pressure imposes the habit on us. We are up against hard facts that can't be Christian-scienced out of existence. Nietzsche talks about the splendid tension of the human spirit resulting from the effort of Europe to throw off the yoke of ecclesiasticism. That tension's nothing to ours—our effort to throw off the yoke of economic slavery. There's the real splendor of the human spirit in our time. You will see it burst out before you die." He rose from his knees and came toward her. She had a little sense of his having dramatically assumed the rôle of protagonist of his class, yet neither that nor the fact that he was addressing an audience of one in cadences approaching those of public speaking seemed odd enough to her to spoil his effect. "We who have borne the burden of the world," he said, "—did you think we would not grow strong? When we had to think ourselves out of your false view of life or perish, did you suppose we wouldn't learn to think? We were forced to forge intellectual weapons for your overthrow or be ground down out of existence. Naturally we forged them. We've come free of your lies with a burning love of truth; we've survived your injustice with a burning love of justice. On truth and justice and the brotherhood we have learned in misery we will build a world a thousand times better than yours—even for you whom we shall overthrow! On our foundation you shall see a human civilization lift into more than Athenian beauty and perfection! For the first time since the communes of savagery the economic basis of life shall be right—and with our power enlarged from stone axe to steam-hammer. . . . *Our* power, mind you. Not Dave Moulton's, and not yours!"

"You are really a poet, Mr. Bradfield," said the girl, so little affected by the substance of his speech that she was free to admire the passionate vigor of his expression.

"And if I am! Do you think so little of the poets as to oppose our vision to fact?"

"I naturally can't help seeing that you overlook some large facts," said Marion calmly. "If it wasn't for my father's factories, for instance, the men there whom you think so oppressed would not have the work they have nor draw the thousands of dollars they get for doing it."

"Do you know your father sells a plow costing him seven and a half for labor and material, for thirty-five dollars? Do you know he has crushed the unions which stand for a little better pay, a little better hours, a little better life for all these working-men? Do you know these workingmen receive less than one-fifth the value of their labor?"

"I don't know just what proportion of the total value they receive. Did these workmen buy the steel and wood to make the plows of?"

"No, the steel was mined and made, the wood cut and sawed by other workers who received only a fraction of the value they created out of the natural earth."

"Why didn't your workers organize the United States Plow Company themselves? Why did they leave that to my father and grandfather?"

"The time was not then ripe. They had not learned to work together in great factories. They know how now. Your grandfather did perform a service to society. Was it so great that society should give him and his heirs forever despotic power over its labor and life? Only a tiny fraction of the human energy of brain and muscle that built these factories and constructed this machinery was his. The savage who first used fire, perhaps a thousand centuries ago, helped him to make his plow. Architects and wage-workers built the factories; inventors, designers, and wage-workers made the machinery. Thousands of men have been forced to content themselves with a pittance for creating the wealth with which the Moultons bought factories."

She was certain the Moultons ought to have the factories, but could not lay hold of a good reason why. "How far back do you go with that?" she asked. "To the Norman Conquest?"

"I could go back to a much older war fought with flint-tipped arrows and stone celts. The Moulton of that time was a war-chief, who, instead of dining on a captive, set him to work and dined throughout the year on the fruits of that work. Slavery, serfdom, wage-work—the last method of living off the labor of other men is an improvement on all others—from the point of view of the exploiters." He laughed, and went back to his basket of moss.

"You seem to be equipped with a very elaborate perversion of the true relations between labor and capital."

"That's funny," he said. "Don't you really see that the economic interest of your class inclines you to look on relations very advantageous to capital and very disadvantageous to labor as 'true'? My economic interest and that of my class makes me brand these same relations as rotten."

"Let me point out that there is such a thing as abstract truth—what the French call the true truth—which is neither your point of view nor mine, but simply true."

"Into the blue!" he exclaimed. "A truth different from what I think, and from what you think, and from what every other human being thinks—existing in no brain—where *does* it exist? What good is it anyhow? In reality there is only you and me and what facts force us to believe. That is the true truth."

She weighed that a moment. "You may be right about that," she said. "Suppose you are also right about slavery, serfdom and wage-work. Do you think you can overthrow these laws of life—the law of stronger and weaker—which, according to your

own view of history, has been working among men
since the age of stone?"

"Not permanently. The present system has tem-
porarily set that law aside since a stupid man with
capital is at present much more than a match economically for a keen-minded man without it. But
my analysis of history shows me that the same economic laws that have made the slave a serf and the
serf a wage-worker are going to make the wage-
worker his own boss."

"Then what will make him work?"

"What makes your father work?"

"He's an unusual man."

"Well, I'll grant that. He happens to be. But
suppose just usual men, the workers, owned all the
factories in common. Can you imagine them standing outside the closed doors of *their own* factories
suffering, perhaps dying, for lack of the things their
factories can produce? No. All there is to it is
this: At present, ignorant, narrow and small-souled
as the view of your class is, you have the power to
enforce it. You capitalist plutocrats had to overthrow the feudal aristocrats to get the power you
have. Very well. As you overthrew them, we social
democrats will overthrow you."

"Oh," said Marion. "Are you a socialist?" She
looked at him curiously. "I'm not sure I ever saw a
real live one before."

"I'll not be the last one you see."

"Very likely not. I understand socialism is growing. But do you really imagine, Mr. Bradfield, that
in Europe the landed aristocracy has no power?"

"Only in so far as the aristocrats are capitalists.

Aristocracy is a survival—like the vermiform appendix. That's why you doom yourself to futility when you attempt to galvanize your Russian."

"How many European nobles have the honor to be acquainted with you, Mr. Bradfield? Do you realize what a cock-sure theorizer you are? It happens that the brain of the Russian nobleman I was thinking of glows with magnificent life. His mind is like a bed of orchids."

Bradfield was evidently impressed for a moment, and then his eyes narrowed keenly. "Why does he need so much rousing, and guiding, and waking?" he asked. "Did you say he was adrift on life? Why is he adrift? The Russian revolutionists are not drifting. Neither are the rulers. They are real—they stand for something vital, they know what they are doing. But your landed young gentleman who is to 'liberalize' the Russian Government! The peasants of the *mir* on his estate will make new Russia— not he."

"I've heard that prophecy is a risky business," she said, not caring to discuss De Hohenfels with Bradfield.

"What is his attitude toward the Russian 'lower classes'?" pursued Bradfield.

"I suppose he considers most of them ignorant and fanatical."

"Risky it may be, but I think I can make a pretty fair forecast of his fate, and yours if you marry him. I do not think you and he will fill the heart of the night with fire. You will certainly not liberalize Russia, and if you did it would do no good. The Russian revolution, the rising of peasant and worker

—whose interests are antagonistic to yours—with that new-found, passionate religion they call Solidarity, they will sweep you away like chaff!"

"How very exultant the idea makes you," said she, smiling. "Well, you are interesting, Mr. Bradfield. You really are an amazing gardener." His expression hardened—in a reaction against her patronizing tone. "But do you know," she added quickly, "I can't see such a vast difference between your rhapsodies and those of the new religionists you are so scornful of."

"They may be alike in fervor. The difference is that mine are based on close analysis of human history, on economic science, on real psychology. Theirs are based on—wind. If you can't see the difference——!"

"It must be because I belong to a muddle-headed class, Mr. Bradfield. Do let it be my class! It is so much more comforting to blame the others for it!"

"It *is* your class. You are the most intelligent member of it I have ever met. You are the only bourgeois person I know that I like."

"Thank you. It happens, however, that I am not a 'bourgeois person.' The phrase sets my teeth on edge."

He looked at her thoughtfully. "I see," he said. "The class feeling of the aristocracy. But consider the angle from which I look. Aristocrat and bourgeois are alike exploiters of us. Now we begin taking the reins of the world from you, you are uniting against us—like you and your Russian. In a few years you will be one class."

"Wrong," she said, exulting because he was

wrong. "I hated all that was bourgeois—in ethics
and wall-paper, literature and hair-dressing—years
before I came in contact with—the aristocracy."
She expected Bradfield to catch the little turn and
smile back at it; but he was busy with a new idea of
his own. Till then he had taken for granted an im-
passable chasm between them.

"You hate the bourgeois instinctively?" he pondered. "Why is that? And you talk of gardening
—of earning your own living. Is it something
deeper than I thought in you? Is it possible that
some day you will be coming to us?"

"What do you mean?"

"I wouldn't think so if you were the ordinary
brainless society girl. You think. You feel. You're
big enough to rise above your class ethics—or you
wouldn't be talking to me. In spite of your wealth
—why, you have even felt in a pale way the lack
of economic freedom! I think you should be coming to *us*—toward democracy, instead of away from
it. Believe me—only on our side will you find the
kind of life you crave—the spirit you love!"

"Just what kind of life and spirit do you take
that to be, Mr. Bradfield?"

"The life of useful work and the spirit of comradeship."

"Awhile ago you were scornful because I wanted
to find useful work."

"Yes, at the present degrading price of human
labor power, someone else taking the greater part of
the value of your labor. That will not be so when
we workers adjust the work and wealth of the
world to our own needs."

"Are you talking of your grandchildren?" she inquired. "And comradeship! Have you the spirit of comradeship toward *us*—whom you regard as your enemies?"

"No, not now. How can we? But there are very few of you—fewer all the time as wealth concentrates. Out of eighty millions in this country not quarter of a million. One in four hundred. But you own everything. You hold everything we must have to work with—to live. You own our working power—mental and manual. We have to sell it to you or starve. You own us. You use us solely for your benefit, not ours. We have to fight you. After we have taken away your power to rob us—we will have no reason to exclude you from comradeship."

"You have your narrowness," she said. "Do you imagine that we—the people you now exclude—do you really think we know nothing of comradeship?"

"Not for us. Not for three hundred and ninety-nine four hundredths of the people in America."

"You are wrong," said the girl. She looked him full in the eyes but met there the glint of a conviction stronger than her own. "How shall I make you feel it?" she exclaimed. An unaccountably vivid desire to shake his grip on that hostile conviction became momentarily the most essential thing in the world. She was leaning unconsciously toward him, exerting all the personal attraction of her serious eyes and earnest voice. Suddenly she held out her hand to him. He looked surprised, took her hand uncertainly, and through his eyes she saw his grip on his idea relax—his attention wavering toward the charm of her gesture and the delicate, nervous shock of her smooth hand in his. "You are one man in a thousand, Mr. Bradfield," she said warmly. "You have plenty of ability. Lift yourself *out of* the class in which you happen to have been born."

He dropped her hand abruptly. "On a ladder of my own people's faces!" he cried with scorn. "No, I prefer to help lift the class in which I was born!"

She drew back. "What folly to look at it so!" she exclaimed, vexed with his rude repulse of an advance she felt to be magnanimous. "Well then—stay down!"

"No!" said he. "I will come up with the other nine hundred and ninety-nine!"

"Try it and see!"

"We are not merely trying—we are doing it."

"A little too unselfish of you for this world as it is," she said, wishing she could lay hold of something that would really cut.

"This world, Miss Moulton, shall not remain as it is. We are not content with a mere mournful, inactive, poetic wish that we might 'grasp this sorry scheme of things entire!' We will grasp it. We will shatter it to bits. We will 'remold it nearer to the heart's desire'!"

"You seem very sure of your ability to do a very big thing."

"As individuals we could not do it. As a class we can."

"A whole class of heaven-stormers?"

"Not at all. Our energy is not directed impotently against God. We have discovered that he is not the responsible party. And you needn't worry about our being too unselfish. To labor for the

super-enrichment of you owners—that's rank unsel-
fishness. What unites us is self-preservation. We
are true to our class because we have solved for ourselves the problem of *alter* and *ego*. We know
towards whom and what we must act egotistically
and where to use our altruism. Light like ours burns
only as a torch in the open night. We've seen too
many labor leaders use their torch for the illumina-
tion of some private bushel. They take place and
pelf and subtler bribes—seats at a banquet—the
privilege of speaking to exquisite women like you.
And their souls—go out!"

"You're not absurd enough to suppose I am trying
to bribe you with my companionship!" She laughed.

"Not consciously. But do you suppose the class-
soul—the social group of which you are one component molecule—does not use you and daily work
through you in a thousand ways you do not understand?"

She had a glimpse of his vision. Since he dropped
her hand she had tried to hurt him, to make him feel
foolish, to shake his faith in his ideas. Whether
they were true or not did not concern her, so much
as her desire to loosen his grip, to weaken him with
self doubt. Each utterance had been a conscious
thrust of her will seeking to break his. He had dealt
with these hostile volitions merely as ideas, unconscious of the easily adequate action of his own resisting will. She gave it up. "It's a little uncanny," she
said. "For a moment then I felt that I was not just
plain me as I comfortably supposed, but—the tip
of a social tentacle stretched out here to you—the
tentacle of another octopus."

"Your octopus very small and quick and open-eyed," he said, his fancy kindling from hers. "Mine gigantic and slow and blind. Yours draining three-quarters of the blood of mine. Mine painfully aware of that weakening drain and slowly opening its long-closed eyes—to see!"

A slight shudder ran through her. "No," she said, after a moment. "I refuse to believe the beautiful world we live in is based upon any such hideous struggle. These social octopuses are not real. Awhile ago you said yourself: 'There is only you and me and what we believe.' "

"You and me—and the other yous and mes. A while ago I merely denied concreteness to an abstract idea. But these classes, of which you and I are at present tentacle tips, are concrete groups of human individuals. The class has no existence independent of its component members. But the members are grouped in certain economic and social relations to each other. A generation dies away atom by atom, and the new generation takes its place atom by atom, maintaining the old relations. These relations, changing slowly, are the growing structure of the social organism."

"*The* social organism! You were claiming two—two distinct and hostile organisms—your class and mine. Which is it—one organism or two?" She thought she had him.

"A half-split ameba may be regarded as one organism *or* two," he said. "Likewise a society split into classes. When our class has *absorbed* yours there will be no doubt about social solidarity."

"And suppose we object to absorption so vigorously that—you fail?"

"We are the immense majority. What shall stop us?"

"Possibly the immense majority's immense stupidity."

"The nail on the head. But events are teachers that reach even the deaf. Stupid or not, I think our desire for the wealth we create will finally prove stronger and better based than your desire for it."

"Please, sir, I'm sorry," said she, tired of seriousness, "but I didn't know I had a desire for the wealth you create."

"No," he answered, refusing to follow her make-believe that she was a schoolchild answering her teacher. "You've accepted your dividends as unthinkingly as you accept the philosophy that justifies them. How much do you spend a year?"

"Do you know that's an awfully impertinent question?"

"You didn't think so the other day when you asked it of *me*. And just now the question seems pertinent to the argument."

"I'm not arguing. It's you. I've never thought about these things you insist upon talking about. I hate arguments anyway." She felt like crying.

"You're not the only one, Miss Moulton. It's a peculiarity that appears whenever a defender of the existing industrial system tries to meet the socialist argument. They never meet it. They evade it. They misstate it. They talk about something else. You have done splendidly."

"The idea of your patronizing me!" she exclaimed.

"You began by patronizing me!" he retorted.

"Aren't you hateful to me!" she protested. And then, mentally criticizing her tone, she grew conscious of the fact that she had become almost incapable of treating this ungentle man in any other way than as an equal. "I am going," she said abruptly. As soon as she spoke she looked furtively to see if he would be sorry.

"Just one more light on the bourgeoisie before you go," he said.

She looked at him resentfully. "So full of your own precious ideas, you don't care whether I go or not!" she thought. She had noticed the lily he had cut for her two days before lying withered on the seat.

"You hate bourgeois ethics and wallpaper and literature, Miss Moulton," he went on, "but you forget to hate the thing that shapes its hateful ideals and tastes. The way it gets its living. There is the root of all its sordid soul and all its ugly evil. Not money itself, as the Christians superficially thought, but the way you private owners of the world's wealth-creating machinery suck profit from the overworked and joyless lives of men, women, and children who have to work for you—or starve."

"I guess you're hopeless," thought Marion. The question "Have you ever been in love?" formed itself in her mind, but she suppressed it, rose, and started across the bridge. Bradfield rose and stood looking after her from among the rocks and ferns.

"Goodbye, Mr. Bradfield," she called back.

"Goodbye, Miss Moulton." His tone had finally changed—and very much.

She stopped and looked back. "Oh," said she with an air of surprise, "are you really human?" He was puzzled—a sight that delighted her soul, and she laughed.

"I don't know what you mean," he said, bluntly.

She stopped. "If you don't understand, you should have the grace to think it your fault, not mine."

"But it isn't," he said.

"Isn't it? Think it over."

"Think over the intentionally obscure expression of some perfectly simple idea!"

"You analytic wretch!" thought she. "How you do refuse to *play!*" she exclaimed. "I *was* going to wish that sometime we might meet and contrive to talk something else besides socialism, but——"

"I'll talk anything on earth," he interrupted. Then as an after-thought, with a secret thrill at his own boldness, but saying it anyway, he added, "——if it is with you!"

"Oh, did you know you were with me? I thought you were conversing merely with a social tentacle. I feel like coming back, now you've stopped arguing and—admitted my personal existence. But be careful. Perhaps you are being bribed!"

She went at once, afraid if she gave him the chance that he would pick loose or break the subtle little knots with which she had momentarily enmeshed him.

V

THE virtues of the absent Feodor?" inquired Lady Diotima, breaking into Marion's reverie one evening before the Pearson hearth-fire.

The girl started. "No," she answered. "I was thinking about a man I've been seeing lately."

"So soon?"

"Oh, I wasn't thinking of him that way!" Her disclaimer instantly striking her as unnecessary, Marion blushed; then menaced her hostess. "I've half a mind not to tell you a thing about this remarkable man—who interests, bores, charms and irritates—all in the same breath!"

"Who is he?"

"Give him one detail, and presto—he has filled in! And his grip on ideas is disconcerting. He's always abnormally right—at least he carries it off."

"I evidently am not acquainted with him."

"He knows what you're going to say, and why it isn't so—that is, why *he* thinks it isn't. He knows what you've done, and what you're going to do, and why it's—why he thinks it's foolish. He loves to tell you it's foolish. Unfortunately his reasons are formidable—unless you're just trifling; then you can fluster him some."

"Marion, does this supernatural male being live
in *Moline?*"

"Yes. He has read out of the way authors you
intended to read and haven't—Max Stirner, Nietzsche, Stendhal, and that sort. He's so absorbed in
his ideas that——"

"That?"

"That to impress him with one's personality—is
an achievement."

"So you took the trouble to achieve. I suppose I
must be patient until you make up your tyrannical
mind to tell me who he is."

"He is one of our gardeners!"

"Marion Moulton!"

"His name is Walt Bradfield!"

"One of your *gardeners!*"

"His father and mother are ignorant Moline
truck-farmers."

Lady Diotima was speechless.

"He is a socialist."

"Does he eat with his knife?"

"I suppose so. I began by patronizing him. Before we get through he promises to scatter most of
my cherished convictions to the four winds!"

"Is he—scrubbed?"

"Well, yes. But his hands feel like nutmeg grat-
ers."

"Feel?"

"The one I shook did," said Marion, laughing.
"His teeth are good and clean and his hair is nice.
His shirt is generally unbuttoned at the neck—perhaps to show his fine throat. And you *should* hear
his vocabulary! Western vowels and r's, of course,

and sometimes too bookish—showing where his culture comes from—but I was astonished. He's given me a new perspective. My quarrel with papa, for instance. I'm going to withdraw my demand about that letter, and see if I can't reconcile him to my marriage with Fedya."

"Marion: did you talk to this gardener about your marriage?"

"Oh, yes," Marion answered, reveling in Mrs. Pearson's consternation.

"What would Hohenfels think of that?"

"I don't know," said Marion, thoughtfully. "Of course, Diotima, I didn't go into the personal side of my affair with Fedya. Our talk was political. Fedya *is* inclined to be a little—leonine. But," she added pointedly, "if I *wanted* to talk intimately with the gardener, and then let other people's cut and dried opinions scare me out, Fedya would be scornful."

Lady Diotima winced a little and changed her tone. "Oh, of course, if he really is such an exceptional man. Does he intend to remain a gardener? How old is he?"

"Perhaps twenty-six. I believe he intends to write."

"By the way," said Mrs. Pearson, "George told me he met you on the train last week. A little rough on him, weren't you?"

"No, Lady Diotima. In pure affection I called him an idiot, and he couldn't conceive the word as kindly meant. It's too bad he and I have such a different set of values. I should dearly love to have you for a mother-in-law."

"Are you sure your values and those of De Hohenfels will not turn out still more different?"

"It is curious—really," said Marion. "Feodor and Bradfield are diametrically opposed in many of their ideas. And yet Feodor and Bradfield and I have passed beyond certain limitations which all three of us regard as harmful to life. George still thinks them essential."

"I know," said George's mother. "But he is not so narrow as his father, and he's more intelligent—except about business. I did use to hope you would take him and broaden him."

"After your failure to broaden Mr. Pearson?"

"I admit I was thinking of George's welfare more than yours. But now I'm beginning to think you have turned your back too completely on convention."

"Because I talked with the gardener? I talked with an intelligent man of unusual power. It's stupid not to know when to ignore convention, and it's cowardly not to ignore it when it ought to be ignored. Do you think George could turn me back into the strait and narrow path?"

"Perhaps not," sighed Mrs. Pearson. "A born rebel like you—any attempt to turn you back—would only drive you farther on."

"Especially if anyone went at it the way George would. He would get behind and push, not lead and lure."

"Would Feodor lead and lure?"

"He'd enjoy making you think the thing he objected to was decadent—your instinct perverted by some herd opinion—your will weakened by too much subservient inhibition of impulse."

"And Bradfield?" asked Lady Diotima curiously.

"Bradfield? If possible he'd startle you with the real simplicity of the matter. He'd bring you and your problem into focus—just for his own intellectual gratification; and not really care a rap what you decided. He wouldn't think you headed for perdition—either way."

"What a tremendous opinion you have of the man, Marion!"

"Yes, I have. I'd like to have you meet him and see why."

"Would you bring him to call?" asked Mrs. Pearson, amused and looking keenly at the girl.

Marion hesitated. Bradfield in corduroys fertilizing lilies and laying moss was one thing, but Bradfield in Lady Diotima's drawing room——

"Bring him to dinner," said Mrs. Pearson gravely. "I should love to see him putting sugar and cream in his bouillon."

"But I shouldn't," said Marion, her protective instinct awaking. "We'll do it some other way. Come over some morning, and we'll talk to him at his work."

The too veracious image of the gardener putting sugar in his bouillon somehow made Marion ask herself again, somewhat irrelevantly, whether she was not rating even his intellectual power too high. It was an absurdly little thing, and yet typical of a lot of little things whose aggregate she was accustomed to associate with human excellence of whatever kind.

She had hastily read up a little on socialism, and in one of her later talks with Walt Bradfield attacked it for the purpose of drawing out his ideas fully.

In Europe socialism was a factor to be reckoned
with, and she knew she ought to understand it. She
had as yet heard nothing of that story of his own
mind which she had promised herself. But the day
after her talk with Mrs. Pearson, intending direct
dispassionate study of him, she went into the conservatory to make Bradfield talk about himself.

He was not there. Irrationally, his absence when
she had come to look for him affected her almost
as a rudeness. She quickly dismissed that. He
was where his work called him—of course. Very
likely he had picked the strawberries she had had
for breakfast. But she found other things to foster
the unflattering suspicion that she was less interesting to him than he to her. One of their conservatory conversations had revealed the fact that her
own *a priori* disdain of him as a "servant" when
they first met had been perfectly matched on his part
by an *a priori* disdain of her as a "parasite woman."
Until then she had supposed the superiority of the
upper classes to be a thing conceded by the lower.
That it was not—that the opposite was firmly believed not only by Bradfield, but as he assured her
by great numbers of working people—was to her
startling, portentous of impending social change and
overthrow. The acquaintance of Marion and Bradfield had caused each of them to make of the other
an exception in their general view of each other's
classes; but the initial prejudice, merely instilled into
her, had been ground into him, and she did not know
to what extent it had yielded to personal liking. The
withered yellow stem of the lily she had loved and
wondered at had fallen into a crack in the rustic

seat. She had left it there beside him, under his eye, within reach of his hand—not intentionally—certainly not for him—and yet men much more important than he would have treasured it. She convinced herself that she didn't want him to be sentimental about her; but the necessity for self-directed argument about it made her wonder if she were not thinking too much about him.

She went back that morning to "Il Santo" and finished it; and that afternoon played bridge at Miss Cowperthwaite's. That evening she went to a bridge party in Rock Island. That night she went to bed sick of bridge but with endless hours of it looming upon her from all quarters of Moline, Davenport, and Rock Island. Human conversation was at a low ebb among the ladies of the three cities.

Next morning the Gildersleeve boys came over in their car and for two hours talked golf—in which fine game their listener was not wildly interested. This experience gave Miss Moulton more respect for Walt Bradfield's taste in hobbies. Another afternoon of bridge; a dinner party with George Pearson beside her, and Marion was ripe for rebellion. George's interest in her had revived on hearing from his mother that she was not actually engaged to the foreigner, and he had contrived to see her every two or three days, heralding his visits with boxes of candy and armfuls of cut roses.

"George isn't very poikilodoros," she mused, after one of Mr. Pearson's prolonged evening calls. "Bradfield would bring other gifts—his own mind—news of big world-wide problems—interest in things

I want to be interested in. I shall shock Lady Diotima by telling her that the big things are as important as the little things. It's nonsense not to make the most of Bradfield's existence in this dreary time. I shall flirt with him if I feel like it. At least I shall hale him forth from his hiding-place and tell him how I hate bridge."

VI

MARION reached the conservatory next morning by nine o'clock. It was a bright day and warm for March. Bradfield was in the long part of the building consulting a thermometer and adjusting a mechanism that opened a row of sash in the roof. He returned Miss Moulton's greeting, and either not assuming or not wishing to appear to assume she had come there to talk with him, he turned his attention back to the ventilator-lifter. Supposing that diffidence was not a permissible explanation of conduct in a professed egoist, she promptly misinterpreted.

"Is your time too valuable to waste talking to me this morning, Mr. Bradfield?" she inquired.

"My time doesn't belong to me, Miss Moulton, but I will steal as much of it as you have any use for."

"That would seem to oblige me to say important things to justify the theft. Important things are what I don't want to say. I'd better wait till you're off duty."

"I have next Sunday off," he suggested tentatively.

In spite of the fact that she admired and liked some of the "big things" about him, she found herself incapable of imagining herself receiving Mr. Bradfield as a caller.

"The Roughers and Finishers of the Republic Steel Company will give a masked ball Saturday," he said doubtfully. "You wouldn't care to see the working class enjoy itself, would you? No, you wouldn't. They don't know how very well. Not enough practice. I wish you could hear Gilroy's socialist talk in Draper Hall to-morrow night."

"I hear enough of that from you," said Marion, smiling. "You couldn't let me watch you work a while, could you? Haven't you something to do while we talk—that I could sit and watch?"

"Why yes," he said. "Someone has to putter around near this thermometer this kind of a day, opening windows and turning off steam. Just before you came in I saw how a thermostat could be put on here with a rod controlling a valve that would automatically shut off steam and turn the windows open—this way—as the temperature started to rise. Like an incubator. It would hold the atmosphere of the conservatory at any temperature you like."

"Isn't that idea valuable?" she asked. "Why don't you work it out and patent it?"

"Perhaps I might make a little something that way."

"A little something? I should think a successful device like that—good enough to put in all conservatories—would mean thousands."

"To the capitalist who floated it and put it on the market. To the inventor—a few dollars."

"Oh dear!" said Marion. "I wasn't going to give you a chance to say 'capitalist' or 'working class' to me to-day and you've got them both in already."

"What shall I talk about?" he asked, laughing.

"Yourself. You are an enigma I wish to understand. But first won't you bring that bench over here for me?" He brought it. "Now tell me where you got your vocabulary," she commanded, seating herself.

"I had four whole years of grammar school," he said, deciding that "vocabulary" meant education. "Trucking then cut school to five months a year, but I studied evenings with my older sister, and made high school at fifteen. Then I discovered the public library. The money I had for clothes went into books of poetry. A student of Augustana College worked for my father summers, and I pumped him of what he knew while we hoed cabbages. He showed me how to study the parts of plants, and I devoured his text-books nights. Time being limited, I had to learn to get the cream of a book in an hour or so, and books being expensive, I had to manage to carry the good of them away in my head. I spent so much time reading I failed to advance out of the D class. My father thought I was wasting time, and so the next year I had to work in the new greenhouse we had built. My English teacher, a lovely woman, was indignant at my being taken out of school. She had me call on her, and loaned me her own beautiful books—Ruskin, Morris, Vernon Lee, Keats, Dante. We read together, and I—wrote verses to her."

"Dare I ask how old she was?"

"To me she was ageless and deathless."

"That's nice of you," nodded Marion approvingly. "I think she accounts for you—nearly. Is she still in the high school?"

"No, she is teaching in Seattle. She sometimes writes. She praised the style of my books, but she wasn't modern enough to—understand them."

"Oh, you have already written books? Where can I get hold of them? Am I 'modern enough'? But if you outgrew her—what gave you the ideas she couldn't understand?"

"First, Haeckel. He taught me the real history and nature of organic life. His savage truth was more inspiring than Alice's gentle fiction."

"So you called her Alice," thought Marion.

He was reddening beneath his tan, and went on rapidly. "As soon as I was clear of the confusing idea of a monarchic interferer in the self-evolving universe, all that was religious in me—and it was a lot—poured itself into a passionate adoration of life itself—life as the pressure of the universe has thrust it up out of lifelessness into ever intenser essence and ever finer forms. After monism, socialism was bound to come somehow—especially after I went to work in the U. S. Plow Company blacksmith shop. The only men there who did anything worthy to be called thinking were socialists. It came to me in one magnificent rush from the lips of a little wizened street-sweeper in the park by the depot. In him first I saw the splendor of impassioned public speech. His grammar was bad, but he had a wealth of fresh and purposeful thoughts— thoughts like the gleam of swords. He was talking to a crowd of workingmen, some of them socialists.

They had a table lit with a gasoline torch and were selling their little red five cent books. I bought the Communist Manifesto. We got into a sizzling argument after the speech, and a dozen of us went over to a saloon and sat there till they turned us out at two in the morning. That was Romance and knightly quest—and I was drinking soda water then too. Till then I had come in touch with intellectual energy only in the quietness and solitude of reading. Here was intellect in battle! My brain glowed with it. Everything was a poem. These were magnificent men. I was intoxicated with high discourse and the leaping play of wits. Of course the socialists demolished the others—all except one anarchist who set up nothing much himself and threw his force into a brilliant attack—from the rear, as it were, while the socialists were faced the other way against the muddleheads."

"Here is where I demand a definition," said Marion. "Is muddlehead synonymous with non-socialist, non-revolutionist, or what?"

"There are overlappings," conceded Bradfield. "Your father is no muddlehead. He knows his class interest—and acts accordingly. Haeckel is no muddlehead in biology. Neither was Mendel, the Catholic abbé. There are socialists who are clear in economics and muddleheads in religion."

"Who are the non-muddleheads in religion? Those who have none?"

"In religion, I think most of the non-muddleheads are what I'd call dynamist monists."

"Sometimes pronounced 'moonists' by the unconverted?" she suggested gravely.

"The unconverted are the moonists," he countered. "Am I boring you with this history of my mind?"

"No. The personal part is exactly what I wanted. But—" holding up a warning finger—"not too much socialism."

"But it is precisely socialism—the crowning, synthesizing science of the evolutionary philosophy—socialism with its riddle-reading analysis of human history, which gives me the key to all that is happening in the life around me. Thanks to it, and the sciences that lie back of it, I am better entitled than Browning's Ben Ezra to cry, 'I see the whole design!' I see the people about me who lack its light stumbling in a blind maze—a welter and confusion of facts they cannot understand. Things happen to them that fill their hearts with misdirected bitterness. Befogging ideas conceal the real source of their misery—the loaded dice with which the employing classes play this game of life."

"So you *do* propose to turn the bitterness of the working people against their employers!"

"No. Against their loaded dice. We will take the dice away—without bitterness."

"Do you imagine that little process will not result in bitterness?"

"Then let it. Would you have us not disarm a burglar simply because he might be embittered?"

"You have things upside down with a vengeance! You propose to take their property away from certain people, and then you have the effrontery to call those people burglars!"

"The burglar's gun is his property all right, but

what use does he make of it? So with natural resources and socially created machinery. When it is
finally beaten into the nation's thick head that it
must—in order to have anything of decent life—
the nation is going to take that gun away from 'certain people.' Miss Moulton: who *ought* to own
those factories—the men who every day put all their
vital energy into the use of them—or you?"

"There's no particular reason for *my* owning
them. But if my father chooses to give them to me
—he may not, by the way—do you expect me to say
'No, thank you'?"

"You'd be a fool if you did—under the present
system. But what do you think of the system, really? And the thousands of men who work there,
every man with a vote, creating an average value
of ten dollars a day apiece, and getting less than
two? What do you think of them for voting year
after year to present your father and you with eight
out of every ten dollars they make?"

"Is it quite so simple as that?"

"Essentially. There's much muddying of waters
to keep the workers from seeing it. Fortunately
the wage-system is only a passing mal-adjustment
in the age-long evolutionary process. It's only a
little over a hundred years old—the state of collective toil by the many and private ownership of
the necessary machinery by the few. As it came,
it will pass—and good riddance! Knowing this, we
are able to work without bitterness against the bitter injustice of it. In place of the bloody, futile out-
breaks my class contented itself with in the past, we
analyze society, discover its laws, work in harmony

with them. We throw our force in the direction humanity must move. Everything groups and relates itself. Facts string themselves ordinately as beads on the sound generalizations of our philosophy."

"Your own mind does happen to work that way with facts. I was trying to express it to Lady Diotima—a friend of mine I would like you to meet. I imagine, though, that your mind would work just the same way whatever your philosophy."

"You imagine wrong."

"So?" said she, resolving to crush him for once. "Haeckel hasn't the socialist philosophy, has he?"

"No."

"Do not his facts string themselves on the lines of sound generalizations?"

"His biologic facts do, because his biologic generalizations are sound. His sociologic facts remain to him a welter and confusion. So would mine if I did not have the socialist philosophy. Take any other social philosophy, and the beads break the string."

She thought hard for a moment. It was too easy for him. "I can't argue with you!" she exclaimed. "I swore I wouldn't do it to-day. I wanted to get acquainted with you. When you argue with me on these subjects it's like a strong man holding the wrists of a child. It's a thing you've trained yourself in for years. You ought to be ashamed of yourself!"

"For self-defense?" he remonstrated.

"I won't argue whether it's self-defense. It isn't, but you'd beat me out of that, too. You are the most

disputatious person I ever met. Did you ever hear
Emerson's saying, 'The gods do not argue'?"

"I wouldn't either, if I were a god," chuckled
Bradfield. "What I said would go—whether it was
so or not. *We* have to make people see things—in
spite of inclination, false education, prejudice. That
takes argument."

"You even argue about arguing."

"Self-defense," he reiterated. "I'm not feeling
argumentative."

"I hope I never see you when you are," she
laughed. "Shall I tell you something? Yes, I will.
You are so egotistic already that nothing can make
you worse. I came in here looking for you the other
day, and was disappointed."

He drew a deep breath and held it while he looked
her in the eyes.

"Well?" she said blithely. "Aren't you going to
say you are honored or charmed or somethinged?"

"I'm somethinged, all right," said he. "But there
seems to be something the matter with my vocal
cords."

"I knew you'd be fun if I could once get you off
your hobby!"

"I think perhaps—I'm safer on it." Tolerant
amusement at himself was his tone—not perfectly
sustained.

"I being one of the national burglars?" she suggested.

"You as national burglar are not especially dangerous to me personally."

"But how about being bribed with my companionship? Is your alarm for your integrity so great that you wish to avoid my society?"

"By no means."

"Is that all you intend to say about it? How unflatteringly moderate!"

"Well, that shows my self-control. My real feelings are not a bit moderate. I'd give a leg or two to know you well, Miss Moulton, but it doesn't look probable that I'll have the chance."

"Now that is what I call being adequate to the occasion!"

"And I refuse to let myself get started wanting things I can't get. It's a waste of energy."

"You *are* economical!" she said unsympathetically. "As for me—Moline drives me mad! I can't tell you how unspeakably I hate bridge."

He looked blank and she laughed.

"You don't even know what it is! Happy man!"

"Oh," he said awkwardly—"bridge whist. Of course I've heard of it."

"They play it morning, noon and night—but not for money. Perish the immoral thought! Think of the inanity—a gambling game without stakes—firing at a target with blank cartridges! I could have stood a little of it. As it is, I'm desperate. I feel like doing something perfectly devilish—something they will disapprove of in me as much as I disapprove of their assassinating half my waking hours. Do you know that pet phrase of harum scarum French artists and writers—'*épater les bourgeois*'?"

"I don't know French."

"You know the word bourgeois. The other means to spat. The idea is to horrify them, scandalize them, do something to shock their deadly sense of propriety."

"May I offer you any assistance I may be able to render in épatéing the bourgeois?" he said, with serious lips and dancing eyes.

There was a flash in her eyes which looked like yes, and he added quickly:

"Shall we go for a long ride Sunday in a speed-boat I have the use of?"

"Oh, I'd like to!" she exclaimed.

"Why don't you? The boss wants me to gather some moss—maybe to prove I'm not a rolling stone. That means some beautiful places I could show you."

She sat a moment thinking. "That would be simply fine—but I'm afraid it would hardly do. We can't do all the things we'd like to, you know," she added, taking refuge in a tone of superior knowledge of the world. "Mrs. Grundy is still a little too strong for us."

He looked at her as though something he had expected had developed, and said quietly, "So you *das*n't épater the bourgeois!"

"You realize very well that kind of lack of freedom common in your own class, Mr. Bradfield," she said, hating to see her courage sink in his estimation, "but I wonder if freedom isn't scarcer than you think—in ours?"

"It's a condition indeed pitiable!" he said. "The university sociologists ought to investigate it."

"Of course you wouldn't understand," she said,

feeling that he was definitely placing her in the very bourgeoisie with which she claimed to have no sympathy. "It's a thing I can't explain. Such things come to be a matter of instinct."

"But I do understand," he said. "It happens to be one of the things I understand best. The explanation, which you are unable to give, is that when it comes to *action* you find you *are* a member of your class and must obey its ethics."

"Is it really no more than *class* ethics?"

He wouldn't answer it.

She saw it was undeniable. It had been too much *of* her to see it herself. She had unconsciously taken it for granted when she weighed right and wrong, what to do, what not, that her standard was simply of humanity—practically universal, because if there were people to whom it did not apply they were of lower orders and did not count. But she had imagination enough to see now how strange that whole standard must look from the outside to one who honestly felt her class to be almost unnecessary, its vital function in the world almost outgrown, its destiny as a class to sink to parasitic rank, and then —be sloughed. That vision seemed to shake the stable world. "Is everything I have unconsciously felt as right and wrong—every act that says 'Do me' and 'Don't do me'—is it *all* class ethics?"

"I wouldn't go as far as that," said Bradfield. "There is common ground way down—deeper than most folks ever get—much deeper than is claimed by those whose interest it is to obscure the chasm. A lot—oh, an awful lot—is of class."

For a moment the undeniable fact of social disunion filled her with sadness and a sense of loneliness—as though she were isolated on some far pinnacle. It gave her a yearning to bridge all gaps—to draw the severed and warring factions of the world together. Then the practical side of her mind took hold. "If that is what the world is," she said, "I cannot change it. That part of my right and wrong which is of class is still right and wrong for me."

"You have this moment become thoroughly class-conscious," said Bradfield. "I predict that from now on you will progressively cease to be a muddle-head."

"Thank you, kind prophet, for your kind prophecy. It seems to me that I have just now felt something much wider than class-consciousness. It seemed cosmic. But you'll admit that it's all pretty far afield from a certain launch-ride. I want to go. Would you care to invite Mrs. Pearson?"

"Why yes. If you *want* her."

"I've been wanting to have her talk with you, you know," said Marion, but then she pondered. The mossy places were good enough excuse for anybody. Lady Diotima would go as *her* guest, but hardly if she realized clearly that she would be Bradfield's. Was Bradfield a man who would at all expand in the presence of a chaperone? Bradfield and chaperonage did not seem to belong in the same boat. And Lady Diotima as friend—Marion feared she would be too keen for signs of ignorance of the unwritten edicts of her class and pounce with joy on any little *gaucherie* betraying plebeian breeding. The girl felt just then that if Lady Diotima tried that with Bradfield she would get the worst of it, but still—"Perhaps I *don't* want her," she said. "But *if* I want her, and *if* she has no engagement, and *if* she'll go—then we'll gather moss."

As she left him that day she had the feeling that between them there had begun a shifting of spiritual hegemony—as though weight had moved from her side of their balance to his—as though the ideal of freedom to which he looked inward had gained on her waning ideal of caste. The meeting of their eyes at parting sent a delicate thrill through her—a sensation as of breathing sudden perfume: but she turned her mind from that at once, and made believe to herself that no such thing had happened.

VII

THE trim, maroon-colored launch "Nancy" lay ready to be stepped into alongside the boat-house wharf on a hot Sunday morning the last of March. The brass would take no higher polish, woodwork could be no cleaner, and Walt Bradfield in his Sunday clothes was looking nervously up the street to the south for a motor car bringing Miss Moulton and Mrs. Pearson. To his surprise Marion arrived alone, coming on foot along the white boulevard through the raw little trees of the new park by the river.

"I telephoned Mrs. Pearson not to stop for me at Hillcrest," she said, joining Bradfield beside the launch. "I didn't realize how hot it was. Shall I get in? That canopy looks good after the mockery of those absurd trees."

He held the launch from rocking as she stepped in and seated herself on the shaded side.

"I couldn't persuade myself you were really coming," he said.

"I was afraid after I started that Mrs. Pearson would get here first. What would you have done?"

"I'm not half as much afraid of Mrs. Pearson as I am—of you."

She looked up the street—perhaps to avoid that

faint thrill of meeting eyes. "There she is now!" she exclaimed, seeing the Pearson car. "I was just in time."

Walt turned to see, mentally preparing for battle with Mrs. Pearson. "No one but the driver in that car," he said.

The chauffeur stopped his machine, saw Miss Moulton in the launch, and brought her a note. She skimmed it.

"Please tell Mrs. Pearson I'm very sorry," she said. She looked out thoughtfully across Sylvan water as the chauffeur went back to his car. She lifted the note from her lap and read it again, then tore it absent-mindedly across. She looked back along the shadeless boulevard. Walt watched her curiously, brightening finally as he saw her look of determination. "Well, she's not coming," said Marion, dropping overboard the fragments of crested note-paper. "We might as well start."

He cast off with alacrity, climbed in, and took his place at the engine. She looked at the slowly widening strip of water between launch and landing. "Can you see Class-Ethics prostrate on that wharf?" she asked.

They laughed together—the laugh of people who have little jokes that other people cannot understand.

"Who's that with Walt Bradfield?" asked a launch-owner of Joe the boat-keeper.

"Looks like the Moulton girl that used to go out with George Pearson," Joe responded. "Guess she wouldn't be going out with Walt, though."

"Marion Moulton? A thirty millionairess! I

should say not. She's going to marry some foreign prince. But that's sure a high-toned girl."

"Prob'ly hired Walt to take her some place," Joe conjectured.

The launch sped away from the dingy wooden landing, Bradfield watching and listening to the engine while he steered with the tiller-lever—a handle set in the line that ran outside the low rail. "It seems too good to be true," he said.

"Good things do happen sometimes. I am escaping some people who'll eat half the afternoon and talk about it the other half. Poor mother! I told her I was going on an all afternoon launch-party. If she could see the party!"

"Would it épater her, too?"

"She might pretend not. She's a new thoughtist, but you can't tell just when she's going to be an old thoughtist. The party might strike her as somewhat unchaperoned." His expression gave rise to an amusing doubt. "Do you know what a chaperone is, oh man of Eden?"

"I've read of it," he answered.

"It!" she exclaimed joyfully.

"It's an institution above my social level and below yours," he explained.

She reluctantly gave up the hope of that delightful piece of ignorance in him. "No," she said, "—not below my social level."

"But below *you*." He liked that even better.

"To-day it is—in the collapse of our friend on the wharf. You see you are giving me the egotism. By the way, is there some place we can get dinner? Not that I'm hungry, Mr. Bradfield. Nothing so indelicate, I assure you, but still—we can't eat moss, you know."

"I don't know any place good enough for you."

"Some woodsy, farmy place? Where would you take me if I were Alice?" Her eyes were mischievous at the name.

"Spinnyville," he said, brightening, but not encouraging her to tease him about his former love.

Deciding to stop on their way down to the island where they were to get the moss, they rounded the head of the government island, went through the new lock, and ran down along a rocky shore. The flawless glades of the golf-links, laid out through rugged woods, were already green with spring. On their right the tree-lined streets of Davenport climbed from river to bluff—churches and residences half emerging from a russet haze of buds. Down-stream, beneath a span of the big bridge they saw miles of blue water bounded by willow-covered shores and towheads putting on new gold. Above the southwestern hills were piled slow masses of white cloud.

As they ran down past the cities and the islands they talked of one of his books. He had given her two of them, small cloth-bound volumes of about seventy pages each. She had yet to read "Social Evolution," but had finished "Organic Evolution" the night before. It was not the cold, scientific treatise the title had led her to expect. She found in it the work of a poet who had based his work on cold, scientific treatises, but he himself had visualized the million centuries of life and written the history thereof with passion. This writing gave her a new feeling toward the world she lived in, a new feeling

toward herself. Life was much more marvelous
than she had supposed, but less mysterious. While
she was under the spell of the book, "soul" ceased to
be a thing apart. It was a function of living matter. But instead of making soul less beautiful, the
intimacy made living matter more so. Instead of
ceasing to exist, the most exquisite spirituality became a glorious phase of material life. Inorganic
matter itself was no longer the inert stuff it had
seemed. It was polarized energy—each atom a
point where complex forces crystallize—each molecule a balancing and interlocking of such atoms into
substance. Matter, as Bradfield made her conceive
it, was as spiritual as her own old notion of spirit.
These forces her mother decried as "earth-forces"
played through the farthest stars of deepest heaven;
but not more wonderfully than through the nearest
grain of earthly dust. The dust itself was force.
And spirit conceived as a something that can float
free of matter was more material than spirit as a
function of matter. A function cannot float away,
and floating is a material process.

When Marion had read the passage on the nature
of "soul" which Bradfield had inserted in his account
of the first trace of nerve-tissue in the Platodaria she
found herself indulging in a curious speculation.
Would a man who felt soul and body to be so indis-
soluble a unity feel as he touched a woman's lips that
it was her soul he touched? And would there be
therefore in his kiss an exaltation——? At this point
she checked that train of thought, and turned her
mind forcibly back to the life-story of her Platodari-
an ancestors. But trains of thought so checked in con-

sciousness are inclined to complete themselves sub-
consciously, and after she had turned off her electric reading lamp, her head sunk in her pillow and
her conscious soul in sleep, she dreamed she kissed
Walt Bradfield on the lips, and was trying to explain
to him that she had made a mistake, but it was the
fault of his book.

As he sat opposite her in the launch this morning,
a casual glance at his lips suddenly and for the first
time brought the memory of that dream of the night
into her consciousness. Mr. Bradfield was talking,
but suddenly lost hold of his idea. He looked at
Marion closely, but contrary to her custom her eyes
would not meet his. He wondered what could have
made her of a sudden so astonishingly beautiful.
That problem he soon solved. The answer was
simply that she was blushing, and there was no sunset cloud that could compete with the fleeting rose
hue of her skin. But why was she blushing? Being
unable to solve that, Walt asked her.

"I'm not," she protested.

He insisted that he had eyes—fortunately.

"Well, then, it's sunburn. I sunburn very easily.
I freckle, too—isn't that dreadful? What is that
stone house over there?"

"That stone house over there is a pretext for a
highly undesirable change of subject."

"Oh," said Marion. "There is a canal lock! And
there's the mouth of a river! That must be the
Hennepin canal. Evidently that's the lock-keeper's
house."

"Nothing I was saying could have caused it," said
Bradfield, reasoning aloud. "Consequently it was

something you thought of just then. What was it
you thought of?"

"Are you acquainted with the lock-keeper?" The
cross purpose conversation amused her and gave her
time to realize that it was no such criminal thing,
after all, to have dreamed of kissing a man.

"Well, I see you're a secretive person—likewise a
stubborn," he observed. "But you can't deprive
me of the satisfaction of having seen it. It was
somewhat the loveliest thing I have ever beheld."

"If that's so, I shall have to cultivate it."

"Have mercy! You are sufficiently disturbing
normally." He noticed that his hand was trembling,
and laughed.

"What are you laughing at?" she demanded.

"People who won't tell things don't get things
told them."

"It's bad manners to laugh and not tell why."

"Not half so tantalizing as to blush and not tell
why. But I'll tell if you will."

She declined hastily.

"Ah ha!" he exclaimed. "That proves you know
why you blushed."

"But you don't!" she exulted. "And that isn't
half. You aren't going to."

"You're doing it again!" he exclaimed. "Good
God!"

She gave a start. "That last remark led me to
suppose the engine was about to explode!"

"The *engine* isn't!"

She could not keep the laughter out of her eyes;
and when he saw it his whole soul laughed, a spasm
of silent, joyous laughter, flooding his nerves in spite

of the protest of reason. The happiness in that was much too keen. Reason said: "Don't do that, Walt. Don't let yourself fall in love with the Countess de Hohenfels." And reason would probably have been obeyed had it not been for certain charming little intimations that the not-yet Countess de Hohenfels was letting herself fall in love with him—or doing it without her permission. He formulated no hopes, but the possibility made her fearfully attractive to him.

"You are fun, Walt Bradfield," she said. "What reader of those deep books of yours would guess how you can laugh?"

He noticed the engine igniting irregularly, stood up and leaned over it, reduced the flow of gasoline: and when he reseated himself, it was beside her.

"Doesn't this make the boat trim badly?" she suggested.

"The boat doesn't mind," he said. "Do you?"

"I wouldn't let a mere boat outdo me in indifference," said she, her eyes fairly crinkling.

He acknowledged the hit with a laugh. "It isn't indifference, though."

"Indeed!" She drew herself up and faced him.

"Not on the part of the boat. My sitting over here really does throw it a little off its balance."

"Supersensitive boat!" she scoffed.

"It never blushes, though. Oh, Lord!" He pulled sharply on the tiller-lever. The boat swung to the left, away from a rocky islet. He looked anxiously at the shore and at the water alongside them and for a moment held his breath.

"What's wrong?" exclaimed Marion,

"We just sidled over the middle of a wing-dam," he answered with a sigh of relief. "Fortunately there was water enough." He looked back, noticing the part of the dam which they had crossed. In turning the boat down-stream again the easing of the rudder drew his arm along the gunwale—past her. He did not think of it as being around her, his mind still being on the wing-dam; but a subtle and lovely sensation stole through him, a faint fragrance from her garments or her hair, a delicate knowledge of her nearness caroling in his nerves. As she turned to look at the island, her face was toward him and her elbow rested lightly on his arm. His sleeve seemed sentient of the touch.

"Look at that cunning cabin!" she exclaimed.

"Lew Anderson's—the blacksmith on Second Avenue. Built it himself. This is his boat we just missed sinking." He was finding articulation difficult.

"Would we have sunk?" she asked.

"Oh, we'd have got her off and run ashore before she filled."

"Wouldn't that have been exciting?"

He forgot to answer, and she looked at him as though to see what he was thinking.

"I am looking at those Rossetti lips of yours," he said. He intended to speak the words lightly, but his voice played him the trick of expressing his real instead of his make-believe emotion. His real emotion made her turn away with a quick, deep intake of breath. Her shoulders drew up a little—with the memory of her dream and the feeling of the danger of its coming true. She seemed to have eaten of the lotus, and the energy necessary to move or speak or think had dissolved under the influence of that insidious flower. The vital electricity which stores and restores itself in living nerves and is wont at a motor thought to pour itself into paths leading to muscular action seemed to have flowed away into the blood that throbbed in her temples and flushed her cheeks.

Walt too had eaten of the flower of enervation. The vital electricity whose total was his soul was raying with unknown spirituo-bodily forces. There seemed to be a glorified form of gravitation drawing them close enough to kiss. She succeeded in turning her face away only by overcoming an exquisite force operating in the opposite direction. He had never known anything so adorable as that ardent, dreamlike bending of her head.

She had let Feodor kiss her once when they found themselves secluded for a moment among the great evergreens of the Pincio with a solemn sunset flaming down behind the dome of St. Peter's; but that had been a voluntary act of hers, a reasonable thing she deliberately decided to do and did, because she loved Fedya and he was dying to kiss her. In that her own nature had played no such part as now, when against reason and will she *wanted* to kiss Walt Bradfield—a desire forming itself into an idea as definite as an act.

"I mustn't, I mustn't!" she told herself, and rose intending to sit on the other side of the launch.

Before he knew it he had caught her hand, but it seemed to her it was not so much by her hand he drew her as by an exquisite invisible net enveloping and drawing her whole body. "I mustn't!" she said aloud and drew away her hand. Her voice, vibrating with unfamiliar emotion, did not seem her own. She steadied herself by taking hold of a rod that supported the canvas roof. "Are you sure you know where this boat is running?" she asked.

He had, in fact, forgotten there was such a thing as a boat—racing twenty-five miles an hour down a river full of just submerged wing-dams. He turned with a start to the indispensable business of piloting, and that turning of his attention seemed to free her a little from the overmastering spell.

She seated herself on the opposite side of the launch, not looking at him, leaning forward on her elbow, staring out with troubled, unseeing eyes across the gray, steel-colored water. The thought of Feodor was linked with a pang at her disloyalty. Till now, since she loved Feodor and did not love Bradfield, she had felt perfectly free to enjoy the companionship of the working-class thinker. Now she began to see that she had formulated the case too simply. Love and non-love were not the two distinct, easily distinguishable things she had assumed them to be. The lovely languor that had stolen through her was telling every fiber that Walt Bradfield's kiss would be sweeter than the one on the Pincian hill. The knowledge was painful. It upset everything. She did not want it to be so. Did it mean that she loved Bradfield? A thousand memories of Feodor said no. The main ideas and purposes of her life were obscured and threatened by this inexplicable allurement. Old feelings rose to defend themselves against the vivid new invader:

but the mental pain of the conflict was mingled with a sweetness beyond violets, gleam of stars, or sound of exquisite chords.

The man's intoxicating impulse to fold her and hold her and tell her he loved her, having been thwarted in that instant when she made him realize the necessity of piloting, all his good reasons for not making love to her came flashing back upon his mind. He looked at her nervously for signs of reaction. One instant he feared that what kept her from looking at him was anger: and the next he hoped it was self-distrust. He was eager to know; but he quickly rejected, when it formed itself in his mind, the question "Are you angry?" It was too likely to convey the suggestion that she ought to be. The only other question worth asking he judged impolitic. If she was not asking herself whether she loved him, there was no use in his asking. And if she was asking herself, then whatever answer she formed in her own mind was likely to be more favorable than any she would voice for him. And after all, he reflected, what difference would it make how near loving him she was at this moment? Her class feeling would keep her from marrying him. Of that he was certain. His own class feeling had hitherto helped him to regard a marriage with her not only as impossible, but even as unwise—from the point of view of his own intellectual and spiritual ambitions.

She was wondering whether she would dare tell De Hohenfels. She tried to persuade herself there was nothing to tell. Nothing had really happened. But how would he take it if he knew she wanted something to happen? It surely would not do to tell him

such a thing in a letter, but she resolved that some
kind of letter should be mailed to him that very
night—in spite of her earlier conclusion that she
could not write until she had talked with her father.
As she sat looking across the slate-colored waves she
was deciding to go to her father that evening and
insist on his listening to what she had to say. Then
she would write to Fedya.

Into her consciousness, interrupting her train of
thought, stole the lovely sensation that filled her
lungs each time she breathed. It was like the scent
of clover in the sun. She remembered the look of
Bradfield's clear, sun-browned skin, the slight rosi-
ness that showed through it, the suggestion of pure,
abounding blood and outdoor health. Was it the
magnetism of health in that tiller of the earth, that
breather of pure air, which so affected her? She
glanced at him. It surprised her somehow to see
that he was absorbed in thought, not looking at her,
apparently not aware of her presence. She remembered the lily he had not taken as a souvenir of her.
He sighed, as though reaching some undesired but
accepted conclusion, then looked at her. Their eyes
met. He smiled a little, in a manner that kept her
from looking away, a tender amusement that took
her into his confidence and compelled the gift of
hers. "Don't you think we had better talk socialism?" he said.

Her face lit up with understanding and sympathy.
She liked his frank acceptance of the fact that they
were attracted, his readiness not to make too much
of it, his ability to take a human, not merely a mas-

culine, view of the sex duel. "Socialism?" she said.
"Well, yes. Or why not try dynamist monism?"

Their attention was drawn by a far-off rumble.

"Just look at that storm ahead of us!" he exclaimed. "Why, there's the Buffalo station! We've passed Spinnyville." He looked around.

"I think you are rather an absent-minded pilot," she observed.

"It does look like it—to-day." He drew the rudder over and the speed-boat wheeled, leaning to starboard and turning almost in her own length. He headed up the river, got his bearings, then looked back at the clouds which stretched from south to northwest as far as the eye could reach. "Funny I didn't notice *that*," he muttered. There was a flicker of lightning reddening the cloud. He quickly pulled out his watch and looked at it until he heard the thunder. "About eighteen seconds," he said. "Over three and a half miles."

"Isn't that fun?" she said. "Just how do you get that?"

"Eleven hundred feet a second." He was trying to judge the speed of the storm from its appearance.

"Can we make Spinnyville?" she asked.

"Easily. One minute's run. But possibly this will be an all day rain——" He looked at her tailored suit.

"Could we make Moline?"

"We could make the lower end of Rock Island in seventeen or eighteen minutes, leave the launch there, and go home on the car."

"Will the storm give us eighteen minutes?"

"If it has just our speed, we are ten or twelve minutes ahead of it now, and of course we'd hold that lead. I don't think it can be traveling enough faster than we to cut the lead to nothing."

"A race with a storm! Try it!"

He advanced the spark to the last notch, showed her how to steer and where to hold, looked over the connections on his coils, tightened a screw here and there, filled up his oil-cups, and once more took charge of the tiller-lever. The boat was at topmost speed, rushing under the drive of sixty horsepower. "There goes Spinnyville!" he said, pointing back over the stern quarter to a country inn. The rapidity with which it receded gave her a sense of security. The storm rampant looked motionless; but Bradfield saw it had grown much higher.

"Goodbye Spinnyville!" she called. "Oh dear! I suppose I'll have to dine with Aunt Farnsworth after all!"

"Will you eat with me—some place in Rock Island?" he asked, hesitatingly.

Marion considered. "Where, for instance?"

He was at a loss. The only place he could think of—Jane's Lightning Lunch—did not strike him as particularly appropriate. "Where would I take you," he asked, "if I were Feodor?"

She smiled at his tit-for-tat, but the question bothered her. She did not know the extent of that fifty dollar a month purse of his; she was reluctant about suggesting an expensive place and unwilling to go to a cheap one. She was perfectly certain poor Bradfield had never in his life ordered a dinner à la carte and was bound to make a botch of it. The question made them both uncomfortably class-conscious. She saw he would attribute a refusal solely to her sense of his social inferiority. "You would take me to The Harms," she answered finally.

He was silent, trying to understand her hesitation, uncertain now whether he ought to ask her to go with him.

"There's the island with the cabin!" she said, looking ahead.

A stab of lightning behind them lit up their faces, and shortly afterward the sound broke on them— much louder than before. Bradfield took out his watch and caught the exact time of the next peal. "That doesn't look very good," said he after a moment. "That was only a couple of miles away." He looked back. "That's all it is, too," he said. He saw a white, contorted fringe of cloud blown out before the black body of the tempest.

"Can't you figure the speed from the two flashes?" she asked.

Seeing that the method of calculating distance by sound had caught her fancy, he took a pencil and envelope. She leaned over looking at his figures. "According to that," he said, "it's making two miles to our one. It will beat us all hollow."

"Perhaps the first thunder you timed came from farther back in the storm."

"Yes, but look at the thing. It must be coming fifty miles an hour!"

The storm-clouds had gained enormously on them even while they were playing with their figures. When they passed the wing-dam they had run over coming down and cleared the head of the island, they saw a great, black arm of cloud above the Iowa hills not half a mile away, and farther back a falling wall of rain. Walt pulled the rudder square across the stern, made the launch whirl, and headed back down-stream. "We've got to get out of that!" he exclaimed. "Us to the cabin!"

From cloud to earth or from earth to cloud there leapt a blinding blade of light, a shocking crash of sound. It fell half way up the hill and split a massive oak-tree into three great gleaming splinters. One fragment of the trunk shot off like a chip from an axe, and two large limbs sank down not wholly severed. Marion gripped the edge of the seat and turned pale. Bradfield's nerves were shaken. An icy wind came rushing up the river piling up waves and tearing off their tops. The canvas roof filled and nearly knocked the boat over.

He was too anxious to get ashore quickly. Rather than turn broadside to the wind by running around the wing-dam which lay between them and the island landing he headed straight across it holding as nearly as he could on the point he had gone over it before. When they reached it the launch struck and stopped with a crash that threw them forward against the bulkhead. Trembling with the futile driving of the propeller, the boat began to swing down-stream. Bradfield picked himself up, and instinctively threw off the power. "Are you hurt?" he shouted.

"No," she called, though she really did not know whether she was or not. "What shall I do?"

"Sit still!"

The water was coming through the stove-in bottom, and the rising waves slapped in as the current swung the stern down-stream. Keel and wheel cleared the dam, but the bow, now pointing up-stream, stuck fast on the rock. Bradfield reversed the engine, threw in the switch, and rocked the flywheel. The engine started backing, but the bow was somehow wedged or impaled on a point of rock. He retarded the spark and opened the throttle for more power, but in vain. "Get clear to the stern!" he called to Marion.

She obeyed, wetting her feet in the water that now covered the bottom of the boat, but the shifting of her weight did not free the bow. Leaving the propeller backing, Bradfield jumped up on the bow deck, lowered himself knee deep in the water, got foothold on the rocks of the dam, and with all his strength pulled up on the painter. She came free with a jerk that made him lose his balance and left him on the dam. He threw himself after the backing boat, caught a precarious hold with his right arm over the bow and clung there half submerged in the icy water. "Can you help me up?" he shouted.

Marion ran forward and climbed up on the little bow deck. The wind nearly swept her off, but she caught herself and kneeling grasped his left arm with both hands and pulled him up till he got his weight on the deck. He scrambled up and darted for the engine. The launch was backing in a circle, her rudder jammed sidewise: and the water was almost up to the base of the cylinders. A little more and there would be no power to run her ashore before she sank. He started her ahead, headed her toward shore, then turned and helped Marion down from the wind-swept deck. "We're all right!" he cried.

"We'll make it!" He shivered with the chill of his watersoaked garments.

Great drops of rain came driving slant-wise: the lightning flashed on the hills. The boat grounded eight or ten feet from dry land. He jumped overboard and waded ashore with the painter, but could not get the bow in far enough for Marion to make it. He came back into the water and put up his arms for her.

"Come!" he said.

She leaned down to him quickly, her arms about his neck. He took her, meeting her expected weight and the unexpected pressure of the wind blowing her damp skirt tight against him and sweeping wet tendrils of her hair across his eyes. As he turned with her and waded swiftly through the water, his purpose of getting her ashore dry-shod could not keep out all joy of even such fulfilment of his desire to have her in his arms. Too incidental to be real fulfilment, too brief to be then quite realized, it was a thing to dream back to afterward.

"Run!" he commanded as she gained her balance on the shore. "To the cabin!"

"What are you going to do?" she demanded.

"Get the boat in. She's going to sink!" He found two round barkless limbs, placed one under the bow, another on the shore, and pulled on the painter.

"Let me help," she said, seizing the rope.

Together they dragged the boat in, the cold rain beating in their faces, and then they ran for the cabin.

VIII

SAFE inside, with the cabin door shut against rain, wind and lightning, Marion wilted into a chair near the deal table, leaned over with her face between her hands, and shivering uncontrollably, began to cry.

Walt looked at her helplessly. Her response had been so quick and adequate when he had called on her in their danger that he had no idea she had been undergoing a strain such as this reaction indicated. "I'm awfully sorry," he said, sitting down beside her.

She straightened up, and caught a glimpse of the solicitude in his face. "How perfectly silly of me!" she exclaimed. She laughed hysterically, then resolutely controlling herself she took off her soiled gloves and dripping hat.

"You've earned the right to be a little silly," said Walt, speaking quietly. "I never would have got back into that boat if it hadn't been for you. And with your skirts—the wind came near taking you into the river."

The little cabin was lit weirdly by three quick angry flashes. Then broke the thunder like a whole sea overhead.

Marion shrank from it. "I had no idea I was such a baby!"

His hand moved with protective impulse to her shoulder. She leaned closer as she would have to Lady Diotima, with a sense of refuge from the threatening river, the rain, and the sudden, sweeping cold. The broad soft coils of her hair lay beautiful against his cheek. He breathed its fragrance. The sweetness that suffused them was lovelier because not sought. For her, not thinking of it then, it made her refuge more complete. But in a few moments it became the main thing, a dear compulsion weaving its fairy meshes round their souls, drawing them close and warm amid the rattling of the water-covered window, the pouring of the rain upon the roof. The idea that she ought not to leave his arm around her did not lead to action. Inaction was too sweet. She let the idea dissolve, closed her eyes happily, and settled herself better— like a child that is content.

Then she knew that if she stayed there another moment their lips would meet. Something powerful within her said "Stay!" She started to pretend to herself that it wasn't so; then broke abruptly from the grasp of self deception, breathing the name of Feodor, and rose as one drowsy, unwillingly awaking.

"How are we ever going to get home?" she asked, going to the window.

Walt had risen with the impulse to follow her. For a moment he could not speak. She turned and looked at him. "A fisherman's house-boat," he said, pointing to the Iowa shore. "We will signal him to take us off. Perhaps we can get a farmer to drive us in to the street-car."

"Suppose the storm doesn't stop? If we were left here all night—it would épater Moline a little more than I bargained for."

"Moline mustn't know."

"My father would. Oh, really, it would be dreadful!"

"It isn't likely to last till dark. We must have a fire."

"You must be frozen," she said.

He glanced at her wet shoes. He started a fire in the stone fire-place, and piled it high with logs. The wind rushing overhead soon made the flame roar in the chimney. From a locker he produced glasses, a bottle of whiskey and one of chalybeate water. "Here's something we need," he said.

He found no argument about it, as he would have with Alice. Marion took the whiskey as a matter of course. "Well," she said, smiling. "Things look better!" She set down the empty glass and moved nearer the fire. "You haven't a cigarette there in your friend's locker, have you?"

"Makin's."

She nodded. He handed her a big sack of tobacco and an orange booklet of Riz La Croix papers. Looking with the eyes of the average American, Bradfield had hitherto regarded girls' smoking as an indication of moral depravity; but as he watched Marion roll her cigarette—the cachet of refinement on every movement of her graceful, efficient hands—he decided that in this opinion he had been a muddle-headed provincial. He thought of the soothing effect of tobacco on the nerves of this girl who was just emerging from a condition of hysteria; and then he rejected that excuse and all excuses as unnecessary. If she wanted to smoke that was reason enough for her, and for him. He fished out a cob-pipe of Lew Anderson's and filled it, and placed a tin box full of matches near her. She tried to light one on the sole of her shoe but it was too wet.

"You must take those off," he said. "Here are a pair of Lew's slippers for you—just the right size."

"The antique jest shall be forgiven you," she answered, lighting her cigarette, "—for the sake of your sensible suggestion." Whereupon, undoing their corded silk laces, she drew off her high tan shoes. He noticed a delicate monogram, two M's in brown silk above her ankle. He placed a box before the fire for her to rest her feet on, then set her shoes and coat and hat to dry.

"How about yourself?" she said. "You must be wet to the skin."

"With your gracious permission," he answered, "I shall now retire to the dressing-room—alias behind the cupboard." He suited the action to the word, opening the cupboard door for additional screened space, and reappearing after a few minutes in Lew Anderson's corduroys, blue flannel shirt, and felt moccasins.

As she sat before the mounting flame, Marion had been contrasting this forthright solution of the wet clothes question with George Pearson's. George would never have dreamed of having either of them do anything but sit all afternoon in discomfort. She reflected that in his own environment Walt dealt with things with firmness and certainty. Difficulties arose only when he approached hers.

Thinking of the girl's fearless, first-hand attitude toward things, the typical attitude Nietzsche called "value-creating," Bradfield went on to wonder how far present master-ethics, the life-expression of men and women economically secure and free, would resemble the ethics of the masterless and slaveless future. Slave-ethics—the product of poverty and economic oppression—would surely disappear. As he came from behind the cupboard absorbed in this, he suddenly became aware that Marion's wide eyes were interestedly fixed on his. She was leaning back luxuriously, the firelight making her hair a glory of gleaming lights and luring shadows.

"What were you thinking about so intently?" she asked.

When he told her, she raised her fair hands in despair. "That soulful gaze!" she cried. "That rapt expression! I supposed of course you were thinking of me! To think that I cannot compete with 'the ethics of dynamist monism'!"

"It was the thought of you which led me to the thought of that," he explained.

"I refuse to be appeased. The thought of that should have led you to the thought of me."

"Fair lady, I have sinned against you," said he humbly. "What shall my penance be?"

"Your penance? Let me see. Your offense was being guilty of prose. You are condemned to improvise a poem in praise of me."

"De Bergerac improvised a ballade while fighting a duel," said Walt. "I will improvise this poem while I roast potatoes." He went and got the potatoes and buried them thoughtfully in the hot ashes.

"No fair!" she said. "You are making it up beforehand."

"I have to arrange my rhymes," he protested. "The poem doesn't have to be done till the potatoes are." He put two bottles of beer out in the rain to cool, caught a kettleful of water for coffee, swung it on the crane, and proceeded to set the table with tin plates, knives, forks and cups. Then he cut pieces of cheese to toast on square crackers, got out a gridiron, sliced some ham, and began broiling it over the wood coals.

"I hope the poem is as good as that smells," she said.

"This poem must be seen to be appreciated."

"Is it done already? What is it—a visible poem?"

"One more line." He poked a potato. He turned the ham, then kneeling and holding the gridiron so as not to burn his hands, he recited:

> "Music of infinite waters descending,
>   Ardors of lightning that gleam in our sky,
>   Richer the music and gleam of my blending—
>   Intricate runes with the meaningful cry
>   Of opulent Love in his subtlety lending
>   Name to his secret of ardor unending."

"It has a noble sound," said Marion.

He made no comment, being absorbed in the problem of not burning the ham.

"But my dear poet!" she broke out. "Am I supposed to *understand* that poem?"

"My occupations clash. If I stop to get my poem appreciated, my dinner will spoil." He hastened to get the dinner on. They sat down together.

"I'm sure this beats Spinnyville," she said. "I never enjoyed anything so in my life. What cook ever prepared a dinner and a poem at the same time—or what poet? But really I couldn't understand it—hearing it just once. Won't you repeat it?"

He reveled in the opportunity.

"The music is beautiful," she said, "but this poem was to be in praise of me. I'm not in it at all. The idea of leaving me out of my very own poem!"

"You are everything in it. Let me write it for you." He wrote it, and watched her read it. "The guarded treasure of the runes," he said, "is—Marion." He spoke the name lingeringly, loving the sound of it.

She saw her name in the initial letters. "You lovely thing!" she exclaimed, and hugged it. Her delight was to him the fitting pay for poet's work. She read it again. "It is lovely," she said, "—the lovelier for being unlockable without the key."

"It gave me the chance to call you Marion once anyhow—in a hidden way."

"Why not do it in an unhidden way?" she said. As soon as she had so spoken, however, she thought of one good reason why not. Feodor! And then, in spite of all her leanings and acceptings and broadenings, all the old other sphere of ideas in her grew uncomfortable at the thought of being Marion to her father's gardener.

He read that like a book. "Don't be afraid," he said. "I shall not call you that."

That made her ashamed of her narrowness. "Here is a man of intellect," she thought, "—a poet, a soul full of beauty and passion!"

It seemed strange to her that she should want to kiss a man, yet balk at having him call her by her name. But so it was.

IX

MRS. MOULTON was alarmed about Marion when the storm first broke over Moline, but hoped the launch party would by that time be safe in the Camanche club house. Since thinking evil things brings evil, it was her duty to believe them safe. Since nothing is but thinking makes it so, thinking of the party as not being at Camanche would very likely cause them not to be there. Her visualization of them there in the grill room became so distinct that she could feel her astral self at Camanche seeing eight people, among them Marion, sitting at a certain table. Had anyone suggested to her that this vision might possibly be the optical memory of a party she had there chaperoned two years before, her will to believe the alluringly mysterious astral doctrine would have scorned the suggestion as emanating from the critical, that is from the Mephistophelian, spirit—"the spirit that ever denies." Yielding to this spirit would be evil because it would project from her mind a powerfully injurious thought-force.

When Mrs. Farnsworth, Mr. Moulton's sister, their guest at dinner, inquired for Marion, Mrs.

Moulton replied that she had gone with a launch-party to Camanche.

Mr. Farnsworth conjectured that the storm would compel them to leave their launch up there and return by train.

"I hope they got there before the storm struck," said Mr. Moulton.

A certain mysterious intonation in his wife's assurance that they had reached Camanche led him to suspect astral information. As soon as dinner was over he succeeded, in spite of the storm, in getting the steward at Camanche by telephone. Then he called Mrs. Moulton from her guests. "No launch party has reached Camanche to-day," said he abruptly.

Her real alarm made him relent.

"And none was expected there," he added. "Now, Anne, don't get rattled, but tell me what you do really know about this launch party. Whose party was it?"

She had to explain that Marion, due at the river at ten-thirty, and not leaving the house till quarter to eleven, had departed hurriedly without giving her any details.

"How did she go?"

"On foot."

"Why didn't she take her electric?"

"I cannot say." She knew David imagined he had shattered one of her intuitions against a stone wall of fact, and resented the air of arrogant, incisive efficiency he always assumed on such occasions. If anything did happen to Marion it would be his fault for creating all this malicious thought-magnetism.

Mr. Moulton sent for one of the drivers and directed him to take Miss Moulton's electric down to the boat-landing. She might be there with no way to get home through the rain. If she was not there, the driver was to find out and report at once what party she went with and which way they had gone.

Twenty minutes later, Mr. Moulton was informed by the driver, Eldridge, that it must have been Miss Moulton who had gone out alone with Walt Bradfield. About eleven o'clock they had gone through the lock, and so down the river, in Lew Anderson's launch "Nancy."

"Bradfield?" repeated Mr. Moulton, trying to place the gentleman.

"He works here, sir," said the chauffeur, expecting to produce a sensation. "Sits beside me in the servants' dining-room. He's one of the gardeners."

"Oh, yes," said Mr. Moulton, "—that plan of my daughter's. I didn't know she was doing that to-day. That's all, Eldridge."

Eldridge turned to go, but hesitated an instant at the door with the idea that he was to be told to keep this matter quiet.

"Was there something else?" inquired Mr. Moulton.

"No, sir," replied Eldridge, getting out. "I wonder if that old fox did know about that Bradfield deal?" he speculated.

Mr. Moulton sank back in his chair, irritation and

perplexity in his soul. "What is that girl up to?" thought he. He looked out at the still driving rain and swaying tree-tops. He was divided between concern for Marion's safety in the storm, and his effort to understand her motive in making a companion of a servant. Stories of refined women infatuated with strapping grooms and coachmen rose repulsively in his mind. He did not accept that explanation; but it remained in the background of his thoughts ready to reassert itself.

The affair looked worse to him when he found the girl had never mentioned Bradfield to her mother. Mrs. Moulton's amazement when she heard Marion had gone in a launch with the gardener made it impossible for her to bring the kindly side of her philosophy to bear. "Earth-forces" was her formulation of the same suspicion that had arisen in her husband. For her, once started along that path of thought, the very occupation of the man was symbolic. Was he not a digger in the earth? And Marion had gone with him upon the water. The affair was of earth and water, unsanctified of fire and air.

Mr. Moulton was tormented with the impulse to do something. Either the launch had swamped, or it had not. If it had, he wanted to know it. If it had not, Marion and her companion must now be some place under shelter waiting for the storm to stop. He did not care to have them wait. He finally sent down the river a big launch with a closed cabin and a searchlight to find the "Nancy" and bring Marion home.

This launch left Moline about four o'clock manned

by two old rivermen in charge of McChesney, a confidential agent in the detective service of the Plow Company. The rain stopped while they were searching. Near dark they located the stove-in "Nancy" on the shore of Round Island; but they found the log-cabin there empty. The old fisherman in the house-boat on the Iowa shore told McChesney that when he came out after the storm to look at his nets, he had seen a couple on the island waving a shirt on an oar. He had taken them off, and they had started to walk to town.

The fisherman had told them they might make it by dark: but they had to pick their way along the edges of muddy roads, finally took to the gravel and ties of the railroad track; and as night fell, the electric lights of Davenport sprang up white out of the blackness of the eastern horizon. They came to a railroad bridge beneath which in the gloom a rain-swollen torrent ominously thundered. They stopped a moment, standing close together. The cold wind and the tumult of that unfriendly elemental force made the warmth and nearness of each other more precious.

"You don't suppose the bridge is out, do you?" said Marion, peering ahead. "No, I can see the shine on the rails." She clasped Walt's hand, and welcomed the support of his arm around her as they crossed, stepping from tie to tie.

He was seized with a wild happiness, a piercing realization of the present moment, an intense feeling of his identity and hers. The two of them crossing that bridge in the black night were to him the only man and woman in the world. When they felt the

gravel once more underfoot she would have drawn
away.

"A man, a woman, and Nature which made us!"
he exclaimed. "There are no classes. There is no
town. There is nothing but you and me and the
night."

His feeling swept her like a poem creating a new
mood. The thunder of waters behind them seemed
no more a hostile voice, but the voice of great har-
monious forces at work through eons and eons creating and maintaining man. She leaned and pressed
her cheek against his shoulder; then, sighing, with-
drew her hand and walked alone. "For me," she
said, "there is town. There is Hillcrest, and in it
another man and woman. They are worrying about
me. They love me,—in a way,—not wisely, not
trustfully, not realizing I must find or make my own
path through life. They do not understand me:
they have no sympathy for the things that I, being
I, must seek and find. They will attack me to-night.
I will have to defend myself. If he had his way,
my father would reduce the real me to pulp."

The great tenderness then filling Walt turned into
the channel of regret that she too should be subject
to all the influences that shape our modern world and
shape it wrong. "Shall I go in and help you defend yourself?" he asked.

"No. The best you could hope would be to defend yourself. After you left I should have my own
fight just the same—or worse."

They caught the suburban car where it crossed
the railroad at the lower end of Davenport. Three-
quarters of an hour later, they got off in Moline at

an electric-lighted corner where the streets were
thickly lined with workingmen's small frame houses,
their paint grimed with soot from the factories.
Back on the bluff towered Hillcrest, its four stories
marked by half a dozen brilliant windows. Well to
the right and left of it stood other great houses, each
aloof on its own spacious eminence—as the castles
of robber barons stood on the hills of Rhineland.

Walt and Marion ascended the hill, walking
alongside a heavy terra-cotta retaining wall, from
the top of which leafless, brittle-looking vines trailed
downward. Between the base of the wall and the
concrete sidewalk stood a row of low shrubs which
Walt himself had planted. The return to use-and-
wont, to Hillcrest, the end of his day with her, affected him gloomily. "I have a wretched premoni-
tion I am not going to see you very much any more,"
he said.

She had the same unpleasant feeling, but would
not admit it. "I should think a monist like you
would regard premonitions as superstitious."

"I did—yesterday. Imagination was reason-
guided,—a light I turned at will upon the world.
Therein lay my power. To-day that monism of
mine is split by war of reason and desire—and reason has the worst of it."

"Is that a reproach of me?"

"An analysis of me. I can no longer distinguish
between the thing I desire and the thing that is true.
I am no better than a bourgeois."

"That *is* humility!" she laughed. "But really,
Walt, a little humility won't hurt you a bit."

He stopped abruptly. Once more, as on the dark

bridge in the thunder of waters, there were no classes. She was woman to him, and he was man. An overpowering feeling of worship swept through him. "I could kneel here at your feet for that!" he breathed. "In fact—I must!"

"Oh, no!" she exclaimed. "No!" She caught hold of his arms to keep him from doing it. "It will make me cry if you do that!"

"No! Don't take it that way. I will be nice and quiet about it. It's a thing I *have* to do." He made her feel it as impulse and compulsion of the depths of life in him, and then he knelt as though it were an act of mere deliberate resolve. She found a beauty and richness in that union, in one act, of simple conscious will and some uncomprehended depth of feeling. The depth, and nothing of quietness, was in his voice when he stretched out his arms to her with the cry, "I worship you!"

She swayed back breathless, leaning against the wall, knowing clearly that this was something more than merely physical allurement. His cry—which she thought no woman in the world could have heard unmoved—and its echo in her were of the spirit, or more truly, of the whole and single being which man is. It felt like a great love. The great desire of all that day, thwarted but stronger inwardly for every thwarting, retreating only to advance through some new path of feeling, seized and subdued her. Not indirectly nor as an accident, not with manner unpurposive, she bent and kissed him—in the mood of answered prayer.

He rose. A beam from an arc-lamp through the young buds showed her his face. In his arms she whispered: "I shouldn't have done it. I don't know why I did. I seemed to have to. It was too big for me, Walt."

"It was star-high above my hope!" he said.

"It's a pity to say it, but you mustn't, mustn't make too much of it. I must go in. I need to be alone and think." She saw a question forming in his eyes and did not dare listen. "Come!" she said, and using all her will power moved on up the hill. She looked down and up the walk. Fortunately—no one! They turned in through the gate of Hillcrest and neared the door.

"Don't let this be the end of things between us!" he pleaded. "It has grown too strong to break."

"I'm utterly at sea," said Marion.

X

SHE would have liked nothing so much as to slip upstairs to her lair, there to get her balance and find out a little where she stood: but her mother heard her come in, and hastened to see if it was she.

"Hello, Mother!" said the girl with rather artificial cheerfulness. "Did you think I was drowned?"

"I knew you were not," said Mrs. Moulton in her tone of occult knowledge. "But I did not know why you had slipped off as you did to spend the day with one of the men-servants."

Mr. Moulton came into the reception-hall, and looked searchingly at his daughter.

"You word it very badly," said the girl to her mother. "Good evening, Papa. I hope you have not been worrying about me. It wasn't necessary."

"I differ with you," he said.

"There's a searching party down the river looking for you now," said Mrs. Moulton.

"Such a fuss!" exclaimed Marion in scornful resignation.

"Where were you during the storm?" asked Mr. Moulton.

"In front of a fire getting dry. We had an accident with the launch, and had to walk home. I would like to get these muddy boots off if you'd just as soon."

"Just a moment, please," said Mr. Moulton. "Have you any objection to telling where this fire was?"

"I wouldn't have the slightest objection to telling everything that happened to-day—were it not for the tone you and mama have adopted. You seem to take it for granted that I am guilty of something. If you wish to make a criminal court out of this, go ahead, and I'll act accordingly." She took off her hat and gloves—frank battle preparations. "I really ought to have a lawyer to take advantage of technical points," she said scathingly. "I believe, first of all, I have a right to know the exact crime for which I am to be tried."

"There's considerable bluff to that, Marion," said Mr. Moulton. "You spent the day alone with Bradfield the gardener—you have avoided saying just where." He paused a moment. "What are you up to?"

"I am not 'up to' anything. I went launch-riding with Mr. Bradfield because I like him." She waited a moment. "Is that sufficient?"

"Hardly."

"It should be."

"Why did you say nothing to your mother about Mister Bradfield?"

"The subject did not happen to come up. I told Mrs. Pearson all about it. She was going with us to-day, and hurt her knee at the last minute. It's absurd to think of Bradfield as a servant. He is a thinker and writer. I have read one of his books. He is much the most interesting man in Moline."

"How did you come to discover all this?" inquired Mrs. Moulton.

"I began talking with him about the Japanese lilies in the conservatory."

"Well, that part of it sounds all right," said Mr. Moulton, relieved of his darkest suspicions. "But Marion, you must be more careful of appearances. The thing looks bad. Don't do it, my girl, don't do this sort of thing."

"If the thing had happened with George Pearson, not a word would be said about it. Why then when it is Walt Bradfield—a man more intelligent and worth while?"

"Look here," said Mr. Moulton. "Eldridge the driver knows you went with this man who in his eyes certainly is simply a fellow servant of his, and he is all ready to start some talk that will make your hair stand on end. If this Bradfield doesn't show a damned sight more decency and good sense than he's at all likely to in answering Eldridge's questions, there'll be a scandal over this affair. You must not let it go any farther. You've got to drop Bradfield!"

"I shan't do it!" blazed Marion, and then she thought it better to be a little more conciliating. "It isn't necessary, Papa. Mr. Bradfield may be relied on for both decency and good sense."

An automobile came up and stopped outside the door, but they were too absorbed to notice it.

"You seem to be completely under the man's influence!" exclaimed Moulton. "I'd like to know how you reconcile your apparently limitless admiration for this gardener with your interest in the Count de Hohenfels."

She had not herself reconciled those two things. If she had only had time to think things out—to find just how far reconciliation was possible! "That is a matter that must be decided by my own conscience," was all she could find to say.

Mr. Moulton was really astonished. He had expected an indignant disclaimer of anything more than friendship for Bradfield.

"Is the trial over?" said Marion patiently.

"I sometimes think you love rebellion for its own sake!" said he bitterly.

"Do you ever love authority for its own sake?" she asked, thinking of his rigid adherence to the time he had set for further discussion of the letter to De Hohenfels.

The doorbell rang. A servant turned on the porch light, and through the plate-glass of the door Mr. Moulton saw a clean-cut gentleman with dark, closely trimmed beard taking out a card-case, the movement displaying white waistcoat and sable-lined overcoat.

There was an exclamation of astonishment from Mrs. Moulton. Marion turned, but the caller had stepped back so as not to see what was going on inside.

"De Hohenfels!" exclaimed Mrs. Moulton. "Marion, it's De Hohenfels!"

"De Hohenfels?" echoed Mr. Moulton. He looked at Marion.

She stood there dazed and speechless.

XI

"JUST look at you!" exclaimed Mrs. Moulton,
almost as upset as Marion by De Hohenfels's
unexpected arrival. "You can't let him see
you like that!"

"Mother, are you *sure* it's Fedya? Did he see
you? *Where* is that footman? Oh, please let me
get away, and open the door yourself!" She fled upstairs. "Why didn't he telephone?" she thought.
"When did he get here? What will papa say to
him? Oh, dear, I *must* dress! Where is Mathilde?"

Suppressing misgivings as to propriety, Mrs.
Moulton did open the door herself. The Count
de Hohenfels thanked her for her kind informality,
but became formal himself on the presentation of
Mr. Moulton, who briefly acknowledged the introduction. The footman, arriving to open the door,
deferentially relieved the visitor of his stick, hat,
and the beautiful warm coat, to get the fur for which
nomad hunters on snow-shoes had lain for days half-
frozen by the holes of the sables on Siberian steppes.

"Won't you come in?" said Mrs. Moulton, turning a key that lighted up the nearest reception room.
"Marion has just gone to dress; I'm afraid she'll
keep you waiting awhile. Why didn't you let us
know you were coming?"

"Things were a little vague," replied De Hohenfels, whose thoughts were then vigorously centered
on Marion's father. Starting to follow his hostess,
he glanced back to see if her husband were coming
too. Mr. Moulton showing no such intention, De
Hohenfels stopped and faced him. Having come
to beard the lion in his den, the sight of the lion
impelled him to immediate bearding. "Do not care
to purchase European title for my daughter" was
rankling.

"Allow me to acknowledge your cablegram," he
said, speaking with the precision of an ambassador.
"I decided to answer it in person. I wish to explain
first that my family makes its daughters independent
of their husbands at marriage in order that the sordid bond of money-asking and money-giving may
play no part in their wedded lives. Should you be
unable or unwilling to do this for your daughter, I
am neither. If Miss Moulton does me the honor
to accept my offer of marriage, I shall be happy to
endow her in her own right with the half of my
estate—which is not exactly the smallest in Russia."

"Very noble of you," said Moulton, wishing to
throw the gentleman off the track of his apparently
premeditated speech.

"Not at all. The satisfaction of making this answer to your polite communication is in itself worth
half of any man's estate."

"Especially when the said half-estate, magnani-
mously deeded out of the family one day, comes
back by marriage the next! I believe, also, that in
Europe a man is the guardian of his wife's estate
and the administrator of her property."

"Not in Russia. There exists there the absolute
independence of a married woman with regard to
her property. But you miss the point. My proposal
effectually destroys the accusation of your cablegram
—that the title of De Hohenfels is for sale."

"Your proposal may also be regarded as a grand‚
stand play of half the De Hohenfels estate now for
all of the Moulton estate later."

"Mr. Moulton, you are at liberty to do anything
you like with your estate except accuse me of improper motives in regard to it. Men accustomed to
wealth take it for granted. With me it is a means,
not an end. I am perfectly willing to throw away
a forest and never see it again for the sake of—let
us say a felicitous revenge. You apparently are
ready to spoil your own life and your daughter's—
for fear somebody other than yourself will enjoy the
use of your money after you are dead."

"I am a creator of wealth, young man; and, by
your account, you are a spender of it. That may
account for certain differences in our points of view."

"My peasants and my land create my wealth.
Your factories and your workmen create yours. Not
so vast a difference, I think. We had better not go
into the subject of political economy, however, since
Mrs. Moulton has been kind enough to suggest that
I follow her. At my hotel I have documents necessary to make the transfer of property I mentioned."
Suppressing a gleam of malicious satisfaction, which
showed his feeling that he had the best of it, De
Hohenfels bowed and followed Mrs. Moulton into
the reception room.

"Clever!" was Moulton's verdict as he turned toward his study. He began to wonder if the man could be interested in the administration of industry, and whether he would live in America. Considering the Bradfield affair, perhaps it was just as well the foreigner had arrived. And still, Mr. Moulton thought it worth while to consider whether there was any way of playing De Hohenfels and Bradfield against each other for the elimination of both and the advantage of George Pearson.

A few minutes after the coming of De Hohenfels to Hillcrest, there sounded through its spacious rooms, with their hard-wood floors and lofty ceilings, the opening of Chopin's Nocturne in G Major. De Hohenfels was playing for Mrs. Moulton, though she was wont to express disdain of "intellectual musicians who spoil the soul-impression by analysis." Since he nevertheless played with all the intelligence, as well as with all the power and taste, which he possessed, it may be surmised that there in the Hillcrest music room Count Feodor was not playing solely for Mrs. Moulton.

The first phrase of the famous Nocturne, rising and repeated in the tonic, he rendered like a question—the descending answer faltering a little to a tentative solution in the subdominant minor. Rearising there, the question was answered in the tonic; but there the eager fairies, knowing another answer, seized the theme, swept it through flitting chords of C and F, B flat and E flat to D flat, transmuted it to esoteric E flat minor, filled it with dew and moonbeams on the borderland of flats and sharps, brought it back as far as F, then gave it to A minor and the gods.

The Olympians said it in their language and sent it back through a thunder of warring sevenths to E minor and friendly C major. There a new movement rocked like a boating song in big slow waves. The yearning question and answer broke out again, developed as before as far as E flat minor, but this time, avoiding the Olympian confusion on the borderland of sharps and flats, the melody sailed smoothly on around the circle of the keys, working through the antipodal key, there solving the mystery of the identity of G flat and F sharp which binds the two hemispheres of the keys into a sphere, and finally, from the other side of the world of music, it emerged Magellan-like in the vassal chords of G and the harbor song.

After enchanted minors the common chords came as the richest change of all, as man, enriched by creative experience, at last emerges into understanding of his own real and earth-born soul—to find it more wondrous than all his mythic gods and heavens.

The recurring question and response hinted of final answer, the music moved toward some climax not to be divined. Gathering energy and meaning, it swept through B flat, E flat, across F sharp, and moved with deepening bass through clear and luminous chords of B and E and A, dropping a sharp at every beat, and then there came, in lieu of the expected D, a chord of stars, the Pleiades, a B flat, E and G, and far below, a mystery and a thunder called C sharp.

The distant phrases intensified Marion's feeling of the importance of life. That pattern of beautiful sound which sadness had woven in the soul of Chopin made more poignant her sense of crisis and unpreparedness. She was afraid of Feodor—not only of his judgment of this day of hers with Walt, but habitually—lest she should fail to satisfy his instinct and intelligence of beauty. Manners, language, ideas, dress, all things expressing personality, were subject of his art-criticism, and she felt that the prize of his approval was a great one.

With Walt she had begun to accept her whole nature, as he accepted his, allowing it spontaneous play; with the return of Feodor, she tried to regain her old attitude of selecting, rejecting, developing favored impulses.

She came down to the room where he was playing, white irises chained to her corsage in a flower-clasp of Roman gold, her red-gold hair done high in a Russian coiffure, the kakoshnik, with which she had once delighted his soul in Rome.

Mrs. Moulton saw in the girl's eyes a troubled look that made her hope she was regretting her affair with Bradfield. There was imperfectly concealed constraint in her greeting to De Hohenfels. Mrs. Moulton left them, and went to tell her husband he had better drop his opposition to the foreigner. Her chief objection to Count Feodor, unacknowledged even to herself, had been that if she would only wait a few years Dave Moulton's daughter could probably aspire higher. It would be very fine to feel spiritually superior to the mere title of a son-in-law who was a duke. But if it was to be Count Feodor or—a gardener——!

Count Feodor's attention was on Marion as picture. "It is impossible to retain a mental image equal to you," he said.

"I can't believe it's you," she said. "*Here* it seems unreal. Why didn't you let me know you were coming?"

"Didn't you know I would have to come after you?" He folded her hands in his, close to his breast, and drew her toward him. She stepped back hastily, and flushed as she realized the idea that made her do it. He accounted for it superficially. She realized then how it would wound him if he ever knew. She had shrunk from him because the kiss of another man was on her lips.

"Tell me," said he, "do you still love me?"

She hesitated.

"You do not!" he exclaimed. "I never doubted that till now. I thought of every other reason why you left Rome."

"Oh, I do. I do love you. But——"

She found herself unable to tell him of Walt. Mentally she made the excuse that she must wait till she herself understood how such contradictory emotions could exist together in her. "The humiliation of that cablegram," said she lamely—uncomfortable with the consciousness of her evasion.

"How can you be so illogical? I thought by next morning you would realize you were not responsible for the acts of your father. The next morning you were gone—without a word, without a line! Not a line from Genoa, not a line from Gibraltar! I had to take your majordomo's word for it that you had gone to America. I wasn't certain till to-night that you would be here in Moline."

"I felt then that I couldn't face you again until you had been atoned to in some way. I came home to make my father apologize to you."

"Make him apologize!" he protested. "That would be a superficial, an empty, atonement. I have already done better than that."

"What?" she asked eagerly.

"Forced him to see that he was wrong."

"You did!" she cried, exulting. "How did you do it?"

He told her of the proposal he had made to Mr. Moulton.

"You—endow—me! Oh, what a shame!" She turned away from him, sank into a chair, and stared before her. "Yes," she said. "You have your revenge. But it isn't fair! It isn't fair to you. You had your sister Vanya's dot to pay. And it isn't fair to me. No; that's impossible, Feodor. We may be barbarians in some ways, but we're hardly so low as marriage by purchase."

"You're confused. The price of a purchased bride goes not to her but to her family."

"Well!" she blazed. "If the price goes to the woman herself—what do you call that?"

He shrugged his shoulders. "American marriage."

She knitted her brows—trying to see in that anything more than a *mot* of his.

"Surely," said he, "it is better that a woman

should be made independent by her husband once and for all and in her own right than to have it doled out to her in the form of support."

"How terribly financial a thing marriage is!" exclaimed Marion. "Americans like my father think the dot makes marriage mercenary. Europeans like you think a dotless marriage mercenary. And what I never saw until this moment is—that both of you are right!"

"Do you think me mercenary?" he asked irritably.

"No. I know you are not. You have had too many things in your life more interesting than the pursuit of money."

"Are you mercenary?"

"No. I haven't had to be. I've taken wealth for granted."

"Exactly. Just as you should do."

"But our being unmercenary makes my point the stronger. We desire to marry, and unmercenary though we are, complication after complication arises about money; and there doesn't seem to be any possible arrangement that isn't degrading or unfair to someone."

"What has started you along this line? It is necessary to settle matters at the beginning—that's all. After that, the question of money will cause us no more trouble than it always has."

She could not help looking through Walt's eyes at the idea that they should have wealth without trouble or thought or any service to the society which gave them luxury and culture. She remembered Bradfield's "you have accepted the profits as unthinkingly as you accept the philosophy that justifies them." She thought of a certain vast, one-story, old brick building in Moline where, from dawn till dusk in Rembrandtesque gloom, lit by the weird, red lights of forges, men with black, sweat-streaked faces and uncanny forearms held and hammered red plow-shares on the ringing anvils. Money was a thing *they* had to think about—and give their whole lives for! "Do your peasants plow with wooden plows, Feodor?" she asked abruptly.

"Hardly. Why do you ask?"

"I thought probably my father was speaking meta-phorically."

"Oh, has he been investigating my estates?"

"I think not."

"It *is* hard to get them to use American labor-sav-ing machinery."

"Why?"

"They are slaves of tradition."

"Why do *they* say they don't want to use it?"

"They? Oh, various pretexts."

"For instance?"

"That it robs too many of work. That they have to have larger holdings of land first. So they dream of nationalizing the land—after overthrowing the monarchy."

"That is not being slaves of tradition."

"Well—no, the social revolutionists are not. They would make muzhiks of us all. But where have you acquired such an interest in this?"

"I was thinking how easily wealth comes to some, how hard to others. Tell me, if you were a muzhik, would you not work for nationalization of the land?"

"What I'd do if a muzhik is too unimportant for

discussion. Being what I am, I shall do everything in my power to prevent the annihilation of present Russian society. It's bad enough in some ways, but as a whole it is on the highest level of individual culture in Europe. Old culture—that of the west—in a new soul—that of the upper-class Russian, not too remote from barbaric vigor—there, perhaps, lies the highest possibility for human development. The muzhik to cultivate the soil, and we—ourselves. But strange as it may seem, my dear Marion, I really can't get my mind on those impersonal subjects. I am disturbed by your unwillingness to back me up in the position I have taken with Mr. Moulton. Unless we carry things through on the basis I have proposed, he will take advantage of the failure to impute insincerity to me. If you are so anxious that atonement be made to me, don't you see that this is the one way that really does atone? Don't you see how strong this makes your position with him? Go and tell him you and I are going to marry next week."

"Oh, no!" she exclaimed, startled by the vividness of the idea.

"Two weeks, then. Three. The point is—say, nothing more about settlement, dower, or anything of the kind. Ignore the subject. If he broaches it, tell him it's quite immaterial."

"That would be delicious!" Her eyes were radiant.

"Good! Do it now!"

"Oh, Feodor!" She sank back despondent. "It's as though you were marrying a beggar from the streets of Rome!"

"Nonsense! Suppose I were an American. There'd be no question of dower. I am able to take care of you. If you love me you should be willing to give me the happiness of doing it—to say nothing of the fiendish satisfaction it will give me to spike the guns of your skeptical pater. Run along and tell him, and come back to me. Or shall we go hand in hand and say, 'Bless us, our father!' "

It was alluring. It was easier to do it than not. She was trembling on the verge of consent. The thought of the cabin and the launch, the bridge, the concrete walk, came over her like a pang. To forget all that before the day was done! It would be desecration. She shook her head. "Not today, Fedya. I can't say 'yes' to that today. That doesn't mean I will tomorrow. No, there are some things I must think out."

XII

WHEN Mrs. Moulton came in after conference with her husband and asked Count
Feodor to stay at Hillcrest while he was in
Moline, the European, betraying no surprise, and
welcoming the indication of a favorable impression
produced on Mr. Moulton, accepted the invitation.
He came up next morning in a motor-car with his
English valet, who unpacked the trunks in a suite
more luxurious than Hohenfels had known in the
manor-houses of Russia. From his windows the
foreign visitor looked across to the heights of suburban Davenport; and in the valley saw the river,
wide as the Volga at Samara, flowing around the
nobly wooded government island. There the arsenal
alined its giant yellow stone gables beneath the
towering flag-staff flying the flag with aristocratic
blue field, its patrician white striped with a color
Hohenfels would have omitted, symbolic of one
blood in the veins of all men—loved by slaves and
serfs and democrats from the days of the labor
unions of imperial Rome.

In the expanse of woods and water and citied hills
the ugliest and most interesting area was the long
crescent of massive brick factory buildings which

lined the Moline water front. Among groups of cylindrical sheet-iron smoke-stacks and tall brick chimneys with soot-blackened tops, the names of plow and wagon and implement and carriage companies stood above the horizontal roof-lines in black or gilded metal letters twice the height of a man.

After luncheon with Marion and Mrs. Moulton, Count Feodor went with them in their car to the golf-links and met a number of society people at the club-house on the island.

When Mr. Moulton, who had lunched at the Manufacturers' with some eastern business men, drove home late in the afternoon, he saw the Pearson car near the door and met Mrs. Pearson coming out.

"Not a soul home!" said she, after Mr. Moulton had returned her greeting. "I came to carry Marion off to dinner."

"Come in, won't you?" said Moulton. "Marion may not go to dinner with you but she will be anxious to have you meet her latest acquisition."

"Yes, she asked me to come over and talk with him," said Lady Diotima, turning back with Moulton to the house and concluding that Marion must have confided in her father as to Bradfield.

"The gentleman arrived last night," said Moulton. "I believe my wife has already domesticated him."

"Last night!" echoed Mrs. Pearson. "Why whom do you mean?"

"Feodor, Count de Hohenfels," said Moulton with a grimace.

"You don't mean it! Hm! So he came. Did you talk with him?"

"A little. By the way: whom did you think I meant by Marion's latest?"

"Oh, a Mr. Bradfield," said Lady Diotima, as though the subject were not worth pursuing.

"I learned of that yesterday," said he. "What do you think of it?"

"She has probably formed an exaggerated idea of his talent, judgment, and so on, simply because in that kind of man one expects nothing at all."

"Sound!" exclaimed Moulton. He offered her a chair. "Tell me," he began, seating himself near her. "I've a hazy kind of notion. Is there any possibility of getting these two—acquisitions—to eliminate each other?"

"Like the two snakes that began at each other's tails and swallowed till they both vanished?" She laughed.

"The analogy would discredit the idea," he said, refusing to think the snakes amusing. "But seriously: women have a talent for such things. Marion has already confided in you. Her mother and I found out about Bradfield only by accident. I wish you would feel your way in the matter."

"I don't want Marion to cast me in the rôle of designing mama," observed Lady Diotima. "If I am to lose her as a daughter-in-law, I don't care to lose her as a friend too. Whatever influence I have with her is as a chum. However: ask her to bring Count de Hohenfels to dinner to-night. In any case I wish to meet him, and George is in Minneapolis."

Lady Diotima's scientific observations at her dinner-table that evening led her to believe that Count Feodor had Marion. She herself liked him. In the conversation there was a sprinkling of smart epigrams, a light tone of graceful false sentiment that made no pretense of being genuine, and not too great earnestness about anything—a kind of talk Mrs. Pearson pined for and seldom attained. The guest followed her lead happily. His easy dignity, his not quite blasé air, his assured tone of man of the world, were qualities whose absence in Bradfield, as Marion recognized, would have meant a constrained party had he been in the Russian gentleman's place.

While Hohenfels and Mr. Pearson, over their cigars, were discussing certain grand-ducal timber speculations as the real cause of the Russo-Japanese war, Lady Diotima, alone with Marion upstairs, innocently inquired if the Count had met her friend Mr. Bradfield.

"No," said Marion, non-committally. The question being not unexpected, she betrayed nothing of her state of soul.

"Aren't you going to arrange a meeting?" asked Mrs. Pearson smiling.

"Goodness!" said the girl. "Your question suggests the duello."

"Do you suppose your philosopher will take it philosophically?"

This pierced Marion's armor. "Don't joke about it!" she exclaimed.

"Dear me! I didn't suppose it was serious."

"I lay awake half the night thinking about it."

"I don't see why Mr. Bradfield's disappointment should bother you so much. You seem quite unconcerned about George."

"I am not worrying about Mr. Bradfield's feelings. He is capable of taking care of them himself. It's my own."

"Is it possible? Do you mean to say you like him better than your Russian?"

"You can call me as weak and worthless as you like, but I don't know. I begin to think myself incapable of real love. I thought I loved Fedya—I think so yet. Yes, it must be that I do. And yet, if I do—how can it be that this other man attracts me so?"

"Has the other man made love to you?"

Marion looked at her reproachfully for asking, but Lady Diotima was unabashed.

"An enterprising person," she observed.

Marion rose to go downstairs. "Perhaps I was the enterprising one. I don't know. My likes and dislikes have always been positive. I imagined I understood myself. Evidently I do not. It's a wretched condition to be in."

"Have you seen Bradfield since the Count's arrival?"

"No, I don't know what to tell him."

"See him, and probably things will clear up. Only for heaven's sake don't marry him. Even if you cared for them both equally as individuals—though I can't believe you do—you ought not to hesitate when life with one leads into the central current—to world capitals—St. Petersburg, Rome—and life with the other leads—nowhere. But you don't have to marry either of them."

"No," said Marion. "I don't have to marry at all. But I think I shall."

"Does that mean one of these two?"

"I do know that these two are different to me from other men—the kind of difference a girl expects to find—and is expected to find—in only one."

As they came down and Marion caught sight of Fedya, immaculate, at ease, as he sat talking in the library, the idea of really marrying anyone else was suddenly painful to her. They left early; and as they rode homeward in the seat behind the driver, Count Feodor, had he known how she then felt, would have prospered.

On the corner of Sixteenth Street and Third Avenue their attention was attracted by a crowd of workingmen. A man standing above the crowd in the light of a gasoline torch was speaking.

"A political meeting?" asked De Hohenfels. "Would you mind stopping?"

The driver stopped on the edge of the crowd. A score of men turned to see what the "buzz-wagon" was doing there. Occupants of automobiles were not usually interested in such meetings. The speaker turned to look at them, and Marion repressed an exclamation of astonishment. It was Walt Bradfield.

When he recognized Marion in her lace automobile veil and saw the man in evening dress beside her, he lost the thread of his discourse. He turned away quickly, groped for his connections, found them, but spoke uncertainly. "Life is too easy," he said, "for those who now own the sources of wealth—that is, the sources of life."

Half a dozen men looked toward the richly dressed occupants of the motor car.

"A socialist?" queried De Hohenfels.

"Hand those plutocrats something, Walt," said one of the speaker's comrades.

"Labor bought with wealth produces more wealth," continued Bradfield. "The possessors of labor-buying wealth call the golden stream which our bought labor pours into their laps the 'reward of brains'! Wake up, you workingmen! That golden stream is the reward of their ownership of your productive power—their power to buy your labor in a labor market in which supply exceeds demand. If it is 'brains" that is being rewarded why does this same ownership enrich imbeciles, children, degenerates?

"The present fight of the Illinois manufacturers against the simplest and most obvious demands for the protection of laborers at their work confirms the old principle that no ruling class can be convinced by reasoning. Only the force of circumstances, the development of society, the awakened intelligence of the oppressed workers can drive them into sense and submission."

"Does your father know he is to be driven into submission to his workmen?" inquired Count Feodor.

"Really they are getting too raw! They have come to rely too implicitly on working-class stupidity. Day before yesterday the Illinois Legislature voted on the Curran bill. If passed, it would compel proper ventilation of rooms where girls and pregnant women must now inhale poisonous sulphuric and alkaline gases. It would compel the shielding of machinery to safeguard factory employees from avoidable accidents. They keep it out of the papers, but in this state women like your own mothers have been mangled by unprotected shafting and belting, and the shafting and belting that did it is unprotected yet. Take a look through the window there in the next block at the exposed cog-wheels in the black-smith shop of the United States Plow Company. Look at their paint shop on the fourth floor, full of fiercely burning materials, crowded with workers, and—without a fire-escape. The company cannot afford fire-escapes. It is fighting the Curran bill to save the expense of fire-escapes. Money spent for fire-escapes cannot go into dividends."

"Is such a thing possible?" demanded Marion under her breath.

De Hohenfels shrugged his shoulders.

"The Illinois Federation of Labor had a lobby at Springfield working for this bill. Did you read in yesterday's papers what happened? The legislature killed it. They killed it in slave obedience to letters written by members of the Illinois Manufacturers' Association, who claimed that the bill gave 'arbitrary power' to the state factory board to demand the reconstruction of buildings and readjustment of machinery. What frightful tyranny that would be! What sort of power to make and enforce such demands shall be exercised by the state if not 'arbitrary power'? What is unarbitrary power? The state exerts arbitrary power to prevent and punish other forms of murder—murders which do not happen to be profitable to the manufacturers of Illinois. The Manufacturers' Association of Illinois is aghast at the despotic restriction of the right of respectable employers to increase their profits by mangling women, poisoning girls, and burning men!"

Bradfield made this point with savage earnestness. There was a sharp, quick burst of applause from the crowd, and then silence to hear what he would say next.

"My father fought that bill," said Marion grimly. She had not suspected in the gentle Bradfield any such fighting power as now rang in his voice. For a moment she saw the whole profit-system and the social structure built upon it through his eyes.

"Women's sympathies make them liable to be carried away by this sort of appeal," observed De Hohenfels.

"They *ought* to be carried away! They ought to make men stop this kind of thing! I see why we ought to vote!"

"Don't you see, you workmen of Moline," cried Bradfield, "that if, instead of a voiceless lobby there at Springfield, you had your own elected representatives on the floor of that house—there with the right to speak and the burning will to speak—we could make the bought slaves on that floor and the masters in their palaces writhe beneath the knout of our criticism? Don't you know that our voices there, speaking as I am speaking here, would *shame* the State of Illinois into an approach to civilization?"

"It's about time the unions found that out," said one workingman to another near the motor car.

When Bradfield closed his speech, he called for questions, and briefly answered half a dozen stock objections to socialism.

"He has it all cut-and-dried," observed De Hohenfels.

"Do you call that cut-and-dried?" exclaimed Marion. "It seems to me I never in my life till now have heard the voice of intense conviction!"

"Well, perhaps when he was dealing with new facts. But these glib answers—he has them by heart. I'd like to ask him a question to make him think, but——"

"Go ahead," said Marion.

"Wouldn't it draw too much attention for you?"

"I don't mind in the least." She sat back, leaving it to him to speak or not.

"Is there any other question?" called Bradfield.

"Suppose you socialists get power," said De Hohenfels in a clear, incisive voice with British accent. "Suppose you really work out your theories in practise. What will then prevent the degeneration of men?"

"There is nothing in capitalism to prevent it," replied Bradfield. "Slums, starvation, overwork, underpay—these cause degeneration, and these we will remove."

"You miss the point. Hard conditions have developed all the virile strength that has ever existed. You propose to remove the source of human strength."

"Have hard conditions developed your strength?" demanded Bradfield. The workingmen laughed, and De Hohenfels wished he had kept out of it.

"What discipline I have had is not to the point," he said. "This is not a personal question."

"Then generalize it. Either there is no strength in what are called the upper classes, or they have developed their strength under easy conditions. You can take your choice."

"It is a well-known fact," said the Russian, preferring not to choose, "that the elimination of the unfit in the struggle for existence has been the chief cause of all race improvement. Socialism proposes to make existence so easy for all that even the most unfit shall survive and breed. Even sincere socialists admit this. You should read Jack London's 'War of the Classes.' "

"I have," said Bradfield. "Jack 's wrong—for once. The same conditions that now eliminate the least fit also reduce the vitality of the most fit. The crushing process that destroys the weak half destroys the strong. It stunts the life of all!"

"You are going counter to the whole science of biology."

"No, I am refusing to confuse biology and sociology."

"Who, may I ask, is your authority for your half-destruction of the strong?"

"I am."

De Hohenfels had suspected as much, but did not imagine the man would dare avow that authority as sufficient. "You will have to pardon me," said the aristocrat, "for declining to accept your *ex cathedra* statement, and for continuing to believe with the rest of the thinking world that the survivors of a severe struggle will be stronger than the survivors of—no struggle at all." He turned to the chauffeur, wishing to end the argument with that, but Bradfield forestalled him.

"A hundred men have malarial fever in Mississippi," he said. "Three die. Ninety-seven crawl around for years—half-men living half-lives. You would retain the swamp for the sake of killing the three."

"That case is too special to base a theory on."

"If you care to listen I'll give you fifty cases parallel. On second thought I won't grant your principle even in biology. The same species of pine that they make masts of where the tree has enough warmth and moisture, grows one inch high and has only three leaves in the hard conditions near the limits of vegetation. Take a human case from Jack London whom you cite—his 'People of the Abyss.' A million people half-starve in the dark, dirty, crowded rooms of London tenements. Many die of starvation, many of tuberculosis. What of the survivors of those hard conditions? Undersized, spiritless human wrecks!"

"The real survivors of that struggle you will find in the West End of London."

"In these days! Too few to count."

"In my counting those few are worth all the rest."

"You are at liberty to count crazily if it amuses you. We prefer to give the millions who are now starved and frozen and stifled into unfitness the chance to nourish and warm themselves into fitness. My proposition stands. Humanity can afford to let more of the 'unfit' survive—for the sake of the heightened splendor of life in all the fit. Observe, by the way, that in this connection 'unfit' means simply unadapted to the present ignoble money game. Through this sieve you lose some of the finest souls of earth. Leisure is good—especially that leisure we shall *earn*—with a moderate amount of healthful, socially useful work. You should have more faith in men, my friend, than to believe it is good for *you* to loaf and invite your soul—but bad for the other fellow."

"And you should have less faith in men. The fact that you are talking here on the street instead of in the Illinois Legislature proves that to the hilt. Why don't your workingmen elect you? They are worth nothing but scorn! Go on, driver."

"They will some day," called Bradfield.

"Ye didn't exactly eat him alive," shouted a workingman beside the car to De Hohenfels.

As the big gray-green car moved off beneath the electric light, the speaker of the evening had a glimpse of Marion Moulton looking back at him.

XIII

THOUGH De Hohenfels had "nothing but scorn" for the socialist speaker's ideals, he was impressed by the man's decided personality and undecadent will. As the car glided up toward Hillcrest, Marion, intently balancing her impressions of the two men she had just seen in conflict, detected a note of unconscious envy in the nobleman's musing question: "Where does he get that passion?"

"From being in close touch with a vital, widespread movement?" she suggested. "Did you feel his intimate relation with the crowd?"

The explanation did not appeal to Feodor. "Do you suppose he is a student of that college we saw this afternoon?"

"No," she answered. "He has had no education."

"Oh, so you know about him?. Evidently a local celebrity."

"His parents are ignorant peasants. His name is Bradfield."

She was about to add that she knew him personally, but De Hohenfels at once became interested in accounting for intelligence from such a source. He thought the man must be regarded biologically as a "sport." His faith in heredity, natural in an aristocrat, had been increased by study of the pedigrees of blooded horses he had ridden at Tsarskoye-Selo and Rome. "Such a man's children are likely to inherit the ox-like qualities of their grand-parents," he observed.

Marion looked away abruptly. For the first time she thought of Bradfield as the possible father of her own children, and De Hohenfels's suggestion made her shrink.

The idea of the brotherhood of man latent in the street-speaker's arguments, and the fear Marion would feel that he himself had rushed in and got the worst of it at the hands of a workingman, stirred De Hohenfels to an eloquent exposition of his own biologic-aristocratic philosophy. He was in full swing when they reached Hillcrest, and contrary to his custom, was so obviously interested in what he was saying, that he hardly stopped while he and Marion were transferring themselves from the car to their favorite fireplace. It was his own esoteric doctrine, cherished the more because really understood by only a few recondite spirits, that some one small class or section of the present race of man is destined to sever itself from the mass and develop into the higher race. He foresaw races of men existing on earth alongside the supermen as various ape tribes exist alongside men. He scoffed at the idea of a feeling of brotherhood toward these hostile lower races, and took for touchstone of moral value the question, "Will this retard or further the coming of the higher race?"

Marion stimulated his idea by saying that what

she had read concerning the superman had appealed to her imagination but not to her reason.

"What you have read!" protested Count Feodor. "My idea has nothing in common with the prevalent loose habit of calling mere superior individuals supermen. The herd have the word and are goring it to death. The real idea never dawns on them. There is no reason for the existence of any such term except to designate a not-yet-existing but possible genus differing from man as genus Homo differs from genus Simia. If the male of one and the female of the other group can habitually reproduce, there is no generic difference. If their offspring can also reproduce, there is no specific difference."

"Would you mind putting that a little less technically?" said Marion, her forehead wrinkling and then relaxing as she smiled.

"What I am driving at is this. Even a specific difference, producing hybrid and infertile offspring, is sufficient, as with horse and ass, to sunder two species forever. There is no more 'brotherhood,' no more race-unity."

"I saw two Madagascar wild men," said she, after some silent thinking. "Their keeper called them *Houvres*. Their skulls were very small and sloped to a point like a pyramid. I was told the bone was three times as thick as ours, and their spines seemed to run straight to the top of their heads. I do not think their brains could be one quarter the size of ours. Their eyes looked human, but their mouths! They are cannibals. Do you suppose they are beyond the boundary line—of our species? I hope they are!"

He looked at her approvingly. "That would be most interesting to know," he said, narrowing his lids in thought. "If it were demonstrated that their unions with highly developed Europeans could not produce grandchildren—it would dispose biologically of sentimental talk about the brotherhood of man."

"But we all come from the same ancestors," she objected.

"Yes. From that one branch of the apes—the Pithecanthropus—which differentiated itself from all the others."

"I see," said Marion. "You have a precedent for your idea."

"A precedent? I have thirty. Every race in our ancestry—back to the plant cytode—offers a precedent." She sat for a moment taking that in. "There is no doubt in my mind," he said, "that the existing varieties of men constitute what biologists call incipient species. Whether these, or some of these, are to become permanent—that is the most important question that can be asked concerning man." He rose energetically from his chair, stood with his back to the fire, and spoke with a curious blending of carefulness and passion. "The amphibian could not keep the ascending section of his race from becoming monotremes. The monotreme had to project out of his tribe the marsupial. The marsupial had to let the placentalia split away and upward. The placentals could not hold down or drag back that branch of themselves who became primates. The primitive primate could not maintain brotherhood with the aspiring prosimæ. Destiny forced the prosimian to bring forth his superior, the simian; and all the ape-tribes could not league together and stop the rise of *us*—the superape! But man—with his democracy, his socialism, his brotherhood, his doctrine of equality, his power of creating an omnipotent majority out of weak, inferior individuals—this race may thwart destiny, sterilize itself, abort, and *not* bring forth the superman!"

"Is that what Bradfield's movement really means?" exclaimed Marion. "I had no idea there was so much real reason to believe we actually will develop a higher race. Why if that is so, Fedya, that rule of the lower bringing forth the higher, then that is the reason for the existence of man. If our race does not give birth to a higher, all humanity will have existed in vain!"

"And we will be the first to fail—the first in a hundred million years."

"The first traitors to the universe! But tell me, Fedya—really your idea is wonderful—have we anything to indicate what the new race will be like?"

"Only speculation."

"But speculate!"

He went and sat in his chair, pushed down its back with his shoulders, and half reclined. "One surmises that intellectually the superman will look as from air-ships—seeing easily all the relations of multitudinous things minutely known. That descendant of ours will draw steadily on such sources of power and knowledge as now open fitfully to trance psychics. He will know the psychology of superman, and man, of ape, and fish, and worm, and even—what the sleeping rocks do dream of. He

will know the laws of eugenics—Mendelian laws,
and apply them to his own breeding. He will exer-
cise self-government, not be governed either by tsars
or by majorities. The unconscious development by
which we have groped and stumbled part way out
of darkness he will replace with clear and conscious
development. He will rapidly shape his race into
a race yet higher, training his children into powers
more perfect than his own. He will know he is not
descended from gods or god-like men who fell. But
he, child of the worm, is father of the gods! The
gods were man's deep dream of what man is to
be."

"It takes my breath, your vision!" said Marion,
low. "I feel the immense past and future! A
child was always wonderful—but now! Think of
it! A link in the chain of life from worm to god!"

"He will be greater in will, in courage, in psychic
power," dreamed De Hohenfels, "—able to control men as men do dogs—or the dog kind of men."

"The idea is glorious!" she said. "You give your
superman a superhuman mind and will. But—why
is he so ruthless, so cold? He will know, he will
know! Is there no superhuman heart?"

"He is certainly no sentimentalist, no non-resister,
no sympathizer with inferiority."

"No," she agreed, "but I see I will have to have
a superman of my own. My superman is going to
be a greater lover and friend than any man has
been. He is going to love supermen, and men, and
animals——"

"And superwomen," interposed Fedya.

"He'd be a superfool if he didn't!" she retorted, her eyes becoming joyous.

"His love can be no sweeter to him than mine to me!" he said with sudden ardor.

She gave him her hand quickly and pressed his, but turned away her face and held him back from kissing. "Over there, over there!" she commanded, pointing to his chair.

"That sweet, sure pride of yours in feminine indispensability—that woman-knowledge of your own value—is simply ravishing!" he protested.

"You will now state the objection I saw in your eyes to my warm-hearted superman."

"My head is too full of a cold-hearted woman."

"You know I'm not. It's too bad you have to go and spoil a good talk. You interrupted a most poetic remark I was about to make and now I can't remember it."

He gave a shrug and sat down. "How," he asked, resuming his wonted, faintly ironic tone, "is this amiable being of yours to dominate, to subdue, perhaps in scornful mercy to prevent the birth of, the hordes of men who threaten his existence?"

She could not say. He made her feel she was too facile with her warm-hearted superman. Ruthlessness, coldness, were traits essential to any dominant race or class which was to develop into a distinct new species. According to Fedya, this was the unconscious aspiration of every aristocracy—the instinctive motive of its effort to differentiate itself from the mass. "The instinct of the mass," he said, "is to drag back and reabsorb all such aspiring life.

In the past, I admit, the mass of mankind has been successful. Somewhere, somewhen,—mankind will be overcome. The lords of war, Alexander, Cæsar, Napoleon, failed. The lords of wealth may not. The intense and successful effort to draw the bulk of the life-sustaining wealth of the world into the power of a tiny social fraction may be, at bottom, a concentration of racial energy, destined to create a special environment, mold the new race, and force a 'chosen people' of nature across the chasm sundering species from species, superman from man!"

She gave an exclamation of comprehension. This vaster vision of Feodor's—was it the other side, the cosmic import, of that class-struggle seen narrowly by Bradfield? Was this the issue underlying all man's battles—raging yesterday, today, tomorrow, and only to be settled in future geologic time? If so, in her recent sympathy with Bradfield's ideas had she been guilty of disloyalty not merely to her class, but also to the highest hope and possibility of man? "Feodor:" she said, "is this tendency of every race to fork and send one branch upward the real cause of that class struggle preached by the socialists?"

"I should say that struggle is a phase of the forking process—yes."

"Then his aim—their aim—with their immense numerical superiority—to wrest control of the wealth producing forces from us——?"

"Is the same old instinct of the mass—its latest, strongest, most dangerous expression."

"But from their point of view—or say from the

point of view of humanity as a whole—isn't their attempt to reabsorb us the effort of the organism called mankind to preserve its unity?"

"Yes. Exactly. Thereby preventing the upward movement of the new and highest branch of the tree of life. Socialism is reactionary in that it blocks the progress of the most powerful few toward greater power. If the socialistic tendency prevails, if humanity retains its unity, real progress will be checked and the new race will not be born."

"But if *we* prevail——?"

"Then the pain and strain and misery of the laboring world are only pangs of the birth of the higher race of which humanity is destined to be— the mother!"

They sat awhile in silence, thinking. The idea the man had somewhat coldly formed by study and constructive thought tended to take on, in the warm imagination of the girl, the splendor of a new and vital myth. Here in the human future loomed a new Messiah, not one to save a little nation in battle, nor yet to save mankind in some mystic, spiritual way by sacrificing himself, but one for whom humanity must sacrifice itself, as parent for child, a Son of Man whom Mankind must either destroy in its own womb—or bring to birth! Marion sighed. "Fedya," she said, "if I looked through your eyes too much I would be terribly sad. I do not think my mind could bear that vast and tragic vision. I wonder if it is really true."

"What makes you doubt it?"

"If it was a question of myself and those horrible Houvres—they are ages behind us—they do

seem another species. But I do not feel even an incipient race difference between myself and—say
Bradfield. In his youth my great-grandfather Moulton was nothing but a common blacksmith. Aren't
you afraid to marry—such a plebeian?"

"You plebeian! You have every mark of the
blood! That astonished me when I first saw you
in Rome. You can't tell where it flows. Everywhere in Europe it has been mixed with Dravidian,
Pelasgian,—oh, all sorts of baser strains of con-
quered peoples. For instance, some think not a
trace of Aryan blood remains in Greece. It died
out there under too much light. That blacksmith of
yours may have carried the old blood in unusual
purity."

"Then so may Bradfield."

"Bradfield?" he said, looking at her curiously.
"No. He's composite—orthocephalic."

"Can you tell so accurately?"

"Not accurately. I know the pure types and can
sometimes guess their intermixtures."

"But if the blood flows everywhere——"

"It generally flows near the top or toward it."

She was inclined to believe it. "How about your
people, Feodor?" she asked. "How do you come
to have a German name?"

"An ancestor—of an ancient German family of
knightly rank—taken prisoner in the reign of Ivan
the Terrible—settled in Courland."

"And is all the rest of you Russian? Oh, of
course, the Countess Xenia—that makes you half
Polish, doesn't it? How about your father? Tell

me about him, Fedya. I am not even sure of his name."

"Lyof Alexievitch."

"What kind of a man was he?"

"Typically a liberal. A university student in the days leading to the Emancipation. Court influence and a railway concession. Lucky thing, for he'd lost money in a paper mill. He was close to Alexander II in the movement for the constitution in '81. A great orator in his generation, but—tastes have changed. I couldn't abide his carefully balanced politico-moral harangues." He looked at Marion for explanation of her smile.

"Were they anything like the messages of our strenuous President?"

"Very much. His model was Gladstone. He was forever standing on some oratorical teterboard and deprecating reaction on the one hand and revolution on the other. In the reaction after the assassination of Alexander he lost all influence, lived on his estates, and spent the winters in Rome. He hoped to return to power in '94 when Nicholas came in, but when he found the young Tsar blowing hot and cold with every wind he gave it up, sold the St. Petersburg house, and bought the Palazzo Zuccari."

"So that is how you came to live in Rome."

"A year ago last February when the Tsar gave out the Duma manifesto and announced his indomitable will to rule through the representatives of the people, my father hailed it as the fulfilment of his old dream of constitutional Russia. Had he lived

he would have had himself elected. Just before his
death, he made me promise I would stand. I am
doing it now. The elections are going on this
month. Am I not an enthusiastic candidate?" Seeing she did not quite like his tone, he added, "I
might have taken some interest, but after the Moscow revolution was safely suppressed, the Tsar began to talk about his indomitable will to bear the
burden of government all alone. I thought then he
was going to throw over the Duma altogether. I'm
glad I did think it, for that is what sent me to
Rome and—you!"

He held out his hand for hers. She gave it absent-mindedly, thinking that if she married him she
would have to get him to take that Duma more
seriously. Just now she wanted more light on the
working of heredity in the Hohenfels family. She
thought of Fedya's Catholic uncle, Prince Razinsky,
a cynical little man she had met at her ball in Rome;
and then De Hohenfels, though somewhat bored,
had to tell her about his grandfather, Alexis Feo-
dorovitch, who, it seemed, had amounted to little
in the army, never sought court favor, married a
beautiful girl of uninfluential family, was something
of a musician and poet, and fond of country life.
The father of Alexis was Feodor de Hohenfels, a
general of the Napoleonic wars, who wore many
stars and crosses and medals, married the Princess
Sarmatoff, one of the great dames of the period,
stood high with Alexander I, and became Governor-
General of Courland. He was a typical bureaucrat,
orthodox, intolerant, bigoted, cruel to his peasants.
Marion could not find what she was looking for—

some unifying thread of character, tendency, or temperament in the various generations. Of course she was following only a single thread of the complex web of Fedya's ancestry, but as far as it went the history seemed to show that each man was chiefly a product of his time—a result of its dominant ideas woven into the soul of each in the formative period of youth. She could discern no definite Hohenfels type nor anything justifying in the least the idea of a tendency toward a distinct and higher variety of the human species, and yet Marion went to bed that night with two powerful impressions—one that Walt Bradfield's children might be like his parents rather than like him, the other that the child of Count Feodor, descending from the master class of eastern Europe, would be likely to begin life higher in the scale.

And through her soul as she sank asleep was filtering that overpowering lonely myth—dynamic as the myths that have given birth to world-religions —the vision of mankind as a female, parthenogenital, big with the embryonic daughter-race that shall replace us as the mistress of the earth!

XIV

E ARLY next morning when Marion, half
awake, began to pick up the threads of yesterday, she felt vaguely as though she had
drifted into some conspiracy against the human race.
She found herself in recoil against the Hohenfelsian
interpretation of life. It affected too profoundly
her feeling toward the mass of people in the world.
It changed things too much. It made the dear old
earth too wild and strange a theater for too vast a
drama. Rising to close her window, she saw the solemn sunrise and felt homesick for her simple old
view of things as they are—things unlit by the weird
light that shines back on them from an immense
and vividly imagined future. That actually existing man there spading the garden beds beneath the
gorgeous, silent sky—she started, seeing that the
man was Walt. Her heart went out to him. For
the moment he was representative of the race of
men. At that dull work! Last night his face and
gestures were expressive of intellectual energy, his
eyes alert and lit, his voice ringing with conviction.
Now his slow, steady movements as he cut and
turned the crumbling soil, seemed to spring from a

totally different temperament. Was this the temperament he had inherited—and might transmit? Or were the temperaments of the digger of the earth and of the man of intellect after all formable and transformable products of their occupations? What would he have to say concerning the powerful new impression she had received from Feodor? Could the magnificent religious idea of the higher race survive his criticism? She dressed without calling Mathilde, and went down to him; but in his presence lost hold of the things she wanted to talk about. She was embarrassed to begin with because she did not know how to address him.

He answered her "good morning" with the same non-committal greeting, and came over to the edge of the concrete driveway along which she was walking. "You're up early," he said, starting to spade up a new bed.

"Yes,—I saw you here from my window."

He glanced up at it unconsciously, showing that he knew where it was. "This is about the only time of day you——" He left it unsaid.

She hastened to break the silence. "I was impressed by your speech last night. It's a shame the employers do not do all those things of their own free will—without legislation compelling them. It's simply barbarous. Personally they seem like good, kind men. I cannot understand their attitude."

"I can," he said, but evidently did not care to go into the subject.

"I did not know you were a public speaker." This too failed, and she became uncomfortably aware of the banality of her remarks. "I suppose you know that was the Count de Hohenfels?" she said, trying to get to reality. "How did he impress you?"

"As being pleasantly situated."

"You aren't in a very good humor this morning. I think Count de Hohenfels admired *you* very much."

"I had the honor last night of dining with his valet. James informs me that the Count has with him fifty-six shirts and he himself fourteen."

"And from that you conclude?" She spoke coldly.

"That the Count is four times as good a man."

"I think you are horrid," she said, looking him reproachfully in the eyes. "I did not expect it of you."

"Did you expect of me the pettily amiable hypocrisy of pretending not to be jealous?"

"Oh," said she, readjusting her ideas. She regarded him thoughtfully, her expression changing. "What an utterly frank thing you are!"

"Why not?" he said, unflattered.

"I wish I knew what to tell you. I could do it now."

"Don't you really know?"

"I thought I did—last night."

"And now you like *me* again?"

"Yes. Miserable jellyfish that I am!"

"Nonsense! Why don't you accept facts?"

"What facts?"

"The big one. That you are in love with both of us."

"But that is dreadful!" she gasped, shivering at his simplicity and directness.

"Dreadful or not, you can't do anything till you face it. Stop muddling yourself by denying what's so."

"But what shall I do?" she pleaded.

He was tempted to take advantage of her momentary helpless reliance on his judgment, but felt instinctively that he could really gain nothing except through clearness and truth. It was these in him which made her rely on him, and confused though she was, he knew she would instantly sense any departure from them in him. "Before you try to decide what to do," he said, "you must unsnarl your ideas."

"That's what I have been trying to do. How is it to be done?"

"In the first place you must accept your nature as it is and stop condemning it for not conforming to ideal preconceptions."

"I'm not aware of having any."

"They are woven right into your thinking. A minute ago I stated the fact, and your thought-process was: 'That cannot be true, for that is dreadful and I am not dreadful.'"

"Well, I'm not," she said defiantly, and then seeing him ready to give it up, she forced herself to follow his reasoning. "Yes—I see what you mean. 'I am not dreadful' is an ideal preconception. You want me to look at the bare facts, and——"

"And nothing else," he insisted.

"It is hard when the facts are one's own heart."

"I think I know the circle you have been moving in, and worrying over. The other night with me—you loved me! Oh, you did!" He paused,, repressing the emotion which had involuntarily found voice. "If I don't look out I can't think clearly either. Here: the fact that you actually are in love with two men calls for revision of your traditional theory that a girl can love but one. You have been trying to revise the fact. It is a false assumption that if one love is true the other must be false. They are both true."

"Both true? But what then?"

"The fact first," he insisted. "Is it the fact?"

"It does seem to explain things. Yes, I suppose it really is the fact. But if they are both true," she said, in the tone of one thinking aloud, "then one, though true, must be disregarded."

He realized which one would be disregarded, and groped for some way to hold her.

"And that leaves everything just where it was to begin with," she concluded.

"Not quite. You have accepted in your own mind the fact that your love for me too is 'true.'"

"I see I have been too completely off my guard," she said. "I seemed to be using your mind to think with as though it were my own. It won't be a bit magnanimous of you if you——"

"If I——?"

"I didn't realize just where that impersonal, scientific method of yours was leading."

"What's the trouble? Have you realized you ought to tell De Hohenfels the real state of things?"

She was silent. She felt she had been trapped into a fatal conclusion. It would be unfair to Feodor not to tell him, and if she told him that she loved "the son of ignorant peasants," expecting him to admit such a man to the equality of rivalry, she felt he would simply decline such competition and withdraw. For, if anything, the class instinct of the Russian aristocracy, implanted in the boy Feodor by social transmission, had gained intensity by the far-reaching philosophic and poetic ideas which he himself had woven into it—or, as he himself would say, had *found* in it. In him class instinct was reinforced by visioned biologic destiny. Seeing no honorable way to avoid losing him, the pain of it taught the girl better than she had ever known it how much she wanted him. Her desperation turned her against Walt. Just then she felt, however unfairly, that he was to blame—for coming between her and Feodor, —for leading her with his seemingly disinterested logic into this position. "I never should have made that admission even to myself!" she broke out. "You took advantage of my openness to force me into it."

"I did nothing of the kind," he retorted, defending himself, but feeling that his cause, hopeless to him always, except for a few wild, exalted moments, was lost. "There was no taking advantage about it. As for forcing you into it—it was your own honesty that did that."

She gave a little gasp of dismay at the sight of Count Feodor strolling from the front of the house, and looking curiously at her and Bradfield. Checking her first impulse to go toward him so as to avert a meeting between the two men, she waved her hand to him as a signal for him to join her. "We have been talking about your speech," she said significantly to Walt.

"You are making a bad beginning," he warned her. "If you can't be frank with him about this——!"

"Please leave that to me!" She spoke low and sharply. "This is *certainly* not the time to tell him anything about you and me."

"That may be. But I doubt if you ever do tell him."

"Good morning, Fedya," called Marion, raising her voice a little.

Count Feodor returned her greeting, throwing away his cigarette, and doffing his cap. His newly pressed English-looking clothes, svelte footgear innocent of wrinkle, and immaculate colored linen were in striking contrast with Walt's russet shirt and thick-soled shoes bent up at the toes.

"This is Mr. Bradfield," said Marion.

Hohenfels stared, not conceiving that Marion could be intending to place a gardener with whom she happened to be talking on the footing of social equality implied by an introduction.

"After last night an introduction seems belated," said Marion, trying to fill the awkward pause.

"Oh," said De Hohenfels. "You are the street-speaker. I didn't recognize you. In the torchlight, you know, you really looked quite fierce."

"I doubt if even a Nietzschian could look fierce making garden," observed Bradfield, and resumed his spading.

It was startling to Hohenfels to hear himself so characterized by a man so dressed, so working. "I doubt if a Nietzschian *would* be making garden," he observed, not concealing his lack of high regard for that ancient occupation.

"I think he would if it was make garden or not eat," said Bradfield with cheerful conviction.

Marion saw that Fedya was irritated at his failure to think of some effective repartee. "Speaking of not eating," said she, "suppose we see if we can get some breakfast." She turned toward the house.

"Oh, very well," said the Count. "Do you work here regularly, Mr. Bradfield?"

"Yes," said Walt. He was thinking how symbolic it was that he was once more to see Marion going away with De Hohenfels.

"Then, no doubt, I will have the pleasure of more discussion of Nietzschianity. But I was thinking what confidence you must have in Mr. Moulton's magnanimity—to agitate against his interests while in his employ."

Was it a threat? Walt was warm and chanced it. "Possibly no one has taken upon himself the rôle of informer!" His hostile look square into the eyes of De Hohenfels left no room for doubt as to his meaning.

"That is a very singular thing for you to say," said Marion, looking back at him.

"Whatever you may mean by that, Mr. Bradfield," said Hohenfels, turning to go, "it sounds awfully—Nietzschian."

As Marion and he went in she told him that she had hitherto found Bradfield interesting and agreeable, but did not like him so well since he made those bitter remarks.

"Why didn't you tell me he worked here and you knew him?"

"I started to last night, but—just then you began philosophizing about him."

He remembered turning the conversation, but—it seemed curious.

Irritated by the gardener's conviction that it was accident and circumstance and not anything inherent in character which relieved the aristocrat from the necessity of digging for a living, Count Feodor had in fact made his remark about Mr. Moulton in order to make Bradfield fear the loss of his job. He had laid hold of the idea only because the gardener was getting the best of their swift exchange of intellectual pistol shots, and he did not fancy leaving the field in defeat—protected by Marion.

He saw it would now have a bad effect to let her know the man had any sort of justification for his cutting remarks. For one thing, it would give her too high an opinion of his penetration. It was easier to let her go on thinking no such idea as Bradfield accused him of had ever crossed his mind, than to try to make her see that even if he really should speak to Mr. Moulton about his gardener's political agitation, there would be no element of baseness or treason in the act. He was not a comrade of Bradfield, and he would not be playing the informer for pay. But it was fortunate for him that he did not try to justify himself along this line, for the girl would have thought it a poor business to use such a weapon against a workingman.

He spent the morning at the piano, weaving on its strings incessant, shifting, complex webs of beauty so unearthly that, felt through them, the present world became at times to Marion no whit less wonderful than that distant, unknown future which veiled the far-off goal of man. Outside on the garden beds Walt listened—and dug.

At luncheon, Mr. Moulton, warming up a little, and Count Feodor found points of contact; and Moulton invited him to call at his office any time he cared to go through the shops. Finding that Marion was going to some reception, De Hohenfels went down that afternoon, and was escorted through the magnificent establishment of the United States Plow Company by the company's salaried inventor, an expert mechanic whose labor-saving improvements were already saving the company scores of thousands of dollars annually in wages. He was a quiet, modest fellow. The company owned the patents on all his improvements. De Hohenfels found he was perfectly satisfied with this arrangement. He had the power to endow machinery with human-seeming intelligence, but did not use it himself in considering his own economic status. "How indispensable to *us* are brainy fools!" the Russian gentleman philosophized.

Mr. Moulton met Mrs. Pearson downtown. Their brief conversation as she sat in her automobile alongside the curb, sufficed to alarm him as to the seriousness of Marion's affair with Bradfield. In the Lady Diotima's opinion, his son-in-law was going to be either Walt Bradfield or Feodor de Hohenfels, and the logical thing for him was to do what he could to make it the gentleman and not the gardener.

Moulton thereupon went out of his way to pick up De Hohenfels at the plow works; and as they came whizzing into the Hillcrest grounds before din-

ner, Bradfield looked up from the fresh black earth
he had been all day spading, and saw his employer
and the foreign visitor together. The Count nodded
to him as the machine went by, and a moment later
Walt saw Mr. Moulton look back at him.

About half past seven, after Eldridge had gone
around with the car which was to take Marion, Mrs.
Moulton and De Hohenfels to a performance of
"You Never Can Tell" in Davenport, Bradfield received a summons to Mr. Moulton's study.

The employer sized him up with interest. "I understand," said he, "that last night at a street meeting you made an incendiary speech against the Illinois Manufacturers' Association."

"If it is 'incendiary' to tell the facts about the defeat of the Curran bill, I did."

"The facts as you understand them," corrected
Mr. Moulton.

"The facts." He might have argued the point,
but was too deeply interested in the source of Mr.
Moulton's information.

"We'll pass that point, seeing you do not care to
substantiate your claim to absolute knowledge of
the facts. You also indulged in some perfervid rhetoric on the subject."

"Did De Hohenfels call it 'perfervid rhetoric'?"
inquired Walt.

Mr. Moulton did not attempt to conceal his interest in this question.

"I believe my informant called it 'hot air,'" he
observed after a moment's reflection.

Walt looked at Mr. Moulton keenly, and set
the remark down as an extremely clever attempt to

throw him off the track. De Hohenfels had certainly never said "hot air."

"Do you think of giving up your job here with
me?" asked Mr. Moulton.

"No, sir."

"I have certain reasons for wishing not to make
a martyr of you, but you cannot work here and go
on talking as you did last night."

"Very well," said Bradfield.

"Does that mean you give up the job?"

"As long as I hold the job I won't speak."

"That sounds as though you didn't expect to hold
the job long."

"I haven't said anything about quitting."

"Let us be perfectly aboveboard, Bradfield. Do
you intend to stay here merely until the next time you
want to speak?"

"I'm not looking that far ahead just now, Mr.
Moulton. That would be a natural thing to do—
if I could get other work."

"I've said all I wish to—this time," said Mr.
Moulton after a moment's thought. "That's all,
Bradfield."

"May I ask if it was the Count de Hohenfels who
told you about my speech last night?"

"As a general thing I do not discuss the sources
of such information. I see no reason for departing
from my custom in this case."

Whether or not Moulton deliberately produced
such an impression, Walt went out with the case
against De Hohenfels proved to his own satisfaction. It made him angry that a man small enough
to use such a weapon should, as a matter of course,

be constantly at dinners, theaters, and in drawing-rooms with Marion, while he, a decent man, was, equally as a matter of course, spading the garden and eating with the foreigner's valet.

At the sound of Walt's footsteps leaving Mr. Moulton's study, De Hohenfels, waiting for Marion to come down, looked out the door of the library. Walt saw him and stopped.

"Good evening, Mr. Bradfield," said De Hohen-fels. "It is an unexpected pleasure to meet you—in the house."

There was a footstep and rustle on the stairs be-hind Walt, but he had no eyes or ears just then for anything but De Hohenfels. "I'm here," he said, "because some informer has really done his dirty work about my speech last night. I don't mind telling you that I think it was you."

"You think wrong," said De Hohenfels coldly: "If Mr. Moulton has discharged you he is well rid of an insolent servant."

"Not like that, Feodor!" exclaimed Marion, speaking from the stairs. She came down as quickly as her trailing gown, which she held through an open-ing in her opera cloak, would permit. "Mr. Brad-field, I am surprised that you should make an accus-ation like that. What earthly reason have you for saying such a thing?"

"This morning you heard Count Hohenfels try to scare me with a veiled threat that he would tell Mr. Moulton about my speech. This afternoon he came in from downtown with Mr. Moulton. They both looked at me, exchanged some remark, and went into the house together. This evening Mr.

Moulton calls me up, and tells me to drop my speaking or my job. He refers to my 'perfervid rhetoric' —a stilted phrase that has a peculiarly Hohenfelsian sound."

"Be careful how you use that name, young man!" said De Hohenfels.

Walt laughed.

"Feodor," said Marion, impressed by Walt's statement of the case, "this isn't so, is it?"

"It is not. Mr. Bradfield and his speech are not of so much importance as he imagines. I have not been thinking of it or of him."

Mr. Moulton came to the door of his study, evidently very much interested in the conversation, which was not being carried on in low tones. It happened that Marion did not see her father, though both Bradfield and Hohenfels did. "Is that enough for you, Mr. Bradfield?" she demanded.

Walt was a little shaken by the Russian's expression when he saw Moulton. He did not look like a man caught in a lie. "I asked Mr. Moulton if his informant was De Hohenfels," said Walt, "and instead of denying it he very plainly evaded the question."

"You were somewhat hasty in your conclusion, Mr. Bradfield," said Moulton suavely. Marion looked at her father. "Since there appears to be need for it, I will state for Mr. Bradfield's benefit that my informant was a private detective employed here in Moline to keep an eye on labor agitators."

"Of course!" said Marion to Walt. In her eyes was a world of reproach and disappointment.

"That gives me the worst of it," said Walt. He

turned to Mr. Moulton. "I wish you had had the fairness to say that five minutes ago when you were asking *me* to be perfectly aboveboard!"

"I think we needn't wait for your next speech to sever our present relations," said Mr. Moulton.

"I agree with you," replied Bradfield.

"Shall we go, Fedya?" said Marion. She turned and went toward the door. De Hohenfels bowed to Bradfield, and followed her, but his silent irony was lost on Walt, for all that Walt could see was Marion in her beauty and her splendor disappearing from his life.

PART TWO

PART II

———

RUSSIA

I

MARION felt it deeply when she found she would not see Bradfield again before her wedding. He had left Hillcrest the night of his discharge. Another interview with him might be hard, but she felt she ought not to let all the splendid threads between them tear apart—with no effort to save and bind them into an enduring friendship. There were things in Bradfield she needed—things she felt she would not soon find elsewhere. She wanted to make him feel better about that unfortunate mistake of his—to admit that her father had not been fair—to keep the thought of that last scene from clouding his whole memory of her. But somehow, for several days her time was so crowded—and she did not know just where to reach him, and when she finally found out his address she found out also that he had gone to Chicago in search of employment. It was too late.

The wedding was hastened by a telegram from Zhergan in Courland, forwarded by cablegram from Rome, announcing the election of De Hohenfels.

The Duma was to assemble in St. Petersburg by the end of April, and it was necessary for Marion and Feodor to spend at least a few days in Rome. At the wedding reception the ladies of the three cities read approvingly the cablegrams from Russian relatives, aristocrats, and dignitaries, and feasted their wealth-loving imaginations on rumors of princely gifts—title-deeds to ancestral estates in the Baltic Government of Courland, stock in the Moscow-Kieff-Vorones Railroad. They debated in low voices whether these unlooked-for accompaniments of the international marriage could be worth as much as that cool million represented by a single entry on a certain stock-book and a single ornate piece of paper certifying that "Marion, Countess de Hohenfels, is the owner of 10,000 shares of the capital stock of the United States Plow Company."

For, of course, Dave Moulton, finding the pair could do very well without his financial assistance, gave it to them.

Ignoring popular superstition, Count Feodor and his new Countess sailed on the Moltke for Genoa on Friday the 13th of April, and arrived without mishap at Rome. They were received by Feodor's mother and her brother, Prince Razinsky, who was some sort of dignitary at the Vatican. He advised Marion to join the Greek Church in Russia on the ground of good form, smiled at the idea that one's private convictions should have anything to do with such a matter, and assured her that Feodor's failure to conform had hurt him in St. Petersburg, and would continue to do so.

The Countess Xenia was glad to see her son devoted to such solid subjects as economics and politics. He had armed himself in New York with works he thought would be advantageous to him in the coming debates in the Duma. He and Marion had studied together in their room-like cabin on shipboard, but the lessons she made him give her in Russian pronunciation were so much more personal and delightful, so much more conducive to kisses as they watched each other's lips pronouncing words, that they did not go very deeply into the "dismal science," as they still called it. At that time he thought her as fascinating as the Duchess di Callignano, with whom in Rome two years before he had had a sumptuous amour.

In Rome, gay with Easter and with spring, the Count and Countess did not receive formally, nor drive on the Pincio, nor appear at the Del Valle Theater, and saw only a few of their intimate friends. Marion sub-let her rented palazzo, and arranged other things left at loose ends.

Feodor translated letters from Ilyitch Kronberg, describing the Zhergan election. Kronberg, who leased a brickfield from De Hohenfels, hoped his landlord would accept his services as political manager in place of certain cash. The manager had been unable to learn whether his candidate was Conservative, Octoberist, or Constitutional Democrat, but Baron Medin of a neighboring estate having come out as a government candidate, the resourceful Kronberg put up his man under the non-committal name of Progressive, and that was enough for the people. They elected De Hohenfels because they hated the Government.

The Socialists had expressed their opinion of the Tsar's Duma by voting for August Rumpe's cow. Count Feodor was not flattered to find he had beaten that political antagonist by only a few votes, and Baron Medin was furious. The vote for the cow was duly included in Kronberg's report. Marion laughed and said she would like to know these villagers of Zhergan. Fedya explained that there had been disturbances. Seventy-five thousand troops had forced out the popular revolutionary officials in Courland and re-established the government of the Tsar, and the country was now theoretically pacified. If it proved to be so in fact, they could go there when the summer became too unpleasant in St. Petersburg.

On the 2d of May, the Count and Countess started for St. Petersburg via Berlin. The Duma was to open April 27th. On May 4th they had their morning coffee on the Nord Express in the suburbs of Berlin, rode all day through agricultural Germany, crossed the frontier at Eydtkuhnen, full of German uniforms and surrounded by broad low fortifications, and reached the Customs Hall at Vierzbolovo after dark on Friday, April 21st. Marion informed Fedya that since their wedding was on April 10th they had been married only eleven days. Fedya thereupon gallantly forgave the Orthodox Church its antiquated calendar for the sake of the thirteen days it added to their honeymoon.

The ex-American's passport was registered and stamped with a notice that she could not leave Russia without a police permit, or if her stay exceeded six months, without a Russian passport. It did not seem possible that these facts could ever become important to her.

Leaving the frontier in a wide, mahogany-paneled railway carriage lighted by scores of wax-candles, they were served with glasses of tea and vodka by uniformed, dignified servants whose gravity was intentionally upset by the Countess practising her Russian upon them. All the night, with the red wood-sparks from the locomotive flying past the windows in the darkness, the train pushed into the unseen. In the weirdness of dawn the bride looked out upon a moorland of endless heather. Later she saw tracts of silver birches, patches of oats, Scotch firs, and occasionally little gray wood-shingled *izbas* —huts not to be distinguished from stables—the homes of Polish peasants. Them she saw at stations standing amid acres of wood cut and piled for locomotive fuel. They wore sackcloth or sheepskins; their shoes were of rope wound round their feet; they had unkempt hair, flat features, mournful eyes —a sad, careworn, hungry-looking people.

On the wooded banks of a river they came in sight of steeples and gilded cupolas, red-tiled roofs, and the gray walls of a fortress. From the station they looked up the narrow dirty streets of the city of Vilna, where palaces of Polish nobles stood side by side with arched gateways leading into dreadful courts formed by blistered, rotting walls that hid the dens and cellars of the Jewish poor. On the platform moved Jews with quick, cunning eyes, greasy black curls, brass ear-rings and long kaftans. Two pretty, fair-haired girls in red blouses giggled and flirted with three or four soldiers in white caps and tunics.

After luncheon they passed, at Gatchina, a summer palace of the imperial family. Truck farms and villages became numerous, and then they saw far-off towers and clustered domes of white and gold and green and blue. St. Petersburg rose somewhat unimpressively from the flat Ingrian plain.

When they pulled into the great, plain, lead-colored station, the Count and Countess, instead of joining the crowd pouring from the train, remained in their railway carriage while Fedya's valet went to locate a certain coachman. A liveried chauffeur, directed by a train-guard, came to their carriage, and respectfully addressed the Count. De Hohenfels shook his head and dismissed the man with a curt message in Russian.

"My sister wants us to come to her house," he explained to Marion. "I can't stand her husband, M. Kokoreff. He's Assistant Minister of the Interior. His father kept a vodka-shop and became a millionaire collecting, or rather not collecting, the revenue on vodka. You'd think now that this Monsieur Kokoreff, who has quadrupled the paternal millions by lending wheat and money to peasants at one hundred and fifty per cent., was the only simon-pure patrician in Russia. He is insatiable. He throws government favor to a certain bank, and they give him bank-stock; he secures exemption from taxation for an industrial company—and becomes a stock-holder."

"Was it money she married him for?" asked Marion.

"And power. He stands high with the administrative clique—the lick-spittle!"

Marion shuddered, remembering her talk with her father about power. "Will you go to see your sister?" she asked.

"Oh, I'll see her. She'll call on you. If you will be good enough to return her first visit—after that we can drop the Kokoreffs."

In the line of droshkies in the station yard De Hohenfels's valet located a big coachman in a padded gown of dark blue drawn in by a narrow silk waist-belt. Feodor assisted Marion into a dark blue droshky drawn by a troika of black Orloffs, and they drove down the league-long, crowded Nevsky Prospect toward the gilded spire of the Admiralty Building. They passed the Annitshkoff palace and the four bronze horse-tamers at the ends of the granite bridge over the Fontanka Canal—half full of broken blocks of ice confined between massive granite quays. The American had a glimpse of Admiralty Square—a mile long, quarter of a mile wide, surrounded by immense palaces, churches, and administrative buildings.

They took a suite at the Hôtel d'Europe, hiring their own maids and lackeys, butler and coachman, and took part in the post-Easter festivities of the capital. Soon after their arrival they were entertained at the American Embassy, and were included in an informal reception—only two hundred guests, and court costume not required—at the Winter Palace, the lodging of six thousand of the Tsar's retainers.

Until that very week, the Tsar had not been in

St. Petersburg for fifteen months—not since Bloody
Sunday, when masses of shivering, half-famished
workingmen, still retaining faith in the "Little
Father," paid for their faith with their lives on the
stones of Admiralty Square, and dying beneath the
bullets of the "Little Father's" soldiers, quenched
forever with their blood the old futile faith of Russia, and began the revolution.

The Tsar's guests at the small reception were
mostly of a class seldom seen in those large pink and
white halls enameled in imitation of marble. There
were men of letters, savants, professional men, many
of them members of the Cadet or Constitutional
Democrat party of the Duma which was to assemble
on the following day. Very likely the Tsar thought
a taste of the imperial hospitality would tend to take
the edge off their opposition to his government.

Marion met half a dozen people of note—a
famous orator and his wife, the editor of the chief
organ of the constitutional democrats, the university professor who had organized the influential
Union of Unions, his wife, the leader of the Russian
woman suffragists, a celebrated old chemist and his
daughter, the Minister of Ways of Communication
—Prince and civil engineer, and a rising novelist, not
yet significant or outspoken enough to be banished
from St. Petersburg.

When the new Countess was presented to the
Tsaritsa, a woman with large features, waist too
obviously laced, and a habit of looking at the floor
when talking with anyone, the imperial lady asked
her a perfunctory question about the higher education of women in the United States. The Countess's

answer led to a less perfunctory question about Vassar, and the next moment the American was called upon to defend her belief that the spirit of a place could be at once exclusive and democratic.

"Democratic!" sniffed a lady of honor, as though the word were a bad odor.

But people so seldom expressed an opinion different from that of the Empress that she found it rather refreshing—at least in an American. She encouraged Marion to tell of her own little group of ten "spirits" at Vassar—from which the non-congenial were excluded by mere natural lack of affinity, and in which the congenial were not excluded by any question of birth or wealth. The Vassarite told how she had brought a neighboring patriarchal nature-lover. and man of letters down from the seclusion of his hills to the frivolity of a dress-suit and an April hop. "He was the center of attraction," said Marion, "and in his droll, quiet, keen way the gayest of the gay. The girls filled up his dance program till he had to 'split' dances, quarreled over his 'cutting' a dance, and made such a fuss over him that the youngsters from Yale and Harvard were quite eclipsed. One disconsolate said he was going to give up football, study the spots on birds' eggs, and grow a white beard."

Liking Marion's way of talking to her as though she were a human being, the Tsaritsa considered the desirability of having the fresh and honest mind of this young woman in her entourage. Then remembering something she had heard, she asked whether the Count de Hohenfels was still inclined to be intransigent in his attitude toward the Church.

Upon the American's unsatisfactory answer, the Tsaritsa sighed and "congéd" her—not so cordially as the tone of the rest of their conversation would have warranted. So Marion lost her chance of becoming an intimate of the Tsaritsa—a lady of honor in the hardened and cynical circle of the Russian court.

The next day, before the opening of the Duma, Count Feodor had a college friend at luncheon, a M. Hertzenstein, who was a fine, scholarly man, somewhat devoid of humor, but an authority on agrarian questions, and well-informed as to the programs and tendencies of the various parties among the deputies. Marion saw how much valuable information Fedya was acquiring with small expenditure of labor. They discussed particularly the probable demands of the Labor Group. Hertzenstein said the muzhiks undoubtedly had to have more land, and pointed out that they could not buy it because existing prices and methods of farming left most of them in arrears for taxes at the end of every year. They talked of the self-educated Kurneen, a clerk in the Moscow branch of the Standard Oil Company, who had displayed such sanity, tact, and skill in organization that he had enrolled over a million in his Peasants' Union with seven or eight million sympathizers.

"How this would interest Walt!" thought Marion. She made up her mind to send a letter to his Moline address telling him of Russia—and the things she had wanted to say to him before she left.

She had to resign herself to staying home inactive while Feodor and Hertzenstein departed for the

Winter Palace to take part in the formal opening of Russia's first Parliament.

The men found twenty thousand motionless white-tuniced soldiers of the Tsar massed about the palace.

Inside, they found the deputies assembled on the left of the throne room, everyone standing, the black frock-coats of professional men and country gentlemen mingling with the dark gray cloaks of brown-faced, bearded peasants. The black-coated men talked in low, serious tones; the men in cloaks talked little, but watched everything with earnest, questioning eyes.

Up the middle of the hall to the throne ran a narrow lane left for the Tsar and his cortège, and on the right of the hall, beyond that social chasm, was a throng of men in scarlet coats and gold braid, their breasts covered with jeweled stars and medals and crosses—honorary generals and admirals, councilors of state, ministers, senators, heads of administrative departments—among them many a flabby face and watery eye and sensual mouth. There was laughter among them—the laughter of arrogant power, as they exchanged loud flippancies calculated to show that they, the inmost circle of the great bureaucracy, were no whit disturbed by all the revolutionary activity which had finally forced the Tsar into this farce of popular government. There was close relationship between the motionless, white-tuniced, still obedient masses of peasants and workingmen alined as soldiers outside the walls and the insolent mirth of the rulers of Russia within.

De Hohenfels flushed as he looked at the two parties and took his place among the people's deputies.

There were not six men of his wealth and rank in
the whole Duma. What was he doing there among
peasants? He caught sight of Kokoreff with his
monocle and his superior stare directed across the
chasm; and Kokoreff, the grafting sycophant, the
son of a brandy-seller, gave him a commiserating
smile. De Hohenfels felt it a shame to him to re-
linquish power in Russia to such hands as Kokoreff's.
And yet, to pay the price for power that Kokoreff
paid would be more shame!

On the other hand the Duma, the people—whose
function it was to be fleeced—what part had he with
them? He felt himself to be in the old inconsistent
position of his father—that position forced upon
him from the grave. Being in that hall at all, he was
doomed to the paternal teterboard, between official
goatdom on his right and popular sheepdom on his
left. It seemed to put his esthetic immoralism out
of joint. He had the pain of a man with an ideal
which does not fit the facts. With his philosophy he
had no logical ground for despising the scarlet-
coated hogs and hypocrites of the bureaucracy. They
were the actual "Overmen" of Russia, but not exactly "arrows of longing" toward a higher race.

There was a blare of trumpets. The Tsar entered, accompanied by gorgeous court chamberlains
and popes. They walked solemnly down the narrow
lane, and reaching the throne, went through an
elaborate religious ceremony. The insignificance of
all ritual was made more glaring here by the mentally made contrast with the significant words which
should have been spoken. After fifteen months of
revolution had shaken Russia, ritual was all the Tsar

had to lay before those thinking university men, lawyers, civil engineers, and toilers. After the wearisome ceremony, the Tsar read his three-minute speech from the throne. Presumably lest he should forget it, he had carefully written down the statement that he loved his people and trusted in God. That was all. Not a word that meant anything—nothing about the land needed by the peasants—nothing about amnesty for men still held in prison for criminal beliefs such as that Russia should have a Duma, an uncensored press, and freedom of speech.

"The kind-hearted Tsar loves his people," said De Hohenfels softly to Hertzenstein, "but he has a little way of expressing his affection with rifle-bullets, and this causes him to be cruelly misunderstood. It is very touching—these lonely sorrows of the great!"

"May God bless Me and you!" said the Tsar, ending his weighty suggestions to his Parliament.

Officialdom cheered the wise words of the Ruler.

The Duma clapped no hand, raised no voice, murmured no approving word.

"Good for the Duma!" said De Hohenfels, taking in the expression of as many faces as he could see. Their silence drew his sympathy as much as the noise of the *claqueurs* in scarlet repelled it.

The Tsar marched majestically down the lane and out, followed by officialdom. The deputies filed out in sullen silence, and went on board the steamer which was to take them to the Tauride Palace. On the way up the Neva they passed beneath the walls of the Central Prison. From many a window waved the hands of men and women whose agitation through the years had made the Duma possible. Their cheers rang out between the stone walls and the boat.

And so, sneered at by the bureaucrats, treated as meaningless by the Tsar, cheered by the prisoners, opened Russia's first Parliament.

Telling Marion about it at dinner, De Hohenfels repeated the epigram he had made about the Tsar, and described the first session in the Tauride Palace where the President, Muromsev, had appointed a committee representing all parties to frame a reply to the "God bless us" throne speech.

"The Duma is composed of abler men than the bureaucracy," said Count Feodor. "It is not in nature that men so stupid should rule the world forever. With the revolutionary nation behind it there is a possibility that the now legally powerless Duma will repeat the course of the States-General under the French monarchy and take the whole power of the state into its own hands."

"Wouldn't that be splendid!" cried Marion.

"I'm not so sure. The trouble is—a movement like that once started doesn't know where to stop."

"Do you mean they may go on to socialism?"

"Yes. Not that these deputies are socialists—consciously. But it's in the air. Things drift that way. For instance these peasants—eight or ten million of them—calmly proposing to expropriate the land for themselves! They think all they have to do is state their case and all the rest of the world will agree with them that the use of the land is a natural right which we landlords have cheated them out of! The Cadets with forty per cent. of the deputies against

the Peasants' thirty-five will insist on their paying
for the land, but even at that—! We don't want to
sell. Why can't they limit their demand to the expropriation of the Crown land?"

Having taken a box for the remainder of the
season, they went to the opera that evening. It was
a resplendent audience; and Marion could see she
was an object of particular interest to many occupants of the boxes. The book of the piece—"Life
for the Tsar"—was irritating to Fedya by reason of
its antiquated patriotic clap-trap; and his humor
was not improved by the visit of M. Kokoreff after
the first act. He went to the Kokoreff box to see his
sister Vanya. There he had to listen to her re-
proaches for his neglect of her, and found no way to
avoid accepting an invitation to a dinner she was determined to give for him and his bride. The Assistant Minister exerted himself to be agreeable to
Marion, telling her her appearance was making a
most favorable impression, and that everyone was
talking of the high opinion the Tsaritsa had expressed of the new American Countess. Kokoreff had
never expected his brother-in-law, devoid of official
influence, to accomplish any such master-stroke as a
marriage with a sixty million rouble American industry.

After the second act, Fedya came back bubbling at
a meeting with two of his old companions of the
Jockey Club, whom he introduced. They were whole-
souled, good-natured fellows, popular in St. Petersburg, laughing heartily over things that were not
very funny. They said "thou" to De Hohenfels, he
called them Mitya and Volodya, and decided that

what he needed was the old care-free, unthinking companionship of men. He had been narrowing himself too exclusively to the society of one woman.

Marion liked these well-fed, happy animals, but when the four went after the opera to "The Bear," the most swagger of the big Petersburg cafés, she knew the three men would have had a better time without her. The need of women friends came over her keenly. That night in the darkness she felt the immensity of Russia—stretching eastward one quarter of the way around the world—so far that in order to look straight toward Vladivostok she must look down at an angle of forty-five degrees into the earth. And in all that immensity not one girl or woman who cared for her! She cried with loneliness and homesickness.

When Fedya had gone next afternoon to the Tauride Palace, and his sister Vanya came to call, Marion disregarded his desire not to become intimate with the Kokoreffs and received Vanya as a sister indeed, and one in need. Unfortunately, with the best will in the world, Madame Kokoreff and the Countess Marion found little in common. The Russian lady cared nothing for books, pictures, music, or politics, and was very anxious to have her brother's wife come under the influence of Father John of Kronstadt in order that he might instruct her in the doctrines of the Orthodox Church. Like her uncle Prince Razinsky she laid stress on the social advantages of conformity, though, unlike him, she would not admit that as her only reason for devotion. Social advancement being in her mind the great end of existence, it seemed to her criminal and suicidal not to do the things that led to it. Marion saw, unwillingly, before Madame Kokoreff took her departure, that Feodor's sister did not have in her soul either the need or the capacity for friendship.

All six of the *grandes dames* Marion met at Madame Kokoreff's dinner were dominated by the same ideals. *Tchin,* official rank, not so much for its own sake as for the standing it gave one in society, was a passion and a longing that left no room in them for much enthusiasm for anything else. Their friendships were calculated accordingly. Fedya said that was true only of "the administrative set"; but after half a dozen excursions into a more fashionable, frivolous, and wealth-displaying crowd, that too proved unalluring. The American girl, her spiritual antennæ out and active, and all doors at that time open to her, failed, during their ten weeks' stay in the capital, to find in all its high society one genuine friend.

The critical spirit, though it did her husband no harm in Rome, and would have helped him in Paris, really isolated him, she began to see, in St. Petersburg. She herself at that time shared to some extent his spirit. Bringing together in her mind remarks he dropped at various times, she found that De Hohenfels scorned the Tsar for his superstition and his pretense that he knew nothing of the terrible things done in his name, the bureaucrats for their sycophancy, militarism for its artificial ranking of natural inferiors above natural superiors, the gilded youth of St. Petersburg for their lack of esthetic and intellectual development, the scholars of the university for their supineness, atrophied life-instincts, and ignorance of joy, the Christian anarchists for their sentimentalism and their unnatural doctrine of non-resistance, and the revolutionists for their futile sacrifice of self for the abstraction they called "the Cause." Did he realize that he was in accord with no one, saying yes to nothing but his own far-off, gigantic dream of a race unborn?

II.

MARION'S hope of a political career for Fedya ended early—in fact on the third day of the Duma, when the committee of thirty-three brought in its reply to the Tsar. The Cadets had yielded to practically the entire revolutionary program of the meek and lowly peasants, demanding not only the rights of free speech, press, and assembly promised by the Tsar in his October manifesto, but also amnesty, responsible ministry, universal suffrage, the abolition of the upper house, and expropriation of all property in land.

The Progressive Party, consisting of De Hohenfels, had hitherto been torn by internal dissensions, but now its sympathies swung abruptly from the center to the extreme right of the Duma. Even there there were only eleven deputies who did not endorse the committee's reply to the Tsar. The eleven, including De Hohenfels, left the Chamber, and the reply was adopted unanimously. After refusing to vote for the reply because of its demand for the expropriation of land, and refusing to vote against it because such a vote would be a vote for the Tsar, De Hohenfels came home disgusted.

On that day the Countess saw just why her husband's inability to join any real and definite movement doomed him to futility in the Russia of their time. He was neither for autocracy nor for democracy, and in Russia no third thing was possible. She lay awake a long time that night thinking about it. She remembered how fine she had once thought his idea that the Russian upper class should "hold the people in check," not by filling their heads with outworn religious superstition and hocus pocus, but by sheer strength of intellect and will—deriving their power not from subservience to an autocrat backed by an army, but from their own individual souls— the natural supremacy of the finer breed. How thin and unreal that idea appeared in contact with actual conditions!

She tried to remember just what Bradfield had said predicting De Hohenfels's political failure. At the time she had attached no importance to his prophecy—it seemed such a snap judgment, based on so few facts. Apparently Walt had grasped their real significance. She could not remount to the exact ground on which he had based his idea, but she knew it was substantially correct. He had seen at once what only the event could convince her of— that Fedya's position as an anti-bureaucratic wealthy landowner prevented his alliance with either of the two great hostile forces of Russian life.

She did not yet understand her own satisfaction in the action of the Duma. To feel so gave her a sense of disloyalty to Fedya's interest, but she could not help it. Perhaps it was merely because she had grown up in a republic. Perhaps her feeling lay deeper in that profound discontent which had arisen in her before her marriage when her quarrel with her father made her feel keenly for the first time that she was of necessity a dependent human being—her only choice being dependence on father or husband. The one escape from that lay in productive, income-producing work of her own, and Bradfield had warned her back from that as being under present conditions a degrading slavery of toil, the fruits of which must flow to other hands. It was probably this in her—the approaching revolt of the Woman—which gave her sympathy with that other world-revolt—of the Worker. The reply of the Duma to the Tsar was one of its thousand voices.

Fedya's first enthusiasm as a teacher of Russian phonetics having waned, Marion hired as tutor a student of philology recommended by one of the university lecturers. Vasili Pososhkov was a pale shy youth with spiritual forehead, bad teeth, and an uncanny facility in mastering languages. Through cold and hunger and poverty in St. Petersburg he clung with demonic persistence to his university career. He came every morning at eleven, treated the Countess with formality, did his work thoroughly and without enthusiasm, and she had set him down as a dry-as-dust sort of person.

One day they finished reading Tolstoi's Sunday-school story about the peasant Ivan Shcherbakof, entitled "Neglect a Fire and It Spreads."

"And if anyone ever did him any harm, he made no attempt to retaliate," repeated Vasili Pososhkov, and tossed the book contemptuously on the table. "What supine rot!" He spoke defiantly. "The peasants have had about enough of being walked on!" he announced. "Why don't you read Gorky and hear the voice of a Russia that no longer intends to 'turn the other cheek' to its enslavers—the Russia that is sick of letting itself be harmed without retaliation!"

"My dear fellow," said Marion, "I intend to read Gorky. In fact I have already read some of his things in English. He is tremendous."

"Then how can you stand 'Neglect a Fire'?"

"I'm learning Russian."

"If you understood Gorky—I wouldn't read that Tolstoi rot if I found it in Chinese!"

The Countess protested her innocence of the crime of endorsing the non-resistance theory of Tolstoi's Christian anarchism, but the humdrum Vasili Pososhkov once ablaze could not be quenched until he had voiced the profound and passionate faith of proletarian Russia in Gorky and the coming social revolution—which would never come so long as people were so morally dense as not to be ashamed of owning copies of "Neglect a Fire."

"Vasili Pososhkov, have you a sense of humor?"

"No, Madame Countess. There has been nothing in my life to give me one."

That gave Madame Countess a thrill of insight into the youth's life, but her sympathy did not deter her from delivering the message she had for him. "You must learn to laugh—especially at trifles. If that kind and brave old man is foolish—smile at him. Save your energy. One can even read 'Neglect a Fire' without destroying the social revolution. To-morrow we will read Gorky."

Gorky (Bitter) gave her a desire to see the life of the workers of St. Petersburg. The first saint's day that closed the University and the factories she took a motor car, a driver, and Vasili Pososhkov, and went to the Vibourg suburb. They traversed miles of slightly sandy driveways winding through the greening woods and budding alder thickets of the island parks of Petersburg; passing villas, palaces, gardens, casinos; skirting granite quays of the Neva arms; crossing bridges from woodland to woodland of silver birch and solemn fir; sweeping around dim forest-mirroring lakelets. From that spacious playground of the rich, used by some of them for a few weeks of the year, they emerged on the north bank into a dismal city of gaunt factories, packed and filthy tenements, damp cellars below the river level where a dozen or more men, women and children lodged in a single room. Sometimes that room was flooded when a hard wind blew a certain way from the sea. Recognizing the responsibility of society as a whole for the welfare of these its cellar-dwelling members, the authorities met it by having a cannon fired when the flood was coming. The cellar-dwellers were accordingly not drowned, but merely rendered homeless till the waters went down and they could bail their apartments.

Vasili Pososhkov regretted that she could not see those warrens of the poor when the Arctic circle spilled its cold down through St. Petersburg, or when the summer stench arose from the low lagoons. She heard him talk with the maimed, the sick, the starving; she saw men dying of consumption on straw pallets on damp and sunless floors, a lunatic lodged in a room among young children, a woman raving—perhaps in typhoid—no one knew. Vasili Pososhkov, coldly explaining everything, held her mind to grewsome details that bit into her soul. She could not stand it. She grew sick. She had to leave.

"One should cultivate a sense of humor," said Vasili Pososhkov.

She could not see the grim humor of that.

In the motor car again, the young Russian renewed his attack.

"Tolstoi knows these conditions and wishes to change them," he said, "yet he is so darkened by his upperclass mind and his Christianity that he has dared to call economic reform nonsense, and to preach resignation—blind to the blazing fact that the one hope of the world lies in the successful rebellion of the class that is now pushed down into that hell!"

The things she had seen were working too deeply in her soul to permit of argument then.

On the way back across the spacious islands held netted in the branching Neva, he told her how they, the proletarians, working for the sake of their own life, and not for other people's profits, would line the woodland drives of all those forty islands with league on league of neat sweet cottages, cleaned and warmed and lighted by the power of the rushing waters.

"I hope you do it soon!" she exclaimed. "You or somebody. All I fear is—that you won't."

That started him on the real weakness of the class whose power, embodied in rifle bullets, maintained the island parks and the Vibourg suburb. According to him their intellects were atrophying. Their incomes came to them with little exertion of mind or body. Their political power was maintained with little more mental effort than it took to command

"Fire!" Justification in their own minds for the present scheme of things was furnished by political economists, editors, philosophers, novelists, who "had to live" and therefore wrote and taught the things that led them upward in the existing social order. He pointed out the inefficiency of the military and naval officers in the war, instancing the childish panic that made them fire on the English fishing boats in the North Sea—taking them for Japanese torpedo boats which were ten thousand miles away. He asked her to read a few state papers of the leading bureaucrats for proof that they were not masters of any language. "With a private income of sixty-six million roubles a year and the Russian army the Tsar needs no brains—and has none!"

"I think you are mistaken about that," said Marion. "I have heard he is not so ignorant as he seems about things that are happening."

"Then so much the worse for him," he exclaimed. "Is deliberate, open-eyed brutality to rule us forever? They pride themselves on strong will-power. It is shown chiefly in their ability to overcome the 'weakness' which makes an 'unhardened' human being loath to order the destruction by rifle fire of a crowd of unarmed men and women coming to tell their rulers they are perishing of cold and hunger."

Marion could not really judge at that time, but felt that Pososhkov underestimated the power of the enemy.

That night she talked to Count Feodor of that damning contrast—the island parks and the Vibourg suburb.

He replied that he could practically match the con-

trast in every great city of the modern world—
including New York. In St. Petersburg there was
no truckling attempt to hide or deny it. In his
opinion the true attitude of the aristocracy of all
time was expressed by Beatrice when Dante wondered if she were not made unhappy by compassion
for the souls she saw in burning hell. She answered:
"God in his mercy has made me such that the fire
of this burning does not touch me."

If the price of the island parks was all that human
misery, he felt that this very fact gave their beauty
added elements of costliness and terror. This idea
struck him as so profound, so true to the nature of
the universe in which we live, that he resolved to
embody it in a tone-poem called "The Islands of the
Neva."

He sought themes expressive of the despair of the
starving dwellers of the mainland and treatment
suggestive of the weakness, ebbing vitality, and
broken spirit, which kept those wretches from revolt.
He had no difficulty with the contrasted movements
full of the joy of life, the sense of power, the pride
of mastery over the world, the exuberance of soul
that overflowed in love of beauty and magnificence.

His inspiration here was his conception of Peter
the Great—the physical, intellectual, and moral
giant whose will had created immense and massive
St. Petersburg there amid insalubrious marshes
where no spontaneous city of men could have arisen.
De Hohenfels strove for strange and Brobdignagian
harmonies and movements to glorify the unnature,
the monstrosity of that creation. He remembered all
he had ever heard or seen or read of Peter—the

life-size, wax-portrait model of him in the Palace of
the Hermitage—sitting in his own chair, dressed in
the very clothes he wore, grasping the very sword he
had wrested from the ruined king of Poland—beside
him the yellow war-horse he had ridden at Poltava
the day he founded Russia upon the ruins of Sweden.
Feodor, the musician, in his own imagination became
Peter, ruining Poland, ruining Sweden, transforming
the Neva-marshes, transforming the Muscovite Russia that had been into the European Russia that he
willed to be.

That destruction and assimilation of nations was
to De Hohenfels's imagination only a vast development of the primitive vital theme—the capture and
destruction and assimilation of one living thing by
another—the theme announced in minute notes by
the musician Nature when the first animal cells turned
from inorganic food and began to suck in, break
down, and absorb the living tissue of their organic
fellows. In the last analysis it was the imaginative
emotion aroused in him by the whole of life as he
conceived it which he was striving to express in
music. He voiced indifferently the tragic hopelessness of helpless victims, and he voiced well the vic-
tor's power and joy of power, but he felt he was failing to make his music express the peculiar relation he
wished it to between this hopelessness and this joy.
The originality and the thrill of his first conception
did not seem to work out in musical form.

He was playing over all he had written one morning when Marion and Vasili Pososhkov were working in a neighboring room. They stopped to listen,
the tutor's interest heightened by her remark that it

was her husband's own composition he was working
on.

"Magnificent!" said Pososhkov when De Hohenfels played what he called the Peter music.

Marion had been deeply impressed not only by
the music but also by Fedya's profound and poetic
verbal interpretations of it. Believing Vasili would
be similarly affected, she outlined the composer's
original conception—the seminal idea of the work—
and some of the branching ideas that had since put
forth.

"That's what he thinks he's doing, is it?" grunted
Pososhkov. "Glorifying Bloody Sunday! The noble
battle! Well, the music's all right. Fortunately
he can't narrow that universal language to his meaning. The dream of Peter nothing! Do you know
what those big, weird chords are really? That's the
giant Labor waking from his strange old sleep. And
that exultant part? Democracy triumphant—the
voice of new Russia. And that doleful stuff? The
miserable Russia which has been—including a wax-
work Tsar and his stuffed horse!"

"Don't you make a mistake in considering such
conceptions dead while they still have life enough
in a human mind to produce art like this?"

"It is good music because he is a good musician—
in spite of his false social conceptions. It is good
because it happens to express our true ones."

"How can the same piece of music express these
opposite conceptions?"

"The musician's conceptions arouse in him certain feelings which he expresses. But in me these
very feelings are associated with opposite concep-

tions. He says that is Tsar Peter's joy of power.
It's nothing of the kind. It's anybody's joy of power.
I like it, not because Tsar Peter had it, but because
the Russian people are going to have it."

She admitted he had the best of that, and they
went back to their Russian grammar, Vasili Pososhkov deciding that the American Countess had a
penetrative intellect and a fair spirit.

When she repeated the young tutor's various
comments to Fedya, he made the point that his
own philosophy and Count Tolstoi's being diametric
opposites, Pososhkov could have no real ground for
rejecting both.

She hurled that at Pososhkov next morning. The
linguist seemed puzzled, but did admit that the two
philosophies really were opposites. Marion then
insisted that he must choose between them, and
when he declined, accused him of being unwilling to
admit defeat.

"But what exactly is the main question upon which
Count Hohenfels and Count Tolstoi take opposite
sides?"

Marion thought in its broadest form it was the
question of egoism *vs.* altruism.

Pososhkov preferred to define it as the actual
practice of the world (mainly egoistic) *vs.* the Christian theory of altruism. "The present practise of
living off the labor of others means island parks for
you and Vibourg tenements for your neighbor. It is
not reconcilable with the theory 'love your neighbor
as yourself.' Your husband escapes this contradiction by accepting the world's actual practise and
throwing away the hypocritical pretense of altruism.

Count Tolstoi tries to escape it in the other direction —by accepting the Christian ideal and throwing away the world's practise. What he actually does is personally half to renounce the fruits of capitalism. He still owns Yasnaya Polyana, but thinks he makes that all right by dressing as though he didn't."

"But does he think so? Doesn't he himself feel that as an inconsistency that exposes him to ridicule?"

"Whether he feels it or not, it is true," said Pososhkov. "He tries to escape the contradiction and fails."

"Well," said she, with a gleam of approaching triumph, "I admit your point against Tolstoi. But I noticed you said my husband *does* escape the contradiction."

"Yes, his position is logical."

"Then why don't you accept it?"

"Because there is an infinitely better one."

"Better than one that is perfectly logical?"

"Certainly. Ours is not only logical, but right. Your husband's is logical and—rotten. It means Vibourg tenements. The whole miserable problem disappears with the system of private ownership of the sources of life. Owning Russia in common, new Russia thereby establishes work and reward on a basis that antiquates both the worldly practise of exploiting others, and the Christian theory of allowing others to exploit us."

But the next day, having thought this over, Marion forced Pososhkov to retreat from his poor opinion of Tolstoi's altruism—for Tolstoi. "I can see now," he said after listening to her, "that in men of Tolstoi's class altruism, non-retaliation, is not socially noxious. Altruism—in him—does no harm. But don't let him preach it to *us*. I know in every fiber of my being that altruism, submission, meekness, on the part of our class means leaving practically all social wealth and power in the hands of the few whose use of it makes such a world as we have. That is socially noxious. The selfish self-assertive desire of the poor, the workers, to hold enough of wealth to maintain life well is socially valuable. The selfish desire of the rich for wealth beyond what is necessary to maintain life well is bad for the common life. Improvement in our society is furthered only by altruists among the rich and ego-ists among the poor. It is retarded by the egoist rich who own the earth and the altruist poor who let them own it."

Marion did not care to go into it with Vasili Po-soshkov, but back in her own mind, unanswered, was the question whether the concentration of wealth he considered socially noxious might not be the world's unconscious preparation for the mighty work of molding the beyond-man.

In succeeding days she saw wider applications of Pososhkov's method of attacking the egoist-altruist problem. She laid hold of tools of thought that were new to her. She had never realized that a posi-tion could be "logical and rotten." She had thought the maxim "Of two evils choose neither" a witty im-possibility. And this new thinking of hers tended to reduce the ascendency Fedya had established over her mind in the blaze of intellectual and artistic power in him when he first conceived "The Islands of the Neva."

His musical enthusiasm had begun to wane even before he was drawn off by his appointment on a commission sent by the Duma to investigate the massacre of the Jews in Bialostok. In that town he helped to gather, sift, and analyze a mass of testimony proving that the butchery of unarmed men by armed, organized, and carefully directed mobs, the raping of women, the killing of children, was done with the connivance of the police and local military authorities, that some of the police were eye-witnesses of some of the murders and made no attempt to stop them, that women fugitives escaping the mob were denied refuge at police headquarters, being told by the chief of police that what they were getting they deserved because of the socialist agitation among the Jews. The commission found that the Anti-Semitic newspaper editor whose paper had carefully manufactured sentiment against the Jews had been given free rein by the Governor-General of Grodno, that this editor and his son had organized the bands of so-called Black Hundreds which were led and directed by prominent citizens of Bialostok. The Governor-General had refused the Jews permission to arm themselves in self-defense, and one band who did arm themselves were overpowered and disarmed by police and soldiers, who then left them to the mercy of the Black Hundreds. The commission found that the editor was acting with the approval of the St. Petersburg authorities.

The Minister of the Interior published a report

on the causes of the massacre which the Duma's commission proved to be wholly at variance with the facts. The final report of the commission placed the responsibility for the massacre upon the Central Government itself.

To the Duma's specific charge of direct complicity in the wholesale murders of Bialostok the only answer of the Government was a manifesto of the Tsar stating in general terms that riot, sedition, and rebellion were rife throughout the Empire, that seventy thousand lives had already been sacrificed, and that this condition had been brought about solely through the dirty work (*skernoye dyelo*) of the revolutionists.

Upon De Hohenfels's return from Bialostok, M. Kokoreff came to him and told him that as his brother-in-law he wanted to warn him that he would find it seriously to his personal disadvantage if he did not use his influence with his colleagues to secure a more "conservative" report.

Count Feodor replied that if Kokoreff wished to indulge himself in the pastime of arranging massacres, to go ahead, but not to expect people of different tastes to help him avert publicity.

Kokoreff said significantly that even for certain unofficial acts he had the sanction of his chief. This should have overwhelmed De Hohenfels, but to Kokoreff's horror, when the report appeared, he found himself quoted to that effect. He saved his official head only by swearing he had never made the remark.

De Hohenfels was protected by a theoretical immunity from arrest enjoyed by members of the

Duma, but "the Tsar's promises" had become a proverb. Scores of men who had accepted as made in good faith the ukase granting the right of free speech and had used the right had been instantly seized and subjected to terrible treatment by the police. Of them and their agents, after Bialostok, Marion began to live in fear.

De Hohenfels's work with the commission having brought him into closer touch with his colleagues, he again attended the sessions of the Duma. Things there were coming to a head. The peasant deputies had reached almost the limit of their patience with mere speech-making. Pressure had been brought constantly to bear on them by their constituents who, in twenty thousand letters and telegrams, wanted to know why they had not secured the land. By the middle of July, after the Tsar's manifesto, which, the peasants noticed, said nothing about the land, committees of muzhiks from all over Russia came pouring into St. Petersburg "to find out what was the matter with their deputies."

Commenting on this, Vasili Pososhkov said to Marion that it showed how really representative the parliament of new Russia would be—"when decaying, capitalistic autocracy is over and done with and the stench of it gone from the earth!"

Their spines stiffened by the knowledge that there were ten million peasants behind them, the Labor Group prepared an appeal to the people stating that the Duma was an impotent body, that it could do nothing but talk, and that the only way to secure any change whatever in conditions was for the people themselves to rise en masse and overturn the existing Government.

That Saturday afternoon, July 21st, the Constitutional Democrats—who had made the long speeches the peasants were weary of hearing—proposed, instead of this appeal, a statement to the people explaining why they could do nothing, but omitting the Peasants' revolutionary call to arms.

Monday morning, the time set for the debate between the Peasants with their appeal and the Cadets with their statement, De Hohenfels went as usual to the Tauride Palace. He found the building full of troops, crowds of excited deputies in the corridors, and on the locked door of the assembly room a manifesto of Nicholas dissolving the Duma.

In the corridor, Hertzenstein, who, as chairman, had signed the report of the Bialostok commission, met De Hohenfels and took him to one side. "I am going to Finland this afternoon," said he. "In fact most of us are. I don't know whether you will be with us in what we may decide to do—from across the border—but take my advice and get out of St. Petersburg. Better get out of Russia. And do it to-day."

De Hohenfels thought him unduly alarmed, but had no intention of remaining in St. Petersburg through the summer, and went home to talk it over with Marion and decide where they were to go. He hesitated about going to his estate in Central Russia, where martial law prevailed, or to Zhergan. Ten days before they had shot eight revolutionists in Riga, forty miles from there. However, he had a letter from Churisnok, his overseer, saying that the commandant of the Zhergan garrison had established his headquarters at the manor-house; and that, he reflected, would assure a guard for himself and Marion.

On his way home in a hired droshky from the Tauride Palace, De Hohenfels secured a copy of the official *Gazette* of that morning, and turned to the Tsar's manifesto, which he had not stopped to read through at the Palace. He read the manifesto, and then, to his amazement, discovered a brief notice of the death of Deputy Hertzenstein, killed by persons unknown in front of his apartment in Vasili Ostrov, Fifth Line. The notice did not specify the hour, but it must have been in type two or three hours; and having talked with Hertzenstein not a quarter of an hour before, De Hohenfels knew it must be incorrect.

When he came in, Marion was writing Russian at a big table with grammar and dictionary at her elbow, getting ready for Vasili Pososhkov at eleven.

"There's some Russian for you," said Feodor, handing her the paper with the Tsar's manifesto. "The Duma is dissolved."

"Dissolved!" She took the paper. "Isn't that unexpected? Doesn't that leave everything unsettled and undone?"

"Of course. That's what the Government wants. Most of the deputies are going to Finland. They may direct the rising of all Russia from across the border."

"Are you going with them?" Her eyes lighted with the hope that he was.

"No. But what we should decide at once is where we ourselves are going for the summer. St. Petersburg is no place—even aside from politics."

They were approaching a decision in favor of Zhergan, when the footman brought Count Feodor the card of the editor Kovalevsky.

Being ushered in, and assured he could speak freely before Marion, the newspaper man said he had only a moment. He was not a member of the Duma, but had been actively aiding it, and he was going to take the first train for Vibourg .across the Finnish border. He had been told by some of the deputies that De Hohenfels had gone home, and passing the Hôtel d'Europe, he had thought it well to come up and tell him of certain things that were happening. "Did you hear about Hertzenstein?" he asked.

"His death?" said De Hohenfels.

"His death!" exclaimed Marion, turning pale.

"It isn't true," said De Hohenfels hastily. "I talked with him myself not over an hour ago, and this paper must have gone to press three or four hours ago." He reached for the *Gazette*, and turned to the notice.

"I know nothing about what's in the paper," said Kovalevsky. "I saw Hertzenstein's dead body at his lodgings half an hour ago. His wife is hysterical. The concierge saw him shot to death by four rough-looking fellows with army revolvers. They were waiting at his door and opened fire as he got out of his cab. After he fell they took time to fire into his body as it lay on the curb. They kept off passers-by at the point of their pistols, and escaped.

Since last night there have been no city police on duty, not even at crossings, within three blocks of that house."

"How horrible!" exclaimed Marion.

"Here's the real horror," said Fedya, pointing to the notice in the paper. "The official *Gazette* printed the notice of Hertzenstein's death three hours before it took place."

Kovalevsky glanced at the notice without surprise. "This was evidently released about one edition too soon," said he. "I don't wish to alarm the Countess, but you also did good work at Bialostok, Count de Hohenfels, and the moral of this story for you is—get out of St. Petersburg."

III.

TRAVELING unattended, the Count and Countess de Hohenfels reached Pskov at nine that evening with sunset still reddening the northwest, and five hours later, in the dawn, looked from the swaying windows of their sleeping-car stateroom to find the train following a swift, cold stream through a warm and winding valley from which rose rolling uplands belted with firwoods. Outlined against the russet sky appeared half-ruined walls with round-arched windows and crenelated turrets—mournful as unburied skeletons—masonic bones of a social structure that had passed away, filling the soul with sudden knowledge that our own crowded and busy epoch will fall silent and foreshorten to a moment of immense antiquity.

They spent an hour in Riga—a large and busy city of electric cars, automobiles, public gardens with electric-lighted band-stands, and solid business blocks like those of Hamburg. After a surfeit of Muscovite domes, Marion was glad to look once more on the architecture of western Europe in the Gothic Peterskirche. They drove past the old Rathhaus of Hanseatic times, and two minutes later, with the imaginative shock of suddenly contrasted ages, they found themselves looking at a steamer from New York.

On a track across the broad paved street from the quay, close to the wall of a five-story stone ware-house, stood a string of dumpy little white freight-cars bound for Irkutsk in Siberia four or five thou-sand miles inland, and on those cars, with a cry of joy, followed by an unexpected choke, Marion Moul-ton that was discovered a row of bright new farm machinery from Moline. The trouble was—it stood just that same way on the cars alongside the Third Avenue warehouse. That warehouse beneath the windowed walls of which she had walked in the days of slates and short skirts—it was there this minute ! She kept her face away so Fedya did not see the sil-ver drops beneath her veil.

Two hours' ride on a slow train brought them to Mitau, a quiet town as large as Moline and Rock Island. Above it loomed the massive castle of Biren, Duke of Courland, a cousin of the Von Hohenfels of his time, a paramour of the Empress of Russia, and the host of the realmless Louis XVIII of France. Mitau was full of black-eyed, high-cheek-boned Cossacks and Polish infantrymen—Catholic Slavs brought here to stamp out the revolution of the Lutheran Letts while Lettish soldiers were shoot-ing the striking workmen of Poland.

It was only twenty-five versts from Mitau to Zhergan, and had it not been for rumors of "Broth-ers of the Woods" in the Hohenfels forest, the Count would have had his coachman meet them at Mitau. They went on a passenger-coach trailed be-hind short, dingy-white, flat-cars whose heavy wooden floors were scurfed by the butts of pine-logs till they looked like hempen mats. After the first ten versts the roughly built spur of the railway ran through their own property.

The logging cars were shunted to a siding in the forest, and the engine, emerging into fields of oats and potatoes and open pastures full of cattle and grazing ponies, drew the coach and some empty "goods-trucks," as Fedya called them, to a little slate-colored railway station in the outskirts of Zhergan—a town whose five thousand people were mostly liberated Hohenfels serfs living now by agriculture, lumbering, and the rural industries.

They were met by broadly smiling footman and coachman in livery, who called Fedya "little father." He called them little David and little Ilya, little David being something over six feet high. They got into a cumbrous gala coach which lumbered out of the village, past Kronberg's brickyard, along a country road between brown hayfields to a large group of stone and wooden farm buildings, beyond which they came through a shady, English-looking park to the manor. It was a large white wooden house with colonnades and terraces and gravel walks not wholly free from weeds, and reminded Marion of the Georgia home of the college chum she called "my glorious Barbara." To the east, in front of an orchard, were the brown shelter tents of a platoon of Russian soldiers.

A score of houseservants were lined up in the manner of the preceding generation to receive the "barin" and his bride, and "Feodor Lefyevitch," greeting them by their diminutive names, found himself drawn back into the patronizing, patriarchal manner of his father "Lef Alexievitch." He drew the line, however, at their kissing his hand.

Yury Churisnok, a Great-Russian muzhik risen by virtue of success as a rent-collector to the long coat of the overseer, performed the important social function of introducing the Commandant Count Tschulitsky to his master.

The Countess acknowledged the introduction of the army officer in Russian, but that gentleman, noting her accent, had sufficient lack of tact to answer in French—as much as to say, "I see you don't speak Russian." Marion gave him a look he did not understand. The Adjutant, Captain Sikorsky, a plump, fine-looking man with blue eyes and brown moustache, spoke Russian and complimented the Countess on hers, thereby winning a look of real interest as she wondered whether he had been keen enough to understand her displeasure with Tschulitsky. Sikorsky said something to De Hohenfels about the inconvenience of finding uninvited guests in possession of one's house.

Feodor replied that on the contrary it was anything but an inconvenience there in the country to be assured of the society of men of one's own class.

Tschulitsky drew attention to the obvious practical benefit of a guard for the premises, at which Sikorsky, raising his eyebrows, looked at the Countess as much as to say, "Well, there's no help for it!"

As Feodor and Marion walked through the old-fashioned rooms with their inlaid floors, ceilings sixteen feet high, and heavy Victorian furniture, he observed that no doubt she would want to modernize her house. He used the special phrase "*sobst-venny dom*," emphasizing her ownership.

"Oh, no, Fedya! Don't try to make a reality out of that legal fiction."

"As you please. I was only trying to make you feel at home."

"I know," she said, and did not explain that bringing up that idea in that way had the opposite effect. "The old nurse is a dear," she said,—"and that jolly Davuidka. The affection they have for you is charming. How much better it is to have cordial human beings for servants than expressionless automata of the English pattern. I can't tell you how glad I am to get away from St. Petersburg to these people who are of the soil."

He said he was afraid she would soon find limits to the charm of the peasant class, and in the days that followed she had to admit that he was right. In the first place she found the "affection" she had noticed confined to a few old Russian retainers among the houseservants. Most of the hired agricultural laborers at the farm, and the numerous tenants, sons of liberated Hohenfels serfs, were Letts, and she could not speak their language. There was an infiltration of muzhiks from Kovno, but though she talked with them, they were suspicious of her friendly advances. For a while the chief impression was one of immense unconquerable stupidity in them, but one morning two muzhiks she knew passed outside the window of the dairy where she was talking to a woman churning, and one of them was criticizing

Count Feodor's attitude on the land question in the Duma as not representing the desire of the people who elected him.

"Don't you know no landlord can understand *any-thing?*" demanded the other.

"So they think *us* stupid," mused Marion, and wondered if the stupidity she saw in them could be a mask behind which they concealed their real thoughts and feelings from "the landlords." From her window she sometimes heard the soldiers laughing, turning proverbs against each other, speaking with voices expressive of shrewdness and humor, but when an officer was near, or when she herself tried to talk with them—the mask! They did not consciously put it on. It was instinct.

The Baron and Baroness Krushcaln and their seventeen-year-old daughter called to pay their respects to the new Countess. They were provincial people and not very interesting to Marion. Baron Von Wikkerstrom and Police Intendant Bratavzinsky were other important neighbors whose calls had to be returned by Count Feodor. Yan Sarin, the foreman of the smithy on the estate, was a manly, intelligent-looking fellow, who, Marion felt, could have helped her get in touch with the people, but he was a Lett. So was the plump, rosy mail-carrier who brought their mail from town. She was reluctant to take up Lettish in addition to Russian, especially since she thought the language had no important literature to reward her for the labor of learning it, but finally took as tutor one of the housemaids. The girl was uneducated and not so much a teacher as a passive, and indifferent, living dictionary.

Count Tschulitsky said he could not understand why anyone should wish to know Lettish, and when she answered, "Because one wishes to know the Letts," he seemed inclined to regard her as a dangerous character. Sikorsky remarked afterward to the Countess that Tschulitsky looked upon the Letts' inability to speak Russian as a kind of treason.

The Captain suggested as tutor the village dressmaker, who spoke Lettish, though she was of a Russian family—now impoverished. She had been educated in France and St. Petersburg. Sikorsky had attempted to make her acquaintance. He said she was a touchy, bad-tempered individual, possibly embittered by misfortune, but no doubt intelligent enough to teach. Moreover if study of the people was the idea, the Countess might find a short cut through this Sonya Demidoff's knowledge of them.

Marion drove over that afternoon to the Zhergan dressmaking establishment, located in one wing of a two-story brick building. It had one display window exhibiting three pathetic bonnets, a trayful of artificial flowers, and half a dozen bolts of ribbon. A bell jangled alarmingly above her head as she pushed open the street door. There was no one in the uncarpeted, littered-up shop; but low sounds as of things being hastily set to rights came from behind a partition of unpainted dressed lumber, in a certain crack of which, unobserved by the visitor, there was one small knot-hole covered, as it happened, on the inside, by a framed lithograph which could be noiselessly drawn aside. The shop was nearly filled by a pine table covered with paper patterns and half-cut garments, two chairs, and a Singer sewing machine

made in the American Company's factory in Podolsk
by low-waged Russian workers. The manufacturer's
name, CИHГEP, in Russian characters, was cast in
the metal.

The door in the partition was unbolted and
opened, a young woman in a black and white checked
gingham waist and short walking skirt came through
it, saw the fashionable customer in her fine linen suit,
and accompanied her Russian salutation with a frank
look out of clear blue eyes. Expecting to see a somewhat sour, old-maidish individual, the Countess was
agreeably surprised. "Are *you* Sonya Demidoff?"
she asked.

"Yes. What can I do for you?" The absence of
any conventionally respectful form of address was
not noticeable thanks to a peculiar friendliness of
tone.

Marion gave an order for a large number of rough
towels and cotton sheets and pillow-cases much needed at the manor in the row of one-roomed cottages
called the servants' wing. The fine embroidered bed-
linen, of which there was an enormous quantity, was
used only on the beds of the gentlefolks, and according to Anna Churisnok, the housekeeper, it
would have been a sure sign of family degeneracy
had there not been enough of it to last a year without a washing.

The dressmaker hesitated about accepting the
Countess's order, but said finally that she would send
to Mitau for the goods—in a day or two.

"It would be only fair if I advanced the money
for the goods," said Marion.

"More than fair," answered Sonya Demidoff,

smiling. "But as I think you guessed, it would save
—my friends the trouble of lending it to me. So you
may if you will."

Marion nodded.

"Let us see how much it will be," said the dressmaker. She sat down and began to figure. After a
moment she looked up, with a shade of surprise, at
Marion still standing, and then at the other chair.

The lady accepted the suggestion and seated herself.

"About a hundred and seventy-five roubles."

Marion opened her silver-linked purse with the
arms of De Hohenfels on one side of it, and laid out
two hundred roubles in clean new notes.

"What a remarkable purse!" the dressmaker murmured.

"It is handsome," admitted Marion, turning it to
view.

"It has money in it! Most abnormal!"

Marion was inclined to view talk about money as
in poor taste, but Sonya Demidoff broke into such
care-free, unmalicious laughter that the lady with the
abnormal purse could not resist its contagion. She
wondered what had given Sikorsky the impression
that this creature was sour or bad-tempered. "I believe I forgot to mention my name," she said. "I am
the Countess de Hohenfels."

"You could be no one else," said Sonya Demidoff,
wondering if the Countess attached much importance
to the title. To find out she observed: "I suppose you
know I am the Princess Demidoff."

Marion's eyes opened wide. "Really?" she
gasped.

The Princess Demidoff smiled. "Is that so wonderful? You will find stranger things than that in Russia."

"Goodness!" exclaimed Marion, smiling. "I hope I haven't inadvertently failed in the respect due to one of your rank!"

"No,—since you have not failed in the respect due the village dressmaker."

"I see. Were you always so democratic?"

"No. I had to free myself of many unrealities."

"Are social distinctions unrealities?"

"Not yet. But they have no weight with me. Individual distinctions are all that count."

"I find the class distinction very sharp in Russia. I know one barin who believes there is even the beginning of a biologic difference between his class and the muzhik—indicated by a totally different set of instincts."

"Such superstition! Do you not know about the *jus primæ noctis?*"

The Countess confessed her ignorance, and Sonya Demidoff opened her eyes by explaining how that institution and the polygamous tendency of the male aristocrats had sent their blood through the entire European population in every two or three generations during all the long centuries of feudalism. "The different instincts are consequently the result of different economic and social conditions," said Sonya. "The same blood flows in the muzhik and the Tsar, and of the two—give me the muzhik."

"Of two evils choose neither," murmured Marion.

"The muzhik is not an evil. He has been made *muzhikavatwi* (boorish), but the root of the word is *muzh* (a man). Did you live in St. Petersburg this summer and not learn the caliber of such muzhiks as Anakin, Jilkin, Aladin, Kurneen? But be more careful how you agree with strangers that the Tsar is an evil. I am not a police spy, but if I were—and you do not know who is—I would talk to you just as I'm talking now—even to this very warning."

The American caught a glimpse of the nature of that great net of treachery and countertreachery whose meshes run through the whole of Russian society. "How do *you* know *I* am not?" demanded she.

"People engage in that dirty business for profit—at first, and finally from perverted pride in their skill as liars. But you are a rich American."

"I will be more discreet. But my instinct for people is quite untrustworthy if you are in any discreditable business."

"That's sweet!" exclaimed Sonya, smiling.

"I am looking for a tutor in Lettish," said Marion. "Will you accept me as a pupil?"

"Lettish? I am doubtful. I have never thought of it as a language to be studied. My knowledge of it has been picked up instinctively."

"It would probably be impossible to find anyone of whom that is not true."

"No, the Letts are cultivating their language. There are poems, novels, romances. There is a Lettish literary society in Mitau. German philologians have made exhaustive studies of the grammar and phonology. You could find masters of the subject in Mitau."

"I want you," said Marion. "You know how to

study language. You would enjoy analyzing your instinctive knowledge of this one."

The dressmaker asked for a day or two to consider.

That night Marion asked Feodor how the Princess Demidoff came to be keeping a little shop in Zhergan.

"She's the daughter of a Siberian exile," he explained. "Prince Ivan Demidoff's estates were confiscated, and he was sentenced to fifteen years' labor in the mines for circulating 'high treasonable' literature condemning the government censorship of books. The girl's stepmother went back to her family. Demidoff was a fine fellow. I heard him speak once when I was in the University. He was perfectly right about the censorship. I hold his view exactly."

"The view he is in Siberia for holding!"

"The same. I didn't print my view. Demidoff was one of the self-sacrificing fools. What good has his ruining himself done for the freedom of the press? Absolutely none!"

The next day Marion was back at the dressmaker's, her sympathy stirred by Sonya's history, her liking for the girl increased by reflection upon what she had seen of her. She was invited into the room behind the partition to have a cup of tea from Sonya's samovar. This room—kitchen, dining-room, bedroom, and salon—was considerably larger than the shop, had a thick carpet on the floor, heavy curtains, semiornamental iron lattices across the windows looking into a side street, and what with the bed, the long divans, and some upholstered chairs, was capable of seating fifteen or twenty persons.

"I see you are looking at my books," remarked Sonya. "Those are for the benefit of the police, who occasionally pay me a little visit when they think I'd rather not see them. You are sitting on my forbidden library—enough to send me to Siberia. If there's anything you'd like to smuggle home with you——" She showed how the divan opened, revealing a secret chest full of books and pamphlets, and watched her visitor's expression.

"I would like to take all your books home with me," said Marion, "—and also their owner." Judging from the girl's pleased expression that the idea appealed to her, the Countess made her an offer of a permanent position at a good salary as tutor of Lettish and Russian, making it plain that she was desired even more as a companion than as a teacher.

Sonya thanked her, but declined, and being pressed for her reason, answered: "Here I am free. Here my friends come and go as they like."

"You can be equally free at the manor. I would love to have your friends come there."

Sonya shook her head and remained firm, not choosing, however, to explain that her friends would not love to go there.

"I haven't one girl friend in Russia!" said Marion disconsolately. "I thought you and I could be—but you don't seem to feel that way."

"Because I won't give up my independence? My dear, that's absurd! You appeal to me strongly. I like you. I will probably love you. Come as often as you will—every morning—and I will talk Lettish to you while I sew."

They drifted into a language lesson that afternoon

over their tea. Sonya gave the words "glass," "lem-
on," "sugar," "spoon," and so on, as she used each
object. She pointed to herself and said "I"—to
Marion and said "you," and by actions taught such
phrases as "I rise from my chair," "I walk," "I roll
a cigarette," "Will you roll yourself a cigarette?"
and "Have•a match." It was a game that called out
the most pleasurable play of invention and imitation.
Words of any language but Lettish were barred.

They were laughing over Sonya's imitation
"sneeze," when the bell over the shop door set up its
violent jangle. Sonya sprang up, closed the divan
book chest, ran to the lithograph on the partition,
drew it back from the peep-hole, and saw—the in-
tersecting head-line and fate-line of a man's hand.

She started back in alarm, stood one instant, then
snatched a lead pencil from her hair and jabbed it
viciously through the knot-hole. There was a yowl
from beyond the partition, and also an unobstructed
view through the peep-hole. Sonya availed herself
of it, and then opened the door. "I might have
known that was one of your small boy tricks!" said
she.

"Sonya, you devil, you've crucified me!" called a
cheerful barytone. "I shall die of lead poisoning.
Why the mischief do you have such sharp pencils?
I always suspected you of being a remarkable woman,
—but now——" The speaker stopped short in the
doorway as he caught sight of the elegant visitor
within.

The elegant visitor was making a heroic struggle
not to laugh in the young man's face.

"Countess de Hohenfels," said Sonya in her stateliest manner, "allow me to present Professor Alexander Bratavzinsky, Doctor of Philosophy, instructor of the youth of Zhergan, nephew of the eminent magistrate A. Bratavzinsky, Police Intendant of Mitau."

"Bah!" said Bratavzinsky. "Give me some tea."

"According to the most recent usage in polite society, Sasha," said Sonya didactically, "the proper formula to use in acknowledging an introduction to a lady is not 'Bah!' "

"In polite society young women no longer perforate callers with lead-pencils, nor introduce them with allusions to their disreputable relatives. I am happy to meet you, Countess de Hohenfels, and trust you will overlook these little provincialisms of our hostess."

"Her methods seem effective," observed Marion.

"I consider them too pointed," maintained Bratavzinsky, glancing at his hand. "Sonya, do I get tea or do I not?"

"Not unless you go knock on Dr. Grenning's door, and ask him to join us."

"All right," mumbled Bratavzinsky. He glanced with lazy regret at the back wall. Grenning's rooms being on the other side of it, he could easily have been summoned by certain taps—the "talk of the walls" used in prison. The status of the Countess de Hohenfels was sufficiently defined. She was well enough known to let her see the use of the peep-hole, but Sonya did not care to have her hear the signals through the wall.

Unlocking a door into a corridor, Bratavzinsky went out, returning after several minutes. "That

Grenning insisted on taking my blood," he complained. "He's putting it 'still alive' on slides in his new high-power microscope and exhibiting it."

"To whom?" asked Sonya.

"Nachman Kaminsky and Trina Ronke. He wants you and your friend to come in and look at it. I assure you it's very superior blood. It has all kinds of astonishing things in it."

"How interesting!" said Marion, ready to go.

"Ask him to bring the microscope and Kaminsky in here," said Sonya, "—where we can all have tea while he tells us about phagocytes and things."

"How about Trina?"

"Her too—of course. Isn't it lucky I stabbed you?"

Bratavzinsky went out posing as a martyr to cold-blooded scientific curiosity.

"Trina Ronke is the mayor's daughter," explained Sonya. Through subtle intimation understood of women Marion knew that Sonya did not like Trina.

Bratavzinsky came back presently with Grenning and Kaminsky carrying the microscope and its accessories.

"Where's Trina?" asked Sonya.

"She couldn't stay," explained Dr. Grenning. He was a man of more than middle height with well-trimmed beard parted in the middle, gray eyes, slightly stooping shoulders, large hands, a peculiar swing in walking, and a rich bass voice which he seemed inclined to use as little as possible. He was the only physician in Zhergan, and did an enormous amount of work for very little pay.

Nachman Kaminsky was the Jewish notary who

had his office across the corridor—a small man with
beautiful eyelashes, hands and voice. He had ob-
tained a costly legal education in St. Petersburg,
found himself excluded from practice by a new ruling against the Jews, and was reduced to writing
letters and drawing contracts for illiterate people
of his blood. He also ran a sort of school for Jewish children. His father was one of the leading
rabbis of Riga, but Nachman was an atheist.

When the microscope was set up and Marion was
looking into it, Kaminsky began to act as barker for
the show, announcing "the blue blood of Bratavzinsky now on exhibition! On the coverslip of this
microscope, ladies and gentlemen, you now behold
thousands of living animal cells. Among the red
corpuscles which look like copecks but unfortunately
are not, you will observe big white corpuscles. Those
are the police of the body, the military caste in blood
society. The large one near the center of the field
is Police Intendant of the Carotid Artery."

"I protest!" said Bratavzinsky. "I won't have
any police intendant in my blood. And I appeal to
Grenning. Have I got any carotid artery in the middle of my hand?"

"No, but don't interrupt Kaminsky's eloquence
with mere facts."

"I am assured by that eminent bloodist, Dr. Ferdinand Grenning, that the red corpuscles of human
blood are entirely without nucleus, while a percentage
of the red corpuscles of *equus asinus* have a nucleus.
Since the specimen of blood before you does contain
a percentage of nucleated red cells, we are forced,
however unwillingly, to the conclusion that the living

specimen from which this blood is taken is a donkey."

"I wouldn't have to take a microscope, Kaminsky," observed Sasha judicially, "to find that out about you."

"Neat!" said Grenning, chuckling.

Marion looked up at Bratavzinsky and laughed appreciatively, her eyes brimming with fun.

"Lovely!" said Sonya, and gave him a glass of tea.

"Annihilated!" groaned Kaminsky. "And by Sasha! Grenning: get me some cyanide of potassium."

Grenning spoke to Marion. "Here is a wet slide with some of Bratavzinsky's blood that ought to show tubercular germs."

"What's that?" demanded Bratavzinsky.

"I've just put them in," said Grenning. "I'm hoping they're still alive in spite of a little stain. Perhaps we can find white cells eating them." Looking into the instrument, he slowly turned the thumb-screws. "Good luck," he said. "In the upper right-hand corner—perhaps you can see that white cell starting to suck in a germ—just a little pink line."

Marion looked and saw it—with awe and wonder at that revelation of the cryptic process. It reminded her of the emotion she had felt in looking through Walt Bradfield's lens at the marriage of pollen and pistil in the Hillcrest conservatory.

"I call that a battle worth fighting," said Grenning. "There is a military caste worth having. If these co-operative citizens of the blood should imitate our present society, the white cells would be sucking the substance from the red."

"That's a beauty, Grenning," said Kaminsky.

Marion looked up from the lens and met the steady eyes of Grenning. "Even bacteriology!" she murmured.

"So you understand."

She was perceiving Fedya's failure to read all the minute notes in the score of the musician nature. He had ears only for the primitive vital theme announced in the individual animal cell absorbing the protoplasm of its organic fellows. The later theme of infinite richness developed in the social cell he had failed to find.

IV

I N Sonya's circle, Marion found what she had
vainly looked for in the high society of St.
Petersburg. She recognized among these free-
souled people a bond like that between her ten
"spirits" at Vassar—an interest in things of the
mind and a comradeship which frequently exist in
youths of college age, but do not frequently survive
the atmosphere and conditions of modern bourgeois
society. She knew, however, that she was not
quite of this group, that they had other standards
and aspirations than hers. Things were understood
between them which she did not understand. She
was half conscious of her desire to make them stop
looking upon her as an outsider.

Thanks to the hour of Lettish every morning, she
and Sonya grew to be close friends—in spite of the
fact that Sonya would not spend the night at the
manor or even accept an invitation to dinner.

Sometimes at Sonya's she encountered Trina
Ronke, a heavy, brown-haired girl whose mouth
often drooped abnormally at the corners, and who
gave the impression of being too acutely aware of
the Countess's rank to accept her as a human being.

Fritz Dumpe, the plump and rosy mail-carrier,
whom Marion rechristened Dumpling, would stop

and joke with Sonya, and tell the news, and talk
Lettish with the Countess. She soon progressed
enough to stop every day or two as she drove by
the smithy and talk with Yan Sarin, the foreman,
whose fine, hard face a sculptor would have wished
to reproduce in bronze. He reminded Marion of a
certain frescoed figure of Michael Angelo's in the
Sistine Chapel. She took pleasure in saying things
like this about Sarin to Captain Sikorsky, who was
pink and white and soft and too obviously trying to
impress her with his graces.

One day the American was struck by a curious
exclamation of Sonya's. They were talking of marriage, and something Sonya said caused Marion to
ask if she did not intend to marry.

"Marry in Russia!" the girl exclaimed. "Bring
a child into Russia!"

Marion did not feel the full force of that. She
said she herself wanted children, but later, in another year or two.

The only one of the Zhergan group to set foot
in the manor was Nachman Kaminsky. He came
to see Count Feodor on behalf of a poor Jewish
family who owed rent on a one-roomed cabin. The
Count tried to refer him to Churisnok, but Kaminsky explained that this was an appeal from Churisnok's already announced intention to evict. De
Hohenfels said since he could not manage the whole
estate at all times it would be illogical to interfere
in one isolated case. Finally he took refuge in the
fact that he was not the owner of the estate. It
belonged to the Countess.

Kaminsky went to the Countess. She explained

that her ownership was merely nominal. She could not overrule Churisnok without recognizing the reality of her title.

His mind full of the misery of that sick woman, those hungry children, that man legally excluded from nearly every occupation, Kaminsky was disgusted with the shifting of responsibility back and forth between the Count and Countess. He told her so, and took pleasure in describing the condition of scores of people on her estate. He told her of miserable hovels, unfit for the housing of cattle, for which she was drawing rent from human beings. He told her of an old Lett and his wife who had just sold their last cow to pay the rent, of families so poor they could afford but one wooden spoon—though a wooden spoon cost only three copecks—of babies born and wrapped in newspapers—the only clothes their mothers could get for them.

She stopped him by giving him the money to give his clients to pay Churisnok to return to her; but she knew well enough how far solving the rent-problem for one family for two months was from solving the problem of five hundred impoverished tenant families paying rent twelve times a year. Ownership of the Zhergan estate became repugnant to her on new grounds.

She went to Fedya and told him she wished to transfer the property back to him, but he would not consent, giving as his reason the opinion her father would necessarily have of that.

Count Feodor was growing bored and discontented. His imaginative emotion, capable of being stirred by whatever he could interpret as tending up

beyond life's present level, was finding little food
in the life of Russia as revolution and anti-revolu-
tion were revealing it. St. Petersburg had given
up fish on account of the masses of soldiers' bodies
thrown into the sea after the betrayal of the revolutionary design of the troops in Kronstadt and Sveabourg.

One day Marion said to him: "We, with no necessary work, are almost as badly off as the muzhiks
with too much. We grow blue and aimless because
there is nothing we have to do. The way we spend
our hours has no relation to the food we eat, the
clothes we wear, the rooms we live in. I am beginning to believe there must be such a relation if
our souls are not to be vague and our lives unreal."

He asked her if she had been reading too much
Tolstoi lately, and averred that for his part he had
long since passed the point where the industry of
the ditch-diggers shamed him.

She said no more, but contrasted the zest, cheerfulness and interest in things which filled the group
at Sonya's with the boredom of Hohenfels, Tschulitsky, and Sikorsky. Hohenfels was reading a great
deal but not creatively, not selectively, not in the
light of any purpose of his own. He was falling
into the vice of the reading idler. For lack of
anything better he spent most of his evenings at
cards with the officers, generally winning from
Tschulitsky and losing to Sikorsky. There was a
different lieutenant in command of the headquarters
guard each week, but Tschulitsky and Sikorsky they
had always with them.

Knowing Dr. Grenning would be a more inter-

esting companion for her husband, Marion wrote
him a note inviting him to dinner. She was surprised and hurt at Grenning's answer, received next
day, in which he regretted that certain circumstances
made it impossible for him to accept an invitation to
the manor.

A day or so later she met him as he was coming
from his office to the street in front of Sonya's. She
bowed coldly to him, and was going on in, but he
stopped her and begged her not to interpret his
refusing her dinner invitation as an indication of
lack of regard.

"I am not overeasily offended," said she, "but it
happens I never before received so singular a note
of regret."

"There are people with whom a man chooses to
avoid even such small insincerities as pleading a
previous engagement when he has none," said Grenning. "You will not be offended at my taking you
for such a person."

"No, Dr. Grenning, that won't quite do," said
Marion. "In such matters one must give either con-
ventional excuses or real reasons, and you did
neither."

"Well, you are right. It's not just in my line,
but I should have written a polite prevarication."

"Why is it impossible to you to accept an invitation to my house?" She spoke impatiently.

"Don't you really know?"

"I do not."

"It is because I do not care to break bread with
professional murderers." His gray eyes were
square on hers.

She returned his look for a moment, but it became uncomfortable and she looked away. His opinion that his remark was justified was stronger than hers that it was not. "I suppose you mean Tschulitsky and Sikorsky."

"The same."

"Are they really, Doctor? Tschulitsky's a boor, and Sikorsky a—an agreeable fellow, but——"

"But they are professional murderers."

"Have they ever done anything but their duty?"

"Perhaps not. It's their duty that's not to our taste."

"So it's the military profession you object to—not these men personally."

"The distinction is unreal. You can't divide a man from his function. The agreeable Sikorsky last October ordered young Juraw taken from his bed at night—a boy of sixteen—and had him shot in the street for refusing to tell where his brother Martin, the revolutionary leader, was. Tschulitsky ordered his Cossacks to take my friend Chelms, the finest soul in Russia, out of his schoolroom and shoot him. It was done—in front of Chelms's pupils."

"Abominable!" exclaimed Marion. "But there must have been some reason, Doctor. Your friend must have been a revolutionist."

"Oh!" said Grenning with a sardonic smile. "I had almost forgotten I was talking with the Countess de Hohenfels. For the same crime your soldiers will have to kill thirty million Russians. However, they have gone at the job cheerfully. Perhaps they will succeed. At least they will destroy all those who are capable of leading Russia out of hell."

For the first time Marion saw clearly the nature of the gulf that separated her from the Zhergan "spirits." Her first thought was that if they were active revolutionists it might be well for her to be a little more discreet about cultivating their acquaintance.

"If you have any curiosity to see how and for what things men are killed in Russia," added Grenning, "just repeat my remarks to Tschulitsky—or to the amiable Sikorsky."

"You don't mean——?"

"I would join Chelms."

"For a remark made to me privately? Without a trial?"

Grenning laughed. "Since last October," he said, "fifty thousand people have been killed by sword expeditions in Courland, Esthonia, and Livonia—not half of them in armed resistance. Think how much time it would take to 'try' all these groups and individuals accused by spies of treason! Why bother with trials when everybody was guilty? It was this whole people that rose. We elected our own revolutionary officers in every town and city and village in these provinces. The Tsar's government did not exist. The Baltic Republic was a fact. Did you know this?"

"No. I heard there were agrarian disorders."

"Agrarian disorders that seized and administered cities of a third of a million people. It is a wonderful thing—the modern suppression of news! But tell me: are my 'real reasons' real enough to win your forgiveness for refusing to dine with the officers?"

She thought a moment. "They are so real, Dr. Grenning, that henceforth I too shall decline to dine with them."

Before he knew it he had caught her hands in his and pressed them. "Don't tell them why," warned he. He turned quickly, and without looking back, went down the street, his head bent forward, his shoulders stooping a little, a peculiar swing in his walk.

V

THE Countess lunched in her own rooms after her talk with Grenning and invited Count Feodor to dine there with her. Weary of Tschulitsky, he did: and that evening she succeeded in reviving his interest in "The Islands of the Neva." The officers had to content themselves with a three-handed card game.

Sikorsky, who had been feeling his way toward an intrigue with the Countess, at first attributed her retreat to her rooms to her dislike of Tschulitsky; but her frigid manner next morning when he contrived to meet her on the terrace, discouraged him. That night when De Hohenfels absented himself for the second time from the card game, the Adjutant observed to Tschulitsky that it was plain they had overstayed their welcome. He began to talk about the three blooming daughters of Mayor Ronke, suggesting that under certain circumstances the house of Ronke, in spite of inferior service and cuisine, might be a pleasanter residence than the manor.

The idea took root in Tschulitsky's mind. He remembered some official business that took him next morning to the Mayor's house in town.

Before Count Feodor was out of bed the forester

of the estate, Robert Guibet, came in from his cabin
in the forest, insisted on seeing the barin at once,
and being admitted to De Hohenfels's bedroom, reported that the night before, cutting through the
woods from the village of Medin, he had come upon
the camp of an armed band of fifty or sixty Brothers
of the Woods not more than five versts from the
manor.

De Hohenfels dressed and went to Tschulitsky's
room, but found he had already gone to town. When
he came back, about eleven o'clock, Count Feodor
told him of the forester's report, and took it for
granted that the commandant would immediately
send an expedition to clean out the revolutionists.

Looking from their windows after luncheon,
Count Feodor and Marion saw that the tents of
the headquarters guard were struck, their army
wagons loaded, and the men formed in heavy march-
ing order.

"Are they going to attack the revolutionists now?"
exclaimed Marion.

De Hohenfels supposed so.

Presently the horses of the officers and of their
orderlies were brought around from the stable.

"Is Tschulitsky going himself?" wondered De
Hohenfels. His interest was aroused to the point
of going down to find out. As he went out on the
terrace he turned and saw Sikorsky coming out of
the house.

"The Commandant has decided we should not
impose longer on your hospitality, Count," said
Sikorsky. "We are transferring headquarters to
town. Please express my regret to the Countess

that I have not had the opportunity of seeing her lately—even to thank her for our entertainment."

"Tschulitsky might have had the decency to say he was going," said Hohenfels, scowling.

"The decision was reached very unexpectedly only an hour ago."

"That is since I told him of that band here in the woods at our door!" exclaimed Hohenfels.

Tschulitsky came out of the house booted and spurred and followed by an orderly.

"Aren't you going to leave a guard for these premises, Tschulitsky?" demanded De Hohenfels.

"No."

"Then you should have given me notice. I could have had one sent from Mitau. In view of the particular danger you know threatens this point your withdrawing the guard to-day looks like deliberate violation of your duty to protect life and property."

"What are you going to do about it?" demanded Tschulitsky. "Come on, Sikorsky."

"Fortunately the telegraph is working between here and Mitau," said Hohenfels, as the officers mounted.

Sikorsky narrowed his eyes, wondering how much influence Hohenfels had in Mitau, and looked disapprovingly at Tschulitsky.

Seeing the troops move off toward town, Marion's pleasure at being rid of the professional murderers was mingled with apprehension. She wanted to see Grenning, thinking he might be in communication with the band in the woods and be able to tell her whether there was danger to the manor. Not wishing to leave Fedya out there, she asked him to drive in town with her. He had her leave him at the telegraph office.

"It will be impossible to get any sort of protection to-night," he said as she left him. "You'd better invite yourself to spend the night with the Princess Demidoff."

"And how about you?"

"I may stay at the inn. There are half a dozen officers there. I'm told it's a jolly crowd."

"I may—" began Marion, starting to say she might find out there was no danger to the manor, "I may stay with Sonya."

She sent Davuidka with the droshky to the inn stable. As she walked toward Grenning's she was considering whether to see him first, or Sonya, when she perceived the girl in the act of locking her shop-door from the outside.

"Are you going to be gone long?" called Marion.

"Well, well!" said Sonya, looking around. "No. In fact I'm not going at all." She unlocked the door. "Come in," she said. "I was just starting for the manor to see you."

"Actually?" exclaimed Marion, following her in.

"I want you to stay here with me to-night," said the girl. "Will you? Your accommodations will be primitive, but——"

"Nonsense! It will be a lark. But what makes you want me to stay with you—to-night?"

"I have my own mysterious reasons," smiled Sonya.

"Won't to-morrow night do as well?"

"Oh, you can stay then, too."

"Won't you let me drive you out to the manor

and spend to-night with me there?" asked Marion, watching Sonya's expression.

"I can't—really I can't. Besides—you practically accepted my invitation, and now I going to hold you to it."

"I want to tell you something," said Marion. "It may make a difference in your unwillingness to come to the manor. The officers left there this afternoon."

"They *did!*" exclaimed Sonya. "Where did they go?"

"Tschulitsky moved his headquarters into town. I don't know where. He took his guard with him— leaving us very much at the mercy of our Brothers of the Woods."

"Won't Tschulitsky be at the manor to-night?" demanded Sonya.

"That seems to disarrange some plans," thought Marion. "He is already here in Zhergan," she repeated.

"Take off your things," said Sonya. "Excuse me a minute. I want to ask Dr. Grenning to take supper with us." She unlocked the door into the corridor, and went quickly to Grenning's.

Marion sat down, her eyes fixed thoughtfully on the floor. "She has gone to tell Grenning that Tschulitsky is *not* to be at the manor to-night," she meditated. "She was going out especially to get me away from there to-night. They hate Tschulitsky. And there are fifty or sixty of them—as many as the headquarters guard." Her conclusion was that perhaps the withdrawal of Tschulitsky and his guard which had so alarmed them might be the very thing

to save the manor from an attack which would otherwise have been made.

Sonya came back.

"Did the Doctor accept your invitation to supper?" asked Marion.

Sonya looked guilty.

"You never asked him!" thought Marion. "You
were too deeply interested in telling him about
Tschulitsky. But I am all wrong unless Dr.
Grenning goes out very soon to get word to the
brethren." She listened for his footsteps in the
corridor.

"I had made up my mind to no more sewing to-
day and hate to go back to it," said Sonya. "Shall
we do some Lettish?"

Marion agreed, but hearing a door open and
close and someone passing along the corridor, she
jumped up, went to the door and looked out. It was
Grenning.

"How are you, Doctor?" she called.

He stopped uncertainly, returned her greeting, and
was going on.

"Are you in a great hurry?" asked Marion sweet-
ly.

"Why, yes, I am rather."

"But we'll have you here with us at supper, won't
we?"

"Why-uh, you'll be here, will you? I think I'll
be back by then, in which case—I shall be charmed."

"Don't let me keep you from your *patient,*" she
said. He saw the door close slowly, narrowing to a
crack, pausing an instant, and then concealing her
smiling eyes and mouth.

"She knows too much," thought he, as he turned toward the street. "I have altogether too much of an impulse to confide in her. But I hope and think she will not tell."

Of course Marion stayed at Sonya's that night. Grenning was there for supper and the evening. She told him as though she did not know he knew it of the withdrawal of the guard from the manor, and asked him if he thought there was any danger of attack.

"I think not," he said in the tone of one who has no special knowledge. He seemed disturbed—probably at the idea of her possessing information leading her to ask that question.

The rest of the evening they talked of books, people, philosophies. Marion told them in some detail of her friend Walt Bradfield, his writing, and his agitation among the workingmen of Moline. Sonya and Grenning found it hard to understand why the American workingmen with their universal and equal male suffrage—the lack of which so handicapped their European fellows—did not control the government, and through it the industrial life of the United States.

The next morning, in Sonya's bed, Marion woke from a dreadful dream—that Walt Bradfield had shot himself! Because he could not get work—? because of her marriage—? because she had not written—? She could not make it out, but somehow it seemed to be her fault. Then she slept again and woke with a new terror filling her mind—the feeling that the manor had been burned in the night—that something terrible had happened to Fedya. As her

thoughts cleared, it struck her as strange and rash
that she should have come straight to these revolutionists, personal friends though they were, and told
them of the unprotected situation of her own home—
which lay exposed to the attack of an armed band
not one hour's march away. She felt as Grenning
had felt about her the day before—that she had
altogether too much of an impulse to confide in
them. If her surmise was correct, these friends of
hers knew of—perhaps had planned—an attack on
her house for the purpose of capturing Tschulitsky.
To be sure they were going to get *her* away from
there, but how about Fedya? What if the activity of
these friends of hers had resulted in his death in
that attack? She rose and began to dress.

"So early?" murmured Sonya, more than half
asleep.

"I'm worried about Fedya. I must make sure he
stayed at the inn last night."

Sonya reached under her pillow, and looked at a
little black watch. "He'll be sound asleep," she
said, but Marion kept on dressing. "Dear me!" exclaimed Sonya, jumping up. "You really must wait
till I get you some tea—I mean coffee. I got some
especially for your breakfast."

Marion finished dressing, waited reluctantly a
few minutes for coffee, then hastened on foot in the
early morning to the Zhergan Inn. She had to
rouse a man sleeping on a bench in his stocking feet,
who had to rouse the innkeeper, who escorted her
to the room of the Count de Hohenfels. That gentleman, having kept it up with the jolly crowd of
officers until a very short time before, was most un-

appreciative of his lady's flattering solicitude. She quickly left him to resume his slumbers, and went back to Sonya's in a frame of mind considerably less tender and self-reproachful.

Of course that other dream—about Walt—was equally baseless. Still it was absurd not to know whether he was alive or not, and this time she really did sit down and write to him.

"Are you angry with me," she wrote, "for the way I left Moline—without saying goodbye? I wanted to see you—truly I did. I hated to leave things so badly—as they were that night. I never dreamed as I went out the door of Hillcrest of not seeing you again and saying goodbye, and telling you—how much I think of you." The letter expressed her desire for his friendship *always*, told of her sympathy with phases of Russian life which she never would have understood had it not been for her acquaintance with him, described the group of friends she had found and asked for his criticism of that doctrine of the higher race which so appealed to her religious sense. "Does not the finest flower of human life," she wrote, "—its superhuman issue —demand at last a divided humanity? Must not root and trunk of the racial tree exist for the sake of blossoming above? The blossoming not for its own sake, but to bear and send up vigorously above the rest one favored shoot, tip of the tree of life, to attain the stage of evolution next above the human and there branch richly out. The idea that humanity by sacrifice of what is lower to what is higher in itself should create superhumanity lays hold of me with a power I cannot describe. To me the superrace looms like a new Messiah, not dreadful, not hostile, not destined to destroy us.   It is not coming to save humanity by sacrificing itself.   For it humanity must sacrifice itself, as parent does for child—a daughter-race which we, the mother-race, must bear and nurse."

After addressing her letter to Walt in Moline, hoping his people would forward it, she became absorbed for the rest of the morning in Sonya's forbidden library.   Some of the propaganda consisted of what struck her as rather mechanical applications of revolutionary and materialist theories, but some of it was based on illuminating study of things as they are, and through this she had glimpses of the whole design—broad and splendid outlines of the freer, finer society which the workers, learning and following their own real interests, ought to develop along definite lines out of the present society based on wage-labor.   She wondered if there was any way of reconciling that with the letter she had written to Walt.   Her own non-proletarian interests and point of view prevented her embracing that proletarian philosophy for herself, but she did not see how its validity for the proletarians could be denied. Passing into their power the world would without question become a place more favorable for their development—the development of all but the chosen few.   She began to feel vaguely, but could not, or did not want to, think out a flaw somewhere in the theory that the chosen few, the present ruling class, could breed from themselves a higher race.

While she sat reading and thinking Trina Ronke came in.   She was returning a book which she had smuggled home, and selected another. As she went out through the shop with it, she asked Sonya if it was safe to have the Countess know of the library.

"Why?" Sonya asked.

"She might tell her husband."

"Do you think the Count de Hohenfels would run and tell the police about my books?" said Sonya, laughing, but Trina Ronke shook her head, saying you couldn't tell about these aristocrats. If anything came up—making it important to destroy her—there was the means!

Sonya said nothing. Secretly she felt there was more risk in Trina's possession of that knowledge.

About noon Davuidka brought the Countess a note from the Inn. The awakened Feodor asked her to take lunch with him there. At table in his own rooms he showed her a letter from the Governor-General at Mitau written with flattering promptitude in answer to his telegram. The letter stated that orders had been issued the Commandant at Zhergan immediately to capture the revolutionary band located on the Hohenfels estate.

"In Courland, at least," commented Count Feodor, "one can still conjure a little with the name De Hohenfels."

"Tschulitsky will have to eat dirt!" gloated Marion.

"He has already. He called this morning. Very respectful. Requested me to send for Robert Guibet to act as guide tonight. They will surround the gang in the middle of the night."

He suggested that until the marauders were captured they had better not return to the manor, so Marion went back after luncheon to Sonya's.

After her first exultation over the idea of humbling Tschulitsky, she began to realize what the orders from Mitau meant. The killing, wounding, and capturing of fifty men was not in itself a pleasant thing to contemplate, and it was still less pleasant to Marion when she realized that in that district it would mean the final triumph of the atrocious government of the Tsar over the Baltic Republic—the triumph of men like Tschulitsky and Sikorsky, who shot intellectual men and heroic boys without trial, over men like Grenning, Kaminsky, and the clear-eyed Yan Sarin, who were working against terrific odds, for liberty and democracy, for freedom of speech and press, for better houses, better wages, and better life.

"The manor will be safer after the revolutionists are destroyed," she thought. It was that consideration which had caused Feodor the landlord to take such prompt and effective steps for their destruction, and it was that which had caused her instinctively to approve those steps. But as she walked along the dusty August streets, catching an occasional phrase of Lettish in the treble voices of children playing, it seemed to her no admirable thing to help the Tsar crush down the Lettish people because a band of revolutionists might possibly burn down one's house. She probably would not have seen that this was what she and Feodor were doing had it not been for Sonya's books. And on second thought it occurred to her that she had not heard of any manor

houses being burned when the revolutionists were in
control of the country. Arms had been taken forcibly by an armed party from the Hohenfels manor
itself, but the house was certainly not burned. Yawn-
ing foundations of small houses were visible in and
around Zhergan, but they had belonged to revolutionists and had been burned by troops of the Tsar.
She had heard of the burning of a house in the
neighboring village of Benen by revolutionists, and
of the shooting of a man and two women among
those who lived in it, but Grenning and Sonya had
told her that those three had been tried by the Zhergan local and condemned as spies whose information to the government troops had led to the burning
of several houses and the summary shooting of many
men. Marion sighed, and without reaching any conclusion, went back to Sonya's books.

Sasha Bratavzinsky came in at four o'clock for
tea from Sonya's samovar. Finding the Countess
preoccupied, he talked cheerful nonsense to Sonya.

Nachman Kaminsky came in looking gloomy.

Marion asked him how the Jewish family was
getting along.

"Your money paid the rent for them. It gave
the woman a chance to die under a roof. She was
buried Sunday."

"Is it that that makes you so blue, Nachman?"
asked Sonya.

"No." He relapsed into silence.

Bratavzinsky talked awhile, but could not resist
the depressing atmosphere, and ran out of subjects.

"Where's Grenning?" asked Kaminsky.

"He'll probably be in for a glass of tea," said Sonya. "I wish he would come!"

"I have news," said Kaminsky. "I've been keeping it to myself on your account, Countess de Hohenfels, but I have decided I want you to hear it. I want you to know how the officers of the detective division of the police examine a witness. Yan Kenim is a man who helped govern the city of Riga last summer when it was in the hands of the people. I have known him since boyhood. Six days ago he was arrested in Riga and taken to the station of the detective division. Night before last he was examined. The officers who did it are Gregus, Mikheyev, Zimmermann, Davus, and Petrov. There were two others whom I shall not name. They read to Kenim a long list of crimes allegedly committed by him, and demanded a confession, if not of all, then at least of a part of these. Kenim denied his guilt. First they struck blows. Then they undressed him, threw him on a bench, tied him to it, gagged his mouth with a rag, and two police officers began— first with rubber whips, then with wire whips. When his back became swollen they covered it with a wet rag and kept on. When he fainted, they poured cold water on him, and as soon as he regained consciousness, began again. Then they untied him, and threw sharp pieces of salt on the floor. Two of them raised him about five feet from the floor and hurled him down on the salt. This was——"

"Oh!" groaned Marion, white and trembling. "What is the use of this?"

"If Kenim and thousands more can endure the

reality of these things," said Kaminsky, "you can endure the telling of them! I am sick of the comfortable ignorance of the leisure class. You don't *want* to know. But I want to tell you that you, every one of you, who maintain and profit by the established order have each your share in the torture of Kenim!"

"I do nothing to maintain the established order!" cried Marion.

"To do nothing *is* to maintain the established order."

She had no reply.

Kaminsky walked across the room, sat down and paid no further attention to anybody.

"What men do they treat like this?" Marion asked. "Not every prisoner?"

"Every revolutionist from whose agony they can hope to wring a confession of guilt or the name of a comrade," said Bratavzinsky. "I know of tortures much worse than this of Kenim."

"If they capture this band in our forest," said Marion, "—will they—torture them?"

"Well rather!" Bratavzinsky answered. He was going to say more, but caught an angry warning look from Kaminsky, and realized he had no business admitting knowledge of that band.

"Do you people know anything about these Brothers of the Woods?" asked Marion.

Kaminsky looked at her. "We do not," he said, positively. "Why do you ask?"

"Because I have been told they are thieves and murderers, and if they are not, I want to know it."

Kaminsky and Bratavzinsky sat keen and silent,

but Sonya broke out. "Thieves and murderers!" she cried. "The very spies that go among them to betray them they try to dissuade from that work. They kill them only when they will not stop."

"Anyone can see," said Bratavzinsky, "that somewhere now there must be in hiding thousands of revolutionists known by the authorities to be such."

"There is no need for me to hesitate," said Marion. "Whatever you people choose to deny or admit, I know that if these men are thieves and murderers you have no interest in them. If they are revolutionists—well, I happen to know that Tschulitsky has information of a band of fifty in camp two versts east of the railroad in our forest. He has orders from Mitau to send a force in there and capture them to-night."

A needle falling on the carpet would have sounded loud while Sonya, Sasha, and Kaminsky were realizing that the Countess de Hohenfels had made herself a revolutionary spy.

VI

KAMINSKY was the first to speak. He asked Bratavzinsky if he had seen the recent address of the rector of the St. Petersburg University urging all poor students to "let science and sedition alone" and go in for manual training. "He refers to 'the glorious battle against the revolutionists' and calls it 'a battle for truth and right.'"

Marion looked at him curiously, smiled to herself, and rose. "There's nothing like discretion," she said. She took her hat and put it on before the mirror. "I have some things to buy, Sonya. I'll be back in time for supper." The bell over the street door jangled behind her.

"It's a quarter to five," said Sonya. "We can reach Martin Mitrevitz by six. Who is going?"

"Is Grenning in there?" Kaminsky asked. He rapped on the wall. There was an answering rap and presently Grenning came in.

They told him the news. His eyes brightened when he heard what Marion had done.

"Kaminsky treated her as though she were a government detective," said Sonya.

"The rest of you are too confiding by half!" protested Kaminsky. "Grenning talks to a woman and thinks he's converted her to the revolution, when all he's really done is convert her to Grenning. Trina Ronke has no more business in your local than her father. She has her cap set now for Sikorsky—the man who shot young Juraw, and she knows it. And now Sonya and Bratavzinsky have let the Countess de Hohenfels see our connection with Martin Mitrevitz! Suppose she has a change of heart!"

"After she has once come square out?" said Grenning. "Kaminsky: she has been leaning our way ever since she came. It's from deep down and of old and by temperament with her."

"How are we going to get word to Martin Mitrevitz?" asked Bratavzinsky.

"I have decided to have a sick-call in that direction," said Grenning.

"See Yan Smika," suggested Kaminsky, "—the forester of the Medin estate. He will know just where they are."

The physician went to the stable, harnessed his horse, and drove out to the cabin of Yan Smika, whom he found getting ready to cook supper. When he heard of the intended attack on Mitrevitz, the forester put half a loaf of black bread in his pocket and took down his rifle.

"I will tell Mitrevitz in twenty minutes," he said.

"Do you think you'll have use for that?" asked Grenning, nodding toward the rifle.

"There's a three-quarter moon. White coats show well."

A new idea struck Grenning. "I believe I will go with you to Mitrevitz," he said.

He and Smika crossed the road into the Hohenfels forest, walked in silence between the thick-set pillars of the pines, and crossed the railroad which ran eastward from Zhergan then turned southwest, so forming a giant figure seven through the forest.

The revolutionary militia lay near a spring two versts east of the curve. They had no tents or military uniforms, and their rifles were of many kinds. The forester and the physician were stopped by an outpost, one of whom knew Smika and let them pass without any military formalities.

Martin Mitrevitz, a lean, bronzed man with several weeks' beard, dressed as a workingman, asked them to share his supper, such as it was. They declined, knowing provisions were scarce in the camp.

"We'll get away at once," said Mitrevitz, when he heard of the intended night attack.

Smika and he agreed that the troops would have to come out from Zhergan on the wagon road past the Hohenfels manor, turn to their left on the railroad, follow it eastward until it swung south, and then through the woods to the camp.

On the back of a letter Grenning drew lines representing the wagon road, the railroad, and the camp. "They will come up the railroad in column, won't they?" he asked.

"No other way."

Grenning put lines on the railroad representing infantry in column. "Instead of finding you, as they expect, here in camp seven versts from town and unprepared," he said, "suppose they found you here four versts from town—like this?"

"They would die," said Mitrevitz, his eye kindling with the idea of the enfilading lines alongside the track. "But we will lie here, still closer to town,

where there is a clearing to shoot across. Here
they will not have begun to move with caution. This
will repay us for not getting Tschulitsky. I am sorry
for these men, but for us to-night they are tools of
the Tsar, not men."

At eight o'clock when Grenning got back to Zhergan after his sick-call at Yan Smika's, he found a
man waiting nervously in his office and had to hasten
out with him to attend a woman in labor. He looked
in at Sonya's a moment. She and Marion sat near
the table reading by a bright, well-shaded lamp.

Sonya rose and came close to him near the door.
"What?" said she, speaking almost inaudibly.

"You'll hear firing to-night," he answered. Then
he raised his voice. "You look so cozy here reading
—I wish I could stay."

"We wish so too," said Marion. "Don't we,
Sonya?"

"Indeed," said the girl absently. "Why couldn't
they get away?" she demanded, whispering.

"They prefer to lie in ambush," he answered, also
whispering, and then gave a warning glance over
his shoulder to remind her that he had an outsider
somewhere there in the hall beyond the half-opened
door.

"Do you share Kaminsky's distrust of me, Sonya?"
said Marion, after Grenning had gone.

"No." After a moment Sonya inclined her head
back toward the door Grenning had just gone out
of. "Neither does he. But wouldn't you rather not
know anything definite about—us?"

"Only this: whether those men in the woods are
warned and can escape."

"Yes, they have been warned." The girl glanced at the alarm clock on her dresser, sat down, and tried to resume her reading. Several times she was on the point of telling Marion what Grenning had said, but did not.

She did not keep her light burning after ten for fear of drawing the attention of the police. Thanks to the iron gratings of the windows they were able to let the cool night air into the room. They could see the moonlit silver birches in the yard of the Lutheran church on the other side of the wide, dusty street. The lights had gone out of the windows, and the streets were deserted save for an occasional pair of lovers in the shadow of a doorway.

Marion was dropping off to sleep, when Sonya, who had remained sitting near the window, called to her in a low, excited voice—"Look here!"

Marion sprang to the window and saw, coming down the street, in a cloud of dust, so silently she would not have known they were passing, the Russian *rotnis* which Feodor's influence had started on their night march against the revolutionists.

"Uncanny!" Marion whispered. "All those men, and hardly a sound!"

"Not the clink of a scabbard!" whispered Sonya. "I'm glad the Brothers know! Thanks to you!" She put her arm around Marion and hugged her.

"I think there will be some profanity when they reach that camp," Marion said. She chuckled happily at the thought of having averted the tragedy.

Sonya's conscience hurt her a little for leaving Marion in ignorance of the ambush. "How many of those men are making their last march?" she thought as the last man passed from sight beyond the corner of the shop.

There was a chill in the night air, but the soldiers did not wear the white coats Smika had said would show well, and Captain Byeletsky had made the men blue their rifle barrels that afternoon lest the glint of them should be seen in the woods from the enemy's camp.

With Robert Guibet knowing every tree in the woods, Byeletsky expected to close in on that camp from all sides and get every man. The main thing he feared was that the rifle of some revolutionary sympathizer among his own men would go off accidentally near the camp. He halted his force on the road outside the town, called the sergeants of his two companies together, and gave them orders to shoot in his tracks anyone to whom this accident happened. The sergeants told the men.

The column left the wagon road and turned eastward upon the railroad track. Reaching the edge of the forest, Byeletsky sent out flankers to move through the woods parallel with the railroad abreast of his advance guard.

This was a thing Mitrevitz had not foreseen. He and his comrades lying concealed behind trees and in shadow on the edge of the clearing in an open irregular line would not be seen by the small advance guard moving along the track, but these four advancing figures out fifty and a hundred *arshin* to the right and left—they must infallibly run into the lines of his ambush. How keep them from giving the alarm—and time for those two hundred men to deploy against his fifty?

Mitrevitz picked two men, explained the danger to them, and told them each to take one of those men, keep square in front of him, and when he entered the shadow, stop him and kill him if he attempted to cry out or discharge his piece. Then, only two or three hundred *arshin* ahead of the enemy's advance guard Mitrevitz crossed the track on his belly, and gave similar orders to two men on the other side. It looked desperate to Mitrevitz. He had done all he could, but it was almost too much to expect to stop all four of those men in silence.

The advance guard thought themselves too far from the enemy to be very alert. The ensign in command was talking in low tones to the forest guard Robert Guibet as the dozen men swung along between the two lines of the ambush. The four flankers, trying not to drop behind, did not slacken their pace as they approached the edge of the clearing.

Mitrevitz, his nerves tense, saw the inner flanker on his side was coming straight for him. "Lie still!" he whispered to the man he had detailed to stop this Russian. "I'll take him." He waited till the soldier entered the shadow of the pines. He sprang up, pointing his revolver at the man's eyes. "Not a sound!" he hissed, in Russian.

The soldier gave a gasp of terror. "Don't shoot!" he whispered, not realizing that Mitrevitz could not shoot without giving the alarm "I'm with you! I'm a Social-Democrat—for the revolution!"

His mind acting with lightning-like rapidity under strain, Mitrevitz seemed to read the man's soul, believed him, and paying no more attention to him, listened with torturing intensity for the shot or shout he feared. To his left, where the outer flanker had come upon the line, he heard a sickening groan—just one. "Whether necessary or not, God knows!" thought Mitrevitz, but that man's death did not occupy another second of his thought.

The advance guard had not stopped. They were fifty, a hundred feet beyond the ambush. On the other side of the track, behind the revolutionary line, he saw a Russian move through a lighted space parallel with the track. It was the inner flanker on that side. He must have closed in far enough to miss the line, and they had let him go.

"Good work!" thought Mitrevitz. "How about number four?" There was no sound or movement in that direction. The advance guard marched farther and farther into harmlessness; and the main body of the Russians was in sight. From the front, at that distance, the two companies in column of fours looked like a single dark object. One would have taken it for a team and wagon. Mitrevitz could hear the deep breathing of the nervous men around him. It was a racking wait till they could see the individual forms, and then the faces of the Russians in the moonlight.

In the silent night, a rifle flamed and roared on the black edge of the clearing—one shot followed instantly by two—a dozen—thirty—visible to the Russians as the blazing arc of a circle of which they were the center—and scores of bullets drawing the short and deadly radii! Men pitched, whirled, stumbled, went down groaning. The column melted down in blood and anguish on the track. From front to rear they were raked and hit by a fire they could not return. To get them out of that focus of slaughter Byeletsky tried to make them execute right and left front into line of squads, but their instinct, far older than modern firearms, far older than military discipline, was to huddle together for mutual protection. When the leaden logic of the 30-30's forced them to see the helpless, hopeless doom of that, the survivors bolted from that litter of warm corpses and writhing human forms in a wild rush for shelter.

With the melting away of their definite living target on the track, the revolutionists slackened their fire, and in the lull heard Mitrevitz shouting, "Forward in line!" He was afraid not to go forward lest the Russians, unpursued, should reform, advance in line, and sweep his still numerically inferior force out of existence.

The Russians, an organization no longer, did not await the charge of their enemies. There were men who had stood the test of Mukden in that crowd of individuals running through the woods toward Zhergan. Mitrevitz did not dare pursue them beyond the forest, for fear of reinforcements—especially the Cossacks.

Seeing the main body scattered, the Russian advance guard, whose carelessness had caused the disaster, did not attempt to return through the revolutionary force. Guided by Robert Guibet through the woods to the road from Medin, they reached town unharmed.

The Brothers of the Woods, whose return from that pursuit was the beginning of their own flight from the neighborhood, saw fifty or sixty dead and wounded Russians on the track and in the ditches where stricken men had reeled. Other wounded men had been able to reach the woods, and had fallen there. Some died there alone. Some had fainted with pain or loss of blood and were to regain consciousness in solitude, or with what grim sense of companionship a man unable to move and feeling the life ebb out of him may have in hearing the groans of comrades in agony.

VII

THREE quarters of an hour after they saw the
troops go by, Sonya left the window and
went to Marion's bed. "Marion!"

The sleeper started, opened her eyes, recognized
her friend, and smiled happily at being called Marion.

"Listen!"

There was the far-off, ominous roar of many rifles
—a sound nearly as horrible in its significance as
any that vibrates in the air of man's still horrible
planet.

"What does it mean?" said Marion tensely.
"Have they caught the revolutionists?"

"I hope for once the revolutionists have caught
them."

"Fifty of them?" She got up, slipped on a dressing gown, and went to the window. Sonya had not
undressed. "That sounds as though it were at the
manor," said Marion.

"The night is still. It is probably in the forest."

A mounted orderly came galloping up the street
from the direction of Mayor Ronke's, Tschulitsky's
new headquarters, and disappeared in the direction
of the firing.

After about ten minutes the fire slackened and

ceased. A little later it began again, more scattering, but louder. Marion shivered.

A drummer at the barracks near the central prison began beating the long roll; a bugler blew first call over and over, and then assembly; the more distant call of the Cossacks came from the northwest quarter; the night air carried hoarse shouts of command weirdly over the town. Somewhere in the distance a door slammed. Lights appeared in windows that had been dark. There was a murmur of wondering voices here and there as sleepers woke and called to each other to know what was wrong.

The mounted orderly came tearing back from the southeast, and five minutes later a *rotni* of Cossacks a hundred strong galloped through Zhergan hurling a great cloud of dust high into the quiet moonlight air.

"Why didn't the Brothers get away while they could?" exclaimed Marion, shuddering at the power of that living, catapultic projectile of men and horses.

"The Cossacks can't go through the woods like that," said Sonya, to reassure herself no less than Marion.

A few minutes later a company of infantry went by in double time, some of the men choking and coughing as they breathed the dust raised by the Cossacks.

"Why do they need so many?" exclaimed Marion. "Is the revolutionary force larger than I said?"

Sonya shook her head. "They made an ambush."

"An ambush," repeated Marion thoughtfully. She realized then that all those drums and bugles in the night, that roar of many rifles, that rush of men and horses, were all the result of one brief sentence spoken by her in this same room seven hours before.

The muffled pounding of the feet of the infantrymen died away in the distance. There were no more audible indications of what was going on among the three or four hundred men who had left Zhergan. The minutes of waiting with strained attention were long. Thirty of them passed with no sound from beyond the town. Sonya and Marion found themselves shivering with cold and excitement. They lay down still listening, grew drowsy, fell asleep.

They were roused and terrified by someone in the corridor kicking violently on their door, and a harsh voice calling, "Dr. Grenning!"

"That's a Cossack!" exclaimed Sonya under her breath. "What if they've come for Grenning?"

"Why should they?" whispered Marion.

"He carried your information to the Brothers."

They heard a match strike in the corridor. Booted feet moved heavily on the flag-stones. Outside the window they heard the hard breathing of horses, the swish of their tails, the champ of bits and stamp of hoofs as the animals bit and kicked at the mosquitoes drawing their blood.

"If somebody doesn't open some door in this house I'll break them down!" roared the man in the hall.

"I wonder if Grenning is in there?" whispered Marion.

"I hope not."

"What shall we do?"

"If they've come to arrest him and find him not here they'll say that proves——"

"He can prove he's been with a patient."

"What chance will he have to prove anything? They may take him out and shoot him against the wall of his own office."

A door on the other side of the corridor opened and the women heard Kaminsky demanding, "What's this racket?" They could see by the gleam of light along the crack under the door that Kaminsky had a light.

"Are you Dr. Grenning?"

"No. That's the Doctor's door over there with his card on it. Can't you read?"

"Can't you see I'm a *jigit?*" retorted the Cossack, scorning the suggestion that he could be guilty of so unwarriorlike a habit.

"What do you want with Dr. Grenning?" inquired Kaminsky. His manner made the Cossack take him for some kind of civil authority, so he adopted a tone of friendly superiority.

"I don't want him at all. The Cossacks wouldn't be such fools as let a few Lettish cattle shoot them to pieces. It's the soldiers. They're spilled all over the woods. I've brought a horse for this doctor to go and cut off their arms and legs. Much good they'll be after that!"

"They want him as a doctor!" rejoiced Sonya.

Marion drew a long breath.

Relieved of the same fear that had upset Sonya and Marion, Kaminsky read the Cossack the notice the doctor had thumb-tacked to his door giving the address at which he could be found. "Did they catch the Letts that did the shooting?" Kaminsky inquired.

"The soldiers? Of course not. They'll let them go till daylight. By then they'll be in as many different *izbas* as there are men. They'll hide their guns in haystacks, and then how are you going to tell who was out?"

"You might shoot them all," Kaminsky suggested.

"We will if we get the word," said the Cossack. "There's no nonsense about us." He rode off, leading the horse he had brought for the doctor.

"I wish the Cossacks had been shot instead of those peaceable-minded Russian conscripts," said Marion to Sonya.

Army wagons half-filled with hay were rumbling and rattling through the streets on their way out to bring in the wounded and the dead.

At quarter to one, Grenning came on horseback with the Cossack, who stayed outside with the horses. The doctor went into his office, packed a suit-case full of bandages, splints, cotton, and gauze, and got ready his instruments, needles, thread, antiseptics, ether cans and hood, hypo tablets and syringe. While doing this, he heard Sonya's rap through the wall, and went to her door. It was held ajar.

"Ferdinand," whispered Sonya, "I was frightened when the Cossacks came for you, and ——"

"I didn't know you knew how to be frightened," he said as she hesitated.

"We were wondering what to do, and I told Marion it was you who carried word to the Brothers. She gave us that information to save the Brothers, and I think she blames us for using it to destroy the Russians. She wants to speak to you. I wanted you to understand everything."

"Thanks, Sonya. She can't expect *us* to stop with half-way measures."

Sonya yielded her place at the door to Marion.

"Are there many wounded?" began the Countess abruptly.

"The Cossack says a hundred. It seems the two companies walked into a trap and lost over half their men."

"Of course your knowledge of that trap comes only from the Cossack!" Her eyes attacked his, but he displayed no qualms. "Do you imagine for an instant that I am ashamed of my share in the trap?" he demanded.

She did not pursue the question. "Is there hospital room for so many?" she asked.

"Probably the army surgeon will secure a building for temporary hospital."

"What I wanted to say was—if there's anything money can buy that the Government fails to furnish, get it. I will pay."

"I understand."

She looked at him, trying to make out why he was not wholly sympathetic. He could not be enthusiastic over her salving a conscience that from his point of view needed no salve.

"Have no fear," he said. "There will be plenty the Government fails to furnish."

"You will need nurses," she said. "Get them. And tell me—shall I come myself tonight? Can I help?"

"Have you had hospital experience?" She judged

from his expression that he hoped she had, but she said no. "Don't come," he said, and looked toward the outer door.

"Don't you feel a curious justice in *your* going to help these men?"

"Justice!" he exclaimed. "Lord!" He dropped his voice still lower. "All that's worrying me is 'aid and comfort to the enemy.'" He thought a moment, then went on. "Today when he saw he would have the Russians in his power the leader of the Brothers said to me, 'I am sorry for these men, but tonight they are tools of the Tsar, not men.'"

"That *is* more human than the professional soldier."

"It was our business to deal with them as tools of the Tsar," said Grenning. "We did it. It now seems to be my business to deal with them as men. But don't delude yourself by thinking I do it to make amends. There are none to make."

"Don't let me keep you from these men who are suffering. I wish I could look at it as cold-bloodedly as you seem to. I can't take so easily the thought that if it hadn't been for me these men would not have been killed and wounded."

"Better men would have been. Yes—and tortured! But you're wrong if you think me cold-blooded, Countess Marion. I have just come from the birth of a child—a thing of unceasing marvel. As I came away it struck me as a ghastly absurdity that you brave, tender women should bear mankind in agony—to have them destroyed in war. But you and I cannot escape war. It is here. We can sulk— we can criticize the ungentle, uncouth fighters, or—

we can take sides. The best we can do is fight on the side whose triumph means the end of war. Yes, and the end of the horrors of peace! You're on that side today. Don't leave it—not for wealth, and not for love!"

Something warm and beautiful seemed to flow into Marion's soul—a sense of rising to a higher spiritual level—a vision or a feeling of practical idealism, of sacrifice approved by reason, of faith that burned not in spite of, but as a result of critical intelligence —a faith that stands the test! "I'm glad you're alive, Dr. Grenning!" she exclaimed. "I'm oh so glad the Cossacks came for you as a physician!" She wished him good luck and Godspeed as he hastened out with his instruments and rode away to his night of toil.

She lay awake a long while thinking of the things he had said. There was something about him that stirred her enthusiasm, made her believe in him and in the cause he placed above wealth and love.

The quiet of the town was not yet broken by the noises of returning troops and wagons. The room and the house were still. In that stillness Marion heard a strange involuntary whisper. Whether from troubled sleep or feverish wakefulness—in either case from her subconscious soul—came Sonya's whispered words—"He loves her!"

VIII

A T dawn, Tschulitsky set out with Cossacks, infantry, and machine guns. Captain Byeletsky
had reported the force he met as not less than
two hundred. The troops spent a hard day scouting
through the forest, but found no enemy. The revolutionists had scattered or circled Zhergan. The soldiers came back to town after dark, exhausted for
nothing.

Marion returned with Feodor to the manor, but
finding it lonely there after growing used to the companionship of her friends in town, she sent Davuidka
to bring Sonya and Grenning out to dinner.

Grenning had been up all the night before, had
worked all day, and was going to bed; but he came.
He was tempted to take a hypo. of morphine, but
finally decided the Countess would have to make
allowances.

The evening was the best De Hohenfels had spent
since coming from St. Petersburg. After the society
of the army officers, it was an inspiration to him to
talk with people of mental range and power. Sonya's self-certainty, her independence, the impression
she gave of thinking more than she expressed, his
feeling that she understood him better than he un-

derstood her, gave her mystery, and attracted him. He did most of the talking, being stimulated by brief comments of Grenning showing comprehension but not agreement. After they had gone, Feodor commented on Grenning's taciturnity, and asked if he and Sonya were lovers.

Marion thought of Sonya's whisper, though by day it did not have the enormous significance it had presented to her nocturnal soul. "Perhaps she is in love with him," she answered. "It's hard to tell about them. They seem more like comrades than lovers, but——"

"I noticed they both look at things from the socialist angle. Do you suppose there is a social-democratic way of being in love?"

She smiled, then considered it seriously. "I had not thought of it," she said, "but perhaps there is. The bourgeois world has certainly failed to create any way of love of its own. Its love, like its poetry, has had to ape the forms of the past. It has imitated the love of feudal chivalry, or finding that false —for itself—has turned to cynical disbelief and disregard of love."

"And what was the feudal way of love?" asked Count Feodor, more interested than he usually was in Marion's ideas.

"The feudal way was to capture a woman, 'dominate' her, set her on a narrow pedestal from which she must not move—then worship her. It was idolatrous because the dominator was worshiping a thing of his own making."

"You will change the nature of man before you do away with domination."

"Willingly," she said. "Fortunately it is changing all the time. In the coming way of love there will
be no domination, no pedestal, no making and so no
smashing of idols, no forming and so no losing of
illusions. We shall love truthfully—with realism.
Love between man and woman shall be love between
comrades and equals. Yes, I have convinced myself
—there *is* a social-democratic way of love."

Feodor de Hohenfels listened with disapproval.
"Then goodbye glamour, mystery and lure!" he
cried. "Goodbye the Dionysian intoxication—the di-
vine madness there was in all great deeds and art and
love! Put out the fire of spring—there'll be nothing
in men's souls for it to kindle! Your social-democratic way of love is drabbest English Puritanism!"

"Do you feel any of that in Sonya Demidoff?"

"No. I didn't feel it. Is it there?"

"Not any drab English Puritanism. But what I
was describing is there. She will love a man as a
comrade, not as an overmasterer. She will play
mouse to no cat-passion of capture. If your Dionysian intoxication is incompatible with sex-equality,
the men of the future will have to contrive some way
to get along without it."

"It dies in marriage anyhow," he said gloomily.

"And the love of comrades does not!" was all
she said, but she was deeply hurt, could not longer
conceal from herself her feeling that her marriage
was a mistake, and her heart turned aching to the
thought of that other "true" love which she had
chosen to erase from her life. "Walt's love would
not have died," she thought.

Count Feodor thought regretfully of Rome and

the Duchess di Callignano, who wrought with the sex-lure like an artist on the souls of men. If to be untouched with modern spirit would enable a woman to retain glamour and mystery, Di Callignano would retain hers forever.

Next day Feodor and Marion had no time to consider the problem of how they were to live together without love. Soon after breakfast sixteen Cossacks rode up the gravel driveway to the manor, and their ensign informed De Hohenfels that it was his duty to escort him to the Town-House.

A court-martial was sitting to determine the cause of the recent disaster. The court could not really succeed in this without finding that had it not been for the torture of Yan Kenim in Riga Saturday night there would have been no revolutionary ambush Tuesday at Zhergan. De Hohenfels asked in what capacity he was sent for, but the ensign could not say.

They found the Town-House full of soldiers, some under arms, some with side-arms—sentries, orderlies, and guards. Robert Guibet the forester was sitting on a bench in the hall-way under guard. He had been imprisoned the night of the ambush. Two private soldiers were also prisoners. Captain Byeletsky and Ensign Khlopov, the commander of the advance guard, were waiting in the anteroom under arrest. The Cossack ensign requested De Hohenfels to be seated in the same room, and sat with his prisoner—or witness. The Count had to wait there during a lengthy examination of Byeletsky, Khlopov, and others.

Byeletsky was let off with a reprimand. He was

allowed to show that Ensign Khlopov was in a position to ascertain the presence of the ambush and had
failed to do so.

Khlopov explained that he had flankers out prop-
erly, but they had failed to give any signal when they
came upon the enemy's line. He had not yet thrown
forward a point, but the point would have been on
the track and would not have discovered the ambush.
He said he was relying largely on Robert Guibet.
He gave the names of the four flankers. The court-
martial recommended that Ensign Khlopov be dis-
honorably dismissed from the service. The recom-
mendation was finally carried out, and Khlopov shot
himself.

Of the four flankers, one—the Social-Democrat
spared by Mitrevitz—was missing, and one had been
found dead in the woods with a bayonet wound
through his throat. The third, the soldier Kazyol,
was drawn by Sikorsky into the admission that as he
approached the edge of the clearing he had closed
in to less than the prescribed distance from the advance guard. This trifling failure to follow in-
structions had caused him to miss the revolutionary
line. He was sentenced to five years in one of the
Siberian disciplinary regiments. When he heard
this sentence, he begged to be shot, but his plea was
not granted.

Dutloff, the fourth flanker, was hazy in his testimony. He remembered walking from the clearing
into the shadow, and the next thing he knew was
that he was on his back under the trees alone, with
a terrible pain in his head. His head was bruised
and swollen. He claimed he had heard nothing of

the battle. The court decided that he must have had some opportunity to give the alarm, and had failed to do so. He was adjudged guilty of neglect of duty through cowardice and sentenced to be shot next day at sunrise in presence of the garrison.

Robert Guibet was brought in and accused of treacherously leading the expedition into ambush. He said he had last seen the revolutionists in their camp at eight o'clock in the evening, and had no reason to suppose they were not still there at eleven. Tschulitsky was presiding, and no one called attention to the fact that he had sent no scouts of his own to find out the exact position and movements of the enemy. He brought out the fact that the forester had full knowledge of the expedition by two in the afternoon. The court decided that if six hours later he was near enough to the camp of the revolutionists to see it, he was there for no good purpose. He was sentenced to be shot next day at sunrise—unless in the meantime he should decide to confess his guilt and name his accomplices—particularly what orders or messages he had received from his master the Count de Hohenfels.

The Count de Hohenfels was summoned. In the small room where the court sat, he found four officers sitting stiffly in full uniform along the farther side of a long table, and a Jewish soldier at the end of the table writing and fussing with open and folded documents. De Hohenfels recognized Commandant Tschulitsky and Captain Sikorsky. The others were infantry captains and Tschulitsky's clerk.

Without making a formal charge, Tschulitsky

pointed out that outside the military authorities the Count de Hohenfels and his forester were the only persons in Zhergan who had official knowledge of the expedition. This knowledge had evidently reached the revolutionists. How?

De Hohenfels replied that he did not know.

He was asked to produce the letter he had received from the Governor-General. He found it in his pocket, glanced over it and dropped it on the table. He was irritated by having been kept waiting so long. "It would be well for you to reflect, Commandant," he observed, "that, as this letter shows, the Governor-General knows you had to be forced into this expedition. If you start any absurd proceedings against me—or against Robert Guibet—I will see to it that a court-martial sits in this case with rank enough to determine why the Commandant of Zhergan had to be compelled to undertake this expedition, and what relation his refusal to attack the revolutionists on Monday bears to the failure of the attack he was ordered to make on Tuesday."

Tschulitsky turned white and red with fear and anger. He saw that this unexpected view of the case looked infernally plausible, and Sikorsky was making him violent signals to keep cool. The Commandant could think of no decent-looking way to drop De Hohenfels then and there. Sikorsky came to his rescue. "It was too clearly to the interest of the Count de Hohenfels to have this band of marauders on his estate exterminated," said the adjutant politely, "to permit anyone to suppose that he intentionally put them in possession of information as to the Government's plans. There remains, however, the possibility of his having been indiscreet. I suggest that the Count be asked to tell this court exactly what persons he talked to concerning this expedition." Tschulitsky put the question directly.

"Only to Robert Guibet," said De Hohenfels.

"What did you tell him?" asked Tschulitsky.

"Tuesday noon I ordered him to keep watch of the band as long as possible to make sure they had not left their camp, but to go to you not later than nine o'clock and guide whomever you designated to the camp."

"That accounts for Guibet being there at eight," remarked Sikorsky.

"Did you tell Guibet the camp was to be attacked?" asked Tschulitsky.

"No. Still, not being a fool, he understood that."

"Did you tell him not to talk about it?"

"No. I was sure he would not."

"What made you sure?"

"I know his character. He is sensible, truthful, and loyal."

"Loyal to whom?"

"To me."

"And to the Tsar?"

"Guibet is a simple man. I have never heard him express his sentiments concerning the Tsar. He is untainted by revolutionary ideas."

Sikorsky leaned over and whispered something to Tschulitsky. "One more question," said the Commandant. "Whom else did you talk to concerning the expedition?"

"To no one." De Hohenfels did not think of his wife as some one "else."

"Did you show this letter to anyone or tell anyone of its contents?"

De Hohenfels remembered the table in his room at the Zhergan Inn where Marion had read the Governor-General's letter. Was it possible their discussion had been overheard by some servant listening outside their door? Should he qualify his statement now by saying, "I showed it to no one but the Countess de Hohenfels"?

"I demand that the Count de Hohenfels be sworn," said Sikorsky suddenly.

A scornful little smile stirred the corners of De Hohenfels's mouth at the idea that if he thought it right to deceive these unfriendly inquisitors he would be deterred by an oath, not given freely by himself, but compulsorily administered by them. He would have been reluctant to violate his own word, but their oath—it was nothing to him.

They administered the oath.

"Count de Hohenfels:" said Tschulitsky solemnly, "did you or did you not show or speak of the Governor-General's letter to any person whatsoever?"

"I did not."

Tschulitsky and Sikorsky conferred together. Tschulitsky asked the captains if they had any questions. De Hohenfels was escorted out by the Cossack ensign, and kept in the anteroom until Tschulitsky's clerk brought him a written notice stating it was the order of the court-martial that the Count de Hohenfels should not at present leave the vicinity of Zhergan without permission from the military authorities.   He was then allowed to leave the Town-House.

Next morning, a few minutes after sunrise, the soldier Dutloff was shot in presence of the garrison at the brickyard.   The sound of the volley that killed him was' plainly audible at the manor-house. The soldier Kazyol was placed guarded and in irons on the morning train for Mitau en route to Siberia—to a life worse feared by the Russian soldiers than the seven hells.   The sentence against Robert Guibet was not revoked, but execution was suspended, and the forester held in prison, to be used as a witness in case the detective division of the police could find sufficient evidence against De Hohenfels to convince the Governor-General, now friendly to him, of his guilt.   For Tschulitsky and Sikorsky had placed the affair in the hands of the secret police.   Starting with the known fact that Guibet and De Hohenfels had the disastrous knowledge which had finally reached the revolutionists, the detectives set themselves to find out if anyone in the town, soldier or civilian, man or woman, had shared that knowledge.

IX

ON the Friday following the execution of Dutloff, Yan Smika, the forester of the Medin
estate, was arrested in his cabin by a party
of Cossacks from Zhergan and sent to Riga for
examination by the detective division.

The revolutionary parties in Zhergan did not
hear of this arrest until Monday morning, when
Kaminsky received word through the Jewish agent
of a firm of grain-buyers in Riga that Smika had
been recognized on the night of the battle by a government spy who fought under Mitrevitz.

Kaminsky went immediately to Grenning's office.
"This brings it only one step from you," he said to
Grenning. "You must get away now—while you
can."

Grenning shook his head. "I was nominated
night before last by the Social-Democrats for the
second Duma," he said. "I wanted to see you yesterday. The authorities have given us only three
weeks' notice, and I hear Medin has been at work
for a couple of months. But if you Social-Revolu-
tionists will deign to vote, and vote with us, we can
take the seat away from De Hohenfels."

"What does the Duma amount to?" scoffed

Kaminsky. "In Moscow they've put fifteen prominent lawyers in jail to keep them from running as
opposition candidates."

"I don't think De Hohenfels will allow that in
Zhergan," said Grenning. "He'd be ashamed to
have the Countess know he'd won that way himself,
and he won't let Medin do it."

"And suppose meanwhile Smika caves in?"

"Your news shows they didn't arrest him for
carrying information to Mitrevitz. Smika shouldn't
have fought with the Brothers that night, or having
done it, he should have stayed with them. But think
of that traitor with Mitrewitz! Do you know who
it is?"

"Yes. Mitrevitz has been notified. The man will
be killed. But that will not release Smika. And if
Smika weakens under torture—it's you next!"

Grenning thought a while. "In the first place," he
said, "I have faith in Smika."

Kaminsky made a gesture of impatience.

"In the second place, they will not be pressing
Smika for information they don't suspect him of
having."

"Nonsense! They will press him for all the information he has and a lot he has not."

"Even so—if I am elected to the Duma, I become exempt from arrest."

"Theoretically."

Grenning laughed and thought of Kaminsky's un-
warranted distrust of the Countess de Hohenfels.
"Nachman: you are 'der Geist der stets verneint.'
It's probably due to your habit of calling yourself
an atheist. Why don't you drop that nineteenth cen-

tury negative—denial of God—and affirm the modern positive—the oneness of the world?"

"What's the difference?" grunted Kaminsky.

"Of mental habit. I call the scepticism which cannot accept a truth no better than the credulity which accepts a falsehood."

"You'll observe I can agree it's better to affirm your own proposition than deny its opposite, and nevertheless maintain you'd better get out of Zhergan."

"I'm not saying there's no risk," said Grenning. "But in my opinion it's worth running. We can win this election in Zhergan. The Socialist parties can return thirty or forty per cent. of the delegates of the next Duma. If we had foreseen last spring the temper of those peasant deputies we would never have boycotted the elections then. If we'd had our delegates there with them we would have made that weak Vibourg Manifesto a call to arms that would have aroused the Russian nation, not in a dozen times and places and unco-ordinated movements, but as one man."

"That has undoubtedly been our weakness," said Kaminsky. He had no idea then that leaders of his own party like Eugene Phillipovitch Azef were tools of the Tsar who were intentionally disco-ordinating the revolutionary movements and scattering the revolutionary strength.

"Will you get your people to vote for me?" asked Grenning.

"If you're still here to vote for." Seeing he could not influence Grenning directly, Kaminsky left him, and went in to Sonya's.

The Countess de Hohenfels was there, but since the others told her everything sooner or later anyhow, Kaminsky did not think it worth while to keep from her the news of Smika's arrest.

"Do they know about Grenning?" was Sonya's quick question.

"Apparently not. Not yet."

"He and Smika went together."

"But Smika stayed that night and fought. It was then he was seen. Now, because they've arrested him for taking part in the fight, and not for carrying information, Grenning thinks they won't examine him along the line that leads to him. The police are not that dense. The main thing they are after is— how Mitrevitz learned of the expedition. In Smika they have a man who joined the band that night. They won't need an abacus to calculate that the information probably came to camp with him. And if so—who gave it to him? Grenning can say what he likes—he lies square in the path of that investigation."

"How about the rest of us?" said Marion. She saw the power of the Russian State working in toward her from both sides—the side of Feodor, from whom she received the information—the side of the Brothers, to whom she had sent it.

"Smika does not know about *us*," said Sonya.

"He won't listen to me," said Kaminsky. "I wish you'd try to get him away from Zhergan."

"He'd pay more attention to you, Marion," said Sonya.

Marion colored. "I think not," she said. "Is Smika a man so likely to betray Grenning?"

"Smika isn't," answered Kaminsky. "But the thing they turn Smika into——!" He shrugged his shoulders.

Marion's face grew gray and her fingers clenched. "I *hate* Russia!"

"Not Russia!" Sonya protested.

"The horror that calls itself Russia! The Tsar and all the tens of thousands of horrible small tsars! I cannot stand this country. I must get away from it to some place where men have a right to think and read and speak and breathe and not smell blood!"

"What is Ferdinand's argument for not leaving?" asked Sonya.

"He has the parliamentary bee in his bonnet, and that's all he can hear. He has just been nominated for the Duma."

"Then he will run against Count Feodor!" Marion exclaimed.

"If he stays," supplemented Kaminsky. "You will be doing a good piece of electioneering if you get him to go."

"Electioneering!" cried Marion. She gave Kaminsky a wrathful look. "I hope he stays—and wins!"

"So?" said Kaminsky, hastily revising his ideas.

Sonya looked away.

"I'm not thinking of the men personally," Marion explained, forcibly. "No anti-democrat like Count Feodor can do anything of value in the Duma, and Grenning—perhaps he can."

"And perhaps no one can," said Kaminsky. "But!" He held out his hand to Marion. They

looked each other in the eye, and for the first time
she liked him. "I did not know you," he said. "I
used just the wrong argument. But for Grenning's
sake, for ours, no, for the cause that is above us all
—since you are a woman who can look impersonally
—get Grenning away. We can't afford to risk him
for the sake of a seat in the Duma. If it was anything vital, I wouldn't grudge him."

"I will try it," Marion responded, rising. "Though
if you could not get him to go, there is little chance
that I can. Is he in his office?"

She went in, accepted the Doctor's invitation to
be seated, and in her talk with him repeated the
arguments of Kaminsky. At one point, as plainly as
though he had done his thinking aloud, she saw him
pause and half-shut his eyes as the idea of "electioneering" crossed his mind; and then, with equal clearness, she saw him dismiss the idea—as being out of
keeping with his conception of her character. His
faith in her gave her a thrill of pleasure. But when
she asked him if he would go, he asked "Where?"

"Out of Russia?" she suggested, uncertainly. She
added half to herself, "That is where I am going."
Realizing the personal interpretation he might give
to that, she looked quickly at him, but saw he did not
give it.

"I am not going out of Russia while there is a
chance of overthrowing the bureaucracy," he said
positively. "For the present they have kicked the
fire of revolt pretty well to pieces here, and in Moscow, and at Sveabourg, but we must be ready for the
new flame. There is still Poland, the Caucasus, the
Black Sea Fleet, the other troops around St. Peters-

burg. The Baltic Republic must be ready to rise again with them. Everywhere the plans of a revolutionary state are being steadily elaborated. The Duma is important because the deputies from all over Russia will be in a position to make the rising of distant districts simultaneous."

"I did not really expect to influence your decision," said she. "I tried it only to satisfy Sonya and Kaminsky. It may sound disloyal to my husband, but you will understand why I wish you and not him to win this election. His position is such that he cannot throw his strength unreservedly to either side in the Russian struggle—and you can. And I hope you overthrow the Tsar. You Russians have suffered so from tyranny that you love and value freedom more than we Americans."

"You Americans? Aren't you a Russian subject?"

"The law considers me one. But it has struck me lately as queer that, whether she desires it or not, marriage should automatically change a woman's nationality to that of her husband. I do not feel myself a Russian, and of all things in the world the thing I am least willing to be is a subject of the Tsar."

"We are not willing either! You speak as though the Americans believe themselves free. If so, they are easily fooled—ruled as they are by the most unmitigated industrial oligarchy in the world. The peoples of Russia have at least the advantage of knowing they are not free."

"If you overthrow this government which has survived out of the dark ages," conceded Marion, "America will have to learn democracy from you.

You and Sarin and Sonya and the rest have more faith in democracy and are profounder democrats than any Americans I know—except one."

"Walt Bradfield?" said Grenning.

"Oh, do you remember his name?" Her face lighted up.

"I would like to know him," the Doctor said, wistfully. "He must be a wonderful man to be loved by you."

"I didn't tell you that!" she exclaimed. "What gave you that idea?"

"You said he was your friend," hedging.

"Oh," she said, subsiding. "I wrote to him two weeks ago." She paused, seeming to listen. "Perhaps he is just this very moment receiving my letter." She turned her watch and looked at it. "I dreamed he was dead. That night I told you about him I dreamed it. I told him of you and Sonya and Russia."

"Be careful what you write," he warned. "The authorities may think it worth while to read your letters these days."

Marion rose to go. "I have a personal reason for desiring your election, Doctor. If Count Feodor is defeated, I think I will be able to get him to live in Rome."

"Rome?" he said. "I will be sorry to see you go." He sat looking intently before him. "I might as well speak out," he said. "I will regret it if I let you go without speaking. I do not think you will be satisfied with life in Rome. It will be a dilettant life—without real significance—and you know what significance is. You know Russia needs this revolution as a man smothering needs air. It's a need greater than religion, keener than the yearning of wife for husband—as compelling as the love of mother for child. This need of the nation comes into the individual's mind—sometimes seemingly against a man's or woman's will—and when it comes it dominates action. Often it comes in the form of an impulse you find yourself obeying."

"You are describing my particular case," said Marion, intensely interested, "—the way I began to tell about the expedition."

"Most of us began in some such way—you when you heard of Kenim, Sonya when they sent her father to Siberia, Bratavzinsky when his uncle cynically condemned an innocent man to death, I when they shot Chelms. Kaminsky thinks the Cause above all such personal considerations. To him these are unworthy reasons; but most of us come to the cause, not as an abstraction, but through the burning need of revolution which we find unmistakably in some particular case that comes home to us, and then we see it everywhere. And when it does come, we grow quiet and definite and unshakable and proceed to do the thing we have to."

"I know you are describing a real thing truly," said she. "But isn't it like madness—such involuntary obedience to an idea?"

"Yes, it is like madness—and like genius. It is the yearning and the struggle for sanity in a nation driven mad."

Marion sat down again. All that she knew of Russia—a thousand hitherto unrelated facts—seemed suddenly to regroup themselves and come into focus. "Am I deserting if I go to Rome?" she asked.

"Not by the mere act of going to Rome. Not by going anywhere. This is a world-struggle. It is more acute in Russia because here oppression is at its worst and in an antiquated form. You spoke awhile ago as though it were here only—as though it did not exist in America. To think that is not to be deserting. It is to have not yet enlisted. Countess Marion: I hold you capable of the only vital conversion left in the world—that which finds one an active or passive supporter of established, powerful, unjust tyranny, political and economic, and makes one a fighter for freedom. This conversion sets you cleanly over from the retarding to the advancing party of mankind—from the world-party of rulers, financiers and magnates who hold the life of the world in their enslaving grip, to the Promethean world-party which means to tear those strangling fingers from the world's throat and give the instinctive brotherhood of man a chance to grow into actuality."

"The instinctive brotherhood?" she repeated. To her now it sounded like a true word—though it opposed her theory that the brotherhood of all would thwart the loftiest development of the few. Her own instinct, her own actions of late did not square with that theory. What was the matter with it? In the light of her Russian experience, Grenning seemed to be defining truly the great real issue of the modern world. She had a keen feeling of its importance and seriousness. But Feodor? She knew his life, his training, his philosophy, made him incapable of that vital conversion. "There are things that hold me back," she said.

"As to Rome," he said, retracting, "I spoke hastily—from personal disappointment. I was hoping to see you this winter in St. Petersburg. As for deserting—you might as well go to Rome. You will not stay there. Or if you do, you will find the battle there. Wherever you go you will find it—the same battle—setting the souls of men on flame!"

"I have a large job of spiritual stock-taking on my hands," said Marion. "A fine lot of unsolved problems I've accumulated. I've been shirking and putting them off. I am indebted to you for a keen desire to attack them. We must see each other again for a good talk before one or both of us leave Zhergan."

As she left Grenning's office, she met Trina Ronke coming in, and received a look of surprise and resentment in return for her greeting. "What's the matter with that individual?" she thought. "Can she imagine I have robbed her of Grenning's affection?"

Stopping a moment to tell Sonya and Kaminsky that she had not shaken Grenning's resolution, she then went by the inn stable, where she told Davuidka to drive home without her; and walking slowly homeward in the autumn sunshine, past the brickyard and the smithy and the fields where women, children, and men were at work digging and sacking potatoes, she thought deeply of her life.

She thought of her old desire, awakened by Lady Diotima, for social and political power, and knew she had missed it by her marriage with Feodor. But that desire had been linked with the supposition that

a woman could obtain and use such power benefi-
cently. When she had come to know upon what
sordid considerations real "influence" in Washington
depended, she knew she could not attain it and remain anything she wanted to be. And power in St.
Petersburg! It was power of darkness, and the
hearts of those who grasped it petrified! Was there
any power in the world which could coexist with
love? With eyes that had seen Russia she looked
back on her father's conception of power—control
of industry—the power of which political power was
but the shadow. She remembered the defeat of the
Curran bill, and Bradfield's burning revelation of
the manufacturers' motives which had made her
want to vote, and Fedya's cold comment—
"Women's sympathies are too easily carried away
by such appeals."

Was power that did not crush and grind mankind impossible? If leaders of the new democracy like Grenning, Sonya, Sarin, and Bradfield attained political power would they make the same
narrow selfish use of it the ruling class made now?
Her feeling was that they would not—but why?
What was to prevent it? She made a mental note
to ask Grenning about direct legislation—the machinery of the new democracy. Then she remembered those peasant deputies whose parliamentary
course had been shaped by the eight million peasants behind them, and Vasili Pososhkov's theory
that collective ownership, aligning the self-interest
of every individual with the common good, would
resolve the undeniable discord now sounding between self and society, and with the discord its re-

flex in men's minds—the apparent antithesis between socialism and individualism. Less definite
but more weighty than all else with her was her
own realization in herself of a new order of motives and passions—the same order she felt in the
souls of all those in whom the social consciousness
had dawned. Through this she felt that she understood the new spirit, the new kind of government, dawning among the peoples of the world.
She felt the bitter need of it.

But Feodor? She had grown accustomed to
keeping her thoughts from him, but was determined
that things should not go on so. Their conversation had grown narrower through avoidance of subjects on which they knew there was between them
a fundamental disagreement. His atmosphere of
cold disapproval, usually unspoken, was slowly
freezing all her affection for him. Her high opinion of his esthetic judgment had at first made her
dread his disapproval even in the least of things.
When she read it in his manner it had then given
her a feeling of her own deficiency. Little by little,
she was forced to feel that the deficiency lay rather
in him. He disapproved of and excluded too
much, he said "no" to too wide and splendid a part
of life, he loved too few things, persons, ideas, and
those he loved he did not love enough. It seemed
some other, dreamier self within her which mentally repeated the words, "He did not love enough,"
as though she were reading the epitaph of a dead
marriage.

"How could he," she thought, "when his heart

grew up in that icy upper Russian world that is based on the crushing of men?"

He was indeed a Hyperborean—a dweller beyond the cold. But the woman needed love. She had to have love or wither. She did not solve that problem as she walked home through the autumn sunshine, nor did she find it solved when she awoke at dawn, hearing the mournful song of a swallow, and feeling the pathos of all far-off things—cities remote, and days gone by, and faces she no longer saw.

X

THE days were shorter, the nights colder, the intense labor of the harvest nearly over in the region round Zhergan. The Count and Countess de Hohenfels and Baron Medin were the only upperclass residents of the district remaining in the melancholy country, and they of course were staying only on account of the September election. Baron Medin argued privately with De Hohenfels that as a landowner he could not afford to divide the anti-socialist strength in the face of a Lettish population honeycombed with socialism.

De Hohenfels smiled. "Considering your small vote this spring, Medin, I don't see how there can be any argument as to which anti-socialist candidate should withdraw."

"There are two arguments. First: the new restrictions of the suffrage will disqualify at least half of those who voted for you this spring."

"Restrictions made in violation of the guarantee in the Tsar's original ukase," observed De Hohenfels.

"The restrictions are now part of the law. The second point is that much of your remaining strength is this time going to Grenning." A third point—that the Government was preparing to use intimidation—Medin did not think it necessary to state.

De Hohenfels had no exact information as to how things were going, but his desire to retain his seat being aroused by the activity of the Government on the one hand, and of the Socialists on the other, he began to give some time, thought, and energy to the campaign.

About a week before the election, Marion, glancing at her morning's mail, carelessly tore open the return envelop of a Chicago manufacturing firm. From it she drew forth a fat letter from Walt Bradfield. She ran off quickly with it to her own room.

It was dated Chicago, Sept. 22d. "Dear Countess Marion," he wrote. "You ask if I am angry with you because you left Moline without saying goodbye and without telling me how much you think of me. How long do you think anger could withstand that question? My answer is that I am fatalist enough to know that all that happened had to happen. All I need to relieve my mind of about that night and morning is this: Count Hohenfels did not do what I accused him of, but he thought of doing it, and in your eyes my great crime was thinking he thought of it.

"You say you have a thousand things to ask and tell. There may be an opportunity sooner than you think. Yes, I have fallen in love a couple of times, but have been too busy to do it thoroughly. It's taboo now, I suppose, but I hate taboos, and the fact is you spoiled me a little for others—or them for me.

"As to that glorious vision of yours—the higher race—I see it must be serviceable to the Countess de Hohenfels in that it will help her to view with indifference (as a thing necessary and ultimately productive of the highest good) the needless suffering and degradation of almost the whole of her own kind—the only beings she ever expects to see. If you and Count Feodor were naturally callous people you probably wouldn't need that philosophic protection against pity. Your doctrine is an apparently well-based substitute for the old idea that God has damned the bulk of the race to hell. For God substitute Nature, and for hell race stagnation and decay, and you have your comforting new formula. Comforting because it relieves you of responsibility for conditions from which you profit. It is Nature at work! The elect, the chosen few of Nature (pretty shallowly identified, I must say, with the present ruling class) are to carry life on up into the earthly heaven of superhumanity.

"That's clever! It could be made to sweep the bourgeois world like Christian Science or New Thought—if only it didn't take so much real imagination and so thorough a comprehension of the big results of biology. I concede at once that all the races of our ancestry have split as you expect ours to. Put on top of all biologic precedent the allurement of the old messianic idea—transfer your religious emotions from a supernatural to a natural Messiah reasonably to be expected in the future and appealing to the most profound instinct of all true lovers of men—the desire for a finer race—and I do not wonder you have yielded to this charm!

"The Count de Hohenfels and you, however, seem to have overlooked the fact that the various ape-tribes, for instance, had no steamships and railroads to bring them together, create among them like ways of life and work and thought, and insure the blending of the blood of all. Thanks to a knit-together world the many branches of mankind must have not many fates, but one. Humanity cannot split as simianity did into lower and higher. There will be no groups left isolated in special environments.

"The Count's idea is worth forming—and rejecting—because it brings into clear light the fact that in *not* branching into distinct species mankind makes a new departure in the history of racial growth. Man must transform not a part, but the whole of his kind into the higher race!"

"Oh, I love that, Walt!" said Marion, half aloud. "There's inspiration of a wider, warmer kind in that!"

She sat a moment loving that, before she went on. "If the Count is looking for the final cleavage to occur, not between different nations or races, but within the highest existing races through gradual widening of the gap between 'higher' and 'lower' classes, tell him to leave that gap to Socialism—and sex-attraction! Europe is not exactly getting ready for Hindoo caste.

"Our race is one, by the test of Fertility, and as one it must attain or fail of the heaven of superhumanity. In a thousand years the blood of the basest must blend with yours. Better not block social progress that will make his children less base! A single pair doubling thirty times would have over a billion living descendants. After the human net is woven through thirty generations, knotting every ancestral thread to every other, you and your worst enemy, if the blood of both of you endures at all, will both be the very great grandparents of every individual alive!

"We cannot say that free men and women—especially women—will never find some way to breed men only from the best. To be the best may be the chief incentive of that time. But it is certainly not from our society of narrow individuals or from the present necessarily selfish and slavish age that a conscious tendency toward a higher race can rise. That time may not come till Capitalism and Socialism are both outgrown and dim as ancient Egypt.

"Having thus wantonly deprived you of the comfort of your new religion (for of course you are crushed!) I feel I should make some slight amends by confessing that you were not altogether wrong about that automatic sash-lifter for regulating the temperature of conservatories. It is on the market, and thanks to some friends I made in Chicago, I was not entirely robbed. In fact I am now extracting royalty from the sweat of the men who are actually making the device.

"You ask for an account of my doings. First, I have not shot myself. Before I 'lifted myself out of the class in which I happened to have been born' I worked in a Chicago greenhouse, did a little speaking, and have had two or three articles in Socialist and semi-Socialist magazines, and a prospect of some money from them for articles from abroad. They would like to know, for instance, why the revolution in Russia is going so badly. It looked like a sure thing. If I were there as a magazine writer—let's see, which is more respectable—I shall also be 'examining the field' for the introduction of the automatic sash-lifter—and since it is in one sense my own sash-lifter, I may prefer to regard myself as a manufacturer rather than a mere commercial traveler. I shall select whichever social status will best enable me to visit you in your Zhergan."

"Zhergan!" exclaimed Marion, and her thoughts flashed. "Here! Walt here in Zhergan! What will Fedya—oh, this isn't Turkey! But we won't be here in Zhergan! What a shame—to come all the way from America—When is he coming?" She glanced on hastily, finding the sentence "I am leaving next week—expect to land in Hamburg. On the map I locate Zhergan near Riga." She looked at the date. "Next week," she repeated. "Not over a week behind the letter—if he comes straight through. But will he?" How much was there to his elaborate intention of coming to Europe and Russia anyway—irrespective of her letter? Would he stop in Hamburg for business, in Berlin for sight-seeing? It would be only decent if he did not rush straight through. But unless he did—he would not reach Zhergan before they left. They were going the day after the election. If she wrote to him at Hamburg—but what could she tell him? She did not yet know where she and Fedya were

going. To St. Petersburg only if he were elected.
And if to Rome—she and Bradfield might not meet
at all.

She laid the letter on her lap and gazed out unseeing across the sere and black-ribbed fields.
"Walt!" Pictures: the island cabin in wood-fire-
light; the launch and the lightning; the white lights
of Davenport; the Hillcrest wall and the uphill
concrete walk. Tones: the rain on rattling windows; music of infinite waters descending; the roar
of that torrent; the sound of his voice saying,
"Don't let this be the end of things between us—
it has grown too strong to break!" She had not
heard again that sincerity of passion in a human
voice.

She rose suddenly, walked through the room and
back, forbidding her mind ever to remember again
those great emotional experiences whose record
must likewise still exist in the memory of the man
with whom she had shared them. Only if these
were ignored and made as though they did not exist
could she and that man have the friendship she desired. She looked at the letter, asking herself, "Can
I show it to Fedya?" She sat down and carefully
reread it with that in view.

"Why didn't he have the sense to observe the
taboo he recognized?" she sighed, and put the letter
in her waist without deciding. She wanted Fedya
to see the criticism of the doctrine of superhumanity. He might have some convincing reply. It
would be best to copy that and burn the original.
As she went about her affairs she began systematic-

ally to reduce Walt's visit to its true importance.
To see a friend or not—important of course, but
not so world-changing as it seemed in her first surprise.

"O Fedya," said she at luncheon, "do you remember Walt Bradfield?"

"Not pleasantly."

"Of course—he was wrong that night. But you
did *hint*, Feodor. It has occurred to me lately that
he took his medicine pretty well. I have a letter
from him. He is in Hamburg, or perhaps by now
in Riga. He has an invention, a conservatory device, that has made money, and he wants to introduce it in Russia."

Count Feodor merely sniffed.

"He is coming here," she said. "Of course we
may be gone, but if not—I shall receive him."

The Count shrugged his shoulders. "One socialist more or less——!"

"I copied the philosophical part of his letter,"
she said, pushing it over to him. "I would like
your criticism of it."

"Sorry you had to take the trouble copying.
Perhaps the original was illegible."

She looked away, shaking her head over the im-
possibility of meeting insinuations which were perhaps not insinuations, and then she turned back.
"Are you criticizing me for not submitting my entire
correspondence to your censorship?"

"How absurd!"

"Then don't say things that sound spiteful!"

"Will you pardon me for reading?" He became interested at the first sentence. ". . . 'For hell read race-degeneration,' " he read, half aloud. "He has it straight. Did you write him all this?"

"Just a hint."

"Now let's see——" He finished reading. "What pleasure he takes in the idea of the basest mingling his blood with the best!" said the Count, tossing the sheet on the table.

"No, Feodor," said she gently. "What pleases him is his proof of our interest in having the basest be less base." Expecting his answer to the main argument, she saw an uneasy look in his face. Self-doubt? She was surprised.

"I never said the higher race is a certainty. It is a possibility—and undeniably it is in the power of the mob to thwart it—if they find out their power. I never said the herd would not triumph. I say it is a pity if they do."

"But who are the herd? Who are the herd's superiors?"

"It would take somewhat too long to enumerate." His tone was an orphic one that usually overawed her, but she had lost her old feeling that not to see what he saw was proof of deficient perception.

"I wanted you to meet Bradfield's objection that the existing class of rulers and owners, say in Russia, does not at all coincide with the human material that should be selected to form a higher breed. What line excludes the numerous men like your brother-in-law and includes men like Grenning?"

"So you want to include Grenning?"

That being mere evasion of defeat, she pressed him no further.

He gave her a hostile look and rose. "I hear you and he are wonderfully thick," he said.

She did not feel like speaking, she was so sorry and ashamed for him, and Count Feodor left the room, the weakness of his great dream mercilessly bare, missing the opportunity to give it heroic farewell.

XI

THREE or four days before the election the Zhergan police and Tschulitsky's Cossacks broke up a meeting addressed by Grenning, threatened him with arrest, and roughly dispersed the crowd. The faces of some of the peasants were cut with whips, and a woman was badly trampled.

In private De Hohenfels expressed scorn of such tactics, but it made him angry when Marion asked him why he did not protest publicly. She had come to regard such a protest as a psychic improbability in any man of his class. This idea of hers irritated him, and yet, as a matter of fact, he had lived so long in the habit of concealing dangerous opinions that he had come to regard anything else as a useless and foolish sacrifice of self. From his point of view, therefore, Marion was criticizing him for acting wisely, and admiring Grenning, who had come out with a scathing protest, for acting foolishly.

"If all men had your wisdom," she said to him, "the present Russian Government would endure to the end of the world."

He reproached her for getting her head full of the ideas of his political opponents.

She reminded him that she was entitled to her own political opinions.

"Herd-opinions!" he scoffed.

"Opinions leading to resolute action. We really should make good and sure of manhood before aspiring to supermanhood."

One word leading to another, she told him she did not sympathize with his desire to return to the Duma.

"May I ask if it is Baron Medin with whom you desire to replace me—in the Duma?"

"Don't be nasty, Feodor."

"If you had any respect for my wishes, you'd quit those daily visits to the Social-Democratic headquarters."

"I do not go to Sonya Demidoff's because it is the Social-Democratic headquarters—if it is. I go there because she and her friends are all that make life in Russia supportable."

"So I supposed. Particularly her friends."

"I'm sick of your insinuations. If you have anything to say, say it—like a man. If not, keep still."

"How delicately you put things!"

"I've heard too many bitter things put delicately. Since we are to leave Zhergan next week, I shall make the most of Sonya in the meantime."

"And her friends?"

"And her friends."

"Your frankness is astonishing."

"Not unless it is wilfully misunderstood. Lack of frankness is spoiling our life, Fedya."

"Lack of consideration for my wishes has something to do with the spoiling."

"There is nothing I would not do," she said with a sudden appeal to him in her eyes and voice, "—if you asked it in the spirit of love."

"Said spirit to be turned on at will like a gas-jet? You say and do things that make such a spirit impossible, and then make my not having it an excuse for the things you do."

"What things do I do?   I hold certain opinions. I see certain people.   These things need no excuse."

They went their ways without reconciliation, but Marion did not go that day or the next to Sonya's. She kept looking for a letter or telegram from Walt.   She thought by now he must be in Europe. The third morning she mentioned to her husband the fact that she had not been to the dressmaker's.

"Wonderful!" he said.

She rang for a page.   "Ironic comment is the only reward for sacrificing one's wishes to yours," she said.

"Must there be a 'reward'?"

"Do you think observing your wishes such a virtue as to be its own reward? I do not." She told the page to have Davuidka bring around the carriage.   "I am going to Sonya's," she said, and went to put on her coat and hat.

It was the day before election.   Marion had almost given up hope of Walt's coming in time.   If he did not let her know where to reach him, the best she could do was to let him come to Zhergan and leave there a letter telling him where she and Fedya had gone.   Her thoughts turning to Sonya, who was about to drop out of her life, she began to get the blues.   It was a shame she had sacrificed—for no result—these last two days.   It might well be that Grenning would now be too busy with the election to have the farewell talk she had planned.

As her carriage passed the brickyard and came in sight of the railway station, Davuidka called, "The soldiers!" and pointed with his whip to a line of white tunics and bayonets. They were drawn up in front of the passenger coach of the train about to leave for Mitau.

As the Hohenfels droshky came closer, a man with his wrists handcuffed was pushed into one of the compartments. Before the door was shut on him, he turned to look back at someone in the crowd. Marion saw that it was Grenning. His face was white and grim, his head held as though the blow of a rifle-butt on the side of it would not have made his neck bend.

Marion ordered Davuidka to turn back to the station gate. He obeyed mechanically, and then, too late for any possible effect, voiced his protest: "Better keep away from there, little mistress!"

She did not even hear him. She sprang from the carriage and hastened through the station with the feeling that somehow she must put a stop to that. There were forty or fifty people kept back from the train by the wall of soldiers. In the crowd she caught sight of Sonya, and started toward her. Sonya ran to meet her. "I want money," she said, under her breath. "Have you money? Quick if you have—I must get a ticket for Riga."

Marion reached for her purse.

"Don't give it to her," said a man's voice at Marion's elbow. She gave a start, then saw it was Kaminsky. "Sonya: they'll spot you if you rush off on this train. You have no permit. You haven't even closed your shop."

"You close it."

Kaminsky turned to Marion. "Don't give her money till after this train goes," he urged.

"She is judge of her own acts," said Marion, and opened her purse.

Kaminsky shook his head, his eyes on Marion's. "They'll get her sure if you do!" warned he. The train-guard closed the last compartment, signaled the engineer, and the train started. A look of relief came into Kaminsky's eyes, and into Sonya's a look of sheer despair. As the coach glided by, they looked, but could not see Grenning. At the window of his compartment sat soldiers. Sonya gave them a look of hatred. "If only everyone hadn't been at work!" groaned she.

"You can go tonight, Sonya," said Kaminsky. "It is ever so much better. I will go with you. Zhergan is getting too hot. I promise you I will do all man can do in Riga for Grenning. But it can't be done in an hour, nor a day. You and I must disappear from the knowledge of the police. Grenning may have to tell them about us."

"He never will!" cried Sonya.

"We will get permits to go to Odessa, but in Mitau our official existence ends—pointing toward Odessa. Another man and woman will arrive in Riga late tonight."

"How about me?" asked Marion.

"Leave Russia."

"Grenning will never tell them about us," insisted Sonya.

"*Grenning* won't," said Kaminsky.

Sonya writhed.

"Sikorsky is looking at us," warned Kaminsky. "He will know Grenning is our only business at this train."

To Sikorsky personally the three were two women who had resisted his charms, and a Jew—the despised race.

"Can you come to Sonya's?" asked Kaminsky.

"Yes. Come both of you in my carriage."

"Not all three. Take Sonya. I'll join you." He turned and walked away.

The two went out and got into the carriage. "Can it be they have arrested Grenning merely to prevent his election?" asked Marion hopefully as they drove away from the station. She spoke French so Davuidka could not understand.

Sonya shook her head.

"What do you hope to do in Riga, Sonya? I know you must go—for your own sake, but what have you planned?"

"I must get poison to him."

Her quietness was uncanny, suggesting to Marion that the shock of seeing the arrest and the thought of what it meant had unbalanced her. How could a normal mind accept that terrible conclusion as inevitable? Was Kaminsky's talk of doing something in Riga meant only to lessen Sonya's despair?

"He may not know enough to take poison—when they finish."

The horror deepened for Marion, but she gave up the idea of madness in Sonya. But what hopelessness! She remembered Prince Demidoff. His daughter had hoped too long in vain.

They left the carriage at the inn stable. As they

drove up, the hostler was saying to a well-to-do muzhik, "Vote for him anyway." When they saw Sonya, the two men gave her a look of comprehension and sympathy.

As they walked to Sonya's, Marion tried to get the girl to think of what she was to do with her books and things. That only made her think of Grenning's books and instruments there in his rooms unused. The police had locked and sealed the doors and taken the keys.

At the shop they met Fritz Dumpe with Sonya's mail. "Oh—our mail!" exclaimed Marion. "Let me see the mail for the manor!" The postman found it and handed it to her. She ran it over. Nothing!

The mail-carrier wanted to know about Grenning. "If Mitrevitz only knew!" he exclaimed. "Mitrevitz would stop the train and take Grenning off."

Sonya's eyes lit up, but only for an instant. There was no possible way to let Mitrevitz know. Dumpe gave her her mail. "You might as well take Kaminsky's too," he said. "No use leaving it lie around. There's a letter from Riga—came this morning. The censor doesn't get a chance to read Kaminsky's letters." He gave a wink. The limit he had placed on the otherwise unlimited power of the censor was pure joy to him.

"Comrade Dumpe," said Marion, "does the censor ever hold out letters for the manor?"

"I never thought to see. I can find out. He didn't use to. Does it matter—much, I mean?"

"I'm expecting nothing political," said Marion.

"I was just wondering—yes, find out if any letter for me has not been delivered. I don't think anything can ever darken the world for you, Comrade Dumpe," she ended, glancing at Sonya. At "comrade" as a substitute for the "master" disguised in "Mr.," the Countess had sometimes smiled—as a piece of make-believe—a pretense that the visioned future was already here; but addressing the mail-carrier, she found no other form of speech that sounded right.

Comrade Dumpe admitted he liked being alive.

When Kaminsky came, Marion gave him the letter from Riga, and waited to see if it threw any light on the arrest.

Kaminsky tore it open, and sat down to read it. It was in familiar cipher. The others watched his expression. "Smika is a maniac," he said. "Somewhere in the ruins they learned of Grenning."

"In the ruins of Grenning will they learn of *us?*" thought Marion.

"Why didn't your man telegraph?" Sonya demanded passionately.

Kaminsky shook his head. "The night operator here is against us. Listen to this. It's from our man in the detective division of the Riga police. 'I can't stay here much longer. If I did, I'd turn monster like Gregus and Davus. I make an excuse to be away from the torture chamber, and then find a horrible fascination drawing me to it. I understand now how the autocracy can get men to do this work. They come to crave it.' "

Sonya sprang up, gave Kaminsky a look of bitterness, and went out into the shop.

"I think she understands," said Kaminsky. "It hits too hard—now. Do you understand?"

"Understand! Absolutely not."

"You ought to. This is good propaganda. He read: 'The shock on the nerves of a man who tears out another's finger-nail and feels his victim quiver is intense. This intense sensation soon becomes an object of desire. I understand the cat with the mouse. I understand the tortures inflicted by savages. I understand Gregus and Davus and Zimmermann. The trade of Gregus has reshaped him —in a way I do not care to be reshaped. The sight of someone's agony is all that gives him sexual gratification. He awaits the hour of torture as a normal youth awaits a night with a woman. For women he cares nothing. Davus is still one step from that. He rushed from the torture chamber to wreak his lust upon the women of the town. I think probably the savages who gave no sign of pain under torture so acted in order to deprive their enemies of actual physical gratification. Gregus and Davus and Zimmermann are not so robbed of their delight by modern victims. There are screams of horror that go to the marrow of whomsoever hears.' "

"Is there no one to kill these men?" said Marion hoarsely. Something that had been soft in her soul seemed to harden into steel.

"Yes," Kaminsky answered, significantly. "Or better—the men who set these at this work. Do you blame the Social Revolutionists for looking coldly on a parliament called by this government? Do you blame us for grasping terrorism as a weapon?"

"I blame you for nothing! I could kill these men with my own hands! I blame the civilized world for permitting such a régime as this to remain on earth!"

"Permitting it! The financiers of the civilized world *maintain* it! The wages of Gregus are paid with the money of New York bondbuyers."

"Yes," thought Marion bitterly, "and Feodor de Hohenfels maintains it!"

Sonya came and stood in the doorway. "Nachman," she said, passionately, "the thing to think about today is Grenning on his way to the claws of Gregus!"

"As though I were not here shaping a force for his deliverance!" thought Kaminsky resentfully; but instead of defending himself, he preferred to let Marion suspect him of lukewarmness, knowing with quick instinct that if she did not place too much faith in him she would feel more powerfully the impulse to act herself. She looked at him expectantly, and he kept silent.

"What are you going to do?" she asked.

"I will not know till I get to Riga and see."

"Why can't your police confederate contrive Grenning's escape?"

"I don't know. But he would have contrived Smika's if he had had the power."

"He can carry poison," said Sonya, softly. "Poison is beautiful, unruining death!"

"Sonya, why do you think of the last resort first?" cried Marion. "Kaminsky, can these insane beasts be bought?"

"Undoubtedly they can," replied the Jew. "Only

—what of the buyer? His offer is a confession of complicity. What is to prevent their seizing him?"

Marion looked at him with a decreasing opinion of his courage and resourcefulness. "Some way must be found!" she said. "What time does your train go tonight?"

"Seven o'clock."

"We are going anyhow day after tomorrow," she mused.

"Day after tomorrow is long enough to make the Grenning you knew a maimed old man!" cried Sonya. "Come to Riga tonight."

"I may have to, to get the money," said Marion. She saw the situation calling for the sacrifice of her last chance of being in Zhergan when Walt arrived. "How much do you think it will take, Kaminsky?"

"I do not know. We have never had enough money to try it."

"Five thousand roubles? Ten thousand? Twenty-five?"

"Really I've no idea. Terrible things are done for much less than five thousand. But the larger the sum the greater temptation—and surer result."

"Could I give you a check on Riga?"

"A check! To establish my connection with you, and yours with me, make me declare my presence officially in Riga, and——"

"No, no," she interrupted. "I see it won't do." She wondered what excuse she could give Feodor. Well, he would have to think what he would. "I'll go tonight," she said, and rose.

"Much the best," said Kaminsky. "They cannot lay hands on you so easily in a large city. Riga is a door from Russia. If necessary we can slip you through on an emigrant ship."

Sonya came and clung to Marion and sobbed convulsively.

"You—of all people, Sonya!"

Sonya tried in vain to stop. "I could—stand everything—till I began to *hope!*"

All that day at home Marion was tense with feeling of danger and uncertainty. At luncheon she could not eat. In her mind ideas independent of her will were blazing, leading to others, passing. "It thought" within her—as one says "it rains." She no longer felt free as of old to choose her way. Her way was being marked for her—by things, events, outside herself. She had to follow the marks. She noticed the visible beat of her pulse in two places on her wrist. She nodded to the servants to withdraw.

"Did you hear about Grenning?" She spoke with a calmness that both surprised and reassured her.

"Kronberg came and told me," replied Count Feodor.

"Are you going to do anything?"

"I?"

"I thought you might wish to use your influence to keep a man like that from being tortured."

"I fail to see——" He paused.

She waited.

"No," he said. "I have no reason to suppose him innocent of the charge against him. If I

thought it was merely pity for the man which moved
you——"

"What then?"

He smiled. "I should then preach a sermon on the
morbid psychology of pity."

She was anything but amused. "What is the
charge against Grenning?"

"Being a spy. Giving secret information to Mitrevitz. Apparently it's about the thing Sikorsky
wanted to accuse me of." He said this nonchalant-
ly; then suddenly looked keenly at Marion. He
leaned abruptly forward, his elbow on the table,
palm up, forefinger pointing toward her, and opened
his lips to speak—then checked his fierce question,
sat back, and was thinking hard.

"I am going to Riga tonight," she said.

"What for?"

"To free Grenning."

He tried to beat down her eyes with his. She
paid no attention, and went on, "I may have to stay
for a time in Riga. I can rejoin you from there
in——" She started to say St. Petersburg, but remembered that that city was located in Russia. "If
Bradfield comes here before you leave, I wish you
would tell him to come to see me in Riga. I will
have to send you my Riga address tomorrow."

"Is this an avowal of your liaison?" demanded
Count Feodor.

"No—since I have none."

"The information Grenning is accused of furnishing was contained in the Governor General's letter
which I read to you. Where did Grenning get it?

Did *you* tell him about that intended night attack?"

"If I had, it would imply no liaison."

"Why then should you tell him?"

She gave a gesture of impatience. "I may as well tell you. I did not give that or any other information to Grenning. He is no spy. That information crossed the chasm from government to revolutionist when it passed from you to me. It reached Mitrevitz—through me!"

"What treachery!" He spoke with loathing. "A spy in one's own bed!"

"Treachery! To what? The Russian government? I hate and despise it! My motive when I did it was merely to save Mitrevitz and his men from its horrible tortures. Since then I have advanced. I would do it now to help destroy your hateful government."

"I am not a supporter of the government."

"What childish folly! You are! You fight the only forces that can end it. And it supports you— your property, your title. For all you have ever done or will do the bureaucracy would go on unchanged forever. You profit by the grinding of the people which it decrees and bloodily enforces. In music you try to exalt existing economic misery—as something beautiful!"

"Don't go into esthetics. You know nothing about it. In all you say about this business you show yourself morally obtuse. That act of yours was treachery to *me!*"

"How unconsciously and completely you identify your interest with that of the government! Don't say treachery to me! A man who sends government troops against the revolutionists is a traitor to the Russian people!"

"And I took you for a natural aristocrat! You are simply crazy with your democratic rot!"

"One must be a block of wood to remain sane in Russia."

"Do you realize that I swore to Sikorsky that I had revealed the government plans to *no one?* What do you suppose will happen when what you have done comes out?"

"Is that all you can think of—that you may be caught in a lie—a lie you were proud of—when what I have done comes out?"

He saw scorn deepening in her eyes, and turned red. "Do you expect to go on living with me?" he demanded.

"I have been wondering. I had not made up my mind. But——"

"Yes, 'but'! You hate the government, and however falsely, you identify me with it. The inference is obvious."

"I do not hate you. I made up my mind this morning to be guilty of no more well-intentioned deceit toward you. I meant to tell you that I no longer have any respect for any Russian who is not a revolutionist. But now—a man whose wife may be given into the hands of insane human beasts——And you think only of some inconvenience to yourself! One can approve the egotism of a large nature. But this! You have a very much smaller soul than I thought possible!"

"That is too much! Insults like these are unforgivable. Our living together is out of the question."

She sat quiet a moment, wondering that the final knowledge of the death of love should be so pain-less. "I thank you—really—for deciding. I give you credit for at least not pretending to feel things you do not."

"I find I have no talent for husbandhood," he said, relieved of his fear of heroics. "Approach and capture charm. Possession cloys."

"Possession? Yes, that is your antique error! Oh, I am glad we have no baby!" She rose quickly, left the room, ran upstairs, and locked her door,—before she broke down.

XII

NEXT morning the Countess de Hohenfels's slumber was broken by the unaccustomed clink of iron-shod hoofs on paving-stones, the rumble of wheels, the melancholy chant of city street cries. She knew it could not be Chicago; she was afraid it was St. Petersburg; and then linking the life of to-day with that of yesterday, she made out the large hotel room in which she lay alone, and murmured "Riga!" Riga, she knew, was more strange and terrible than St. Petersburg, but why? "Grenning!" Somewhere in this city lay Grenning. Already Gregus must have laid eyes on him—eyes of terrible lust! That was the overtowering, difficult, immediate thing—to free Grenning! She looked at her watch. It was too early to do anything, but her desire for action, her feeling that an unforeseen emergency might arise at any time, forced her to rise and begin dressing.

The events of the night before crowded through her mind—her departure alone—driven for the last time by Davuidka—the lights of Feyda's manor far in the night—last seen from her car window—the railway journey with Sonya, tense to the breaking point, and Kaminsky, watching everyone without showing it—her open farewell to the two, acted for the benefit of detectives in Mitau. There the revolutionists were to help Sonya and Kaminsky change their names, passports, destinations, clothes, professions, personalities. They would leave Mitau a third-guild leather-merchant and his wife. They must be now in Riga—in rooms over a German bookseller's in the Kaufstrasse. Marion wanted to rejoin Sonya as soon as possible. Sonya had urged her to leave them what money she could and get away from Russia at once, but the girl was under terrible strain, was likely to go all to pieces if they failed to save Grenning, and Marion definitely declined to leave the best friend she had in Russia like that. She was going to stay till Grenning was free—or all hope gone. The Countess de Hohenfels was to exist just long enough to get her money from the Riga bank. She had written from Zhergan that she would call personally this morning. As soon as she had that money the Countess would disappear.

She was sorry for Walt—and for herself—after his long journey from America. He would try to trace her and would lose the trail. There seemed to be no help for it. The nets were being drawn too tight to risk exposure a single unnecessary hour. The hotel people might already be asking how it happened that the Countess de Hohenfels came in in the night alone. Wishing now that she had learned to use it better, she took from beneath the bed and put into her handbag her automatic pistol. Fedya had given it to her. The thought of Fedya, the memory of the first days of their marriage, swept her soul. She stood still, thinking; then slowly

shook her head. The thought of him had nothing
for her but deadening of heart. It was over!

Her soul had been arctic yesterday afternoon in
that final, formal conference in which Count Feodor discussed the question of divorce. He assured
her that under ordinary circumstances he would of
course think of nothing but of allowing her to obtain it—though the Russian law would not in that
case permit him to remarry. "Not that I wish to
remarry," he explained, "—at least till after I have
lived the best of life. But the time will come when
there should be an heir to the name of Hohenfels.
Of course legitimization is possible, but—since you
will not live in Russia, and will therefore not be
subject to the restrictions of the Russian law——"

"Of course," she had answered. "Obtain the divorce yourself."

"Thank you. Is there any reason for delay in
the matter?"

"I have none." It did not seem real to her—
the iron tone between her and the man who had been
her lover and her husband.

She had impressed even herself as a person without emotion. Mayor Ronke had come at her re-
quest to the manor. She empowered him to act as
her advocate in the suit to be brought in Mitau, in-
structing him not to contest. Through him she com-
pleted arrangements for the transfer to the Count
de Hohenfels of the Zhergan estate and her Kieff-
Vorones stock, and the Mayor, dazed by the magnitude of his realized and prospective fees, sent her
her police permit to leave Zhergan and the passport entitling her to leave Russia. She was dubious,

in view of her known friendship with Grenning, whether the national and Riga authorities would permit her to leave. She was not at all sure that Tschulitsky and Sikorsky, connecting her flight with Grenning's arrest, would not today be taking steps through the detective division—— She shuddered, opened her handbag, made sure again of the readiness of the pistol.

She met no obstacles, after her coffee and rolls, in paying her hotel bill, conveying the impression that she was leaving that day for America, and getting away in a cab for the Bank of Riga. Watching the sidewalk crowds it struck her that Bradfield might this very day be passing through Riga on his way to Zhergan; and as soon as she began to look for him several men at a distance resembled him.

At the bank, a distinguished-looking polyglot gentleman with frock-coat and monocle received her with formal hospitality in a room with semipartitions of hard wood—a room carefully unsuggestive of bookkeeping. After waiting a few minutes in trepidation lest they should require inconvenient identification, the Countess learned that they had received her letter. She made out a check for the exact amount that stood to her credit in the house— nearly thirty thousand roubles.

The bank-clerk asked in what form she desired the money, noted her reply on a small piece of paper, touched a button, and with no word spoken, handed check and note to a uniformed bank messenger, and made a polite remark about the weather. In a few minutes the messenger returned with a few gold and

silver coins, stacked on a little green felt mat on a
salver, and three packets of bank-notes—ten one
thousand rouble notes, the rest in hundreds—the
largest denomination the men for whom the money
was intended might be willing to accept.

Noting her dismay at the bulk of the packets, the
clerk observed it was quite a sum to carry personally.

She explained that she was about to make a visit
to America—whereat the financial gentleman looked
surprised. "We can furnish you with American cur-
rency," he said.

She mentioned obligations to be met before she
sailed, put the Russian money in her handbag, and
left the bank uneasy. No one appeared to be following her, but instead of driving to her rendezvous
in the Kaufstrasse she went to the warehouse of the
United States Plow Company, leaving her cab in
front of the office.

Introducing herself to her father's Riga agent,
and incidentally saying things that convinced him
she was really the president's daughter, she arranged to have her trunks and boxes coming from
Zhergan received and held subject to her order.
The American gave her sailing lists of the steamers
out of Riga. She noticed that there were none after
November, the gulf being ice-bound in mid-winter.
On the pretense of wishing to see it, she went
through the warehouse. Recognizing a young man
she had known by sight in Moline, she felt like hug-
ging him. She asked him his name, and inadvertently left him full of visions of romantic promotion.
She gave him the money to pay off the cabman

in front of the office—after awhile—and went out
on the other side of the great warehouse.

On foot, suit case in one hand, in the other the
handbag whose loss would be fatal, she found the
crowded Kaufstrasse, and the number, and the near-
sighted German bookseller's, and climbed to a not
very elegant third-story furnished flat. Sonya was
there waiting. Marion held her in her arms. She
would hardly have recognized her. Poor Sonya! It
was not wholly the artificial changes that disguised
and aged her. Thoughts that came in the night
must have been dreadful to her.

Kaminsky had not yet returned from an interview
with his informant of the detective division—the
revolutionary spy in the third section of the Riga
police, from whom he expected to learn just what
could be done for Grenning.

Sonya had already been out and located the prison
in which Grenning was confined. It stood in a small,
irregular, cobble-stoned plaza. The narrow, pre-
Russian streets that led to it ran up-hill, and from it
there was a distant glimpse of the Dwina sliding
to the gulf. It was a long, gray-plastered, three-
story building with iron-shuttered windows, not much
different from the surrounding buildings except that
its walls bore no crudely frescoed pictures of boots,
keys, clothing, or other objects for sale. From the
front the only places Sonya could see into were a
wide doorway opening into a corridor paved with
square brown bricks or tiles, and beside this a small
uncarpeted business office with roller-top desks, low
pilastered wooden railings with gates, and two or
three black horsehair sofas somewhat humpy and

worn through in spots to dingy once-white canvas. There was an ikon in one corner, and a gilt-framed, fly-specked lithograph of Tsar Nicholas II on the unpapered wall.

There were buildings or blind walls across the streets and alleys which, at one time, had led past the rear of that tragic, commonplace-looking structure, in some dim cell of which sat Ferdinand Grenning, still a high-souled, unmutilated man with surgeon's fingers still sound and flexible. Walking past casually, her eyes taking in everything with the intensity of fever, went Sonya Demidoff, who loved that man, and knew her native land as a place unfit for the mating of man and woman.

Sonya going to answer a knock at the door of the apartment, Marion instinctively caught up her handbag, thinking how useless her pistol would be shut away with the money inside the bag. The tradesman Sonya permitted to walk in past her looked at Marion with a grunt of satisfaction. "I see you got it," said he, nodding at the handbag, and she finally realized it was Kaminsky.

He told them there were fifteen revolutionists besides Grenning and Smika being held in the central prison and in the station of the detective division for trial by a field court-martial which might not sit for several weeks. It was illegal extension of the powers of the field court-martial, but seeking legal redress was futile. The third section would have ample time in which to secure "confessions." He did not tell the women that Grenning had already been taken to look at the glaring, cowering wreck of the forester Smika—in order that a vivid picture of what was in store for him might be working on his mind.

"What's to be done for Grenning?" demanded Sonya.

"We thought of two things," said Kaminsky. "Comrade M. will be in charge of the station next Wednesday night. If he ordered the warder and turnkey to release Grenning there is no way to keep Thursday morning's investigation from locating responsibility."

"Let M. do it and leave Russia with us," Marion urged.

Kaminsky shook his head. "He is much too valuable where he is." He looked at Marion. "No one man among *us*," he said, "need expect to have the interests of many sacrificed for him. Let me do Grenning justice—he would not have it."

Sonya and Marion exchanged a glance recognizing the predominance of the Cause. "I do not see that he's of much value if he can't keep men from being tortured," said Marion unreasonably.

"Do you remember he let us know of Smika's arrest? And when Smika told of Grenning, Grenning was warned by M. through me."

"Is that warning to be made a reason for doing nothing for Grenning?" flashed Sonya.

"No, Sonya. M. will try the other thing we thought of. It's this: the first chance he gets he's going to let Davus know there's ten thousand roubles for the escape of Grenning—non-political source—personal interest of a wealthy noblewoman. Davus is chief—would investigate himself. M. will merely mention as a piece of gossip that this offer has been made to him. Davus may look it up himself,

The drawback is—someone has to be named finally as the person who will pay the money, and if Davus double-crosses——"

"Tell M. to name me," said Sonya. "I am here for just that thing."

"Not exactly," said Kaminsky. "If that has to be done I'll do it—with every precaution. We might be able to leave the money in a stipulated place. The whole thing depends on how Davus reacts. You mustn't expect the very first thing we try to succeed, Sonya. You must be patient. It may be two or three days before M. can find the right time and place to speak to Davus." He turned to Marion. "Are you going to sail?"

"Why no," she answered. "We settled that last night."

"Are you sure you don't want to? Do you realize the risk?"

"I realize. I can't leave."

"All right. In that case a woman, an English governess out of a place, will sail to-day for London as Countess de Hohenfels. We pay her passage and five hundred roubles in consideration of risk of arrest. Give me the money, your passport, etc., and I'll bring you hers. No, I'll bring new papers and you'll not risk being found ignorant of your own history. You are Miss Baker, fresh from England, looking for a governess's place. Make yourself older, not so good-looking."

Marion gave him the money and papers.

"You understand the advantage," he said. "The police mark you down out of the country and won't

look for you here if Grenning—if in any way—
through your husband, through anyone in Zhergan—they trace to you that message warning
Mitrevitz."

He went to close the bargain with the Englishwoman and came back at noon with Miss Baker's
English passport, registered and stamped with the
regular notice that she could not leave Russia without a police permit. He also had the police permit
—signed but undated, and proper papers for Sonya,
Grenning, and himself—though he said he himself
would not leave the country unless some new de-
velopments made his stay too risky.

An event next morning made Marion think it
risky enough as it was. She was playing the un-
wonted rôle of housemaid, cleaning her room after
breakfast, when she heard Sonya and Kaminsky
talking with some men in the front room. She looked
in, and nearly dropped at the sight of two police
officers, questioning Sonya and Kaminsky and making notes of their replies. "Traced from Zhergan!"
thought she. "They've established our connection
with Grenning."

"And you?" demanded one of the officers, glaring
at her.

"I don't understand," she said.

"She doesn't speak much Russian," said Sonya.

"The Englishwoman?" asked the other officer.

"Yes," said Kaminsky. "The roomer."

Marion saw a gleam of hope.

"They'll want to see your passport," said Sonya
in French.

Going to get it, Marion had a moment to recover, to hide her thirty thousand roubles, and throw herself into her part.

At the close of their domiciliary visit the officers informed the leather merchant that he was fined one hundred roubles for taking up residence without permit. Kaminsky protested that the party who sublet him the apartment told him he would make everything straight with the authorities. Finally yielding the principle sullenly in the face of mysterious threats, he made the officers think he could not scrape up one hundred roubles between himself and his wife, and appealed to their roomer, Miss Baker, to advance them enough to make up the fine. The officers pocketed it and departed, satisfied they had secured all the traffic would bear.

As soon as they were gone Marion nearly collapsed.

"They might have caught us at a worse time," said Kaminsky consolingly. "These petty grafters are not the ones we have to look out for. They consider us dry for the present. It was a little hard on you, Countess Marion, because you didn't know their brand. You'll have more confidence next time."

They scanned the evening paper for indication whether the sham Countess de Hohenfels had been intercepted at the dock.

"Here!" exclaimed Sonya, catching the name Countess de Hohenfels. They found it was a dispatch from Mitau announcing that Count Feodor de Hohenfels had filed a petition for divorce from the Countess Marion, his American wife, and that the case would be heard at an early date before the Magistrate Intendant Bratavzinsky. Count Feodor, the dispatch added, was being detained, until after the hearing, from an important journey to Rome.

"What an inconvenience!" murmured Marion.

Sonya came and put her arm around her. "You didn't tell me this," she said reproachfully. "Have I been too full of my own fear and grief?"

"How could you help it?" answered Marion, shuddering. "I am not so much in need of sympathy now—for this—the mere legal forms. The real end of things was when love flickered and went out."

To Kaminsky, who would have allowed neither Russian state nor church to sanction or dissolve a marriage of his, Marion's view of it was so much a platitude that he took refuge from it in the election reports.

"Here's a dispatch from Zhergan," he said, and read: "The judges of election threw out the votes of Dr. Ferdinand Grenning, Social-Democrat, issuing a statement that he had furnished secret information to a band of outlaws and marauders guilty of armed resistance to the authority of Holy Russia."

"But he hasn't been tried!" cried Marion. "How can those election judges say that?"

"The odd thing about it is that for once their statement happens to be true," said Kaminsky.

"Outlaws and marauders isn't true."

"Marauders isn't. Baron Medin, Conservative, was declared elected, he having a majority of the legal votes."

"That's why Count Hohenfels is going to Rome,"

said Marion, adding mentally "—and Callignano."
She found no pang of jealousy in the thought.

"Grenning is legally a member of the Duma,"
mused Kaminsky. "Unless we buy his way out, it
will be a member of the imperial Duma here in
Riga that they———"

"It doesn't say he had a majority," objected Sonya.

"They would not otherwise have bothered to
throw out his vote."

"Oh!" cried Sonya. "Just one more day! If
Smika had held out another day Ferdinand would
have been protected by uncontested Duma member-
ship!"

"Do you think that would have stopped them,
Sonya? Don't break your heart about that!"

"And here we are doing nothing!" cried Sonya.
"We ought not to rely on M. He does nothing
because of his idea it's wrong to single out one man
and do anything for him!"

"Only when doing something for one will hurt
the others. M. is doing what he can. I didn't tell
you because it came to nothing, but yesterday he approached the officer who will be in charge of the
station tonight. He let him know there was ten
thousand roubles for the escape of a prisoner, thinking this particular officer, who has not yet acquired
a taste for torture, would consider ten thousand
worth more than his job. The man did, too. He
would have been ours but for his fear that M. was a
government spotter."

"The revolutionary police spy feared as a government spotter!" thought Marion, seeing more clear-

ly the great net of treachery and countertreachery whose meshes run through Russia.

Kaminsky found out that evening that the ostensible Countess de Hohenfels had not been prevented from sailing. But two days later, on Sunday, they learned from Sasha Bratavzinsky, just from Zhergan, by how narrow a margin she had got through. Yan Sarin, informed of it by the Zhergan day operator, had sent Sasha to tell Kaminsky of a cipher telegram sent to the Riga police that morning calling on them to arrest the Countess de Hohenfels. Riga had replied that the Countess had sailed for London Thursday. Sarin supposed she had, but for Kaminsky's sake and Sonya's, wanted them to know just how much the police knew. Bratavzinsky was astonished when he found Marion still with them.

"What made them call for the Countess's arrest, Sasha?" asked Kaminsky.

Sasha glanced at the Countess. "The testimony in the divorce case yesterday in Mitau. I suppose you know about it."

"No," said Marion, her lips setting firmly. "How should we? Was that in the papers too? What was it?"

"I didn't see it in the papers, but the divorce was granted—by that unspeakable uncle of mine—on the ground of improper relations with Dr. Grenning. Sikorsky and the Zhergan detectives jumped at a political connection."

A hard light came into Marion's eyes. "So he did that!" she exclaimed. "He never told me there'd be such a charge as that. I left it to him, taking it for granted he'd be decent."

"Give the devil his due," said Kaminsky quietly. "There had to be such a charge if there was to be a decree. Everybody understands that."

"I didn't understand it!" blazed Marion. "Count Feodor knew I didn't. My people won't understand it."

"Need they hear the details?"

"What possible evidence could he present?" she demanded of Bratavzinsky.

"Trina Ronke testified to seeing you come out of the doctor's office one day and—she gave the thing the proper color."

"The little beast!" exclaimed Marion. "Her father in charge of my case—did he let that testimony of hers stand?"

"Did you instruct him to contest the case?" asked Kaminsky.

"I did not know it would be *such* a case!"

"What's the difference, Marion?" said Sonya. "The whole thing is of that dreadful shackled world we're out of. If chains are cut or broken, what's the difference?"

"Even in your own Russian circle, Countess Marion," said Kaminsky, "since they *have* to have divorce, and since they will not leave it to the people who best know whether it's necessary, this kind of testimony is simply a legal necessity and is so understood. Of course with your double standard—the men of your class don't suffer and it's usually the woman who gets the divorce. Outside of high society most thinking people no longer bother with the law at all. The serious thing in this case is the political significance they attach to your connection

with Grenning. Count Hohenfels should have waited till you were out of the country."

"He may have heard she sailed," said Sonya.

"And he may have been in such a hurry to get to
Rome, he didn't care!" retorted Marion.

She sat down and wrote a letter to her father,
though she dared not mail it till after she was out
of Russia. The real facts would set her straight
with him at least, though she could hear his inevitable "I told you so."

Imbued as she was with the ideas of her American
training, she could not accept the point of view of
Sonya and Kaminsky. They discounted the crude
complication forced by the antiquated divorce law
into the delicate human problem. Her it embittered
beyond all possibility of future reconciliation with
the man who had accused her falsely before the
world.

XIII

SHAKING snow from their hats, Sonya and Marion came into their apartment after luncheon; and Kaminsky, stretched out on a lounge, woke up, looked at his watch, and growled because he had been asleep. They paid no attention to him.

"Snowing?" he said, looking at their coats. "I've had no lunch." He went to the window. "Say, I meant to tell you last night. Bratavzinsky threw me off. M. told me yesterday. Might interest you."

"Well, out with it," said Sonya.

"They've got an American in the station."

"An American?"

"Yes. They arrested him yesterday—day before yesterday."

"What for?" asked Marion, stopping.

"They read some letter of his saying he was going to write up the Russian revolution for some American socialist magazine."

"What!" gasped Marion, dropping her coat. "What is his name?"

Kaminsky had not asked.

"But I have a friend coming! He wrote that very thing in a letter to me. Was this man's name Bradfield? Walt Bradfield?"

"Didn't hear his name."

"Your gardener!" exclaimed Sonya.

"What a thing to arrest a man for!" cried Marion. "They must have read his letter to me. How long have they had this man? Where did he come from?"

"Saturday's steamer from Hamburg."

"But Hamburg is where Bradfield landed from America last week! Oh, it's he! Kaminsky, what will they do to him? What can they do to him?"

"They probably expect to change his mind as to the desirability of studying contemporary Russian history in Russia."

"I am going to the American consul," said Marion.

"You are an Englishwoman," objected Kaminsky.

"I am Dave Moulton's daughter!" Her eyes flashed with pleasure, picturing the energy she would put into that consul. She went to the mirror and rubbed energetically at Miss Baker's make-up.

"Don't you realize you can't possibly appear in your real character in Riga?" demanded Kaminsky, thoroughly awake. "Do you think the business we're in here is some fool girl's masquerade? You'll upset everything. If the police learn you're in Riga —it's sheer madness!"

Marion stopped and thought. "The consul is not going to compare the time I see him with the time I officially sailed. What's more, I'll tell him I'm incognito for personal reasons. He probably knows about this wretched divorce. He'll keep still. There isn't one chance in a hundred that the discrepancy will ever come to anybody's attention. If it does, somebody's memory for dates is poor. I can't afford to throw away the influence of my relation to one of the most important American interests in Riga. My father could have this consul removed if he wanted to. It won't take me an hour."

Kaminsky argued in vain. She restored her youth and good looks, took a cab to the consul's office, saw him, charmed him, convinced him of her relation to Moulton of U. S. Plow, informed him that she was strictly incognito in Riga, swore him to secrecy concerning her and her interest in the Bradfield case, made him call in one of the best lawyers in the city— to be paid through the office of the Plow Company— and sent the two of them personally to the detective station to secure Walt Bradfield's immediate release. Having arranged it, she departed charging them to bring Mr. Bradfield back with them to the consulate. There would be a man there to take charge of him.

Ten minutes at the U. S. Plow Company office and she had the attorney's fee provided for and the services of the Moline youth, Mr. Benson, at her disposal. She sent him to the consulate to meet Bradfield and take him to the warehouse. "I'll send a man here," she said "—a Jewish leather merchant— he doesn't speak English. Turn Mr. Bradfield over to him. Send them out the other side of the building—to shake these vile Russian detectives that watch everybody."

She returned to appease Kaminsky, assure him there was no harm done, and coax him to go to the Plow Company office. When the time came he went, coerced by her threat to go back herself, but told her it would have been a thousand times better for them all if it were the real, and not a sham Countess

de Hohenfels who had steamed out of the Gulf of
Riga.

"If you could only do that for Ferdinand!" sighed
Sonya, as Kaminsky went out.

Marion clasped the girl's hands. "I wish I could!
How I wish I could! I'd give up anything, Sonya.
I'd give up—seeing Walt. I'd give it up forever!
Do you grudge my seeing him? I don't want to turn
bitter at my age. It seems to me now he's my only
chance of not hating the world. I had forgotten
how much I ought to see him—till I heard he was
here in prison. Sonya, my heart has been simply
frozen all these months! Frozen, frozen!" She
stood a moment silent by the window. "Walt's coming! Walt's coming!" whispered some hidden joy
within her that would not, could not, kill itself because another woman's joy was in danger of dreadful
death.

"I should think so!" muttered Sonya. "That man
of ice!" Her thoughts snapped back to Grenning.
It hurt. If it were only Grenning who was to walk
out of that grim building! It did not seem fair.
"They wouldn't torture Bradfield if he did stay!"
cried she, the words wrung out of her.

Marion winced. "I feel utterly selfish," she said,
and sat down searching her conscience. How was it
she had suddenly laid hold of so much power to save
Walt when she had so little for Grenning? She explained it point by point to herself, and proved it,
and yet felt wretched. Her father's name was magic
with the consul; theoretically the consul *should* have
taken up the case of an arrested American anyway.
Walt's case was trivial beside Grenning's in the eyes

of the Russian authorities. Though she filled the
cables with appeals to her father, he would not
touch the Grenning case. Kaminsky had said lawyers
for Grenning would be futile. "Sonya!" she demanded, "is there anything I can do for Ferdinand
—beyond furnishing money?"

"I wish you had waited a day or two, and somehow—perhaps they couldn't. But M. in there *might*
have arranged the mistake of sending Ferdinand out
as Bradfield. Afterwards they'd have had to let
Bradfield go just the same."

"Unless they held him for conspiring to release
Grenning. But it's too late now, Sonya. Walt must
be out by now."

An hour later Kaminsky returned from the warehouse. Marion sprang up radiant as she heard him
coming, but he was alone.

"Where's Bradfield?" she said, turning pale.

"The consul couldn't get action on the case till tomorrow," grunted Kaminsky. "So your Mr. Benson
said. Profitable time I've had sitting there."

"What's the matter with that consul?" demanded
Marion. "Do you think he intends to act tomorrow?"

"Yes. I heard your lawyer telephoning the Plow
Company to make sure he'd get his fee. They told
him you were really Moulton's daughter. Your
man will come out fast enough."

Sonya looked eagerly at Marion. "Sonya wants
to know if Comrade M. could cause a mistake that
would let Grenning out in place of Bradfield."

Kaminsky gave thought to it: "Grenning doesn't

speak English. How could he pass for an American? The consul would have to be in the plan."

"But no!" cried Sonya. "Let M. not make the release till after the consul is gone."

Kaminsky shook his head. "I'll ask M. tonight," he said. "He may be willing to try it. We have other things, Sonya. Davus may want that ten thousand."

Davus, as Kaminsky found when he went to M's that night, did want it. At first when M. told his chief of the wealthy noblewoman, Davus said, "Take her money. You fail to secure Grenning's escape. What then? Has she influence enough to hurt you?"

The detective said he didn't care to risk it.

"She evidently hasn't enough to get orders in here to release him."

"She may be handicapped by not wanting her interest in the prisoner known," surmised M. "I won't risk taking her money and making her desperate."

"I will," said Davus. "Who is she?"

M. replied that he had not heard her name, and had difficulty in withholding the name of his informant—on the ground that he himself would get the blame for any double cross. The incident did not improve his standing with Davus.

M. told Kaminsky he would make no more attempts of that nature for Grenning or anyone else. He was hurting the confidence of the men of the division in him. He also declined to try to substitute Grenning for the American. "Their cells lie pretty well for it," he said, "but it's a good deal too complicated to put through."

"Oh, here!" exclaimed Kaminsky, impatient with himself. "The proper man to offer these bribes is Grenning himself. That implicates nobody; he has nothing to lose."

"Why didn't you say that last week?"

"Let Grenning get the turnkey and the warder. Their jobs are not valuable like those of the officers. They can leave right after Grenning. He can tell them he has friends who can get them out of Russia if they wish."

"It looks good," said Mitiukhin. "All I have to do is get the money to him. When can you get it?"

"I'll have it here in three-quarters of an hour."

"I'll go with you and bring it myself. I am armed."

M. had the dress and manners of a Germanized commercial traveler, though his speech at times was a little too scholarly. Kaminsky took him to the Kaufstrasse flat, where Marion and Sonya were waiting on edge.

"Did Davus consent?" asked Sonya, as soon as she learned who M. was.

"No."

"Then Marion and I have thought of a way. Get the money to Grenning. Let him buy the guards."

Kaminsky and his companion exchanged a glance, laughed, explained that they had the same idea, and whether it was telepathy or coincidence they took it as a good omen. With low voices, gas turned down, and curtains drawn, they worked out that night everything they could think of—Grenning's disguise by shaving as soon as he reached Kaminsky's room,

his pseudonym, his passport, their steamer tickets—
each of them had something to do next day. As
Marion placed the ten thousand roubles for Grenning in the hands of M. she realized as never before
the meaning of money. The sweat and weariness
and pain of glistening forearms at red forges in
Moline—the endurable torture, spread across years,
of muscles aching and stiffening under an ever accel-
erated pace of work—this was the price of one man's
rescue in Riga from concentrated hours of soul-
destroying, body-breaking anguish!

As M. took that money they all felt that Grenning
would sail for London Wednesday noon with Sonya
and the Countess.

Marion went to the door with the detective. "I
want to ask about Bradfield," she said, "—the
American arrested Saturday. Have you seen him?"

"Yes. Stubborn chap."

"What did he do?"

"Refused to take the hint and leave Russia."

"Do the police require that? Surely they have no
legal right——" She saw the man of the third section smile at her naïveté. "What did the consul say
to that?" she asked.

"Said there was powerful pressure on him to get
the man in. Seems funny—an American socialist
writer. We hadn't heard of the Socialist Republic
taking control in the United States. The police told
the consul the man was free to go as soon as he made
up his mind to leave Russia."

"But do they refuse to liberate him anyway, un-
conditionally, whether he agrees to leave or not?"

"No, not if the consul insists. It would make unnecessary trouble to refuse. But——." He stopped.

"This man's a friend of mine, Comrade M. I in-
fluenced the consul—who knows my father could
crush him. Tell me what Bradfield had better do."

"He'd better leave. You can have him released
tomorrow if you like, but he can do nothing now in
Russia! He's spotted. He'll never send any articles out of Russia, and—he'll never take any out—
neither in manuscript nor in his head."

"Would they kill him?"

"Someone will somewhere, and the police will be
mystified. They'll never be able to discover who did
it. Or he may be arrested some place and get shot
'attempting to escape.' There are numerous ways."

Marion remembered the fate of Hertzenstein.
"Bradfield must go with us," she said. "Let him tell
them he'll go on the London steamer Wednesday.
Will you tell him I ask him to go? Tell him I'm
going Wednesday." She began to color beneath
M.'s penetrating look.

"No," said M. "I'd rather not risk being seen
talking to him. My English is none too good. He
wouldn't believe anything a police officer told him
anyway."

"But then you'll flick him a note, won't you—an
unsigned little note? Won't you please?"

M. consented reluctantly, and Marion flew to
write it before he could change his mind. "Don't
say anything the police shouldn't see. Tell him to
swallow the confounded thing as soon as he reads it.
Tell him not to recognize you at the dock."

To facilitate the swallowing process she borrowed

one of Sonya's needle-pointed pencils and wrote her missive on half a cigarette paper.

"You can do nothing in Russia now they have you spotted," she wrote. "They read your letter about the superman. What do you suppose they made of it? Tell them you'll go. Take the K. and F. steamer for London Wednesday noon. Marion sailed for London last week. Do not recognize any-one you know at the dock. Wait till the ship is at sea. Swallow this paper. I've chewed up the other half to see what it's like. That makes this a philo-pena. I mustn't sign this, but remember the Nancy."

M. put the tiny scrap of paper in his pocketbook, made sure of the packet of bank-notes, and took his leave.

Next morning, choosing a moment when none of his colleagues or subordinates were there, he came down the corridor between the cells of Grenning and Bradfield, laid his hand carelessly on the hori-zontal iron bar across the bottom of the American's window, let fall the folded flick of paper almost con-cealable beneath a long thumbnail, and tapping swiftly three or four times on the bar to draw the prisoner's attention to the paper, stepped across to the nearly opposite cell of Grenning. Bradfield, picking up the note, intently sized up the message-bearer. M. slipped the packet of bank-notes to Grenning. "Buy the turnkey and warder," he said in an undertone. "Go out about quarter past twelve tonight. Go straight down the hill. Meet Kamin-sky disguised as a leather merchant. Got it?"

"Yes," whispered Grenning.

The officer, having stopped only three or four

seconds, went on through the brick-floored corridor, the eyes of prisoners staring at him sullenly through their little windows.

Gratitude and love swept Grenning. The Countess Marion—what liberality! Kaminsky and perhaps great-hearted Sonya here in Riga risking for him the same horrible fate that threatened him! What greater love could man or woman show?

Bradfield picked open his minute missive. As M. had said, he was not disposed to trust anything that came from a Russian police officer. In two days he had come to hate them as he had never hated a human being. The tiny handwriting on the crumpled paper gave him no clew. The query about the effect of the superman on the police suggested Count de Hohenfels to him, and the statement: "Marion sailed for London last week,"—who else in Russia could have written that? "But why so friendly, so familiar, De Hohenfels? Why want me to go to London if Marion is there? 'I've chewed up the other half to see what it's like,' " read he. " 'That makes this a philopena.' " That was pure Marion to him—and "remember the Nancy!"—It was she! He did remember the Nancy—with a thrill. He went back and started to read the note through as Marion's. It could be her hand, writing as small as this. This time he accounted for "Marion sailed for London" as a precaution to throw off possible police readers. Why was the Countess de Hohenfels forced to such mysterious secrecy? "If she really *is* the writer of this she did *not* sail for London last week," he thought. "But the note tells *me* to. De Hohenfels would like nothing better than to send me

off to London if she was here. But that philopena!
He hasn't playfulness enough to invent that. She
might have told him in a general way about our
launch-ride—but the name Nancy!" "Recognize no
one at the dock." Who could there be to recognize? Herself. It looked as though she herself
was going on this ship Wednesday. He formed a
dozen theories, none of which he could disprove
or verify. He wanted to speak to the police officer
who had given him the note. He tried to attract the
attention of the prisoner across the corridor to
whom the officer had spoken. Once he caught his
eye and whispered: "Can you speak English?"

Grenning shook his head, laid his finger on his
lips, and drew back from his window.

At noon the turnkey unlocked the door of Grenning's cell to admit an attendant with a prison dinner. The attendant came out. The turnkey closed
and locked the door, and was going on.

"Wait," said Grenning in a low voice.

The man gave a start, looked around and shook
his head.

"I have something that means big money to you."

"Forbidden." The man went on.

Twenty minutes later he reopened the door, and
the waiter took away the bread and soup almost untouched. The turnkey was slow about locking the
door. "Why don't you eat?" he asked.

"I expect to get something worth eating tonight.
Look!" He showed a bulky roll of bank-notes, held
them to the light, and counted them back one by one
so the 100-100-100 struck the turnkey's astonished
eyes.

"Bozhe moi! In the name of Christ! Where did you get that?" He looked around guiltily, saw a prisoner peering out of his cell on the other side, moved his body to cut off the man's view, and whispered, "That's only the American. He understands nothing." He looked longingly at the money. "Why didn't they get that when they searched you?"

"Well, they didn't. If you report it you get nothing. Otherwise you can get all this for yourself."

"All that? How much is that?"

"Two thousand roubles."

"What do you want?"

"See that this door and the corridor door are unlocked just after midnight."

"Yes, and have them find you gone and the door unlocked at two!"

"You can lock it again before two. What's more, you can be out of Riga before two. How long would it take you to save two thousand roubles on this job?"

"I never would. I never saw that much money in my life. It must pay to be a revolutionist."

"Yes, it pays the best of all. It gives a man friends such as no other man has."

"When do I get that?"

"When you unlock the door. Is it a bargain?"

"Sst! Yes. Here's the waiter!"

Grenning sat down on his blanket on the floor, momentarily unnerved in his relief from the strain. He had still to get the warder who would come on at four o'clock that afternoon.

Soon after three, the American consul and the

Riga lawyer hired for Walt drove up to the station. A few minutes later and Walt was taken from his cell to the office. There being no charge against him, the consul, the lawyer, and the police came to an agreement very quickly when Walt announced his intention of sailing next day for London. They very affably turned over to him his passport, most of his other papers, his money, an order on the custom-house for his much searched trunk, and made out his police permit to leave Russia.

Walt drew a deep breath as he left the office with the consul and attorney. "What ghastly tyrants life can turn men into!" he moralized. "I wonder how those hell-hounds would check me up if I didn't go to-morrow?"

The consul looked alarmed. "But——"

"Oh, I'm going," said Walt, with the mental reservation: "Unless things turn out very different than I think."

"Don't worry about their checking you up," said the consul. "They'd do it eighteen ways. This isn't America by a long shot. Everybody has to be accounted for everywhere. The police can let you drop and are sure to pick you up again the first place you go."

Walt looked at the consul's cab, into which the Riga lawyer had already climbed.

"Where to now?" inquired the consul.

"To a bathtub—if I can make some cabman understand."

The consul laughed and hailed a cab for him. "Benson of the U. S. Plow Company was waiting for you yesterday at the consulate," he said. "He speaks German and Russian. You'd better look him up and make him steer you around."

Walt assented, and with twenty hours of freedom to spend in Russia, drove first to the Plow Company office and inquired for Benson.

"The Countess de Hohenfels had a man here waiting for you yesterday," Benson told him. "She forgot to leave us her address. I've no idea where to reach her."

Counting on her note to insure Walt's sailing on her ship next day, Marion had renounced as too dangerous the attempt to see him sooner.

Half an hour after Walt left the prison, the warder who would be on duty between midnight and two came down Grenning's corridor on his first round. He stopped and looked into each of the occupied cells. Hearing how brief a time he paused at each door, Grenning was nervous with the realization that he would have no time for leading up. He was close to the grating when the warder looked in —so close the man threw his hand to his revolver.

"Do you want to make three thousand roubles?" asked Grenning tensely.

"Shut up." The man came close, and peered past the prisoner into his cell.

"I have to pass you tonight as I go out," said Grenning. "It will be worth three thousand roubles to you if you fail to see me."

"Don't talk to me, I tell you. It's against the rules."

"One breaks a rule or two for three thousand

roubles. Pay attention to what I told you and you
get in your hand thirty hundred-rouble notes."

"Are you crazy just thinking about—things?
Wait till they happen!"

"I don't intend to wait," said Grenning, resisting
the paralyzing image of cruelty and fear the warder
was trying to force upon him. "I'm going out to-
night. Look, man!" He pulled out his roll of bills.

"So. You have real money in there? It goes to
the office."

"Where you get not one rouble of it. Keep still
and agree and it's yours—right now."

In vain! The warder said he had a wife and two
children in Riga.

Grenning told him he could go abroad and have
them follow.

"No. If I let a prisoner escape and went myself,
the woman and my son and my daughter would never
leave Riga alive."

Grenning promised him they would—within
twenty-four hours. "You're crazy, man!" he exclaimed. "Here's a chance for you to make more
for your family than you could save in a lifetime. By
doing what? Something bad? No. By saving a
human being from this hell on earth."

"You wouldn't be here if God didn't want you
here. You can't buy God off—no matter how much
you got."

"Are you sure God isn't trying to get me out of
here through you?"

"God trying? No. I report what I see to the
office."

Grenning raised his offer to eight thousand roubles and showed them.

"I don't care if it's eighty thousand! You won't have it long!" His footsteps died away down the corridor. Then the prisoner heard low voices and heavy, hateful steps returning. The warder was bringing the officer in charge and brutal guards the prisoner knew would not be gentle.

"The Countess's money gone!" was Grenning's first thought, and then despair swept his soul. All the thinking, planning, co-operating of his comrades, their wary approach, their love and sacrifice, wiped out in a moment, leaving him to suffer worse than death—through a blockhead's incorruptible fidelity to the cause of hell!

XIV

C OMING to their apartment after supper in
a Kaufstrasse café with Sonya and Marion,
Kaminsky found a man waiting for him with
a crushing message from M. that Grenning had lost
his ten thousand roubles and his best chance of
escape. They could not bear to look at Sonya.

"As far as the money is concerned," said Marion,
finally, "if it will do any good we can still spare
another ten thousand."

Unable to endure an hour without some definite
plan, Sonya made Kaminsky set out with her for
M.'s to try to form some new idea. Marion offered
to go with them, but Kaminsky said two were already too many. On the way Sonya stopped to buy
her vial of poison.

Marion was left alone to realize that she and Sonya and Grenning would not sail next day and that
her note to Walt would not only send him off on
that ship alone, but would set him looking in vain for
her in London. She knew he had left the station,
but did not know where he had gone. "Why didn't
I have the nerve to keep in touch with him as I
wanted to!" she exclaimed. "I've missed my chance
to see him!" To send a message to him at the dock
where the detectives would be watching to see

whether he got off would immediately direct their suspicion against anyone who communicated with him.

She put on her hat and coat, turned out the gas, locked the apartment, went down to an apothecary's where there was a closed telephone booth, called up the American consul at his residence, and asked if he could tell where Mr. Bradfield went that afternoon.

"Oh, yes," answered the consul, "is that——"

"You recognize my voice, I see," interrupted Marion with significant quickness.

"Excuse me. Yes, I do, of course. It's not easy to forget."

"Thank you so much for your interest. Could you tell me where the gentleman went? Or where he intended to stop?"

"I think he was going to some hotel. I told him about Mr. Benson waiting for him yesterday, and when he left me he was going to look up Benson at the Plow Company's office. Benson might tell you where he is now. If you'll hold the wire a second——" In a moment he gave her Benson's number.

"Thank you so much," she murmured.

She got Mr. Benson.

"Mr. Bradfield?" he repeated, answering her. "Yes. Who is that?"

"I prefer not to say just now. You are a poor guesser, Mr. Benson."

"Oh, of course," said Benson. "Excuse me. Yes, Mr. Bradfield is here with me. We got to talking

Moline—and Russia. He is going to stay with me tonight. He leaves for London tomorrow."

"Yes. Will you call him to the phone?"

Mr. Benson did.

"Hello!" came Bradfield's hearty, open voice.

"Walt," said Marion.

"Yes?" He was all hushed attention.

"Can you find 534 Kaufstrasse, third floor, right-hand apartment?"

"Yes."

"Come. Try not to be followed. Do you understand?"

"Yes."

"Goodbye."

She went back along the brightly-lighted sidewalk, covered with trampled snow, crowded with middle-class shoppers, to her room. She changed Miss Baker's clothes, removed Miss Baker's years. Walt was real. His one word—yes—thrice spoken —what depths it stirred!

Alone in the German-Russian apartment with its ugly, ornate gas-fixtures, its blue and white porcelain stove, its pious ikon in the corner, she listened for Walt's step, and heard instead the mournful sirens and dim bells of steamers, the hum and chug and rumble of tram and motor and train far off, the chink and grind and murmur of hoof and wheel and voice, the thousand tremors and reverberations not definable but blending in one faint throbbing roar— the sound of Riga. The modern Baltic city, meshed in tyrannous authority—a daily woven web of fear and lies and violence, of insane cruelties and pangs and bitter deaths—was suddenly as strange to˙her as Sidon. Through that city of Moloch—of spies who might track him to her and drag her to worse than death—came Walt.

At his knock she called softly, and heard his answer before she unlocked her door. She drew him in quickly, her hands on his arms—leaned and looked past him down the stairs, not noting how the life in him intensified at the touch of her and the remembered fragrance of her hair.

"Shut in Elysium!" The phrase flashed, while his eyes etched on his glowing mind her coronal of red-gold hair, the tendrils of it gleaming on her white neck, behind her ear, the undulation of her noble figure as she bent to lock the world out. Her hands trembled when she turned and pressed his. He read her eyes of welcome—full of reviving memories. He looked at her firm, rich lips, which had once met his —the day they had eaten of the lotus—and even as then his thought of her love for De Hohenfels was an invisible barrier shutting her away. The golden mist half-lifted at her tense question: "Were you followed?"

"Yes. I shouldn't have noticed it if it hadn't been for your telephone, but there were two of them sitting in a cab opposite Benson's—out there in the cold. I was surprised. Why am I so important to them? They drove after me, and when I got a cab, kept right behind. When I stopped and got out, they did too. I lost them doubling through a crowded department store."

"You must go on that ship tomorrow."

"Are you going on it?"

"I was. I can't."

"When are you going?"

"A week—a month. It can't be long." She shuddered with the horrible, absorbing thought dominating those days.

"What queer thing has hold of you?" he asked.

"Russia—almost."

He had an uncanny feeling of terrible, vague danger threatening her. He looked at her critically. "You don't use cocaine, do you?"

"Why no. Do I seem so strange as that? Walt, Walt, I am so glad to see you! I thought tonight I had missed you. You don't know, you don't know!"

He drew in his breath and held it—as though her words had fragrance.

"Your mind is so clean—so free from—you've never had your soul screwed out of shape—by lust of blood. I need you so—your comradeship—the warm interpretation of the world you can help me make."

He felt, but read it as illusion of his own desire, that she needed most—his arms around her and long kisses. He could not gauge the loneliness, the bitterness, the fear, from which he was refuge. He looked away to keep himself from being drawn depth below depth by the look in her eyes. He had thought she would know she must not use her power to make love ache in him. She turned slowly and seated herself on the lounge.

"How do you expect me to go?" he demanded.

"They will kill you if you don't."

"If that's all," he said, smiling and sitting down beside her, "I think I—will manage to go."

"I want you to wait for me in London or Paris. Will you?"

"I must find out first whether *you* ought not to go. What are you doing here—writing unsigned notes—wording them so the hell-hounds of police will think you're in London—staying in this place where men are killed for—I don't know what! Why are you here in this queer flat in this murderous city?" He looked around the room for signs of Count Hohenfels, and saw her pistol lying on the table.

"It's a long story," said she, with a quick sigh. She leaned toward him and lowered her voice. "The heart of it is that five weeks ago I gave a small party of revolutionaries a warning that resulted in a military disaster to some troops of the Tsar."

"You did! The Countess de Hohenfels!"

"Ssh! Don't use that name! I am Miss Baker. I am here to get a man out of the prison where you were—the man who carried that warning—one of my best friends—threatened with torture unspeakable!"

He clenched his hands. "For carrying the secret you sent! Then if they get you——!" He saw her lips shut tight and her eyes turn steel. He had the maddening picture of her cherishable body writhing beneath the hands of fiends. He looked at her pistol. "London is no place for me until you're there." He spoke with finality.

She saw it was useless now to try to make him go. She had not meant to let him know so much. Ignorant of the country, the language—marked and tracked by the police—he would be more trouble to them in their enterprise than he was worth. Yet her unreasonable soul rejoiced that he was there.

"Do you have to stay here?" he asked.

She nodded.

"What is it—friendship for this man?"

"That too."

"Were you drawn into all this accidentally?"

"Yes."

"Then you're not yourself a revolutionist—on principle?"

"I've hardly stopped to realize it, but I am—yes! With my whole soul! I'd die—I'd be tortured—if that could destroy this Russian despotism!"

He gazed at her, stirred, disquieted, convinced. There was a terrible fire behind her eyes. Too far down that road——! But who, capable of magnificence, is not capable of madness too? "I've called myself a revolutionist," he said. "Henceforth I think I'll save the word—for the reality."

She laid her hand quickly on his, her eyes softening, her tense soul unclosing a little in the sweetness of being near him. "I seem unreal beside some men and women here," she said. "Of me—such as I am —you were the beginning. Walt: after you, as I went on, I kept on looking at things from my own old point of view, and Count Feodor's—but then, just for fun with myself, because I liked pretending to be you, I'd shift the angle and look at things from yours. A dangerous game, sir! From yours I could read men and women who from mine would have been meaningless scrawls. I could account for the hollowness and falseness of high society: I could see through the self-deceptions and hypocrisies of ruling classes—the dreadful governments they maintain—with a disgusting pretense that it is for the people's good that they 'keep them down.' "

"You've traveled far," he said, his half-closed eyes looking afar—at his new picture of her mind.

"Had you not touched my eyes, dear man," she said, leaning close to him, "I would have been blind for life—like the rest—to our utter and eternal disregard for the life and welfare and liberty of the millions who are and must ever be of our own blood and nature, but who are without the little trained-in traits of our own class! Those would have been the all-important things to me—not the big human things!"

It moved him deeply to hear her—the most desirable woman he knew in mind, in will, in bodily loveliness, voicing out of her own experience and heart one phrase of his own belief. His left hand was shut tight, a result of his determination not to put it around her as she sat beside him. He still thought clearly but with an effort like that of a man refusing to let the wine he has drunk affect him. "You'll never get back to the view of the world that prevails in your own class," he said. "You are not of the working class. Where will you land?"

She had a sudden exalted sense of glorious answers to be reached some day—if Russia did not end all. "All I see left for me," she said, smiling her way back from that somber, intruding thought, "is the viewpoint of—the social whole. Your own letter opened my way to that. If I can get life that will let me grow out of the bitterness recent things have forced into me—I may become, not class-conscious like you, but socially conscious."

"And what will that lead to?"

"I'm not sure. From that viewpoint I may have to agree with you that everything beautiful and true and free in life is being blighted by our profit-system —without which most of us who are used to it and benefit by it think the world would stop. You class-struggle socialists seem to be the only ones who now desire to end it. But wouldn't it be a lovely joke on you if the private owners of the world's industry should themselves see it ought to be socialized—and do it themselves?"

"Can you imagine your father doing that?"

"No. But can't you imagine me doing it?"

"Yes, if you had the power—bless your big heart! But it's your class that has the power, and a ruling class, even though doomed, cannot surrender. It is against the law of the world. It is there to make the rising class develop—struggling. Your class is an organism much too tenacious of life to drink the hemlock you think of offering it."

"I haven't thought it out," she said. "I'm not so sure the workers will ever win. I would not like to see the present wage-workers, degraded by bad conditions, secure control of the world."

"Are those now in control running the world so well—for human welfare?"

"They are running it for their own welfare—and very badly from every other point of view. Would the workers as they are do better? If they are to gain power I hope men like you will first have made them more fit for it—than the present rulers. If I can help you do that, I will. I do feel in you, Walt—oh, with love I feel it—a great hope of a clean, sweet world!"

A surge of feeling made thought difficult for him. His arms ached for her. He started to speak—cleared his throat—let his criticism go.

"Walt," she said, pouring oil on flame.

He turned his eyes to hers.

"Are you glad to see me?"

"You know I am." He could hardly speak.

"But why don't you tell me you are? Why do you pretend not to be?"

"Because I'm—a thousand times too glad!"

"You can't be! Oh, I need a monstrous gladness for me in someone—someone!"

"Do you know what will happen if you—how does Count Hohenfels feel about your revolutionary activity?"

"What he feels about all things and persons but himself—exalted scorn!"

"So on account of *him* you're lonely and unhappy? Where is he?"

She drew her forearms back against her breast, lowering her head so her knuckles hurt her cheeks. "I have left him."

A diamond turning on her clenched third finger revealed its deepest unsuspected gleam. To the impassioned man beside her, life in that instant changed. In his soul a trumpet blew.

"He has a divorce—on a miserable false charge of improper conduct with Dr. Grenning—who is here in prison, facing death and worse."

He saw her indignation against De Hohenfels blaze out even through her anxiety for Grenning. He could not instantly adjust his own ideas, nor follow hers. She looked at him. He felt her feel through his shifting thoughts his underlying joy. "It may be a sorrow to you," he said, "but don't ask me to sympathize. To me it means that you, Marion, who loved me once on the other side of the world—are free! You are a woman unmated!"

Her attention focused on him with that intensity in her which was new to him. He did not want her to think that merely because she had left De Hohenfels he thought her his. For all he really knew she did love Grenning—or loved no one. So reasoning he tried to keep himself from her. He could not. His soul knew she was crushing her throbbing fingers against her cheeks, her yearning breasts against her arms in lieu of—to keep herself from—him! He leaned and gathered her against him, feeling her body shake with sobs as she opened her arms to fold him in beauty and wonder. Through her nerves, made tense by days and weeks of mental pain and dread, saving her from threatening hysteria, flowed the deep magic of love-liesse.

She raised her head and looked with glittering eyes at him.

"I knew nothing of love," she said, as their lips neared. "It is strong as death."

XV

THE evening roar of Riga had died away to discontinuous nocturnal sounds when a knock at the apartment door startled Marion from her hour's oblivion to the cocaine-like Russian fear.

The sudden pallor of her face as she rose from her lover's side could not conceal the stirred and vivid beauty of kissed lips and shining eyes. A throbbing languor underlay her quick movements as she twisted into place a fallen strand of glinting hair and closed the fragrant bosom of her gown. Echoes of exquisite sensation, sweet throes inflicted by caressing lips were vibrating in her as she went to answer the unwelcome summons of the outside world.

She opened the door.

There, dumbly waiting, stood Sonya—with stony eyes. From them the forgotten thought of Grenning leaped and stabbed the love-intoxicated woman. Sonya did not speak. In her nostrils Marion heard the quivering breath indrawn by shuddering lungs. Kaminsky drew her by the arm. As they passed in, Marion caught his eye, and flashed him her dreadful question.

"Yes," he said. "They examined Grenning this evening."

Her gesture begged him not to drive it into Sonya's mind by speech.

He did not think much of the policy. "I don't think she hears anyway," he said. "We need a doctor."

Sonya turned as though to speak, looked at Marion, shook her head.

Encircling her with arms of infinite compassion, Marion went with her to her room, bending to kiss her, pressing her to her side, talking to her in the voice new love had taught her, trying to woo back to life her friend's will to live. She could not make the life-creating sweetness throbbing in her veins reach that shut heart as Sonya's dumb agony reached hers. In glimpses that seemed to open and flame upon her from the inferno of Sonya's soul she saw the prison room, the intent look of torturers at work, the strapped-down victim, the distorted face of—Grenning! Stifling a sudden desire to scream, she felt back for Count Feodor's prophylactics against the infection of pity—its morbidity and futility—the ideal of the hard, heroic heart—beatitude unscorched by the flame of another's burning. Those cobwebs might shield the intellect that spun them, but not— a woman's midriff!

She came out to Walt and Kaminsky. The latter sat with his shoulders hunched up near the stove, his mouth occasionally twisting. He straightened up when he saw her and became matter of fact. "Better not leave that there," he said, nodding toward her pistol on the table.

She picked it up mechanically, considering where

to keep it out of Sonya's way. "Did she hear—everything?" she asked.

"She got everything out of M.—made him tell her everything. She loathes him. He had to help."

"Help———!"

"He had to. Davus suspected him. M. had to try to force Grenning to tell who gave him that ten thousand—sweating blood for fear he *would* tell."

"And he didn't?"

"No. Nor about us. Nor his own connection with Mitrevitz. They got nothing out of him. The only evidence they have against him is Smika's—and for all the police know that was mere insanity."

"Is there a hope they will release him after all?"

He shook his head. "Sonya hoped that too. When she realized—she made M. go back to the prison to give Grenning that little bottle. M. came back and said the doctor wouldn't take it. In spite of Smika, Grenning thinks his nervous system is strong enough to pull him through alive and sane. He hopes we will find some way to get him out before they re-examine him."

"Oh, we must, we *must!* But why—if they think he had nothing to do with Mitrevitz———"

"They daren't let people see the marks. They put out cigars against his flesh. They could hold him till the holes are healed, but—his hands. They are ruined. The broken bones of his fingers will reknit unset and his nails are gone."

A tigress sound broke from the woman, and her hand clenched convulsively on the pistol. Walt sprang up—not understanding—ready to fly at

Kaminsky. "Are you going to kill them?" demanded Marion.

Kaminsky's gesture indicated there was nothing to gain by it.

"What is it?" asked Walt. He held out his hand, wanting to take the weapon himself. "What are you going to do with that?"

"Nothing—oh, just nothing! They tore out Grenning's nails,—but we submit! They broke his surgeon's fingers—what did they do with those nails, Kaminsky? Just throw them on the floor? They must look pretty. Wouldn't you like one as a souvenir of Grenning? I never saw the root of a man's nail!" She looked at her own pink nail.

"Pull your mind straight off of that!" commanded Nachman Kaminsky sternly. "Go baresark and kill Gregus and what have you done? Your life's worth more than that!"

"Think of it, Walt!" cried she, again speaking English. "That girl, Sonya, loves him, and can do nothing!" She looked at Walt's hand, not yet soft and white like a gentleman's. She looked at his nails. She shuddered and her face was screwed out of shape by imagined pain. Suddenly she reached and drew Walt's fingers passionately against her breast and kissed them, and then for an instant, unexpectedly, her life flamed toward him. There was a sudden all-meaning look between them on their narrow ledge of joy above the world's swimming pain. Her voice dropped. "Even now I am drunk with your love," she said. "Even this ghastly news——! If I could only give poor Sonya the least bit of this unquenchable sweetness! Don't leave here tonight. They would pick you up again at Benson's. I'll be with Sonya. You can have my room. Tomorrow we can make a place for you."

"Elysium in the midst of hell!" he muttered. "I don't like the way you handle that gun. If shooting has to be done, give me the job."

She turned to Kaminsky. "What is to be our program?" she asked. To his relief she spoke now like a sane person.

"Get Sonya to go with you tomorrow as planned, minus Grenning."

"Heaven and earth couldn't make her! She'd die ten deaths first!"

"She'll lose her mind."

"More likely if she went."

"Be careful yourself," he warned. "Terrible forces are ready to break loose from you. Don't make pictures—as you were doing. Don't let them make themselves. Don't let your thoughts concentrate on finger-nails. Keep your rudder; use judgment how you handle your mind. If the whole pack of you would get out of here leaving what money you can, I could do just as much—with one quarter the risk."

"You're right. But she won't go! How can you ask it? I wouldn't in her place."

"Being in your own, you'd better go. Bradfield can leave tomorrow as he agreed, and you with him—that is, on the same ship. He will have trouble going later."

The unquenchable sweetness rose through her lungs. To escape from the horror of Russia into love—just love! "What would Sonya do?" she asked.

"I'll take care of her."

"If ever a woman needed another, she needs me. If I let her make her fight for sanity alone—no, thank you! Walt won't leave me either. There's no use preaching sense to any of us, Kaminsky. We must keep Bradfield here. The police have lost him. Get him some papers for the benefit of the domiciliary gentleman. Let him be my brother come for me from England—or my betrothed." The tones her voice found for the word surprised her. She looked at Walt, and across her flashed the vision of a sympathetic marriage—years together—in Western Europe, in America—he and she touched with the same flame—working together for the same great social ends—bringing their vision of a fairer society to bear upon the one in which they lived—carving their dream in the resisting block of hard reality—helping to lead the world into the coming time. Then the shadow of Russia fell on her—the difficulties of frontier and port—the ghastly tragedy of capture—Sonya alone there in her room. "I must get back to her," she said. "I'll show you where you are to sleep. Start something for Grenning, Nachman—if only for effect on her."

Kaminsky smiled after her and Walt. "Lucky for you you *have* got something to take your mind off—Grenning's nails on the floor!" he thought. His mouth twisted again. Was it out of his own experience he knew one must not think of nails? "Grenning should have drunk that bottle," he muttered.

Four days later, Kaminsky was hopeful again. The day after his examination, Grenning, in ceaseless pain, had been transferred to the Central Prison. In a vodka-shop Kaminsky gained the confidence of one of the prison guards, excited his cupidity, got him to draw in a pal, and the two agreed to get Grenning out. The guards intended to take a fishing boat and sail to Sweden. Sunday night was set for the escape, and arrangements made for leaving Russia Monday; but Sunday morning Grenning was unexpectedly sent back to the detective station for reëxamination.

After that it was hopeless. He could not have walked out had all doors stood open and unguarded. For in the second examination, determined to get something out of him before the field court-martial, they strapped Grenning to a bench, placed a plank across his back, jumped on the ends of the plank and broke his spine.

He made no confession. He told them nothing. He did not die. Day after day they let him lie—the agonized wreck of a man—still sane.

At every opportunity Kaminsky talked to Sonya of the revolutionary plans and activities going on in Riga, told her how the peasant deputies of the first Duma had come to the second Social Revolutionists, described how the waves spreading from the Russian revolution were stirring Turkey—Persia—India— all of them testing the strength of their chains. In every way he sought to relight the fire of what had once seemed Sonya's strongest passion—Russian freedom.

It all seemed to mean nothing to her.

Marion got her occupied preparing breakfast and lunches, but could not make her hold her mind to the game of teaching Walt Russian. It was a fearful pain to Sonya to do anything that kept her from her own thoughts. Her "pictures" drew her to look at them always. They were jealous of any interruption. Even the danger of detection in a second domiciliary visit of the police drew her attention only while the officers were present. Kaminsky being away Marion herself had to deal with them in exaggeratedly meager Russian. Walt was superficially disguised by spectacles and changed dress, and the visitors were not of that section of the police who could have identified him. Fortunately Kaminsky had supplied him with papers that satisfied them.

It was eight days after the reëxamination of Grenning, on a dark mid-October afternoon, the east wind whirling snow-flakes down the streets of Riga, when Kaminsky brought word to the Kaufstrasse that the field court-martial was sitting. Russian officers and gentlemen—men with the old culture in a new soul —were passing upon the evidence submitted to them by the detective division, deciding the fate of the seventeen revolutionists then in the toils in Riga.

It was reported that night that two were condemned to death. Grenning and Smika? Their friends did not voice the hope that they were the lucky ones. Sonya, Marion, and Walt rose before daylight next morning, went to the reeking wharf of the fishing boats, and gazing with a glass across the sands between them and the Central Prison, they saw both prisoners march out and stand before the firing squads. Neither of these new corpses could be Grenning's.

Soon after breakfast they learned that Grenning and Smika,—a maniac and a man with broken spine who would not die—had been sentenced to fifteen years' hard labor in the Siberian mines. Thirteen other prisoners left at eight o'clock for Siberia, but the doctor and the forester were not among them. They were not in the detective station or the Central Prison, and in neither of those places was there any record of where they had been sent. They must have been removed in the night. M. was not in the secret.

Kaminsky mingled with the Jews of his father's synagogue after the morning service. Among them were secret revolutionists, merchants who had all kinds of codes and modes of communication with others of their race throughout the Baltic provinces, Kovno, Grodno, and the governments of the Pale. They had no information, but by nine o'clock that morning the question "Where is Grenning?" began to spread in curious ways through western Russia.

After a midday meal with a Jewish friend, Kaminsky, returning to the Kaufstrasse flat, found no one there to let him in. "All at lunch together again and taken the key!" he reflected. He looked at his cheap watch, sat down on the top step, and pulled out a newspaper. Presently he heard someone running up the lower flights of stairs. It was Sonya. She came up breathless, frightened out of the introspective look of melancholia. "We've been recognized!" she exclaimed.

Kaminsky clenched his fingers, fighting for control of the panic that started in him. "Where are the others?" he asked.

"I don't know. I hoped they'd be here. We separated. It was in the Alexander II café. Trina Ronke came in with Captain Sikorsky and took the next table. We kept our faces away and did not let them hear our voices, but we had to pay the waiter. Ronke looked harder and harder and finally she was sure. We got out as fast as we could, but she had Sikorsky convinced and he was up looking for an officer. In the street we went opposite ways. What if they've got Marion!"

"If they have, Trina Ronke will die."

"As if her miserable life could pay!"

"Is her money with her—or here?"

"Here—I think."

"Has she the key?"

"Bradfield has it."

"Then we'll have to get a locksmith—or break down the door. If she has the money with her we will have none for getting her out."

"Oh, they can't have been caught!" exclaimed Sonya. "They must have mixed up in some crowd to avoid being followed."

"I'm going down to look," said Kaminsky. "Was it——"

"Listen!" exclaimed Sonya. There were footsteps below—two persons coming up fast. It was Walt and Marion. He had hold of her arm and was talking low, emphatic English. Sonya sat down on the step with a sigh of gratitude. That strain of danger and relaxation of relief were perhaps her salvation.

They saw Marion's white face, compressed lips, and eyes turned up to them, and heard her relieved exclamation, "Sonya's here!"

"You've heard," she said to Kaminsky, as Walt unlocked the door.

"Yes. When are you going?"

"The first ship. Sonya, you are coming, too."
She followed Walt in.

"No," said Sonya.

Marion sat down by the marble-topped table and
scanned the sailing lists. "The F. and K. steamer
Kursk for London. Three o'clock." She looked at
her watch. "An hour and three-quarters. Sonya,
there's no time at all to lose. Get ready."

Sonya shook her head. "No, dear Marion," she
said. It was her old, reasonable, loving voice.

"She recognized you too!" exclaimed Marion.
"They'll know you're not in Odessa. They know
how close we've been. She knows you loved—Sonya, won't you come? I want you!"

"We've done all we can for Grenning," urged Kaminsky. "It was our best, but it wasn't enough. We
may never hear definitely what happened. It is
certain he is dead or will soon die—beyond our
knowledge or power to help him."

Sonya bowed her head. "I know that," she said.
"He should have died as he was when he came here.
But Marion—my place is Russia. I'd love to go
with you, but I'd have nothing to do—but think.
Here there are things to be done that can't very
well be done by people who care to live. I can do
these things."

Marion looked away suddenly.

"The revolution seems all tragically futile now,"
said Sonya, "but no matter who is killed, it can never
end—till it wins."

The eyes of Sonya and Marion met, and they

knew for the first time, in the moment of farewell, the full depth of the love between them.

Marion came and embraced her. "God bless you," she said. "Don't throw your life away! Will you get away from Riga to-day—in a good new disguise?"

"Yes. Perhaps to Libau."

"You make me see my place is America—not Rome—not Paris. On the other side of the world I'll be on your side of the world-fight, Sonya!"

"Look here!" said Kaminsky. "This ship doesn't leave soon enough. It will be two hours after Sikorsky saw you. The police will have telephoned the dock. They'll have a description of you in that disguise."

Marion turned—saved from breaking down. "I'd better leave off the wig and look young," she said.

"I'm afraid no disguise is good enough now. There are too few English-speaking people going out. You have some accent. Half a dozen of them can identify Bradfield."

"Walt," said Marion, "Kaminsky says we can't get through at the dock. They will have telephoned about me, and there are half a dozen men who can identify you."

"In fact, all of them," said Bradfield. "They took my measurements. How far is it to the Swedish coast?"

She asked Kaminsky.

"Less than two days' sail with this wind. Tell Bradfield he's right. A fishing boat's the thing. But tell him the Swedish Socialists have to fight to keep our refugees from being sent back by their government. Best keep in the steamer route and get an English ship to pick you up."

Marion looked at the sailing lists. "There seems to be no English ship till—day after tomorrow."

"Better go now," said Kaminsky. "It will be harder tomorrow when every detective knows of you. Try the Kursk. It's her last trip. She won't be back till spring. If we go at once we should get a boat and get you off an hour ahead of her. I'll go down with you and help get you a crew. You might as well be in the hands of comrades."

Quarter of an hour later they were ready. Marion made Sonya say she would make a good new disguise and leave Riga at once. There was a knock at the door. It was a messenger from M. at the detective station warning them that the police had information that the Countess de Hohenfels, wanted for complicity in the Zhergan disaster, was disguised in Riga. They were looking for her. She turned pale, and translated for Bradfield. "Let's get to that wharf!" he said. Marion turned to Sonya for a last kiss. Then she went down with Bradfield and Kaminsky into the wind-swept, daylight streets of Riga. Armed all three, knowing death was better than capture, they passed at every crowded crossing one of the *gorodovoi* with his visored cap and boots and saber. Kaminsky went twenty or thirty feet ahead.

They passed Benson on the sidewalk. He stopped in astonishment, a danger to them, but Marion gave no sign of recognition and kept on. Ever since Bradfield had left his trunk there, a representative of the third section had been living in Benson's pension.

A Jewish pony-buyer wanted to stop and talk with Kaminsky, who would not have it. The man walked along with him. They saw Kaminsky give a nod of comprehension, and then the man turned back the way he had been going.

Down a squalid street they saw the black hulls of vessels, their spars and yards white with sticky snow. The shores of the Dwina were lined with thin, blue ice. Passing through a line of carts and wagons, they reached the wharf. It was built along the length of its center with low forecastle-like cabins, and was covered with trampled snow and scales, cluttered with frozen coils of line, piled high with low, heavy barrels. There were only a few boats in. Kaminsky made some inquiries and got the Americans into one of the shanty markets smelling of fish and tar, of vodka and bad tobacco. They quickly struck a bargain with a skipper and his one-man crew. The cabin of their boat was a dire-looking place to spend a day in, but the sight of the walls of the Central Prison across the snow-covered sands made it alluring. A hundred rouble note persuaded a wharf detective who had not yet heard of the Countess de Hohenfels that this man and woman could want a fishing-boat for none but laudable and lawful ends. Walt helped Marion down from the icy wharf into the boat. Kaminsky went with them into the little cabin while the fishermen made ready to cast off.

"I have something to tell you," said Kaminsky. "Did you see that man that walked with me? He was coming from the freight-yard. Among the mar-

ket reports the Jews send each other chalked on the
sides of freight-cars, that man saw a message in
Hebrew on a car just in from Kokenhausen. It
said, 'Grenning and Smika were brought here alive
in the night. This morning they were dead. They
were reported shot attempting to escape.' "

The slap and swish of little waves against the
sides of the boat—the creak and strain of pulleys
as the sail went up—were for a moment the only
sounds.

"Thank God!" breathed Marion. She laid her
hand on Walt's. "Grenning is dead. Shot attempting to escape—a man with——! Walt, did you
know Sonya thought he loved me? You know how
she loved him. And look at her love for me! She
has the greatest heart I have ever known!" She
turned to Kaminsky. "Nachman," she said, clasping
his hand goodbye, "take care of Sonya! She is the
most precious thing in Russia." She gave him an
envelope containing ten thousand rouble notes.
"This was for Grenning. Now it's for the cause.
It means that you and Sonya shall have a little freedom for a while to work for Russian freedom. And
can't you have Grenning's body cared for? The
cause owes him burial."

Nachman Kaminsky hesitated an instant. "Yes,"
he said. "I will." But he knew that Grenning
would lie that night in a bed of quicklime. No man
of the future would read in the broken, half-knit
bones of that skeleton how men were governed under
the Tsars.

Two hours later, Marion and Walt Bradfield,
sailing northwestward through the Gulf of Riga in

the track of the outgoing ships, were helped over the rail to the deck of the steamship Kursk, loaded with ponies and Jewish emigrants bound for London.

Before night fell, breathing deep breaths of cold salt air, standing close and warm together in the lea of the cabin on the after deck, they saw the white shore of Russia fade into a cloud beyond the sea-rim of the Baltic.